KING'S CROSS

A STORY OF REGICIDE

Other Mystery Fiction from Quarry Press

Great Canadian Murder & Mystery Stories
edited by Don Bailey and Daile Unruh

Sinister Gambits: Chess Stories of Murder & Mystery
edited by Richard Peyton

A STORY OF REGICIDE

D.G. COURTNEY

Quarry Press

The Highland echoes in this book are dedicated to Lord Fergus and Lady Glencora, my collies, best in heart and breed . . . .

The publisher gratefully acknowledges the assistance of The Canada Council, the Ontario Arts Council, the Department of Communication, and the Ontario Publishing Centre.

Canadian Cataloguing in Publication Data

Courtney, D.G.
King's Cross: a story of regicide

ISBN 1-55082-082-6

I. Title.

PS8555.08264K46 1993 C813'.54 C93-090514-8
PR9199.3.C69K46 1993

Front cover illustration by Jack McMaster.
Design by Keith Abraham.
Typeset by Quarry Press, Inc.
Printed and bound in Canada by Webcom Limited, Toronto, Ontario.

Published by
Quarry Press, Inc.,
P.O. Box 1061, Kingston, Ontario K7L 4Y5.

PROLOGUE

Regicide

One

Christmas Eve • New Bond Street • London

AND HECTOR MACKENZIE was here to conduct the most difficult task anyone, even a Marine Commando, Deputy Chief of British Anti-Terror, could undertake: the purchasing of Christmas presents for people who had everything.

Or if they didn't, MacKenzie thought, gazing at a gold and saphire peacock behind his own plain-clothed reflection in Aspell's window, they could if they wanted to... but of course that was the point: the people on his mental shopping list would never dream of giving each other such a conspicuously gaudy bauble. The glittering objects in the Jewelers' window were for the world's nouveau riche, not one of its oldest reigning Royal Families.

By Appointment
To His Majesty
KING GEORGE VIII

The Lion and Unicorn beneath the Merchant's proud boast made MacKenzie pause for an extra moment. The last week of the year was a time of reflection for everyone, if not for everyday shoppers, about saphire peacocks! But for British subjects this past year was especially memorable, this Christmas in particular. Not only was it the first anniversary of the new King's unexpected accession to the throne: it also marked a whole generation since his Great Great Grandmother, the Old Queen, Elizabeth the Second, stunned the nation by announcing her intention to abdicate in favor of her son, then still a middle-aged, frustrated Prince of Wales, too-long-in-waiting, and retire to concentrate on raising bloodstock racehorses, "Like my own extraordinary and beloved Queen Mother."

"Nice ring for the Little Woman, Squire?"

The broad accent accosting MacKenzie was born-and-bred Cockney; the even broader grin on the guileless black face looking up at him must be Caribbean Trader, descended from pirates. Who else would have the nerve to peddle undoubtedly redhot rings and watches from a flap under a jacket outside the Royal Jeweler? MacKenzie was amused; he wasn't going to encourage such a life of crime. Then, about to shake his head and move on, he spotted a brooch of a crouching silver leopard, the central heraldic emblem of his own ancient Highland family's coat of arms. It would make a perfect present for Liz Ponti, the unexpectedly serious — and because of her freewheeling broadcasting background, most unlikely! — new woman in his disciplined masculine life.

"Pure sterling," the pavement pirate lied with bland assurance. "But only thirty quid, or forty in Euro-bucks. Either toss, stuff this number in her stocking, Squire, the Missus'll love Santa that little bit extra when he rolls over in bed beside her tomorrow morning."

A suggestive male-bonding wink didn't help the brigand's pitch. Liz wasn't Missus to anyone except her anchor job at the BBC; and far from a roll-over in bed, MacKenzie wouldn't even be able to lay eyes on her until after the heightened security of the holidays! But when the two of them could meet again as lovers, Liz's Neapolitan raven hair falling on her shoulder would certainly show the silver leopard off to advantage ... and the added touch of probable larceny would appeal to her Glasgow newshound's soul. MacKenzie encouraged further London petty crime after all, by settling at twenty in the Euro currency he still had on him from a flying trip to Anti-Terror Headquarters in Brussels that morning, and crossed Liz off his mental shopping list.

THE NEXT PERSON on it proved even easier. A toy shop immediately around the corner on Stafford Street had one model left of an armored Range Rover, complete with rubble-plough and working turret-hatch, exactly like the one MacKenzie would be driving during his perimeter patrol at Sandringham upon his return this evening. The request for exactly such a vehicle had been made to Father Christmas (on the back of a one-time-cypher message pad) inside the full-size vehicle by the gift's eight-year-old recipient last week, just before the Second in line to the Throne asked MacKenzie to be sure and mail it, "To the North Pole with super extra-special quickness, Colonel Ken," directly from the Military Postal Unit attached to the Estate.

The young Prince's letter (accompanied by a last-minute addition from the next Heir, his two-years-older sister) had actually gone in the bombproof A-T pouch with the hardcopy backup of the online computer-file on Terrorist Possibles at Sensitive Locations. A euphemism for the other Royal residences, as well as Downing Street.

MacKenzie glanced at his watch. He was due there in ten minutes, for his personal report under his second hat, as Special Aide to the Prime Minister. He postponed the most difficult gift selection, for the King... which would have been simple, a few Euro-ounces of Dunhill's finest blend, if His Majesty's Scandinavian wife, otherwise an utterly charming Queen, hadn't made her husband give up the Royal Briar for her bed!

But as he walked briskly beneath the overarching Christmas decorations brightening the Burlington Arcade, MacKenzie, far more than any of his fellow British subjects doing their same last-minute buying all around him, was only too aware how fortunate the country was to have such a sound Royal marriage for such a small bargain. Queen Elizabeth the Second's act of surrendering her throne had been one of great personal generosity — astutely timed at the start of a New Millenium — but the late Queen's maternal gesture to her oldest son had unwittingly launched him, the rest of her family, and the country they ruled upon a course of constantly upsetting Royal change, interwoven with a far darker thread of Household tragedy.

MacKenzie's own father had died still unable to make himself able to accept the subsequent decade's events, and feeling personally responsible for one of them. At Charles the Third's Coronation he had been made Senior Equerry to the King, one of the posts MacKenzie now held with the present monarch: like his father also, the position was based on schoolboy friendship in the Royal early years as well as military proficiency. "Looking at it all from inside, as I could, most of what happened stemmed from sound motives," his father always insisted. "You have to understand, in those days we had such an apparently inexhaustible stock of hellraising young Royal possibles frontpaged in the Tabloids. The saying was you couldn't buy fish and chips without getting them wrapped in scandal by an Heir! But there were also full-length leaders in the *Times*. The first incoming Social Democratic government removed all but the two adolescent boys directly in line, William and George, from receiving State grants from the Civil List, the taxpaying public trough. After that, of course the other young ones didn't give a damn — they all had too much money of their own from land anyway — and now no sense of responsibility to the Nation whatsoever. Booze, drugs, fast cars, divorce, homosexual affairs, and sex with women in Hollywood and Down Under. All this was before gays became accepted in the Church and Armed Forces, and Australians stopped recognizing a King in Britain as their Monarch, after mine was killed in the avalanche on our Austrian skiing trip — the thing I feel so terrible for. I'd just gone down to Salzburg on official business, and I know of course I couldn't have changed the condition of the snow, but I might have done *something.* But even then, after all that, I suppose the Family, and me personally, could have gone on pretty much as before if it was only the sins of human nature we'd been hit with ... but the whole world got hit by the global flu pandemic from the Russian gene catastrophe, which cut through inbred families like a grain harvester. All King William's side went, with most of his Great-Aunt Anne's. And I lost your mother ..."

MacKenzie could still hear his father's defeated voice reciting that bleak litany of loss in front of a peat fire and peat whisky on those howling, lonely Highland nights with only the pair of them left in the old Highland manorhouse on the gaunt Skye coast at Blairloch. The personal crisis, coming after the string of Palace tragedies, had also prevented his father from attaining his Marine heart's desire to become Commander of the Regiment.

"Good King Wenceslas looked out ..."

Passersby sang the familiar words as a band of the Combined Household Guards marched along Oxford Street, playing carols for the holiday shoppers. And once again there *was* a good man as King, an almost overlooked surviving second cousin of William's from Princess Anne's line, MacKenzie thought, more cheerfully. A small but sound Succession ... and if he kept his own professional long Scottish nose in the trenches and out of gutter politics that final, and greatest Regimental personal career possibility won by his Grandfather, and Great Grandfather, was still open to himself.

Downing Street

OPPOSITE A DUNHILL'S tobacconist, the steel dragon's teeth and concrete blast-shields forming the outer anti-mortar ring installed at Whitehall Place to guard the Prime Minister's residence put the risk of death from smoking in its true place on the Royals' hazard scale. And not just for Christmas. Since the assassination of the King's distant relative, Admiral Earl Mountbatten, now more than fifty years ago, for Britain's Security Forces assigned to protect the Throne, an unspoken Fear of the Ultimate Attack had been constant everyday reality.

"You're cleared, sir."

The last human backup for the automated ID checkers waved MacKenzie past the machine's video scanner. The final set of dragon's teeth dropped down to the cobbles retained for the tourists whose already unbelievable number had grown even more so now that there was once again a stable Monarch and assured Succession for them to personal-video with the Bearskin Busbies at Buckingham Palace and Windsor Castle.

"Even for the Black Force, access to Master's ear will have to be curtailed this morning, Colonel."

The Downing Street barrier now blocking MacKenzie wasn't military automation. It was a snide little gutter turd from politics called Roger Slade. The Prime Minister's Principal Private Secretary was wearing his habitual smirk; it made granting access seem a personal Slade favor.

"The PM will see me," MacKenzie said curtly. "I have his message confirming our meeting."

"Master is otherwise engaged."

As Slade gave an arch nod towards the sound of a flushing toilet, the Secretary's high-pitched voice had an assumed Oxbridge accent which disguised something a lot lower on the social scale. In "Master's" place, MacKenzie would have fired Slade on assuming office: not because the PPS was gay but because Slade was a bitter man. Secret envy was the worst vice in any subordinate, but the PM, with his old-fashioned Officer's Mess adage of "Keep the Staff," didn't believe in sudden change.

"Ah, on the button as always, Hector. Good man." The Prime Minister was disengaged. Oblivious of his Secretary's openly jealous gaze he shook MacKenzie's hand brusquely, before gesturing him ahead to the private inner office, saying as he always did, "Sit down for a moment while I take stock."

General Sir John Gore, VC, sat himself down with a stiffness to his spine that had been with him since a bullet lodged beside it when he started his long career of service back in Queen Elisabeth's reign, winning his Victoria Cross for highest gallantry in recovering a remote patch of bog and sheep in the South Atlantic for her; only to see the Falklands given back to Argentina by the last government of her Grandson, William. Gore's most recent fight was constitutional. The Social Democrats' latest national referendum for a Second British Republic had been defeated by a squeaking two percent because of Gore's stump speeches in the Monarchy's defence.

His battered military campaign desk from his time as Chief of Defence Staff in the Second Gulf War was cluttered with photos of Royals past and present. For MacKenzie, who also knew so many of them, the PM's victory for the Throne had almost put the kiss of death on the already unlikely romantic relationship of a Lowland Republican Reporter and a Highland Royal Marine!

"I'm glad to see you smiling." Gore looked up from the hard-copy of the current A-T Threat Possibles, which was flanked by a faded color portrait of King William visiting Canada before that country also cut its ties to the Monarchy, to keep Quebec in the Maple Leaf's Confederation. "I agree with A-T's assessment," the Prime Minister said. "Except for the usual Holiday fanatics, things at home don't look too bad, this year."

"A couple of these Greater London's seem worth taking seriously," MacKenzie replied, pointing his lightpen at the telescreen on the PM's desk; the console supported a pensive portrait from the brief reign of the late King Charles. Gore was not a graduate of the computer age. He grunted at the screen and returned to the hardcopy.

"At least no IRA this year," Gore said. "That must be a first for this century. If I do say it myself, some of the credit lies here. I truly believe my latest talks with Dublin have settled the Irish Question once and for all. We finally are a United Kingdom."

Barely. As part of the wave of Nationalist devolution which swept Europe after the end of the Cold War (and one too many Australian Royal scandals by the last man to visit there as a Prince of Wales) the Welsh had dumped that thousand year office to retreat with their impenetrable language and virtual independance behind the Red Dragon flags along their border. MacKenzie's Scots, particularly Liz Ponti, were hot on their heels with the blue Cross of Saint Andrew. As for the Irish! With both Britain and Ireland as political equals in United Europe there was nothing left for any sane person to add on the bloody madness behind that thousand-year-old Question ... but the names in his file under Belfast Council showed that even with equal votes and freedoms some hard-core IRA were still prepared to carry on their obsolete struggle.

"Well if that's all," Gore said, "I'm off to Chequers with the grandchildren. My wife's managed to round up our whole tribe this Christmas, otherwise assure the King that I would have accepted His Majesty's gracious invitation to carve the bird at Sandringham. As it is, I suppose you'll be doing the honors?"

MacKenzie nodded and smiled. In all the years since he and the man who never thought he would be King had been at school together, his boyhood Royal chum's many skills had never encompassed either shooting birds or cutting them —

FLASH BLACK ALERT

The telescreen suddenly went dark, with vivid orange letters.

Belfast rumors Anniversary Special:
No What or When yet.

Gore stared at the message, then at his collection of Royal pictures. He picked up the portrait of the new Family and looked at the diffidently smiling, gentle man at its head. "Like his Second World War forebear, George the Sixth. The country has finally got a good one again." The Prime Minister echoed MacKenzie's earlier thoughts, then added, "I don't need to tell you to watch your Single-Malt sessions this holiday, Hector. Whatever it is — whenever: don't let it happen."

Two

Christmas Eve • Sandringham

MACKENZIE LANDED HIS jet-helo outside the village bordering the Estate. The local constable reported that there had been no sightings of anyone suspicious in this part of Norfolk "as far north as to Burnham Market, south to Barton Bendish, or east at Horningtoft." West didn't matter, it was the Wash; still, MacKenzie took a swing along its closest coastline to make sure for himself that the arm of the North Sea was clear.

The frozen broads and marshes were deserted. The setting sun was low enough that anything moving would cast a large shadow. Nothing did. He made a second pass using infrared for body heat, just to be sure, but the only signs of life the sensors now detected against the background skim of ice were one fallow deer and a badger just starting out on their own evening patrols. He decided to follow their example by setting the chopper down at an auxiliary pad beyond the Main Gate where a parked Range Rover was waiting.

As he drove the Rover along the Sandringham southern perimeter, he slowed down by a scrub-willow thicket and he concluded that the toughest part of his job in fact wasn't buying Christmas presents in Bond Street. The real nerve-cutter was trying not to overreact because of the secret Fear. He took this latest Belfast rumor seriously; he didn't assign it top —

"This is an ambush! You're taken prisoner!"

MacKenzie slammed to a halt and raised his hands.

"I really got you this time, didn't I, Colonel Ken?"

"You did, Your Highness," he replied, in a tone of suitable chagrin, although it was hard to keep a straight face when the bright yellow gumboots and tousled fair head looking up at him so triumphantly from the side of the Rover had been as visible as a Highland raven on a snowbank for the last five minutes!

"Can I have a ride now?" the Prince asked him. "My feet got a bit wet waiting for you to inspect my new tree fort."

MacKenzie saw that the gumboots were overflowing. His first urge was to give their gutsy young owner a hug, but going by the Dutch Uncle's rule book for Royal upbringing he instead said sternly, "The tree fort inspection must wait. I've told Your Highness before about thin ice on the stream."

"I know, but I wanted to be sure about the North Pole. Do you think Father Christmas really got my letter?"

MacKenzie tucked the brightly colored packages from Bond Street under the seat before allowing a smile: "Aye, lad, pretty sure — and you can ride this time. But no more polar explorations. We don't want you to catch a cold and miss your first New Year's party."

"If my father is really going to let me stay up for it."

"If His Majesty said so, then it will be so," MacKenzie reminded the boy, bulling the Rover through the willows to emerge on the edge of the new polo pitch. "Your father always keeps his word."

Which was more than could be said for the Monarch's own late male parent — the final Prince of Wales — but the less thought about that unfortunate example, the better! The present King's slight figure was standing on the terrace, shoulders hunched against the raw cold from the North Sea. MacKenzie smiled in sympathy. Whenever his Sovereign arrived at the Estate the King insisted on following the Spartan code of his maternal ancestors: Cold Baths, No Overcoats on Walks, No Central Heating. The invariable result was a chill which ruined the rest of the Royal holiday. Fortunately, his young son had a hardier constitution.

"What was it like, the very first New Year's Eve you ever stayed up for, Colonel Ken?"

MacKenzie swung the Range Rover around the edge of the polo pitch towards the small cottage of the Main Gate keeper, trying to remember his own initial experience of bringing in a brand new year. "It was in my family's house on the Western coast of Scotland, Your Highness, about two hundred miles north of Balmoral. My mother served a roast grouse with all its feathers on, and there was a haggis."

"I hate haggis."

"So did I." MacKenzie grinned, allowing the postponed hug from the gumboots warning. "On Robbie Burns' nights I still always hope there'll be a dog around somewhere to take the damned sheep's stomach off my plate."

"We have enough dogs at Sandringham to eat the *whole* sheep!" The Prince peered surreptitously into the classified message compartment below the Anti-Terror radio, then said in disappointment, "Sergeant-Major Wallop didn't leave any chocolate biscuits."

MacKenzie's regimental right-hand man had a secret sweet tooth but Wallop always saved one biscuit in case of being ambushed by this Royal passenger. The Regiment and the Family, MacKenzie thought: his life had been interwoven with both — military backbiters bitched that he was married to both! — from the day of his birth. The snide jab was untrue. He conceded that the boy in the passenger seat was a temporary substitute for the son he hadn't yet been able to have, but he intended to change that situation in the immediate future, by asking Liz Ponti the vital question as his first act of the New Year.

"My sister always eats her haggis," said the proxy son at his side. "She says it's because when she grows up she's going to be the Queen."

And she would make a great one, MacKenzie thought, but with a touch of sadness at how quickly a Royal heir had to leave childhood behind her for duty. For the Fear...

"Blink the headlights, Colonel Ken. My father's seen us."

On the terrace, the slim figure of the King waved in their direction before turning back gratefully to the warmth of the Drawing Room. MacKenzie saluted, feeling relieved himself for a moment of the secret burden.

"King George the Eighth has just been shot....!"

He heard such imaginary announcements in his head every day... and despised himself for allowing them to linger even for an instant. There was no sniper here. There could not be a sniper. The complete Estate perimeter, outer and inner, had footfall sensors and body-heat detectors; even the foxes of the Sandringham Hunt were picked up and located on the automated Anti-Terror status board.

"May I steer for this bit?" his passenger asked. MacKenzie nodded, keeping one hand close to the wheel as the two small ones grasped the spokes. "It must be really fun to drive the Rover yourself," the youthful driver said, barely squinting over the top.

"A lot of fun, Your Highness," he agreed. To defuse the accusations of privilege he kept hands-on the active service side as much as possible. MacKenzie had never wanted to be a Palace military lapdog — had always gone to great lengths to succeed in dangerous spots on his own merits — but being chosen as Senior Equerry to the Monarch was a non-declinable honor, and he had had no option other than to accept it. But taken together with his other post as Special Military Aide to the Prime Minister (doubling up of regular and Palace positions was routine in Britain's sharply reduced armed forces) the combined task was both enormous and a potential career killer. So far he had managed to balance on the professional seesaw...

"Sergeant-Major Wallop's waving at us now, Colonel Ken."

The boy was pointing at the mobile Anti-Terror command center parked under a camouflage net and some screening elms on the edge of the park. The sergeant-major's bulk completely blocked the door at the back of the vehicle. MacKenzie drew the Range Rover up beside it. Wallop saluted.

"Sorry to bother you, sir. Update on that other matter."

His subordinate glanced at the young figure sitting in the passenger seat. The Royal children might have to eat what was put before them but the security staff could still try to shield them with euphemisms from the worst of the reality that would hem in their future lives.

"Very good," Mackenzie said casually, getting down from the Rover. "See His Highness back to the nursery in the personnel carrier, would you Sergeant?"

"If Wallop is going to help you catch a real live bomber, I want to be there too," the boy protested.

"How about a chocolate biscuit first, Your Highness? I think we might find one in the troop carrier."

WALLOP'S ALTERNATE OFFER succeeded. MacKenzie watched the pair drive away happily in the armored vehicle, then he entered the mobile Command post. The computer state boards were quiet except for an amber Preparatory Warning arc extending about a mile along the Estate's southeast perimeter. It was unchanged from the last time he had seen it. He keyed in the latest All-Clear he had obtained from his personal reconnaisance. The arc changed to flashing dotted green, indicating that extra caution should still be taken in that sector.

"What about this other update?" he asked the duty signal woman.

"It's a verbal, sir. Holding on the Whitehall personal."

MacKenzie walked across to the video phone reserved for the Combined Intelligence net and keyed his identification code. He was unpleasantly surprised to recognize the male figure approaching on the screen. Even before he saw the face he recognized the hand. The face was early forties, boyishly handsome, with smooth Slavic cheekbones, and a thick wing of graying dark hair. The hand, placed on the Whitehall desk immediately in front of the transmitting camera, had a uniquely ragged scar across the back, as though an animal had ripped it. If that identification wasn't already excessive for an anonymous secret policeman, its possessor also walked with a marked limp.

"MacKenzie. I've been waiting. How are you?" The voice was cool, with a neutral accent not identifiable with any specific British region.

"Well, thanks." He managed to keep his own voice noncommittal. The last time the two of them had met in person had been at a formal board of enquiry, headed by MacKenzie, to investigate the death by torture of a terrorist suspect, a female. The accent of the chief witness, now facing him on the screen, in fact was the result of a Czechoslovakian birth, followed by a top-quality British education. The man's name was a similar amalgam: an unpronouncable collection of doubled Middle-European consonants; when reduced by his naturalized parents to plain English, it became Love. The bizarre name had added to the obscenity of the torture case, although no direct participation by Love had been proven. MacKenzie's unpleasant surprise was to see such a man back so close to the civilian center of Intelligence power at Whitehall.

He said tersely to the screen, "I've just come in from responding to the alert in the southern sector, promulgated by your people in London. There was nothing there. What is your update?"

"A correction. It shouldn't have been south. We have a new Suspect Irish sighting in a village called Weasenham St Peter. That's about twelve miles east of you. He was seen carrying a shotgun case with a silencer sticking out."

"The average Norfolk pubgoer on Christmas Eve wouldn't recognize a silencer from the bottom of their beer mug," MacKenzie answered. "It was probably a golf club."

"Probably," Love shrugged. "I thought you should know. The physical description could match Sean McDermid."

A name as Celtic as MacKenzie's own. It haunted his sleep, but he said, "They all match McDermid. His picture has been up in local post offices so long that every person buying a packet of stamps thinks they've seen him."

"I agree," Love replied. "If McDermid ever showed up in this country he would have new plastic fingerprints and a voicebox synthesiser, but dealing with the opposition's Killer One, we can't be too careful. Royal Security up there is your show, MacKenzie. I just pass it along."

Excessive threat incident reporting was another byproduct of the secret Fear. No one in the security bureaucracy wanted to be the one who missed the vital warning. As the scarred hand in the picture from Whitehall went dark, the weight of responsibility descended even more heavily on MacKenzie's shoulders.

The "opposition" were not the random maniacs who showed up at an Opening of Parliament with a water pistol or streaked in the buff past the Royal Enclosure at Ascot. The people behind the Fear were MacKenzie's lifelong opponents, as they had been for his father, and grandfather: the last fanatical renegade cells of the obsolete IRA.

"A man carrying an anti-tank rocket was observed..."

That was a greater imaginary threat than a marksman with a telescopic sight. On the flat Norfolk countryside Sandringham made a target which couldn't be missed by a drunk dart player! The rambling Edwardian structure had one hundred and fifty rooms — added on at random since the time of George the Fifth — with no proper firewalls and a second-thought sprinkler system haphazardly installed forty years ago. To make matters worse, once any fire started its flame would be fanned by the almost perennial wind off the North Sea.

Because of the new warning MacKenzie reassigned the extra Estate patrol from the south to the east, with particular care for the duck shooting area of marsh which was still used for that purpose by one or two of the more shellbacked Royals. All the other members of the Family set blameless examples of environmental awareness for the British public. If a Royal fox was chased these days, it was only for charity and blood was never spilled.

"His Highness is safe home, sir. He asked me to remind you not to forget the new tree fort inspection."

Wallop's reassuring mass had returned. MacKenzie put the grinning Sergeant-Major in charge of the Eastern sweep, which included the tree fort, and went to put on his third party hat.

Christmas Day

IN WHAT WAS almost part of the longstanding Sandringham Tradition for the Season, the big day dawned not white, but raining — a typically steady Norfolk drizzle with a raw edge from the sea. It did nothing to dampen the spirits of the Family in MacKenzie's charge. Like all the others in the Kingdom, Royal Stockings were opened as usual — far too early! — in the Nursery Quarters, and too noisily shared with tolerant Royal parents in their bedroom. By the time MacKenzie returned from receiving an all-clear overnight Security report and making his equally uneventful dawn perimeter patrol with Wallop, the King and Queen were downstairs having a

Traditional "First Real Present" Breakfast (opening one gift, with a boiled brown Estate Farm egg) before the next Traditional item, Attending Village Church, with their still excited children.

"Only another pen set? I asked for a Range Rover!" The young Prince stared in disappointment at the eagerly torn wrappings in front of his plate.

"Even Range Rover drivers have to write properly," the King said, with a light smile that included MacKenzie, whose handwriting scrawl was a joke that went all the way back to their first shared days as New Boys at boarding school.

"Besides," said the Prince's mother, with the charming touch of Scandinavia still present in her otherwise perfect English, "Father Christmas hasn't finished yet. We must all be patient until after Daddy makes his Speech."

The Christmas Address was as old as the house, dating from the beginning of radio in the reign of Queen Victoria's grandson, King George the Fifth. Then it went crackling around the globe to the red-painted quarter of it that formed the British Empire: now, thanks to a population explosion, it was heard and seen via satellite by five times that number in what was left of the loose confederation still called the Commonwealth.

A SMALL BATTERY of transmission dishes was waiting at the church. The local members of the congregation paid no attention to technology as they filed in to the ancient Norman structure. Despite the well established composition of both groups, all of them — and the new Vicar — were scrupulously vetted nonetheless by Security ID and metal detectors. MacKenzie entered last, sitting in the pew directly behind the one reserved for Sandringham's First Family and listening to words of Confession from a blameless monarch.

"*We have left undone those things which we ought to have done...*"

The only possible fault the trendily modern Vicar might find in the current Defender of the Faith was the King's insistence on using the archaic Old Prayer Book order of worship for Family occasions! The God being defended didn't seem to mind. By the time the service was over the drizzle had stopped. The cavalcade drove back through puddles under a clearing sky. MacKenzie appreciated the change for comfort's sake but rain or shine didn't matter to the infrared sensors. With the King safely home to give his televised Speech from the study, his Chief of Household Security prepared for the most nerve-racking part of Family tradition.

THE GREAT TREE, cut from the Estate, was topped as usual with an Angel handpainted by Queen Victoria, and flanked as always by a clockwork Drummer Boy given to her at their first married Christmas by her Consort, Prince Albert. The modern Royals waited beside the Drummer who was wound up to deliver a ratatatat as Father Christmas — a.k.a., in Anti-Terror clearance, that Department's Deputy, MacKenzie, Col. Hector — in white beard and pillow, carrying the scarlet flannel Present sack, entered the Drawing Room to further traditional wild young Royal applause.

Which got a lot wilder when the toy Range Rover package, the tantalisingly last of the afternoon, was opened.

"You got my letter! I mean the real North Pole one!"

The Prince began to drive the Rover at maximum velocity around a pinelog Dolls' House given to his enchanted sister by their mother's relatives in Norway. The King and Queen gave each other matching sweaters to combat the English weather. At the bottom of the Family pile MacKenzie found presents addressed to himself: a battered pewter antique Highland drinking mug, "For Father Christmas's off-duty midnight malts!" from their Majesties, and a crudely framed and hand-drawn crayon picture of Santa and his helper in an unlikely position, "Coenel Ken and SargantMajor Wallop Inspecting My new TreeHouse."

"I'm sorry the frame isn't better," said the Prince. "I ran out of pocket money at the last minute."

MacKenzie looked at the rest of the objects around him... the splendid Tree, decorated with its museum-piece Victorian ornaments; the scarlet-berried Estate holly on the tops of the Stubbs' oil paintings of thoroughbred horseflesh; the comfortably overstuffed Edwardian armchairs and layers of faded Turkey carpets too threadbare to be kept in any upscale Better Home... and this lonely little boy he loved, waiting uncertainly for a grownup's gruff military approval. "Your Highness," he said, swallowing the lump in his throat, and planting a most unmilitary kiss on the Prince's forehead, "Under such circumstances, the frame is perfect."

"Colonel sir," said a voice over the mini-receiver in the white beard behind his ear, "Wallop speaking. Sorry to bother Father Christmas, but it's that Mr Love again."

OUTSIDE THE CHRISTMAS lights of the drawing room it was dusk. As Wallop materialized like a wraith, MacKenzie reflected that for a man with the mass of a battle tank the Sergeant-Major's surprising ability to hide was a useful commando attribute which had saved his superior's life on more than one occasion.

"All quiet otherwise?" MacKenzie asked him.

"Not a peep anywhere, sir. I've just come back from the duck marsh. Three tits-up mallards, and a water rat, nothing else."

Inside the mobile Command center the screens were equally dormant. The amber arc to the east was also showing dotted green, like the previously cleared segment to the south. West was the Wash, the safe arm of the North Sea. But the update must be urgent. This time MacKenzie didn't have to key in his ID code: Love was calling clear on the Direct line.

"Didn't mean to spoil Santa's party." Love curled his lip in a way that managed to remind MacKenzie of two things simultaneously: how much he had disliked this Special Security bastard on their earlier meetings... and that he was still wearing his red Father Christmas suit for this one!

"Tell me," MacKenzie said, ripping off the cottonwool beard.

"We've just had a Positive from a place called Holme next the Sea. Confirmed Irish. Timing critical. A suspect quote: 'Wait till bloody Brit midnight, if you want a Happy fucking New Year!' "

MacKenzie saw the hamlet on the screen. Due North. Eleven miles. A Perimeter Breached signal was showing from a northern footfall sensor! On his way to the door MacKenzie said to Love's screen image, "The same one as yesterday, with the guncase?"

"Larger. A golf bag. That could hide an anti-tank."

Which could pierce a brick wall. MacKenzie shouted at the Duty Officer, "Black Alert, north sector! All screens Red!" and raced from the Command center.

Wallop already had the Range Rover pointed in the Threat direction. As they roared away from the main house, MacKenzie caught a glimpse of the family he had sworn to protect with his life when he was commissioned a Royal Marine. The father was standing beside the piano again. He was wearing his new sweater. His matching wife at the keyboard was smiling up at him. The Heir to the Throne, their daughter, was concentrating on moving a tiny sofa in the pinelog dolls' house and —

"Where's the Prince?" he asked Wallop.

"System's showing His Highness with the present you gave him sir. Says he's gone to play with it in his tree house. But that's clean, while you were inside we re-swept it."

MacKenzie saw the clean co-ordinates. Half a mile north. Next to a man with a bomb.

THE MOBILE DATA link screen in the Range Rover was still showing the footfall sensor. The intruder was moving towards an area of trees first planted for an Edwardian pheasant shoot. Now, like the rest of the Royal Estates, it was a nature preserve, dedicated to protecting the wildlife of Britain.

"There's a woodcutter's path," MacKenzie told Wallop. "Hard right, a hundred yards!"

The Rover took the corner on two wheels, at an angle which almost had it over... but the Sergeant-Major was a superb driver. The vehicle slammed four tires back on the frozen track. The ghostly silver trunks of birches reflected in the headlights. The blackness of Scotch pines hid anything behind them.

"Looks like he's going for the old charcoal burner's hut, sir."

Wallop nodded at the data screen. The sensor signal was only half a mile ahead, approaching a small clearing in the trees.

"Lights off!" MacKenzie snapped. "Change places!"

When he took the wheel the silver trunks were gone — but the Rover's speed increased. Only the night-vision image of the track on the infrared screen prevented an instantly fatal collision. A narrow opening, not much more than a footpath, appeared on the screen, north of the track. The sensor signal showed each tread of the intruder as a blue dot. The charcoal burner's hut was marked as a green circle.

"His Highness, sir! Hostile's between him and the tree house!"

The blue dots were moving to intercept a row of yellow ones, the color of a small boy's gumboots...

SOMEHOW MACKENZIE MISSED the trees. He saw a ditch and didn't bother. He smashed the pedal to the floor and flew over it. His skull hit the roof when the Rover landed. His neck might have broken but that didn't matter either. He had saved thirty seconds. At moments like this all he heard in his head was his own father's voice saying of a King's death, *I could have done SOMETHING!* — half a minute extra was all that counted. He saved two more by not opening gates. The Rover crashed them, hurling the shattered pieces sideways with its armored plough-blade. He rounded a stone wall with the temperature boiling from a tach dial jammed at the end of the Red Line —

"Okay now, sir. We've past attacker's point of intercept."

Only Wallop's huge fist, still clenched hard enough to snap a gunbutt, showed that the Sergeant-Major had also been under a certain degree of driving tension.

With the Prince's track safely behind them, MacKenzie let the Rover coast to a halt. The wood was quiet. They were at the western edge of the clearing. The blue dots would enter it to their left, at a pointblank range of fifty yards. He took a night-sighted automatic rifle from its stowage at his elbow and settled the barrel into a support on the Rover's dashboard.

"I've got the bastard on my scope, sir."

In front of Wallop the pale red electronic outline of a human figure materialized above the blue dots at the edge of the green circle. MacKenzie saw the figure in his own telescopic finder. It was kneeling on the ground, dropping an object from its shoulder.

"Lights on!"

The headlamps flared. A man was caught in them. His face was darkened with soot. His white teeth showed in a grimace that mixed fear and rage. The object he had dropped was not a golf bag. Two fresh carcasses lay on the frosted grass of the clearing.

"Gosh!" said a piping eight-year-old voice behind them. "Have you caught a real live bomber?"

"Shit no!" Wallop exclaimed with disgust. "Begging Your Highness's pardon, just a bloody local rabbit poacher."

New Year's Eve

THE STUFFED PILLOW and long white beard act was safely over. So was a week without further threat. Continuing Royal Tradition, the Monarch had been joined by other immediate members of the Family to welcome the new year. Once again, as MacKenzie looked at the small group gathered in the Drawing Room, he thought what a contrast it was to the huge Royal clan assemblies in King Charles's time, before the Epidemic, when his father had this job...

But at least this annual celebration in the heart of the Norfolk countryside still allowed a special informality not possible under the gilt of Buckingham Palace or within the six-foot-thick walls of Windsor Castle. For one week of the year a British King could let his thinning hair down enough to sing archaic pop ballads in a slightly flat tenor, while his Anti-Terror watchdog vamped the Household's hundred-year-old Steinway piano — backed by a squawling musical partner, in another Victorian Tradition like her clockwork Drummer Boy. This was the ear-shattering live presence of the Household Bagpiper, and MacKenzie's late-night malt partner in Highland laments, Major Jock MacGillivray, Royal Scots Guards, brought from Balmoral.

"Surely that's enough musical ability until Auld Lang Syne!" A laughing woman standing between the King and the Pipe Major backed up her suggestion by turning on the Drawing Room television set. As the image materialized she added with more amusement, to MacKenzie, "My Intelligence sources in the nursery tell me that you also play your piano for this bright lady, Hector."

The image was Liz Ponti, anchoring the global New Year's show for BBC from Trafalgar Square on satellite. The woman across the piano was the King's first cousin. When MacKenzie was only twenty-one, taking a course on military history at Cambridge, they had appeared together in a revival of *Evita*: she had played the lead and he had been the low-life pounding the piano in the bars of Buenos Aires. Now, as well as Liz, two decades of life separated them, but the turn of a year didn't turn thoughts back to just life's political and military might-have-beens...

"We can only be good friends, Maam," MacKenzie replied deadpan to the Nursery Intelligence query. "I'm afraid the bright BBC lady is tone-deaf."

Jock MacGillivray guffawed, even as he discovered that this tonal fact *was* how MacKenzie first met Liz. She had been interviewing a legendary American bass player at the end of a spectacular riff in a smoky Soho cellar, and she congratulated him for the wrong notes. MacKenzie, accompanying on piano, corrected her... and that unlikely meeting place matched the oddness of their consequent relationship. He was Royalist in every bone and sinew, with a thousand years of Highland family background. Liz was born and bred in a middle-class suburb of Glasgow, trained in film at the University of California, ardently in favor of a separate Scotland, a written Constitution in British politics, and totally republican in sentiment. With that almost treasonous political mixture and her half-Italian, jet-black hair her conquest of him was complete. She gave him her view of priorities in bed after their second meeting. "Jamming in a cellar shows an exploitable little kink in the Royal Marine armor. How about letting me do a program on women going through Commando training...?"

"I'm relieved to hear that you're still married to the Regiment," the woman behind the piano murmured now, with a trace of a smile that hinted at something good they might both have missed.

"Play the Saints marching for us, Colonel Ken!"

The young Prince dropped the model Range Rover and grabbed his older sister's hand to drag her forward. The solemn little girl held back, looking at her father. The King smiled encouragingly. Only then did she allow herself to let go and join in as a normal ten-year-old. It was a rare flash of the unique bond between a present and future Sovereign of Britain. One that could not be fully comprehended by anyone who would not themselves wear a crown. Even MacKenzie, with his lifelong Family association, realized that there were areas of Royal experience he would never enter. He might have, almost, he thought, if he had pursued the possibility offered once before by the woman at the piano.

"And now we're joined by the Prime Minister," Liz, the other woman in his life, told her worldwide viewers.

A face probably more familiar than the King's appeared on the screen. The silver hair, brushed in a wing to the right; sideburns clipped sharply at the center of the ear; military moustache, trimmed just as correctly to the corners of his lip; blue eyes, ruddy skin . . . this old man behind a campaign desk *was* England.

"His moustache is all blurry," said the young Prince.

"Damn it!" the King exclaimed, in a rare show of temper as Gore's picture remained skewed. "I wanted to see President Nimitz's party at the White House. Send the bloody thing back and get another first thing in the morning."

To outsiders, MacKenzie realized, it would seem absurd that the television belonging to the country's wealthiest family was not owned but rented. The reason was a typically Royal mixture of penny-saving and tradition. Elizabeth the Second had once possessed a set which broke down at a critical moment during a horse race. To avoid any repetition of the problem, a local rental firm was engaged to provide a new set, in perfect condition, immediately in advance of a Family arrival at any of their principal residences.

"Colonel Ken had a Great Grandfather who burned down the White House!" his Princely admirer informed the rest of the party.

"Only scorched it, Your Highness." Fortunately MacKenzie had warmer personal current links with Washington: he had played real jazz last year at the Inaugural bash for Maureen Nimitz, America's second female Chief Executive. In return the new President had graciously forgiven him for the historically accurate but still awkward fact that in the War of 1812 MacKenzie's regiment, commanded by one of his direct forebears, had indeed razed her predecessors' capital.

"Wherever you are, this is Liz Ponti, from Trafalgar Square, reminding: Fifteen seconds to the Witching Hour! And let the good times roll for Hogmanay! Unless you're driving! Now start counting: Five, four, three, two..."

The wildly excited Prince blew a noisemaker and shouted, "Last minute! Everyone put their Witch hats on!"

MacKenzie laughed. With both hands engaged in Auld Lang Syne he bent his neck for the boy to slip a paper tricorn on his head, as a screeching blast in his ear announced the year's main event for the Household Piper. MacKenzie checked his A-T watch with Liz. 23:58:59. They agreed to the second —

"Look, everyone! A shooting star at midnight! Colonel Ken, make a wish!"

MacKenzie glanced out through the double French Windows at the black sky beyond the polo pitch. At the end of a small boy's pointing finger he saw a streak of light that any other watcher in the Norfolk winter fields might think was a lucky shooting star, and wish...

Or pray.

We have left undone those things we ought to have done. Whatever it is — don't let it happen!

MacKenzie had shared a King's prayer of confession and a Prime Minister's last warning. He could answer the first part: this lethal *it* was an incoming missile, his military training told him... and that there was no time left in the frozen, eternal split second of horror which always separated battlefield life from death. Human prayers were too late to stop this lethal star from falling. Once a homing ground-to-ground missile reached the end of its guidance plan trajectory, even God in Heaven couldn't stop it falling.

Or the Unthinkable from happening.

MACKENZIE HAD TO. Unlike his father, absent at Salzburg, he was *here.* If his Highland sixth sense could just alert him, give him some slightest hint of the missile's programed point of aim he still might —

Wait till bloody Brit midnight...!

Love's IRA warning. He saw the countdown clock from Trafalgar Square behind Liz. The missile was locked to the rented television! The King was closest to it, with the Queen, their daughter, the Bagpiper... but that group was fifteen feet from MacKenzie at the Steinway.

The Prince was in the curved bay of it, right beside him.

So, at the end of the timeless instant of ultimate Fear and bottomless self-rage that coincided with the inevitable shattering of French door glass: — at 00:00:00, on New Year's Day, as all the system sensors in Southern Britain recorded overload at Sandringham, Hector MacKenzie made the only available, unthinkable, almost unspeakable final choice that even his agonized father had been spared.

Bellowing, "MacGillivray! Take Their Majesties...!" he hurled his own useless body across the piano to save their vital boy.

The Witching Hour

THE PIANO SAVED MacKenzie. He was not aware of that at first. He was only aware that he could not move because something large was blocking him. When his hand recoiled from the heat of the hinge he realized that he was behind the lid. But the lid was on the floor. The piano was on its side. Balanced perfectly on edge like an upright, except that in an Alice in Wonderland scene the ivory and ebony keyboard ran vertically towards the ceiling. What was left of the ceiling. Most of its Edwardian woodlath and horsehair plaster seemed to have fallen on the English Oak parquet floor and Turkish carpets all around him. He heard a crackling noise in his right ear. His left ear didn't hear anything except a thin inner screech like endless Morse Code. Both his eyes worked, although lumps of grit scratched the lenses every time the lids blinked. Through constant tearing he saw the hair on the back of the hand that had touched the hinge begin to sizzle... and realized that the crackling noise was fire.

He was burning!

He pulled his hand in sharply. The curve of the up-ended Steinway formed an arch just large enough for him to crawl through. He began to move and discovered that the piano stool was still on his head. He shook it off and eased forward beneath the arch... to find that only now was he seeing the true side of hell that used to be peaceful Norfolk.

THE DRAWING ROOM was blazing from its center, outwards. He got up and moved forward. The heat took off his eyebrows. He moved forward. The French doors were flaming on their hinges, the glass was melting. He moved forward. A burning beam from the ceiling fell across the piano. It fell over on its back with a twang of death as all the strings snapped like MacKenzie's frozen moment of sanity.

He stopped moving forward.

HIS KING AND QUEEN were dead. The King's brother was dead. So were the King's uncle and two aunts, and the aunts' two children. And the woman from Cambridge, who once played *Evita*...

MacKenzie saw all that might-have-been in a single glance. He was not surprised. In the super explosive power generated by a High-Oxygen warhead no one at the point of impact could expect to live. He understood that because the military side of his brain was not mad. But because he was a man as well as a soldier, the human part of him still hoped insanely: *At least not the other children. Not the two Special Ones*...

THE DEAD TEN-YEAR-OLD girl who would have been his next Queen was under the body of Jock MacGillivray — but that still did not mean that all hope was dead in this region of hell that used to be peaceful Norfolk. The Estate firemen and Emergency crews had already arrived.

"Get out, Sir!" Wallop's voice called. "You can't stay in there!"

MacKenzie could, his mad part wanted him to — *to die beside them* — but the sane part paused long enough to think seriously about grabbing the closest fireman's protective clothing. Instead, he turned his back on the bulky silver boots and heavy mica-glass visor to re-enter hell unprotected and find what he must look for.

THE SMALL SHAPE WAS lying where MacKenzie's last-second lunge must somehow have managed afterall to place it: on the blast-protected side of the fallen piano, in the outer darkness with the scorched model of a Range Rover... and one small outstretched hand holding a clockwork Drummer Boy. MacKenzie fell to his knees. He bent his head... and in this roasting hell felt a tiny breath from heaven cool his cheek.

"Wallop! Bring up the evac team! The Heir is *alive!*"

BUT HE COULD not hold the Heir's small hand for comfort. Both hands were skinless. He could not hug the small body: it was too badly blistered. MacKenzie could only weep, as he wrapped it in his own still-smouldering Marine dress jacket, and carried the priceless, featherlight burden with the Drummer Boy... and repeat over and over again, into a little boy's one unburned ear... as he bore him out through the shattered doors, and placed him on a stretcher... and crouched beside him in the medic Evac chopper taking him to London —

"Be strong, Lad. Be brave. You will be King! God bless and save Your Royal Highness."

PART ONE

Interregnum

One

New Year's Day • En Route Reality

TEARS AND PRAYERS were not enough. Even in this unthinkable tortured moment the military side of MacKenzie's brain was working through the concrete implications of this atrocious act.

The first thing was the Prince's safety. Of course the boy would receive the ultimate in medical treatment that it was currently possible to obtain. But that generated another immediate problem. His bedside would become the focal point for the nation, which would immediately make it another target. The deranged intellect behind this rocket could launch one again. MacKenzie did not yet have confirming forensic evidence but almost certainly the radius of the kind of hand-launched missile which could inflict such damage must be up to twenty miles. That meant it could be fired from anywhere on the circumference of Greater London into the center of the capital. Complete security for such an area was impossible. Already, as the Evac helicopter was lifting off with its irreplacable cargo, MacKenzie realized what he must do.

He would ask no one's permission. He would tell no one the whole truth. At this terrible turning point in British history his position was unique: he alone could protect this boy and preserve his Crown.

He got on the scrambled Anti-Terror line to Central Command. "Send a second Medic chopper immediately," he ordered. "Rendezvous soonest, at Special Forces Base Chedburgh. Then alert hospital authorities at the new South London Burn Center to receive His Highness as a patient. Estimated time of arrival, forty minutes."

Chedburgh was south of Bury St Edmonds. It wasn't as isolated as MacKenzie would have wished but it had adequate facilities and was on the direct flight path to London. He fired off a flurry of deep-code messages: to the Prime Minister's Office; to the War Room, personal, the Chief of Staff; to his superior at Anti-Terror; to the head of the new civilian National Police. By the time he was finished every radio frequency in Britain was being used. Except this one, from the stretcher side, which he kept for his exclusive use.

"Chedburgh field in sight, sir."

The Evac pilot indicated a beacon ahead. Navigation lights of the requested second helicopter were approaching from the starboard side.

"There's a Special Forces field hospital with a roof landing at the far end," MacKenzie said. "Put down there and tell the other helo to come in beside us."

From his crouched position next to the stretcher he had no way of knowing whether his other instructions had been complied with but, as the craft banked for the landing, halogen floodlights suddenly illuminated a large red cross on the roof of the building. A team in white coats emerged. The chopper touched down. MacKenzie jumped out. A man in one of the white coats ran towards him.

"Surgeon General Walker," the man said. "I only have half what you asked for but it's enough to get us started. The rest will be here by the time I need it." He turned to a pair of nurses behind him, "Bring out His Royal Highness."

MacKenzie watched the little figure on the stretcher pass by him. He said to the Surgeon, "That is the last time anyone here uses the title. From this moment, for everyone else, he is to be known only as the patient."

The doctor raised an eyebrow, but didn't argue — except to say, "Have you seen your own condition?"

MacKenzie's ear was ringing less. The rest of his body was starting to feel as shattered as the ruined piano. He said, "I can get patched up later," and went inside the building where a soldier in combat fatigues stood waiting. Like the Surgeon General, the Brigadier's pips on his shoulder epaulettes showed that he also outranked MacKenzie. He was also prepared to take his orders.

"I have received the Prime Minister's special authorization," the Brigadier told him. "We already have two anti-missile companies in close position, and a third at extended range. One of your Royal Marine squads is managing the gate and perimeter security."

MacKenzie nodded. "And the change in cargo?"

"Ready down below." The Brigadier gestured to a second flight of stairs, "I'll come with you."

"That won't be necessary, General," he said tersely. "You have better things to do."

"Not for the next thirty seconds," the man replied.

MacKenzie doubled down the stairs. At the foot of them he saw what he had asked for. Another bandaged figure lay on a mobile stretcher. Only the figure's lips were visible.

"He looks a little too tall," MacKenzie said.

The Brigadier agreed. "He's a year older, but I thought it was close enough and there wasn't time to look further. And security with his dependants won't be a problem."

"Why not?" asked MacKenzie.

"He's my son."

The Brigadier looked him in the eye. They understood each other. They might never have thought they would have to honor it in such a brutal fashion, but this was what their oaths to serve the Crown had meant when they first took them.

Mackenzie said, "I'll get him back to you as soon as possible." He turned to the bandaged boy, "What's your name, son?"

"Robert, sir. Bobby, actually."

"Right, Bobby. We're going to give you a ride in that other chopper out there. Don't be worried, I'll be right with you."

The lips between the bandages managed a smile. As the Brigadier bent to kiss his son, a door opened behind him. Another stretcher with another bandaged boy, a Royal one, was wheeled in. MacKenzie said to the Brigadier, "I have two final instructions, General. Once anyone arrives at this establishment, they stay here. No one leaves. And except for yourself, on my coded line, there will be no communication whatsoever with the outside world."

"Understood."

MacKenzie turned to board the waiting second chopper, then turned back. He bent again to the stretcher from Sandringham and repeated his incantation to the little figure with the Drummer Boy. He knew it was only superstition, that God had nothing to do with saving the child beside the scorched toy. If there was a God this atrocity would never have happened. He repeated it again, *"Be brave, Lad. Be strong..."* This time, as he was about to straighten, the one blue eye that wasn't swathed in bandages, opened very slightly, and saw him. The expression in the eye was one MacKenzie would never forget: deep fear, overcome by pure courage. It was an expression worthy of a boy who *would* be King. The small head nodded, once, in a movement that was barely perceptible, before the eye drooped and closed.

MacKenzie squared his shoulders, saluted his titular superior and said, "A personal request, sir. Even if there's no change, I would appreciate those reports on my coded line as often as you can make them."

The Brigadier's adam's apple bobbed as he gulped, hard. "Hector," he said, "that too is understood."

INSIDE THE SECOND chopper, the second boy had already been strapped into place by two army medics, and given a sedative. He would remember nothing further of his trip to London. For MacKenzie it seemed endless. Half his mind was with the child he had been forced to leave alone behind him. The other half boiled with lust for action.

Meanwhile he could do nothing but let the medics patch up his superficial burns, and know that he had failed. And reproach himself over and over again for not expecting the flaming track of the missile threat to come from the wrong direction; from the safe side, the West side, from the sea...?

He watched the lit-up houses going by beneath him. Not just the towns, like Colchester, or even the villages, Great Commard and Little Horkesley: in this darkest hour in the middle of the night every home in Britain was awake. Every person watching would be feeling the same emotion. Every heart would be howling to heaven for Revenge.

"Army One, this is Chelmsford Police reporting. London Burns' Unit is fully ready to receive you."

"Army One, this is Air Force Central Region. You may proceed direct: all London approaches are clear of civil traffic."

There was no more room in MacKenzie's mind for introspection. Their position was known. From this point on, anything could happen. He scanned constantly for the telltale flare of a ground-to-air missile. The message traffic kept building. A blaze of light filled the approaching horizon. The capital was waiting.

If a missile did fire now, he wouldn't see it. They banked in across the new Broadcasting Tower at Hampstead Heath, then due south. He saw the contrasting darkness of Hyde Park, and off to his right, a building which would normally be floodlit, also waiting. Buckingham Palace. Now it was also dark, the yard behind the toy soldiers' sentry boxes in front of it, deserted...

"Oh, bloody good, sir! That'll show the murdering bastards!"

The voice was the chopper pilot's. He was pointing at the Palace roof. A single spotlight had come on. It was shining on a white needle. As the helicopter went past, almost at eye level, MacKenzie recognized the dumpy male figure of a Palace coachman standing at the base of the mast. His name was Stubbins, an amiable oaf, who had no business being there: the man's normal duty was just to carry a daily despatch box... but then Stubbins yanked a halyard. At the eye of the needle, the top of the mast, a scrap of color suddenly unfurled. Gold and Scarlet. The Royal Standard.

The coachman gave a ragged salute.

The King is dead. Long live the King!

The chopper's downdraft snapped the flag taut to prove to the world that a thousand years of history continued: once again a British Sovereign had returned to his capital.

But he hadn't. He was in Chedburgh. At the same time that MacKenzie felt a new lump in his throat from this display of loyalty by a simple Palace servant, his mind returned to the boy battling such pain, alone, a hundred miles north.

"Ready to disembark the patient, sir."

To save a few valuable seconds the onboard medics had already released the straps holding the stretcher. One nurse threw the hatch open. Night air rushed in. Another red cross moved up towards them as the chopper touched down. Even before the undercarriage had absorbed the full weight of the landing a Trauma Team from the Burns Center was rushing the stretcher into a mobile Crisis Unit waiting on the roof. They passed a single BBC video photographer: MacKenzie's instructions had been to allow one Media camera through Security to record the scene. The Crisis Unit was a mini-ward, with state-of-the-art burn support and monitoring equipment. Once the stretcher and patient were inside it, the entire unit descended in an elevator. The BBC photographer moved to follow.

MacKenzie blocked her. "Sorry. No closer!"

The lift doors closed. The elevator stopped after a single floor. The doors opened. He saw troops in combat gear guarding a hospital passageway. A major saluted him.

"Medical team has been cleared. The area is sealed, sir."

"Very good." MacKenzie acknowledged the salute and accompanied the Crisis Center into a regular Burns Trauma ward. The Major hesitated, looking at the bandaged figure on the water bed.

"Sir, if you don't mind, but all the rumors, my people are wondering: it isn't really possible? The bastards didn't take out everyone? There can't be just His Royal Highness left?"

"It's not a rumor, Major."

"But it *was* Paddy?"

"We don't know that yet."

"My Christ. When we do know — !"

"We will do our duty, Major." MacKenzie told him firmly. "We will not let our imaginations run away with us. You and your men's present duty is to protect this building, and this floor, and this room to the limit of your ability. No one enters. And after I've gone, no one else leaves. The medical staff will remain in-house until the crisis for the Prince has passed."

"So he will get better?"

"Of course."

The Major breathed a sigh of relief. MacKenzie thanked the power of military discipline. Nothing else could hide his own terrible uncertainty from anyone.

"I forgot, sir. A pool group of Media are waiting below. Do I have your permssion to let them through?"

"Absolutely not! Bulletins on the Prince's condition will be released to the Press by the medical advisor for the Royal Family, in consultation with the senior burn specialist. They already know from the BBC that His Highness has arrived safely. You can add that the best possible treatment has started."

The double doors of the Trauma Ward slid shut behind him, blocking off further questions from the outside world. A woman in sterile surgical clothing stepped forward. MacKenzie recognized the King's Physician — the *late* king's! The self-reminder was like getting a football boot in the gut. He had seen the bodies in Norfolk: he still had not begun to grasp the fact of death.

"Good," said the Physician, looking down at the stretcher. "Our patient is still sleeping. I think we'll just ensure that he continues."

The eyelids of the Brigadier's son were blinking rapidly in dream movement. While the doctor administered further light sedation intravenously, a male nurse swiftly began removing the dummy bandages. MacKenzie tried to control his impatience. Although he had a thousand urgent things to do, he owed it to the boy's father to see the lad safely on his way home. There was no necessity to risk another brave child's life by keeping him here. If a second attempt was made against the Throne, the adults apparently helping to save its Heir at this Burn Center were all volunteers.

"There we are," the nurse said. "All ready to travel."

Dressed in jeans and a sweatshirt with a popular cartoon character, the sleeping boy looked like any other nine-year-old going home from a hospital. The nurse thrust a stuffed toy into his arms to complete the picture, then wheeled him to a second elevator door at the rear of the Trauma Center. It was marked: DIRECT TO SURGERY.

MacKenzie looked at the now empty Trauma Center and waterbed. He said to the Royal Physician, "I'll leave you with your invisible patient. Thank you, and your staff, for the risk you're taking."

She waved it aside. "I understand the military necessity for the cloak and dagger. We'll keep up our end of this charade until —" Her professional calm shattered. "Dear God! It's unthinkable! It cannot have happened."

But it had.

INSIDE THE SURGERY elevator, MacKenzie watched the indicator lights showing the lift's descent to the operating theater in the hospital's first below-ground level. When he had checked that the space was deserted he nodded at the male nurse. He wheeled the Brigadier's boy through an equally empty post-recovery room to a sign saying, AMBULANCE RAMP. In the underground parking area beyond it, an ordinary civilian ambulance was waiting with its engine running. Not quite ordinary: the driver and attendant were from Special Forces, and both armed.

The boy and his stuffed toy were embarked. MacKenzie followed.

The driver said, "It's Chedburgh then?"

He nodded. The vehicle began moving smoothly up the ambulance ramp. The male nurse waved, as though he was saying goodbye to a regular patient. Then they were part of the anonymity of Greater London. But it was not the usual late night hangover atmosphere in the capital. All the lights were on in the windows. Groups of people milled aimlessly in the streets. It was the kind of random movement that could turn to violence in an instant. All it needed was a target for its pentup anger.

"Just show me anything bloody Irish," said the Special Forces man, supposed to be a neutral ambulance attendant.

MacKenzie didn't envy the person responsible for controlling such national anger. The other man he worked for. It was time to put on his third hat, as Military Aide to the Prime Minister. At the fourth set of traffic lights past Westminster Bridge he said to the driver, "Stop here."

The ambulance halted at a pair of steel gates. They had first been installed thirty years before, after an earlier part of the Irish Problem tried to assassinate their arch enemy of that time, Britain's legendary female Prime Minister, Margaret Thatcher, the Iron Lady.

That was then. The ultimate horror was now. MacKenzie got out. The rear door slammed. The ambulance became part of the stream of red tail lights heading north on the new East Anglian Motorway. North to that other hospital bed, where there was a real patient. MacKenzie's heart cried out to let him be there too, holding the boy's hand, to comfort him.

Duty, and a lifetime's discipline, commanded otherwise.

10 Downing Street

INSIDE THE STEEL gates the street and the building were iron-tight with Black Alert security. After double-checking that with the Officer in Charge, MacKenzie proceeded to the Prime Minister's Office to make his report. Once again he was halted by Slade's snide voice:

"The Black Force will have to wait for Master's decision to address the Nation, but I'm sure you'd like to watch this particular performance, Colonel."

The Secretary smirked and flicked a switch on his desk intercom. Even though the Video Privacy bulb was lit and the telescreen should have remained dark, an image appeared of the inner office. Gore was seated, studying the battered military campaign clock on his antique desk. A BBC television camera was focussed on him. An off-screen voice said,

"In five seconds, Prime Minister...!"

MacKenzie suddenly understood Slade's last jab. The voice belonged to Liz — and the little bastard PPS had just caught MacKenzie's momentary personal pleasure in recognizing it. He forced himself to show a neutral expression instead, while he looked at Liz's lefthand fingers that he had so often kissed. Now they were unfolding each second on the screen, until she said,

"Down to one...!"

FOR ANOTHER HALF a minute the microphones transmitted only the ticking of the antique clock. Then Gore spoke, without hesitation, without notes:

"People of Britain: by now every one of you will have heard partial reports of our catastrophe. You will have been numbed by shock, as I was, and have wept, as I did. You will be asking yourselves in disbelief, *'Can it be true?'*

"My terrible duty now is to tell you that it *is* true. The sole surviving Heir, in direct succession to the Throne, is now our young Prince. At this darkest hour in our national history he is battling for his life in a London hospital. He will receive all the medical care that is presently possible from science. For the rest, as our forebears did in another Battle of Britain over London years ago, we can only pray.

"As for your government, tradition requires that on the death of the monarch, the heralds proclaim: 'The King is dead. Long live the King.' In the present circumstance the heralds cannot make such a proclamation. To ensure continuity in case of the worst, I have formed a Council on

Succession, headed by the Chief Herald and Garter King of Arms, his grace, the Duke of Dorset. On their advice, until we have at least a Regent, I shall stand as interim ceremonial Guardian for the Nation, in addition to my position as Prime Minister. I shall also take the post of Minister of Defence until the investigation of the terrible act at Sandringham is complete and the appropriate judicial sentence has been imposed on the perpetrators.

"This is a time for measured actions... But have not the slightest shadow of doubt, people of Britain: with our gallant young Prince, this is *our* battle and, like our forebears, we shall win it! Under the powers granted me by the Defence of the Realm Act, I have already ordered sealed every exit from our islands. And to all of you, my compatriots, who listen and watch, I make this pledge:

"No matter how much time and treasure it may take:

"No matter where, or with whom, the assassins may hide:

"They will be found. They *shall* be dealt with."

THE SPEECH WAS the right mix. For the time being, MacKenzie thought while swallowing yet another lump in his throat, it should work in the country at large: even the hard-bitten camera crew with Liz had broken into spontaneous applause at the end.

"Master will see you now, Colonel."

Only Slade was still unimpressed. MacKenzie decided it was overdue to squash the sarcastic little sod. He pointed at the illegal bypass switch on the office intercom's video circuit , and said tersely, "That thing is a breech of the privacy laws. Get it fixed."

As he went through to the private anteroom he met Liz coming out. She was wiping away a tear. When she saw him an expression of enormous relief filled her face.

"Hector! Thank God!" She reached for him with both hands. "I knew you were up there. Until I saw the feed from the hospital, I thought..."

She saw the bandages on his own hands. "You were there," she said, in a new shock of understanding. "With them, when it happened..."

MacKenzie hugged her to him. They had only a moment alone. He said, "We knew there was a threat. I should have stopped it."

"There's always a threat," Liz said. "You can't blame yourself for a national disaster." She studied his face again, "Those lines around your eyes..."'

"I saw everything," he said. "Sweet Jesus, Liz! I saw *you* just before it happened. My last glimpse of the Family, they were watching your show from Trafalgar Square..." He almost broke down.

While he made himself recover, Liz said, "At least we still have the Prince. You've just come from his bedside. How bad is he?"

MacKenzie couldn't lie to her. He couldn't tell the truth either: that he had left an empty bed in London. That the boy was fighting the pain and terror alone, a hundred miles north...

He changed the subject abruptly. "How do you rate the PM's speech?"

"The country will think it was magnificent," she said. "As a Scottish Nationalist, anti-monarchist, I clapped and cried like everyone else at the time."

"But now?"

"The professional part of my brain tells me that if we cut the bullshit, the last man to give himself such total power in Britain was Oliver Cromwell. Today, with the power of my medium...?" She gestured at her camera crew leaving the inner office. "If it was anyone other than rock-solid, dead honest, blue-eyed Sir John Gore, VC, we should be scared shitless of anyone who sets themselves up as Guardian of a nation."

IT WASN'T POSSIBLE to have such doubts about the man inside the office. Gore looked up from a sheet of paper on his desk and wordlessly extended his hand. As MacKenzie shook it he saw the word *Casualties*, and observed that the normally unbreakable figure in front of him had also been weeping.

Gore passed the list and said, "Half the names are children..."

"My apologies, Prime Minister." Slade's nasal voice intruding on the intercom was business as usual. "Because of the holiday season, a full meeting of Cabinet cannot be convened until noon at the earliest. I have instructed the broadcast media to hold an open-ended slot at fourteen-thirty — half-past two this afternoon."

"Mr. Slade, I am familiar with the twenty-four hour clock!" Gore was not usually a sarcastic man. His sharp response to the secretary's petty condescension was another symptom of the terrible pressure. Sensing MacKenzie's own negative reaction to Slade he added, "I only kept that man on because in my book, functionaries already in place know the mechanics of making the beds."

Slade certainly knew how to make his own, MacKenzie thought. The old-fashioned hands of the Campaign clock on Gore's desk stood at three forty-five.

"I wish the Cabinet could meet sooner," the Prime Minister said heavily. "With every minute that passes on this clock, the people will be getting further alarmed and fragmented by rumor."

MacKenzie agreed. The waves of newcomers from the former Commonwealth and, more recently Eastern Europe, had vastly altered the old patterns of the British population. Another fax list fed out of a computer. Not casualties this time: he saw *College-of-Arms* at the letterhead, *Duke of Dorset* under the signature. There were two other names above it. Gore picked up the message.

"The possible alternate Succession list, from the Chief Herald. Edward Marching and I were at school together. The same regiment."

"The Duke says that the Succession is assured then, sir?"

"Not quite," Gore replied, with grim understatement. "This piece of paper tells me that if the Prince's injuries prove fatal the country has the choice of persuading an excessively devout Roman Catholic woman to renounce her faith, or putting a mentally defective male on the throne."

The time had come for MacKenzie to bite the bullet for his actions. "Sir," he said, "about the Prince — "

"It's insanity, Hector!" Gore smashed the Casualties paper with a clenched fist. "Year by year, while Britain and Ireland become further linked together in United Europe — while Irish workers and their families from the South are allowed unlimited British entry! — this butchery has continued. Well now it shall cease."

He pressed a button marked NAVY on his videophone. MacKenzie saw the weathered face of the First Sea Lord; another old friend of Gore's, and a fellow Falklands veteran.

"Can you see me?" Gore asked.

"Clearly, Prime Minister."

"Good. At the soonest possible hour I want you to impose a total blockade on Ireland."

"International waters?" One naval eyebrow was raised a fraction. "The complete island?"

"There would not be much point in half measures, Admiral."

The senior officer of Britain's navy might have the spirit of Nelson, MacKenzie thought, but he no longer had even a tenth of the massive fleets of a century ago. The First Sea Lord said with deliberation, "That will require the Reserves."

"You now have authority for whatever is required."

"Aye aye, sir."

Before MacKenzie could cut in again, Gore had pressed INTERNAL SECURITY on his video. The Chief Commissioner of National Police replaced the Admiral. Isaiah Dayman, a former Suffolk village boy, had started as a London bobby on the beat and had come up through the ranks of Scotland Yard with two university degrees and phenomenal speed. The other thing which made Dayman unusual for a cop was that he was an openly professing evangelical Christian!

He said with a strangely sunny smile, "Good morning to you, Prime Minister."

"It seems like the middle of never-ending night, Commissioner!" Gore replied. "Until the Home Secretary returns I shall be wearing his hat as well as my own. Under the powers of the State Order which I've had my PPS send across to you, I want you to ensure two things. First, that until further notice not one person leaves this island from any point without Security vetting. Secondly — and 'a moderated response' is the key phrase here, which is also being stressed in my communique for the Media — nip any hooliganism against Irish immigrant enclaves in the bud."

"A moderated response, yes, I have read the Order. As you can see, Prime Minister, I've already taken steps." The policeman's image swung away on the screen to indicate an illuminated computer simulation of the British Isles behind him. "For civil unrest — outside Belfast, which is of course number one on the urban list — South London, Liverpool, East Birmingham, and Bristol are probably the most hair-trigger over Irish immigrant labor at the moment: fortunately, the event at Sandringham occurred after the pubs' closing time. As far as unauthorized exit is concerned, remote shoreline areas are the biggest concern. However, the entire East Anglian coast has already been sealed tight. All Rural Auxiliaries elsewhere have been called up, and God is on the side of the righteous."

"While I try and explain that to the electorate," Gore said to MacKenzie, shutting off the screen with an air of frustration, "go back to Norfolk. Before this country finds itself at war against the IRA I want to know in the plainest barracks language that they are the flaming bloody bastards who caused it." The Prime Minister pointed at a section of bookcase wall in the corner of the office. "Use the back stairs."

MacKenzie couldn't avoid it any longer. He said, "Sir, I'm afraid there's some personal action tonight which I haven't revealed to you."

"Personal?" Gore looked sharply, then his face softened. "Forgive me, Hector. You were almost part of the Family. I haven't made enough allowance for the frightful shock it must have been to see that horror. And escorting the Prince afterwards, to hospital here in London. You need rest. I'll send someone else to Sandringham."

The Prime Minister reached for the intercom PPS button. Slade was the last man to be trusted with the secret! Before Gore could press the key, MacKenzie used the main OFF switch to kill the whole system.

He said, "It's not the shock to me, sir. You should know: His Royal Highness is not in London."

"The boy is dead, too?"

Gore slumped in his chair. Now it was MacKenzie who felt sorry for not taking sufficient account of the emotional strain the man in front of him was carrying. As quickly as possible he explained his actions and the reasoning behind them.

"I should have been consulted first," Gore said, but his tone was less harsh than expected. "Given the risk of leaks you did the right thing, I suppose. How secure is Chedburgh?"

"Nothing is totally secure from a ground-to-ground missile," MacKenzie replied. "At the moment we have the advantage of concealment."

"Which must be kept," said Gore heavily. "I shall not tell the Cabinet."

"Thank you, sir." MacKenzie saluted. "I'll leave immediately for Norfolk."

The Prime Minister activated a foot switch beside his desk. A section of the wall bookcase swung open. As MacKenzie moved towards it, Gore added in a choked voice, "When you see our boy, if he can hear it, give him my love."

Two

Dawn • Chedburgh

THERE WAS NO change at the bedside. MacKenzie flew his own chopper, solo, from London to reach it. Inside a sterile, clear-vinyl oxygen tent only the head of the little figure was still bandaged. The rest of the small body lay in the specially constructed water bed, under featherweight burn dressings. Through two slits in the bandages, the Prince's eyes were closed. His breathing was regular, but also feather light. Remembering the trace of breath on his cheek from the last visit, MacKenzie was reminded of a moth whose beating wings could stop at any time.

"We have him heavily sedated," said the Surgeon General. "Without it, even the weight of these airpack dressings would be unbearable."

MacKenzie looked at the mass of dials and pumps of the automated equipment filling the ward. "And this is everything that can be done for him?" he asked. "There's nothing else, anywhere, that could help, that you aren't using?"

The Surgeon shook his head. "Anything Medicine knows about burn treatment is in this room."

In one corner of it MacKenzie saw the wreckage of the model Range Rover lying beside the blackened clockwork Drummer Boy. He picked up the Victorian toy. The charred drum sticks gave a single, *rat-tat*...

"We can heal the burns, with time," said the Surgeon. "Our enemy is shock. Whether, and how, the body copes with that depends on the human spirit — which is still as great a medical mystery as it has ever been."

Like faith, MacKenzie thought, placing the Drummer Boy on a shelf where the closed eyes in the bandage slits could see it when, or if...

The Surgeon General squeezed his shoulder gently, and left the ward. MacKenzie sat on alone for a few moments at the bedside. His officer's training and duties as Equerry involved constant attendance at ceremonial Church functions, but he had not been religious since he was himself a child. Silently, he began to pray to whatever unseen force might make the difference between supporting, or quenching, this fragile human spirit beside him. He closed his prayer by repeating aloud the same personal litany:

"Be brave, Lad. Be strong. You will be King!"

But there was no sign from the bed that his message got through.

Aftermath • Sandringham

THE ATTACKERS COULD NOT have chosen a more vulnerable target. MacKenzie agreed with the Chief Forensic Officer's conclusion as he stood with him and Wallop surveying the burned out shell of the building.

"If the family had used Windsor for its Christmas gathering, as they used to in the Old Queen's day," said the C.F.O., "the damage and consequent fatalities would have been only a fraction of those here in Norfolk."

MacKenzie knew every inch of Windsor. The six-foot stone walls of the Castle, many of them dating back to William the Conqueror, could have taken a direct hit from any portable rocket launcher currently in use, and scarcely been dented. And although the leaded roofs of Windsor were more fragile, the spread of damage would have been limited by the physical separation of the living quarters, as it had been during the big fire at the end of the last century. Then, each principal family member had a Castle tower of their own.

"Their traditions were so damned predictable." With an air of professional frustration the Forensic man held out a half-melted object. MacKenzie felt his stomach churn again. The object was the mouthpiece from Jock MacGillivray's bagpipes, his drinking companion for those Highland laments...

"The Royals' tradition of TV hiring ensured the success of the attack," the Forensic officer continued. "A voice-activated, pre-tuned micro-oscillator fitted in the set installed for this Christmas season was the homing beacon for the guidance system of the terrorists' missile." The C.F.O. compared a recovered circuit-chip to the bagpipes' mouthpiece in his gloved hand. "The combination of the late King's voice and the set's built-in, real-time clock countdown to midnight, New Year's Eve, ensured a perfect hit."

The television had been destroyed in the smoking ballroom rubble; the oscillator chip, built to military tolerance, was virtually unscathed. The Forensic Officer led the way into a mobile lab guarded by additional troops from the perimeter detachment. The local Commanding Officer joined MacKenzie as the Forensic man placed the chip under the microscope lens on a bench, and said, "You can see for yourselves, gentlemen: made in Pakistan, for a division of ITX."

MacKenzie saw the magnified logo of the American supra national conglomerate formed some years ago as a protective measure against the Far East competition.

"Well?" demanded the local unit commander. "Is it Paddy?"

"It's similar to circuits the IRA have used in Northern Ireland," the C.F.O. replied, "but I can't tell for sure. When we have more pieces of the missile, perhaps —"

"Give me Defence Central." The unit commander was barking at a young female operator on the mobile lab's video phone. The image changed to a man in camouflage fatigues, wearing the shoulder pips of a Lieutenant General, whom MacKenzie also recognized.

The local man said tersely, "It's Paddy."

The on-screen General nodded briefly. "Confirmed?"

"In my book. His homing system."

"Good enough."

A tightening of the cheek muscles was the only sign of emotion in the General. The local man said to the screen, "It's gone on sixty years, but we're finally going to take Paddy out, aren't we?"

The General's image nodded again and said slowly, "Yes, I rather think we are."

MacKenzie found a wakeup pill in his pocket. He agreed that the atrocity was IRA, and that at last that group enemy must be dealt with: but the individual name he was looking for behind this act was not the cartoon racist stereotype of "Paddy". It was a real name, once recorded for an infant in a Galway baptismal register: *McDermid.* And when he found its adult, blood-soaked, terrorist owner, he vowed silently to the ghosts rising from the smoking rubble, wherever, and whenever, on the Oath of a Royal Marine, he would personally destroy him.

"If you don't mind my saying so, sir," Wallop said, as he swallowed the benzedrine pill, "coffee and bennies may have to do the rest of the day, but you're going to have a bite of proper breakfast first."

The Black Pig

THEY SAW LIGHTS in a rural pub not worried about legal closing time. MacKenzie walked with Wallop under a sign that had a white-tusked black boar painted on it. A rugger match crowd of players and supporters from the playing fields of a famous Public School nearby was having a wake, eight hours late, watching the satellite New Year in San Francisco!

"No matter where, or with whom, the assassins may hide:

"They will be found. They shall *be dealt with."*

Without warning the picture cut to a home-taped replay of Gore's speech ending.

"Run the whole thing again!"

The publican rewound and hit the play button. Pumped up by the warped emotional reactions of too much booze, the girls at the bar were all crying. So were half the guys, including both team captains.

"Fucking murderers!" Masculine embarrassment snapped to fury. "Nuke the fucking lot of them!"

The last threat was meaningless, Britain had no nuclear weapons any longer. The Home team captain swung his head thickly, like a thwarted bull, and grunted, "There's a bunch of the IRA bastards in the trailer park past School — !"

His girl said, "Building that new shopping mall!"

"Deal with the sodding micks!"

A group roar put it together. The center forwards of both teams crashed the Black Pig's front door without opening it. The hinges pulled out of the woodwork. The door and half its frame, with the two Elevens and all the supporters, fell into the street.

As MacKenzie grabbed a phone to call the local police, the Away team captain led the charge in an antique V-12 Jag. MacKenzie joined Wallop, who was already running down the road after them until a police car screamed up to make an arrest.

"Not us!" MacKenzie showed ID. "The rugger players! There's a trailer park with Irish."

The police driver hit the accelerator. At the next corner they passed an even older MG roadster nose-down in a new sewer ditch. The caravans beyond the wreck were dark, except for one with a single light above the rear side-door.

"Up and over, boys!"

The bellow came from behind a fence. The police car rounded it. Twenty-two pairs of pumped-up shoulders were under the wheel housings of one trailer. There was a moment's pause while the electrical and sanitary connections held... then a *snap*, and a whooshing noise as the caravan rolled, followed by a child crying.

The side-door, which was now on the roof of the trailer, flipped open.

A frightened male face appeared, then a terrified little girl in flannel pajamas. Two of the largest rugger tackles got the man and hurled him over their backs to both waiting scrum lines. As his child watched, the man's head split open on the concrete.

"Deal the same way with the rest of them!"

"Let me, sir."

With MacKenzie on his tail, Wallop bulldozed through the bellowing scrum. The two tackles at the front lowered their stoneage skulls in unison to flatten the Sergeant-Major with a double forehead butt. Wallop waited... then sidestepped. One ham-hand grasped each neanderthal's neck. Their brows came together in a crash of solid bone which rolled their stunned ox eyes for a long enough moment to let MacKenzie gather the unconscious man's weeping daughter up in his arms and get her clear.

The police did not make any arrests until the fourth trailer went over, and then they took the little girl with the rest of the Irish families into close custody, for their own protection. After promising to pay for the damage to the Black Pig's door, the neanderthal rugger teams were let go with a caution. The local sergeant said to MacKenzie, "Thanks for your call, sir. Boys will be boys. We'll book it as 'Moderated Response to Unusual Circumstances'."

Reactions • Whitehall

MACKENZIE PRESENTED HIS personal report to Gore on the IRA rocket confirmation, and anti-Irish hooliganism. At the Prime Minster's instruction he stayed to sit in on the emergency meeting of the Inner Cabinet. With a military man's distaste for rule by committee Gore had drastically curtailed the central body to a mere six members, of whom only four were seated at the long table: the two absentees, the Foreign Secretary and the Minister of Defence, were still airborne.

"Good afternoon, everyone."

"Good afternoon, Prime Minister."

The group's voices shared a forced normality. Their eyes studied the leader's smallest movement for traces of uncertainty. Gore reached for the leather and silver photograph frame containing the pictures of his grandchildren, and said without preamble:

"First, the Funeral. There will be no wake with multiple, and children's, coffins; just a simple National remembrance to honor the dead with a minimum risk of further inflaming passions. For the living, I have arranged with the Chief Commissioner that special additional security be provided by the National Police to the immediate families of all prominent political, military, and judicial leading figures in Britain."

"Thank you, Prime Minister."

MacKenzie sensed that the group's response this time was less strained. Jane Lear, the Home Secretary, a beak-nosed little wren of a woman, as Minister responsible for the administration of justice, appeared particularly relieved. Her two youngest children were still at school: her oldest boy was a pilot in the Royal Air Force.

"You mean you expect further attacks?"

The question came from Henry Roper. The casually polished, six-foot two-inch Chancellor of the Exchequer seated to MacKenzie's left preferred "Hal" — typical of a man who came to politics from the laid back atmosphere of a broadcasting and tabloid empire. As Liz put it, "Tits and arse for Sunday breakfast on three continents!" Roper had surrendered all his media business interests to a blind trust upon first election as a Member of Parliament. If the post of Prime Minister was "First among Equals" in cabinet then, given the sensitivity of the pound and international finance as well as his personal clout in the City of London, the Chancellorship was second. Roper was divorced, but apparently happily remarried; had two children, a boy and a girl, both nearly adult, studying in Japan and California.

"No, Chancellor," Gore replied calmly to Roper's disturbing question. "It is only prudent to guard targets of opportunity, but I do not expect another terrorist incident."

"Then what *do* we expect?" Lawrence Brown, the Minister of Health and Liason to the National Assembly in Edinburgh, epitomized the sort of interchangeable political-bureaucrat that MacKenzie most disliked.

"I expect," Gore said, still in an even tone, "that the forces who perpetrated the horror at Sandringham will shortly be making a political demand which they will expect to be granted."

"Leave Ireland." Wilfred Jamieson, the Minister of Industry and Technology and a Belfast Protestant bachelor, spat out the last word as though it were poison. "Surely it goes without saying, Prime Minister, as it has for five centuries, that such a request for abandoning innocent British subjects living on soil that is part of the United Kingdom, will *not* be granted."

The murmur of assent was interrupted by Jane Lear. "Surely the most important question is: if the Prince dies, will we still *be* a Kingdom?"

"Don't be so bloody wet!"

"Damn fool woman!"

"Gentlemen, enough!" Gore hit the Cabinet table with the flat of his hand. "Honest difference of opinion, very well. Rudeness to a lady, I will not abide."

"I appreciate your solicitude, John, but it isn't necessary." The diminutive Home Secretary had prosecuted a thousand criminal trials. She wheeled on her two male opponents. "Emotion is no answer. In the narrowest legal sense, upon the death of the sovereign, without the proclamation of the next, the throne is vacant."

"An Interregnum," said Roper.

"Exactly. Without a proclaimed Heir, we have what the Prime Minister has called his temporary Guardianship. That is not a functioning kingdom. The next question, if this disaster worsens: does the country wish to continue being one?"

All four ministers looked to Gore. He held up the alternate Succession list and said, "Since midnight, I have been asking myself the same thing. Suppose, for example, that the Lady named here should refuse to convert from her Catholicism, then an heir is determined but he is patently unsuitable. Is he to be ruled out by whim? And whose whim? Ours, at this table? Or by a vote in the Commons?"

"A popular referendum," Brown said.

"A referendum on an individual," said Gore, "would be tantamount to an election."

"Clearly," Roper interjected smoothly, "there is an absolute difference between an elected official and a hereditary monarchy."

"It's called a Presidency." Brown lurched to his feet. "Like Australia now has. And I'm all for it."

"Well I'm bloody not!" bellowed Jamieson. "King and Country forever, and be damned to you!"

Gore had to strike the table with his gavel. The shouting stopped, but the men from Glasgow and Belfast remained standing, glowering at one another.

"From the effect this question of the Succession has on ourselves," said the Prime Minister, "we can imagine all too clearly what would happen if it were presented now to the country at large. The population must be given time to assimilate what has already befallen them. They must be permitted to mourn; then the British people can be faced with the Throne problem, and relied upon as always to reach a sensible conclusion." He looked at each cabinet member in turn. "Before we proceed to the Commons, I will now ask for a vote on my proposed course of action."

"I would like to offer one amendment, Prime Minister. On the question of your leadership, and specifically your new function as National Guardian —" the other ministers stared at Roper — "I move that Mr Slade, in his capacity as clerk, record in the minutes this quorum's vote to be unanimous."

It was done smoothly, but at the word *clerk*, MacKenzie caught a sudden look from the secretary confirming the depth of his insecurity and hostility. A weak and dangerous man.

As he left Downing Street's murky world of politics to fly north for a few more precious moments at the Prince's bedside, he passed the exact opposite. A figure he had last seen hoisting the Royal Standard on the roof of the Palace. Now Stubbins was in his traditional coachman's dress, carrying his regular, blue-leather, Royal despatch box. Although there was no Monarch to receive its contents, through such continued expressions of simple loyalty, MacKenzie knew that one day soon, there must be. The Slades of Whitehall, playing their bureaucratic games, were an annoying irritant. The backstage people like Stubbins were the real living core of British history.

Two Bit Players

ROGER SLADE DICTATED the latest hollow victory for Cabinet solidarity into the voice-activated computer system which managed all the inner circle paper housekeeping of modern government in Whitehall. The Chancellor of the Exchequer's bold gesture of personal loyalty, Slade thought contemptuously as the divided ministers and the starched military jockstrap, MacKenzie, left for the predictable Commons debate, would not be made public to "Hal's" constituents until a safe thirty years later!

As for Roper's use of *clerk*...

The humiliating description typified for Slade what was still so infuriatingly wrong with this country. The position of Principal Private Secretary to a modern British leader was vastly more than a mere pen-pusher. A "clerk" was something out of Dickens! He turned away from the computer and went to his own desk, a genuine Hepplewhite, *circa* 1770, with graceful legs... and a secret compartment at the back of the upper right-hand drawer. Slade pulled out the drawer and pressed a carved rosette above the knee-hole. With a sharp click, the compartment popped open. He withdrew the leather diary he kept there.

Today's date was delineated by a matching leather bookmark and had already seen several entries. He placed the diary on the desk's blotter, uncapped his fountain pen, and began to write. His script was extremely small but, by its neatness, would still have been legible to a casual observer. To circumvent such nosey parkers in the unpleasant East End school where he had begun his long climb out of the rathole slums to higher education, Slade had devised a simple code. For certain key words (names and sexual preferences) it required merely the replacement of a consonant, or vowel, by the next one to it, in the normal alphabetic sequence. Thus, Roper became "Suqis", Lear became "Mies", and Gore was "Husi" —

There was a knock on the door.

Slade swiftly slipped the diary beneath the blotter. The door handle turned. A male voice said in a Cockney accent, "Excuse me, sir: it's Stubbins."

A short fat man dressed in an absurd uniform appeared around the door.

"What on earth are you doing here?" Slade demanded.

"Well it's time, sir, isn't it? For you to, like, give it to me."

The man was pointing at the desk.

"Give?" Slade was nonplussed... Then his mind caught up: the fool in front of him was here for the Despatch box. With typical British idiocy and worship of the past, it still went daily from Downing Street by coach through the streets of London to the Palace, for a bored monarch's listless and useless perusal. The archaic uniform, which presumably titillated the hordes of tourist morons, was the Household stable livery, complete with ridiculous knee breeches, a top hat and, at this time of year, a heavy felt cape.

"The King is dead," said Slade.

"I know that, sir. But there's still the Box."

Like old Gore earlier, the coachman (who was probably only thirty and, if he'd had better legs to show off in the breeches, might even have been interesting) had apparently been crying. His eyes were red and watery.

"There is no point in taking a State paper half way across London," Slade said, with sharp annoyance for such bovine stupidity, "if there is no one to read it."

"But there will be, one day, sir, won't there? And I always take it. What else would I do?"

"I'm damned if I know. Ask your superior."

"The Sergeant Footman is away in Spain, sir, and with this morning's news the Master of the Household's gone and had a stroke."

The man stared slack-jawed at Slade. The secretary had wasted too much time on the fool already. With mounting impatience he unlocked and opened the blue leather despatch box at the side opposite its handle, removed its contents, relocked it, and returned it, empty.

"Thank you, sir." The oaf touched his braided tricorn hat, crossed to the door, paused...

"What now?" Slade snapped.

"Well if there's no one to read it, sir, what shall I do with it?"

"What do you usually do?"

"Bring the Box back again."

"Then do it."

"Yes sir!"

With a huge sigh of relief the moron finally left, his enormous stable boots clumping. Slade kicked the office door shut and retrieved his diary. He wrote a terse few lines for each coded name present at the Cabinet meeting — plus the obvious deduction from last night that MacKenzie took his tartan jockstrap off long enough to screw the television woman, Ponti! — recording approximate dialogue where it revealed animosities or alliances between ministers, knowledge which might prove useful in the very near future. Replacing the diary in its secret drawer, he stared down at the absurd sight of a British Prime Minister talking to a horse in the courtyard below him.

Dolly

SAMUEL STUBBINS SALUTED the PM as Sir John passed by on his way across to Parliament. The PM saluted back, like always, but without his normal smile. It was these kind of moments that made Stubbins remember how lucky he was to have the job. He'd wanted to be a London taxi driver, with his own cab and a licence to prove it to all his passengers in a frame screwed just above the dashboard, signed by the Senior Licence Inspector himself. Sadly, although he sat for the Theoretical and passed the exam a hundred percent three times, on the equal number of occasions for the Practical — the actual driving bit — he failed.

"But it's an ill wind, Dolly," he told her, as he patted his horse's bay-neck and adjusted the black ribbon on the bridle at the back of her head. "If I'd of got the cabbing, you an' me, luv, and Sir John over there, we wouldn't never 'ave met."

Dolly whickered and pushed at his pocket with her velvety lips.

Stubbins fed her the sugar lump she expected, climbed up on the driver's bench and flicked the reins, which he didn't really need to because Dolly knew their route by heart. They moved forward at their usual slow clop, turning in a circle that took their antique Hansom carriage from the back door of Number 10, and out along the lane leading into Downing Street. There they had to stop for Security, because of the Black Alert.

After Sandringham…

Stubbins still couldn't believe it, even though he could see Dolly's black ribbon. No one on the Staff at the Palace could. With the Sergeant Footman away on holiday in Madrid, Stubbins didn't know what else to do except harness Dolly up and go on as usual.

"Muddling through, luv," he said to her, as Security waved them forward. "That's what we call it, don't we, muddling through?"

A pair of tourists from America on the corner heard him while they were taking his picture, and Dolly's. There were always tourists in Downing Street, but today there was a crowd of real people as well, Londoners, who came out whenever there was a National Crisis, just in case. Dolly turned left, between them, towards Birdcage Walk, flanking the south side of St James's Park. Her breath steamed, and there was still frost on the grass where it was shaded by the trees. Wellington Barracks was next, with the flag at half mast. Samuel Stubbins sat a little straighter and pulled the blue Despatch Box close beside him.

"Mabe there ain't nuffink in it, Dolly-luv, like that bleeding Whitehall secretary pansy-arse said. But what does that matter, eh? The PM told us last night, God bless him! It's our Battle of Britain now."

Three

Chedburgh

MacKENZIE RENEWED HIS vigil with the clockwork Drummer outside the sterile tent protecting the Prince from further infection. There had been no change in the hours since his last visit. The boy had not surfaced from his heavy sedation. His eyes remained shut. Occasionally, in a sound that tore MacKenzie's heart, he moaned.

"It could be days like this," the Surgeon General said. "Or he could go tonight. We just don't know."

The portable mini-fax machine which MacKenzie carried with him was spewing out a constant stream of priority messages, but nothing had higher priority than this: *To be here, when, or if...*

He turned on an unused hospital television at the foot of the bed. All channels were carrying the Prime Minister's address to Parliament. Gore was standing at the Treasury bench, waiting for the applause to subside. MacKenzie inserted one earphone, leaving his other ear free to hear the bed, *just in case...*

"Mr Speaker," Gore said to the Chair, "Members of the House, and beyond those here in this Chamber, people of Britain. When I spoke to you from my office, immediately after our catastrophe, I had just issued certain orders for the deployment of British forces. I can now tell you that those orders have been carried out. As of this moment, a Royal Naval blockade is imposed against all Ireland. The Royal Air Force will prevent any movement into, or out of, both the Northern and Southern spheres of influence on that unhappy island. In the North, from the border to the sea all available British Army units of armor, and foot-soldiers, are in place on the ground."

Gore paused. A collective intake of breath could be heard from all sides of the Chamber. In the Burn ward, as MacKenzie glanced to check his patient, the only sound was the rhythmic pumping of the oxygen and saline systems.

"Despite the scope and nature of our recent loss," Gore continued, "our troops are *not* in place to exact a terrible revenge. There has been too much killing for revenge already in Northern Ireland. It must be stopped — it shall be stopped — but it cannot be stopped while the small core responsible for attempting to impose a terrorist solution to a political problem, on a largely innocent population, remain.

"They shall not remain. So that there shall be no doubt in any quarter, I will now read to you my latest Order of the Day to the General in Command of our Combined Forces, and to the entire civilian population of Northern Ireland, Protestant as well as Catholic."

After Gore's emphasis of the last words in the House of Commons, there was only a silence so complete that it seemed solid. In the ward, MacKenzie suddenly thought he heard...! Nothing important. It had only been fresh oxygen rustling the sterile vinyl canopy. The Prime Minister picked up a copy of the numbered Order and began:

" 'One: commencing at dawn, the day after tomorrow, the forces under your command will advance, from the border to the coast, in a concerted pincer movement. Town by town, village by village, street by street, house by house, farm by farm: urban or rural, every dwelling will be ordered evacuated by its residents.

" 'Two: any resident whose name is on the comprehensive list that has already been widely posted throughout the territory, shall, at this time, have free right to step forward.

" 'Three: any named person who does so will be escorted under safe conduct to the Southern border, if Catholic, *or* to a place of their choosing in the Home island, if they are Protestant.

" 'Four: such persons are to be informed that three years from today, upon request to this Government, and providing that they undertake to refrain from any further violent act, they have this Government's solemn pledge before the world that may return to the northern part of what will be by then a United Ireland, free and independent, with a full pardon.

" 'Five: any weapons on the premises evacuated shall be voluntarily surrendered under the same terms of safe conduct.

" 'Six: once such search has been completed, the balance of the unlisted population may return to their homes.

" 'Seven: any person on the aforementioned list of names who does not come forward voluntarily; or any person found as of this time of Proclamation to be carrying a weapon or munition of any sort; or any dwelling found upon search to contain even a single such item; together shall jointly be considered the Enemy and, whether person or residence, dealt with accordingly.

" 'Eight: should the Enemy attempt to evade by crossing the border to the South, your forces will employ the doctrine of Hot Pursuit.' "

Gore put down the document. The Chamber was still in total silence. He turned slowly towards all of its members, and then back to the camera.

"I now ask for your vote that, under the rules of engagement and conduct in the Order I have just read to you, a State of War exists between the duly elected government of this country and the terrorist substructure — of both-sides! — in Northern Ireland."

The silent House of Commons plugged into MacKenzie's right ear became pandemonium. He didn't notice. Because to his left, from the bed, beside the clockwork Drummer Boy, he heard in a tiny whisper:

"Is that really you, Colonel Ken?"

He swung around. In their slit of the bandages, both blue eyes were open, fixed on him. Every fibre in MacKenzie's body yearned to take the live boy in his arms... but even the slightest touch was impossible. Instead of love, it would bring agony.

"Aye, Lad," he said, feeling tears prick his own eyes. "It's really me."

"I don't know where I am."

A look that was part bewilderment, part terror, came into the eyes. MacKenzie knelt down beside the bed so that his face was only inches from the bandaged cheek he longed to kiss. To prove that something human, and loving, existed for the child in this terrifying sterile world.

"You're in a hospital, Your Highness. You were hurt, but now you'll get better."

The eyes stared at him. They had always believed him.

"Where are Mother and Father?"

He could not lie to these eyes, but the truth could kill them. He said, "Their Majesties cannot be here..." and could manage nothing else. The portable fax chattered at his side. He glanced down, glad of the respite, to regain his composure.

"They're probably opening Parliament," the whisper said.

The eyes had seen the House of Commons image on the television screen. MacKenzie turned it off before it could show the other scene at Westminster. The one described in his fax message. The preparations for the Funeral.

"It hurts!"

The whisper had changed to a high cry of pain. As MacKenzie reached to hit the alarm button a nurse was already in the doorway. She said, "I'll boost his sedation," and pressed a key on the automated intravenous system attached to the waterbed.

The pain in the eyes faded.

"Colonel Ken, I want to tell you..."

The voice dropped back to its thin whisper.

"Aye, Lad?" he said. "I'm here. I'm listening."

"It's what you said before. About being brave. When I look at my Drummer Boy, I *do* try..."

The nurse's professional composure broke. She turned away to hide her tears. MacKenzie said through the plastic to the small figure in the bandages,

"I know you do, Your Highness. Always."

"Will you wind up my Drummer for me, please, Colonel Ken?"

MacKenzie would walk through hell again if it would bring the voice back from a whisper. He turned the charred key in the toy's back. The scorched metal arms that held the sticks began to rise and fall in the military rythm that had marched British regiments to battles for almost two hundred years.

Rat-a-tat. Rat-a-tat...

MacKenzie remained until the Prince's eyes closed again and the breathing was regular. Then he took the example of a little boy's gallantry back to the Capital of what was still a Kingdom. Through the following bleak hours of other muffled drum beats and draped flags, it helped him endure the unendurable.

Whitehall • Anti-Terror Annex

WINTER HAD COME to London with the funeral. It brought a benefit: eighteen inches of wet snow stopped any hotheads wanting to create a further incident. Three hundred feet below the snow MacKenzie stood with the A-T duty officer in the underground Annex, adjacent to the main War Room, monitoring a real-time video intercept from the IRA Council's safe house headquarters in Belfast.

The building was in the heart of what had been the Catholic slums in the last century, before the British government spent a large portion of the Defence budget providing sanitation. It was considered "safe" by the IRA because the house was so old that although it now had an indoor privy, it was one of the last structures in Belfast still without any form of electric wiring. No power, no phone, no cable TV: swept regularly for bugs, the house was believed by the enemy to be electronically neutral. It was not. The silicon particles of the ancient horsehair-and-lime plaster could be made to resonate on a sympathetic frequency so that the rooms acted with light, and radio waves, in much the same way as the sound magnifying horn on an antique gramaphone.

"An Internal for you, sir," said the duty A-T. "About the Sandringham investigation."

MacKenzie pressed Video and found himself looking at the Chief Forensic Officer. He said, "Proceed."

"It's the Attack Initiation assessment. The homing mechanism was provisionally classified — "

The audio stopped. The video face looked awkward.

"This is a secure line," MacKenzie said, "you can speak openly."

"I did caution the local Army people in charge of the security perimeter. One can never be positive at the outset..."

The voice died a second time. MacKenzie said grimly, "If it's negative, don't fart around, man. Spit it out."

"I have now completed my analysis of the missile fragments. They come from a ground-to-ground weapon known as Hugger, manufactured by a Korean firm. That type of missile has been used for similar incidents, in the Far East, but it has never previously been employed by the IRA."

"Which doesn't mean it couldn't be," said MacKenzie. "You've confirmed it was their preferred beam-guidance method."

"Unfortunately there's something else. A fingerprint — a thumb, to be exact. I have a firm identification: a man called Asao Nakano. He belongs to an organization named Kōfuku-na Museifu-shugi-sha.

" 'The Happy Anarchists'." MacKenzie knew them. "Asian terrorists have worked in random international groups many times," he said. "There's nothing to say they shouldn't have linked with the IRA on this occasion."

"No material reason, I agree. But psychological, although that isn't my department..." The image shrugged, "Well, Irish pride."

At which point the duty A-T said, "Sir! The safe house are on."

MacKenzie turned to the intercept monitor. The known Council members were assembled in the tiny parlor, across from the tinier kitchen: a white-haired old man, two younger, and one woman, obviously waiting for someone else to arrive. All had quilted weather-jackets and gloves. The A-T duty officer hit fast forward. The group on-camera looked suddenly towards the kitchen's outer door. It opened. A full-bearded figure entered, sodden with rain.

The old man said as a greeting, "You're here, then. You've heard?"

The new arrival nodded. The woman smiled. She had unusual hair for IRA, long and blonde.

"Sister — !" the old man said sharply: the enemy used no names at their Council meetings — "you can wipe that smile off right now. The Government in Exile didn't want this to happen, ever. It's going to mean catastrophe for the Cause, you all know that." He looked at the woman. "So it was you, then, your lot?"

She shook her head so that the blonde hair swayed. "I've wanted it with all my heart, and I would have died to see it done myself, but I follow orders — *you* know that." She pointed at a tabloid with a huge headline:

PRINCE SURVIVES!

"I just wish we could still take their last one and make a it a grand slam."

"So which of you?"

"None, Brother." The man in the center of the trio answered. "We all wanted it, but we know why it could never have been permitted."

"It means wipe-out." The younger man across from the woman was pale with fear. "What the hell are we going to do?"

"Take as many of the Brit bastards with us as we can," said the woman. "And afterwards, the Cause wins."

"If there's ever going to be any bloody winning," said the old man, "and if nobody in this room organized bloody Sandringham, then the outside world needs to know bloody quick: Who bloody did?"

"Ask Whitehall." The bearded new arrival spoke for the first time. He tapped the headline, and added in a calm, thoughtful tone, as though considering a routine move in chess, "With this one that's left from Sandringham, maybe it's not too late yet, to make a thorough job of it."

THE VIDEO INTERCEPT broke up as the storm took out another circuit. The A-T officer turned a huge grin to MacKenzie. "Fantastic, sir! He's using a speech mini-synthesizer implanted below the beard, and he's had plastic surgery to the nose again. But Jesus Christ Almighty! After seven years of trying ...!"

The duty A-T hit a computer key.

MacKenzie stared at the laser hologram now superimposed on the recorded face of the bearded man as he considered the headline. It was the image of a man without a care in the world. A man with a smile on his lips and a shotgun blowing off the head of a rope-bound captive. A man incapable of conscience, with a degree in English Literature and History. A man who said, in his only recorded interview, after a bank robbery using extreme violence, "George Orwell's *1984* Big Brother came to Northern Ireland, not to reborn, godfearing, moneygrubbing modern Russia!" A man responsible for a decade of carnage. A man whose hundred known victims included some British soldiers and diplomats, but mostly innocent wives and mothers, priests and children. A textbook-perfect psychopath. With this man back in Ireland all the red herrings of Asian or Whitehall involvement at Norfolk could be discounted.

"Isn't it bloody marvelous we've got him, sir?"

Twenty-four hours earlier, a lifetime ago, MacKenzie would have shared the young watch officer's wild enthusiasm. After Sandringham, and the Funeral, he felt only an iced rage that gripped his gut so hard that he winced.

He welcomed the pain. It was only a fraction of the agony being endured by a boy trying to be be brave in the Burn bed at Chedburgh, but it would serve as a reminder until he got his hands on the living throat of the surreal image in front of him. Until he had personally wiped from the earth this psychopathic piece of filth the computer identified simply as:

Killer One • Sean McDermid

Four

H-Hour • Ireland

THE MASSED BATTLE circuit screens in front of MacKenzie were dark, apparently blank. But as his eyes grew more used to the illumination level of the Belfast War Room for the Officer in Command on the ground in Northern Ireland, faint images became discernible, shadows within shadows. He touched a laser pointer to "Night Vision". The ghostly shapes were revealed by infrared as houses, trees, the figures of waiting troops, and tanks.

ADVANCE

Gore's word for history flashed on all screens. MacKenzie watched the first tanks roll out simultaneously from their staging posts at Balleycastle, Ballintoy, and Benbane Head. At H+5 minutes he saw a trio of men from the Balleycastle infantry contingent slide helplessly off a snowbank, straight towards a moving vehicle's tracks. The face of the tank force commander ordered his driver to slam reverse. The tracks screeched. The engine roared. Too late. The closest infantryman disappeared beneath the steel skirt of the side armor. A splash of red spray on the snow marked the first British casualty.

At H+10 the force had advanced to Grid position, Moyle map, Alpha Alpha, Tango Charlie: the first "Location for Inspection" was a farm, comprising house, cottage, two outbuildings. One name listed. Banned Designation, Protestant: Ulster Defence League.

The inhabitants had made an effort to plow out the lane, MacKenzie noted, but the ice had made the approach worse than it would have been through the undisturbed snow. The leading tank skidded again, clipped the lane corner, and brought down a stone gate post. A dog barked furiously. A light came on in the farmhouse front window. The commander maneuvered his vehicle to block the front door, and directed his other units to cover the back and each outbuilding. He took up a bullhorn and began reading the Warning clause from the interrogation Order.

"Attention! The resident of this dwelling whose name is shown on the list that has been posted in this District, shall, at this time, and for the next two minutes, have free right to leave said building and step forward."

Another light came on, this one in an upstairs window. A child's frightened face looked out. The front door underneath it remained closed. The commander read the Warning again, in accordance with instructions, but with the time limit reduced to thirty seconds. The dog abruptly stopped barking. In its place, a male and female voice could be heard arguing behind the curtains.

The commander called through the bull horn, "Your time for free passage has expired."

He waved a detachment of his infantry forward: a sergeant and three men for the front door, two for the rear and each outbuilding.

He called out again, "Final warning! If you do not immediately leave the building, an explosive charge will be placed at the front entrance."

The adult voices inside were louder, but there was still no sign of any movement. The child's terrified face was pressed to the upper glass. MacKenzie thought of the boy at Chedburgh. The sergeant squatted down to apply the plastic explosive to the lock. When the charge fired, the child above it by the window would...

"He's coming out, the great fool."

The woman's voice screamed it. The front door opened. A man's figure appeared, disheveled in denim overalls and long woolen underwear. The woman pushed the man ahead of her through the doorway into the arms of the sergeant, who asked politely:

"Are there any weapons, missus, or munitions on this property?"

"No — " she looked sharply at her husband — "are there?"

The man shook his head. The sniffer squad went inside the building with their ion detectors. The house was clean. So was the barn. The illegal ammunition was found in a cache under the hearth in the cottage. The two men were placed under safe custody in the armored personnel carrier set aside for prisoners of Operation Clean Sweep. As they were leaving, the tanks swung around together and, with a single salvo, blew the cottage at Alpha Alpha, Tango Charlie, off the Moyle District map.

At H+20 the unit in the Fifteenth District was a regiment of the elite Irish Guards: "The Shamrocks". MacKenzie was a War College classmate of their Brigadier. The storm's parting thrust in the south had brought down all the power lines from the weight of black ice. The Shamrocks' Commander got out of his armored carrier to give some moral support.

"Things under control, chaps?"

"Just about, sir."

"That's the ticket."

The regimental spirit was sound. MacKenzie watched the on-screen Brigadier watching a pair of engineers, wearing rubberized gauntlets and standing on a mat of the same material, snap a jumper between the two broken sections of the hissing high tension line. The Brigadier gave his engineers an encouraging wave and walked back to his vehicle. The mobile HQ was ten yards past the repaired powerline when the road beneath the ice exploded.

BECAUSE OF THE weather damage in Belfast, the computer switching unit automatically re-routed the report to London. The C-in-C, standing next to MacKenzie in Ireland, found himself televisually face-to-face with *his* Commander in Chief, the Prime Minister, direct from the War Room.

"At Drumcard," Gore said, without preamble. "The Headquarters vehicle for Fermagh District has just been destroyed. The Brigadier, his Number Two, and five other ranks are killed. Two wounded, one will probably prove fatal. The cause appears to be a landmine, detonated from ambush by remote control."

The C-in-C said, "We saw. I'll send my Deputy down there immediately, by chopper, Prime Minister. He's ex-Irish Guards and talks their language. He'll keep the lid on."

"I trust so, Field Marshall. To this time," said Gore's tight-lipped image from the War Room, "only two Protestants have been arrested."

At H+25 the count was even.

"I have absolute respect for my superior as a man and as national leader," the C-in-C told MacKenzie in strict confidence, "if anyone can be trusted not to get carried away by his own importance as a 'Guardian of Britain', John Gore can. But when it comes to his ability in current warfare?" The C-in-C echoed Liz's earlier doubts. "Give the old boy a straight military objective and he would swim the South Atlantic or climb the Himalayas to reach it, but you know yourself, MacKenzie, in the quagmire of modern Anti-Terrorism it's often necessary to take the long way round: to try odd tangents, even go along with intuition!"

Finally, at H+30, MacKenzie moved. The message came through that he was waiting for.

"Wallop here, sir. We've sealed off St Mary's Square."

THE SAFE HOUSE was still in the dark when he arrived. The square had been sealed so tightly that not even one of the rangy cats which ran wild in the neighborhood could escape.

"The bastard isn't on-camera, sir," Wallop reported, "but Surveillance say he's definitely still in there."

The roadbed shook from tracks grinding on the cobbles. A massive gun barrel appeared from each of the four streets entering the Square. All four turrets swung around and locked on the safe house.

"Attention! The residents of this dwelling whose names . . . !"

The list crackled through the bullhorn. There was no movement from the safe house.

"Final warning! If you do not immediately leave . . . !"

The front door opened. The old IRA man stepped out. He waved up to a purple-cheeked young lieutenant manning the bullhorn from the conningtower of a tank beside MacKenzie. "You can lay off all that, Tommy. I'm the man you want."

The young officer looked down at him from the top of the turret. "Murdering IRA swine. You bastards took the Shamrocks from ambush — !"

The lieutenant leveled a pistol.

"Shall I be turning my back for you, Tommy?" the old man asked with derision. "Isn't that how you Brit buggers like doing it?"

The pistol shook with fury. MacKenzie put it aside. "That's enough, Lieutenant!"

Wallop jumped down from an armored personnel carrier.

"Two at a time, then? Sure, and why not!" said the old man.

"Don't try and pull my pisser, Mick. We're not making martyrs for the Struggle on this one. In the coop with your opposite numbers."

The Sergeant-Major snapped shut a pair of handcuffs. A hatch in the front of the carrier swung open.

"Mother of Jesus," the old man said, looking inside it, "not you!"

Five seconds later he found himself locked to the boss of the Belfast Protestant Defence: a man he had been trying to kill for five years.

The two young IRA males came out next and got the same treatment. The blonde woman made a move to try escape from the back door, which was caught on the A-T monitor.

Leaving only McDermid.

The name was read through the bullhorn, followed by the warnings, repeated twice. There was no movement outside, or on-camera.

"I'm going in for him," MacKenzie told Wallop.

"They could have the place rigged to blow when you enter, sir. Let me put a sniffer through first."

The situation was dangerous enough without false heroics. He waited impatiently while the robot risked its life for him on the ground floor. No trace of explosives there, but the ancient twisting stairs barred the machine's access to the upper floor.

MacKenzie tightened his flak jacket and stepped into the building. With only the primitive stove in the kitchen, the other rooms were almost as cold as the Arctic air outside. He put a first foot on the stairs.

Crack!

The sound came from behind him. Metallic, sharp. His body flinched, waiting for the thud of the bullet, until his brain caught up and realized that if it was one it would already have struck him. When he opened the door the stove pipe had contracted from the change in temperature.

He moved to the bend on the staircase. Beyond, and above, the space was dark: training-manual territory for a booby trap! He kept to the wall and took the first of three winders. Two doors appeared dimly. Both closed.

He took the next winder. The tread broke. His foot went through the rotten wood and was caught by the support below it. If he was McDermid, this was when he would act...

"Are you all right, sir?" Wallop asked, behind his shoulder.

His foot came free. He lifted the latch of the first door.

Something dropped on his arm. A starling, frozen stiff. Otherwise the tiny bedroom was empty. MacKenzie took a deep breath, and smashed open the other one.

The stink of human feces struck his nostrils. The only trace of his opponent had been deposited in the center of the floor, half obscuring a foully smeared and crumpled page of the names list from the Guardian of Britain's Proclamation.

That scrap of paper was nothing to MacKenzie. McDermid had taken with him the front page of the tabloid with the headline of the Prince's survival.

Whitehall • Club Lunch

WITH HIS MASTER playing at tin soldiers underground, Roger Slade decided to take advantage of the opportunity for a leisurely advancement of his own more vital interests. His table partner was a senior civil service mandarin who had been passed over for even higher promotion, and missed a knighthood on the last Honors List, because of an indiscretion in a public lavatory at the new Museum of Nature and Man. Thanks to a little help from another obliged party at the Human Rights Tribunal, Slade had already managed to have the toilet episode formally removed from the man's file. Now there was just the matter of getting him back on the promotion track.

"The job I've always had in mind," the mandarin mused over a balloon glass of cognac, "would be twofold: Postings and Careers, as a sideline, and Commercial Investment Review, full time. Getting C.I.R. would give one a chance to sort out the winners and the shady stock market runners from the City — not always mutually exclusive, of course, as our present Chancellor of the Exchequor shows."

"Of course," said Slade, sipping his Perrier. "But I don't think I get the reference to Roper?"

"The required divestiture of his assets in a Blind Trust, old boy. All Hal's worldwide filthy tabloids and his American cable telly interests. Going by the book, it's not *quite* as arms length as one might wish. Whereas — " the mandarin continued with a swirl of the amber liquid in his glass — "looking after Careers is just good-housekeeping. Squaring off who's classified as permanent Whitehall staff, indexed pension benefits and so on — and who isn't. Take your own very important, but unofficially recognized, career position, for example..."

At which extremely relevant point a Club waiter arrived with the Prime Minister's call. Slade reluctantly excused himself and stood up from the table.

"Ah yes," said the mandarin, with the kind of shit-disturbing little smile that got him into trouble in public pissers, "there's a war on."

UNDERGROUND, WHEN SLADE returned with a plate of Prime Ministerial sandwiches and his portable speechwriting machine to the War Room, there was a spot of trouble with the toy-soldier games in the Twelfth District, west of Belfast. A child had been hit by a gun carrier. Otherwise, the players seemed to be happy. There was a lot of Boys Own talk about "Closing the ring!," "All over by teatime!," "Immensely proud of the British Army's discipline!"

Slade yawned from the lunch, managing to disguise it as a look of suitable respect for military accomplishment when Gore said to him, "Take down the following: 'To Commander in Chief, Northern Ireland: for relay to all troops in the field. Your performance today has been one in the very highest tradition of — ' "

"Excuse me, sir." The flow of self-congratulation was interrupted by a pretty boy from the Signals duty watch. "A special report for you on Battle Circuit Seven, that's Command South, in Fermagh."

Slade remembered that there had been some sort of fuckup there, before lunch, with the troops wearing the quaint green shamrocks on their helmets. One of them came up now on the big screen.

"Deputy C-in-C, sir. I was sent down to investigate from Belfast. Prime Minister, the explosion at Drumcard this morning was caused by a planted mine. However, it was *not* detonated deliberately from ambush, as people reported in the initial confusion. A high tension line had been temporarily repaired. As the HQ vehicle passed below it, the wire parted again. When it hit the road, the voltage spark melted the asphalt and set off the mine's primer by mistake. A prisoner taken later in the morning confirms that it was a leftover from an IRA attempt six months earlier. It misfired on that occasion. My sappers tell me the chance of a dud going off in this way is one in a million. Bloody bad luck for the Shamrocks, but fortunes of war, sir, I'm afraid."

Gore actually appeared to be relieved by this evidence of military incompetence! "Thank you, General. Ensure that the details you have just given me are immediately transmitted, in plain language, to every level of your Command."

The PM turned away from the screen and saw the plate of delicately prepared smoked salmon and cucumber sandwiches which Slade had brought from the chef at Number 10. He wolfed down two of them.

"When you're ready to continue, Prime Minister, we were at 'Highest Tradition of the Service'?"

Gore slurped some scalding coffee. "Good. Message continues: 'Your professional competence, your discipline, your restraint and perseverance in the face of the worst weather conditions, and provocation — ' "

"Excuse me, Prime Minister." The interruption this time was a snippy young woman holding out a red telephone. "Your ear only, sir."

Gore missed the first words of reply. The reception was bad, and the hearing in his left ear had been shot to hell years ago. He transferred the instrument to his good ear and turned up the volume, allowing Slade to catch the word, "...marching."

"Marching where?" Gore snapped. "Which unit?"

"Edward Marching. Sorry if I got you on your wrong side."

Slade recognized the Duke of Dorset's voice. Gore laughed. "I'm the one who should apologize, Ted. My dear wife has tried to get me to change my hearing aid for months. This is rather a Shakespearian turn. What's the College of Heralds doing in the War Room?"

"The alternates' Succession List. I thought you'd want to know immediately — "

"Prime Minister! Belfast Circuit!"

An open-mouthed and flat-chested female Colonel was pointing at the big screen. It showed a wire compound in the snow. Slade saw that it was crowded with prisoners. The compound was divided down the middle. Black lettered signs said, IRA and ULSTER. An armed guard on the Protestant side was patrolling a locked gate leading to the Catholic side.

"A possible third candidate ..." came over the misplaced Ducal conversation Slade was eavesdropping. Gore was ignoring what the Chief Herald was saying. Now Slade saw that the figure with the automatic rifle in the compound was not a guard: it wore no uniform.

"One of the Protestant insurgents!" said the out-of-her-depth, flat-chested Colonel.

"Illegitimate Australian ..." said the Duke.

"God save us," Gore said in an appalled voice to everyone present. "They've been armed. There will be a massacre."

The un-uniformed man turned to the compound's dividing gate and shot the lock off. Something had obviously gone wrong with the game. Slade observed that the Protestant side of the wire did indeed all have weapons. His employer was flicking the Belfast C-in-C video circuit desperately with his laser-pointer, but all the Command pictures remained blank, except for the one showing the compound. The first bodies were dropping in the IRA enclosure. Those still alive froze in panic. Except for a few in a corner, led by a woman with long blonde hair. She threw herself directly onto the spitting muzzle of a gun.

Slade turned away in revulsion.

"An actor ..." the Duke's voice said.

"You're bothering me about an Australian bastard actor?" Gore looked as though the sandwiches were going to vomit from his gullet. On the screen, the Catholic prisoners' bodies were falling in a spraying welter of scarlet on the white snow. But the image that was making the Prime Minister ill, Slade realized, was the old man's play Army: his disciplined, dedicated, professional British toy soldiers were standing outside the wire of the prisoners' compound. Laughing.

"Mutiny."

As Gore whispered the word another voice broke in unnannounced to compound the War Room madness.

"Prime Minister, Commissioner Dayman here, National Police. Norfolk Detachment report that they have taken a prime suspect in the Sandringham bombing. A Japanese."

Five

Belfast

LONDON HAD A mutiny to halt. MacKenzie's only goal was stopping McDermid. Although the killer had to be still on the Island, and any IRA remnants elsewhere couldn't know the Prince's actual location, he ordered extra detachments moved to Chedburgh, for additional protection. At the same time he took a moment to talk on scrambler to the Surgeon General.

"The patient is stable," the doctor told him, "and we've been able to reduce sedation. Your visits obviously helped, but he's also been asking more often about his family. I don't know how long we can hedge. Do you want me to have the psychiatric staff handle it?"

"No," MacKenzie said heavily. "That's my job."

But not yet. He alerted London Anti-Terror that another attempt might also be launched against their scapegoat Burn Center by the Thames, then turned his full attention back to Ireland. An inner and outer ring of Royal Marine steel encircled Belfast's docks.

"Any last minute instructions, sir?" Wallop asked him.

"Just one, Sergeant-Major. When McDermid is intercepted, I want him taken alive."

McDermid would *be* taken! The assassin might be able to get into the North by using a cowpat to cover his tracks from the sensors, and escape with a shit of derision from the Safe House but, with no IRA allies left to call on, and a quarter of a million troops with authority to follow in hot pursuit across the Border, final escape back to the South was not possible.

Even the weather was helping. Outside the mobile A-T control center a full gale had hurled itself inland from the Irish Sea. The killer's capture, and then due execution, called for only one thing by MacKenzie...

"Sir!" Wallop shouted. "Codhead Lane! We've just had a visual!"

Cool Customer

RUNNING DOWN THE lane, full speed, McDermid felt it was more like taking a Sunday stroll. Since the time he was a kid, it had been this way: the tighter the Brits turned the screw, the more his nerves relaxed. And he knew this place like his grandmother's antimacassar on the back of her favorite rocking chair. The fireblackened debris and melted glass of the Lane's gutted fishpacking plants crunched under his feet; rain slashed his face with the sting of wet leather. He didn't care about that either. The storm was a bloody sight worse for Tommy Brit and his electronic booby toys. The surveillance cameras hanging from the power lines were twirling like boleros on the pampas of —

Lights.

An armored car was approaching from the Falls Road. And then another, and another... McDermid counted forty! And then the trucks started coming. He thought they were endless, but there were only a hundred and fifty! Before almost as many enormous battle tanks, rumbling, crushing the storm litter of black plastic garbage bags like bodies on the cobbles in front, and under them. The whole bloody Brit Army, and all he had on him was two rounds in a pistol! It was enough to let him take at least one of the shits with him. He removed the pistol from its hiding place, strapped inside his sock, with the newspaper headline ...

They weren't stopping!

In the heart of the Catholic ghetto which the swine themselves had created there were enough troops to wipe it as flat as the fishplant behind him — yet they were moving on.

McDermid continued to stand, dumbfounded at their Brit stupidity and his own good luck, until the rain hid the last of them. Then, gathering his wits, he tucked the pistol back in his sock and ran across the road and down the alley formed by the back wall of a new supermarket complex. Equally heedless of the downpour, a trio of mangy Belfast cats foraged in the tipped-up bins of rotting food waste exposed by the wind. The stench was foul but, once he was past it, the gale carried a different, quite magnificent odor: Sea-spray. The smell of escape!

The sound of waves crashing against the breakwater at Holywood filled his ears: now, only a wide-open school playing-field was between himself and the scenic drive that flanked Belfast Lough. McDermid crossed his fingers and made a dash for it. Safety! For a moment anyway. He lay up and got his breath back in the lee of the school. He estimated that he still had five miles to go to his exit point.

But would the comrades be there? Would they be loyal?

The invading Brit army must be scaring the living Jesus out of all helpers of the Cause this night. No point in thinking about it, he told himself, you'll find out soon enough. He passed a house where the occupants had their backs to him, watching television. He saw an image of Westminster towers, and the face of John Gore, the old Army whoremonger, shooting from the lip. The watchers inside suddenly applauded. Protestant sons of bitches! The house must be as Orange as the flames of hell. The picture changed to the Capitol dome of Washington: America, bloody fence-sitting as usual! But the Cause had ten million voters in the States who had been waiting a hundred years to vote for Ireland at this moment and send President bloody split-tail Nimitz a message for her next election! A dog barked from inside. McDermid turned and ran east along the road.

Traitor's Gate • Lust for Power

ROPER'S BEDSIDE TELEPHONE rang in his condominium penthouse overlooking the Thames below the Tower. He kept the place for late-night Parliamentary sessions. He also kept a few of his best Old Masters and a mistress in it. The paintings needed absolute privacy because although they cost what most people called a fortune, they had been purchased without a legal bill of sale.

Prestige from conspicuous display was the turn-on for average collectors. For Roper, showing off his acquisitions meant nothing. The magnificent hidden paintings on his penthouse walls filled a psychological gap which first opened forty years ago when he saw the contents of his nursery bedroom being hauled away in a bailiff's van. As he stood with his parents in the street and watched, the last item to be tossed in the van had been a gift from Roper's grandmother: a faded print of a Beatrix Potter illustration... the wily red fox outwitting the foolish Jemima Puddleduck. The original of the same picture was the first thing he purchased as an adult after his first successful business merger.

The naked woman lying on the bed beneath his current Art black market favorite — a Titian preliminary study for the Dresden *Venus*, which hung in the Vatican Library until its recent "liberation" — needed privacy for a different reason. In contemporary Britain a man could get away with a second wife and hold cabinet office: a third marriage was still pushing luck for any man with wet dreams of becoming Prime Minister. The living beauty in his penthouse was instead of another divorce. Roper looked up at the Titian, and the elegant creature sitting on top of him, gently rotating her pelvis about the pivot point of his groin, and ignored the bedside phone for another thirty seconds.

"I can stop," she said, squeezing softly, as she smiled down at him.

"No." He gritted his teeth. Her auburn hair traced his chest and then his stomach as she swayed her body. First one side, then the other...

"Oh Christ."

He felt her muscles contract, and himself explode into her.

"Christ," he said again.

"You liked?"

"I always like. You're bloody marvelous."

"Blame my Oxford education," she said. "Your machine is still ringing."

She kept him inside her while she leaned over to pass the receiver. In the most regular tone he could manage under the circumstances he said, "Roper speaking."

"I'm sorry to bother you, Chancellor."

He recognized an edge of implied superiority as Slade's voice. "No bother, Principal Secretary. Go on."

"While the Prime Minister is fully occupied in the War Room — the Americans have just recalled their Ambassador — I'm keeping senior cabinet informed of events on his behalf."

There was a slight pause. The clatter of trays and cutlery filled the background. Slade must be calling from the War Room Cafeteria. "Very helpful of you," Roper said. "The Ambassador's recall is news. I know about Belfast."

"Not Belfast, Chancellor. At Norwich, the police suspect in the Sandringham affair."

"The Happy Anarchist connection." He knew about that too. Slade was fishing. "Has the man confessed?"

"He's committed suicide. Before he could be interrogated, apparently."

"Suicide while in police custody?"

"Yes, Chancellor."

"And no interrogation?"

"No, Chancellor."

"I see."

"There is one last thing..."

There would be! The secretary's nasal voice had gone up in pitch. Roper waited for the true reason for this disturbance.

"In the event of the death of our beloved young Prince, the College of Heralds has produced a possible Australian alternate candidate as heir to the throne. Although we don't yet have a name, Chancellor, apparently the person is an illegitimate male, an actor — I thought you might wish to know."

"Not in the middle of the night, to my private, ex-directory number." There was a slight hiss of breath on the other end of the line as the man balancing there wondered if he had tilted too far. Roper decided to throw Slade a first-names scrambling net. He added, "But as you have this number, if you get an identity for this unpromising possible heir, don't waste it... Roger."

"Absolutely not! and thank *you*, Chancellor."

Roper dropped the phone onto its cradle and looked at the necklace of lights on Tower Bridge reflecting across the stolen *Venus* of Titian and the perfect hips of his mistress. "First rule of politics," he told her, running a finger over a velvet fold of skin, "Be underestimated."

"I could never be in politics," she said, and moved his hand down.

Mobile Anti-Terror • Codhead Lane

MACKENZIE KNEW HIS target was gone by the time he got there. The armored command center received a non-stop stream of information from its data links. A footfall sensor and a camera had both detected McDermid's presence entering the Lane, tracked him through it, then lost him when a fiber-optic cable supporting the camera crashed down from the storm.

The fallen line was directly in front of them now. Wallop halted the vehicle. MacKenzie flipped back the conning tower hatch. Iced rain struck him with the sting of shotgun pellets. The wind was blowing full gale force.

"On foot, a night like this, sir," Wallop said, immediately below him, "we're only five minutes late on datum. The perimeter's tight. The bastard won't make it much further."

Over the sound of the storm, to the east MacKenzie heard waves crashing against a seawall. Belfast Lough. Escape by small boat was impossible in these conditions. The buildings on the land side of the coast road had all been cleared and sealed. His target would be desperate, trying for any kind of rathole to wait out the weather.

"What patrols have we got in this sector?" he asked Wallop.

"Not the best, sir. No Marines. The closest group is Taffies, just behind the school."

Welsh Fusiliers. MacKenzie could trust them. They and the Guards regiments hadn't been affected by the Compound incident. He closed the hatch and flicked the microphone of his tactical circuit, to transmit a signal putting this sector on highest alert. The command vehicle rolled forward. The tactical screens acknowledged his message. The one reserved for Special Strategic was flashing as well. All hell was breaking loose diplomatically. Official Protests from Dublin and Washington, over what they were already calling the Compound Massacre, were sharply stepped up. The latest Hotline message from Maureen Nimitz to Gore, protesting the Prime Minister's Order authorizing hot pursuit across the Border, sounded almost like an American declaration of war. The Strategic Net screen could only be opened for viewing after entry of MacKenzie's private code. He keyed it in again.

Personal from Chedburgh. Condition worsening.

The vehicle lurched like his heart. For the first time in his life MacKenzie could not tell where his duty lay. Should he go? Or remain? Even by jet, it would take an hour to get to the bedside. If he kept on, his opponent was only five minutes in front...

"Infrared just got a positive, sir! Bell Street. One thousand yards!"

He looked at the map of Belfast showing on the local screen. Bell Street was en route to the military airstrip where his reserved jet interceptor waited.

"Go!" he told Wallop. "We'll take McDermid."

Belfast Lough

THERE WERE THREE murdering Taff pigs in the patrol which stopped him: a fat sergeant and two skinny lance-corporals. The Fuseliers' armored Jeep had been hidden from McDermid by a clump of gorsebush. A Welsh sing-song voice said to him, "A damp night to be jogging, boyo. Papers now. Look sharp!"

Papers were better than having to speak, he decided. His false beard was sodden; the synthesiser unit, to fool their voice recorders, was totally drowned. His forged documents were dry, and the best that could be made. He passed them over nonchalantly.

"A butcher iss it?" said the pig sergeant, with their Welsh snake hiss on the s. "Out running for your saussage, wass you?"

McDermid smiled, shaking his head, appearing to be winded, and pointed at his identity card.

"Keep 'em up!"

One of the lance-corporal pigs prodded him with the barrel of an Israeli crowd-controller. The fat Taff sergeant examined the card again.

"Volunteer?" McDermid nodded. "Need a medal you lot do, on a night like this. What happened, car break down?" McDermid croaked. "Never mind that talking. Sit you in the Jeep and catch your wind." The sergeant held the vehicle's door open and turned to his pig subordinates, "You two stay here, see. I'll only be a minute, taking him. Any killer micks come by, hold 'em close up by their short and curlies till I get back."

The Jeep accelerated into the wind. The headlights showed the tops of breaking waves. The radio was filled with non-stop Tommy talk from the invasion force. They passed yet another mobile command center approaching doomed Belfast. McDermid's driver said to him conversationally, "Like bloody D-Day at Normandy, all over, issn't it? Sooner you than me, out there now! Here we are."

The Jeep swung hard to the left. The headlights illuminated a red and yellow sign, with its first word missing:

The sergeant leaned across helpfully, to open the passenger door with a spare left hand. McDermid smiled and slipped his own right hand down his leg to his sock, and his pistol with its last two rounds, wrapped in the tabloid with the Target headline. For all the Brothers and Sisters about to become martyrs in the North, he decided to put one of the bullets behind the thick ear on the Taff pig's head.

But then he saw again the magic words in the headline — *Prince Survives* — and the discipline of a soldier took over. The Taff pig's body would be found and focus attention on this location. One day, given the fortunes of war, a member of the Struggle might even need to use the Station again, or another one like it.

The sergeant straightened up. McDermid stepped down into the storm and coughed. The Taff pig tapped him soliticously on the back and said, "Look after that chesst, see. And good luck!"

Mobile Anti-Terror

THE SYSTEM HAD drawn another blank. While Wallop interrogated a pair of Fusiliers found huddling from the wind at the last target datum, MacKenzie tried to think. It was almost impossible. The volume of electronic intelligence material pouring in on the Command vehicle's circuits — Strategic, Diplomatic, National Police, Tactical Ground — was overwhelming.

"GREEN TEAL TWO, this is Anglesey Control: vector three-one-five for new target."

Now the Tactical Air net was adding to the communications madhouse. A target image appeared on the Air Intercept radar screen.

DESIGNATION: COMMERCIAL, AJ 1027.
FROM: BOSTON
TO: SHANNON.
VOLUNTARY DIVERSION: MANCHESTER

Another regularly scheduled flight, MacKenzie noted, an American-Japanese airbus, not taking any risks with its insurance policy. This was the third similar action the RAF had taken this morning. The Irish air blockade was already almost routine.

"They had a suspect, sir." Wallop indicated the two Fusiliers. "A Protestant, carrying Vital Occupation papers."

"A-J Ten Two-Seven, this is RAF patrol. Please maintain present heading and take no further action until you come under Manchester umbrella."

"Royal Air Force Patrol, I cannot comply your last. We are a civilian flight. Our nationality, United States of America. Regularly scheduled point of landing, Shannon."

MacKenzie reached to get rid of the Air Command clutter by removing the pilots' chat from the tactical nets.

"Ten Two-Seven, this is RAF! Regain your original heading immediately, or face a single shot warning."

Astonishingly the US airbus banked the wrong way on the screen. In a split second reflex the British fighter pilot followed in the same direction, reducing his extra speed for weapon acquisition.

"RAF, this is US Navy escort. Break off, pal. We have you covered."

A flat New England voice had burst in on the military combat circuit. Three radar blips appeared from nowhere. Designation, ACZ: US carrier-borne Stealth-10 interceptors.

"The Fusiliers' sergeant took the suspect to his place of work, sir. Do we follow?"

MacKenzie heard Wallop's question but his eyes were rivetted on the Pilot's View image coming from the RAF cockpit. For an instant the leading American Stealth blip on radar became a visual sighting, dead ahead, closing... then the screen went black.

He had just witnessed two men's deaths in a midair collision. Before that shock had fully sunk in, the automatic State board produced another: the British pilot's identity. Flying Officer Francis Lear. It was the oldest son of the Home Secretary.

"Disregard my last, sir. The sergeant is back."

A Jeep appeared out of the storm. To MacKenzie the fury of the elements was a pale reflection of the manmade chaos resulting from Gore's Irish policy. Wallop waved down his Welsh opposite number. The Jeep pulled alongside.

"This Protestant you took up the road?" Wallop asked. "Did you double check his Vital Occupation status with a thumb print?"

The Fusillier shook his head. "My portable print reader got buggered in this storm. But the boyo was genuine. I ticked him off after, against the Lifeboat List. He was on there."

The Whitehall message screen was already calling an emergency full Cabinet meeting. MacKenzie's name appeared in front of him, to report immediately, in person, to London.

"Do you want to go to this lifeboat station, sir?" Wallop asked him.

MacKenzie was about to shake his head when he saw a torn scrap of paper on the floor of the Range Rover, in front of the passenger seat. One word, in heavy block capitals: **PRINCE**

He snapped at Wallop: *"Fly!"*

Belfast Lough

EVEN IN THE ENCLOSED waters of the Lough, the lifeboat plunged, bucked, and rolled with unbelievable force and discomfort. McDermid couldn't imagine what it must be like farther out in the Irish Sea. The interior of the lifeboat resembled a barrel-shaped coffin with the crew strapped into it by body harnesses. The skipper and navigator had seats like an airliner's cockpit which gave them a view of where they were going. The rest of the crew — except for himself, all good practicing Catholics! — could only grip the safety rails and trust in a dead God and the marine architects who designed the coffin.

"Sure, and can't she roll over every which way, and still come up all standing!"

The mate of the boat shot McDermid a wide grin, and offered a fatty ham sandwich. He gave a wan smile back and felt his stomach move up into his head. Under such circumstances, the good humor of the crew was incredible. A faint glimmer of a January dawn began to filter its way in through the heavy quartz-glass windows at the front. The skipper stared with a fierce concentration, both hands on the throttles.

"Trying anything with the rudder is pointless," the mate shouted in explanation, "even when the sea's running as slack as this."

"Slack is it?" said McDermid. "Sweet Jesus, I'd hate to see what's bloody rough!"

"Cartwheel. Going over."

The sea took them before the skipper's warning. For a moment there was a weightless feeling...the boat seemed to float in air...then McDermid felt flung by the neck in three dimensions, and found himself looking at the floor beneath his head.

"Coming up, lads."

Miraculously, impossibly, the forward end of the coffin rose in front of him. He heard the thunder of a thousand drums, and then the light brightened. For a moment he saw the outline of an enormous wave surge past a small round porthole by his elbow. The light went out. This time the boat rolled sideways, but only halfway under. It came up again... and there was a shape beyond the skipper's window.

"Is it a bloody whale then?" McDermid asked.

"Bangor lifeboat, this is HMS Defiant. *Take off your way. Over."*

The radio crackled. The skipper eased the throttles. The navigator responded. "Lifeboat Bangor speaking. Good morning, Royal Navy. Our way is off. Have you seen Lifeboat Larne for us, over?"

"Good morning Bangor. Dead ahead, one half mile. They have no radio. Proceed."

"Bangor, wilco."

The engines revved. The monstrous shape disappeared. The mate of the boat said in McDermid's ear, "She's the Brits' newest nuke sub. The bastards have brought out everything except the kitchen bloody sink."

But no stopper! McDermid thought. Sink or swim he was through the blockade line of the Royal pisshound Navy! Even as he threw up into a barf bag he felt an enormous exhilaration. When he wiped his mouth, he saw the Larne boat passing for home in the other direction, just as planned.

"May day, May Day. Man overboard. Man overboard."

Another strident radio call resounded inside the steel hull. The Bangor crew came to an even higher state of alert. The navigator said into the microphone,

"This is Bangor Lifeboat. Signal position: where are you Mayday?"

Another of the giant drumming waves crashed over them. When it was gone...

"Rocket away! Bearing, Red one-zero!"

The navigator pointed. A flickering green flare was dropping outside his quartz window. The mate gripped McDermid's shoulder. "Ready?"

He nodded. *This* was why they were here. All the co-ordinated planning. All the bravery. The rumble of the diesels lessened. The mate fitted him with a second inflatable life jacket, slipped over the rigid foam one he had on already and the full-body immersion suit. His hands were gloved, his head was hooded. When they went outside, only his face would be exposed to the elements. A second green flare fell by the window.

"Five hundred yards," said the navigator.

The skipper eased back on the port throttle. The boat began swinging in that direction. They dropped into a trough, rose out of it. A rusted trawler hull came up to meet them. Ragged, once-white letters on the stern said, *Constancia.*

"Ready?" The skipper asked it this time, over his shoulder.

The mate looked at McDermid. He said, "As I'll ever be."

The skipper went full ahead with the port throttle. The hull of the trawler came parallel. A wave slapped them sideways and passed on. The mate opened the hatch. The other ship was fifty yards away.

"Too far!" shouted the mate.

"We'll crush from the Venturi effect," the skipper answered. "I can't let her get closer."

The sea did it for them. When the next wave was gone, McDermid found the hull of the *Constancia* on top of him. The skipper hit full reverse on both throttles. A line with a horse collar on the end of it snaked down from the upper deck of the trawler. High above it, McDermid saw the contrails of two jet aircraft, lit by the rising sun meet and become a blazing ball of fire!

"God speed."

With aircraft wreckage plummetting from the sky, and those pointless words from the mate behind him, McDermid jumped over the lifeboat's side into the winter fury of the Irish Sea.

Deep Water • Anti-Terror

THINGS MOVED TOO fast in modern war, MacKenzie thought. As the Mobile Command Center raced along the coast road events outside were overtaking it. An American pilot was dead. In answer to Dublin's request and US voting pressure, President Maureen Nimitz had authorized the deployment of her last European paratroop brigade to act as a fire break against further British hot pursuit operations into Southern Ireland. Whitehall had just informed the C-in-C at Belfast that Gore was arriving to take personal command of the Northern situation.

The radar relief map of Ireland, transmitted from the Prime Minister's aircraft and projected onto the mobile Command Center's tactical plot table, revealed the terrain moving swiftly below the plane in real time. MacKenzie saw that it had just crossed the coast at Dundrum Bay, and now the Mourne Mountains. There was an Irish folk song about them, an old Celtic woman's lament, which he had learned as a child.

"The Mountains of Mourne..."

He recalled the tune but the rest of the words eluded him. North of the mountains on the Tactical Ground screens was the Americans' closest drop point. Dundalk was on a river and a rail line, just below the smaller Northern towns of Forkill and Crossmaglen, and bounded on its eastern side by the sea. The US paratroop commander would not want his men to risk the water; and the steel rails and rough roadbed of a railway, combined with the power lines that flanked it, were almost as hazardous as drowning to a parachutist hurtling down on them at twenty miles an hour. MacKenzie knew: he had done it.

"Lifeboat Station coming up, sir!"

He saw it just ahead of Wallop. They were too late. The steel launching ramp was empty. He switched to the Naval Operations circuit.

"Wreckage sighted. Closing now. This is HM Submarine *Defiant*."

The Navy was already on the job, in case of a miracle for either of the crashed pilots. The Maritime Forces screen showed the submarine's position — and two lifeboats! The one to the south was labeled *Bangor*. MacKenzie picked up the scrambler phone and sent a Flash message to the submarine's captain ordering him to board the lifeboat.

"We'll do our best. It's tough out here."

Ashore, the waves were breaking right over the top of the lifeboat station. Salt spray covered the Command Center's windshield. Northern Air Control broke in, advising the Prime Minister's Flight to keep clear of the newest US drop zone at the central farming area around Monaghan.

"A-T Command, this is *Defiant,* Captain speaking. Bangor crewman matching your suspect, lost overboard."

MacKenzie's pursuit of the vermin called McDermid was finished. But in Ireland...

"Colonel, sir! The Yanks are jamming the PM's flight!"

Fifty miles to the west, the air-to-air radar screen showed two rapidly fading concentric rings of electronic blips. The inner ring of large blips, MacKenzie realized, was the first wave of the approaching US paratroop transports. The outer ring, the smaller blips closest to the Prime Minister, were the transports' protective fighters.

They vanished. All that was left on the screen was a blizzard of snow. McKenzie hit the anti-jamming switch. It made no change to the picture. He wasn't surprised: the sophisticated equipment British forces used had been made in America.

"A-T Command, this is *Defiant.* Suspect's life jacket recovered. Further search impossible until seas moderate."

Survival times were measured in minutes in winter northern waters. MacKenzie switched from the Maritime net to his personal circuit for the Special base at Chedburgh.

"The patient is stable," said the Surgeon General. "Perhaps a little stronger. Another visit from you would do more than we can at the moment. And of course he still doesn't know about his parents."

That terrible task was still hanging over MacKenzie. But in Ireland there was a lull on the ground. The air screens were still blank.

"I shall be back shortly," he told the Surgeon, and added to Wallop, "Take us to the strip."

The Command Center rolled away smoothly from the Lifeboat Station and returned to the Coast road. The main storm front had passed. In the eye of its center the Irish countryside sparkled in bright sun. People appeared in windows. Kids snowballed. Except for the handful of houses closed by the Clean Sweep operation, life was back to normal.

"Incoming on the Prime Minister's line, sir. For your Ears Only."

A red light was blinking next to Wallop. MacKenzie put on his headset.

The light went amber. He pressed, Ready to Receive. The light went green. He heard the C-in-C, Belfast, say, "Good morning, Prime Minister."

"I wish it was, Field-Marshall," replied the somber voice of the Chancellor of the Exchequor. "This is Hal Roper. The Prime Minister is dead. As acting Head of Government I am ordering an immediate halt to any further military action."

PART TWO

The New Britain

One

Aunty Beeb

LIZ PONTI WAS waiting with her BBC crew for their van to disembark from the ramp of an arriving charter when she saw Hector. On this second accidental meeting since the crisis started he was doubling across the tarmac to board his own special military jet for London. As he caught sight of her, and halted in mid-stride, she felt again the irrational sharp tug of her unlikely attachment to a Marine Commando. It wasn't his unexpected and considerable musical ability, or dry Highland humor, that had finally hooked her. The chink in his armor that proved he was more than a military career automaton was finding out from her BBC research staff that Hector financially supported his divorced sister, paid her two kids' school fees, and in the children's holidays managed to take time out of his incredible work load to act as a surrogate father.

"I guess we should thank whoever is organizing our schedules," she said, giving him her best personal smile, before switching to business. "I'm here because we got an incredible rumor at Beeb London Central about Gore being shot down by the Americans. Is it true?"

"You know I can't answer operational questions."

"Meaning yes," she said. "The informant reported it was in a beet-field, near Monaghan, across the Border?"

His strong face looked straight at her, and she saw the new small pain lines radiating from the corners of his eyes. To the vast majority of people the Royals were remote fairy-tale or Hollywood figures, but this man she loved and cared for had known them as ordinary mortals, as friends.

"I can only tell you," he replied in his clipped Official-Military voice, to her last query, "if you're thinking of driving in the vicinity of Keady, the area is still closed to all civilian movement."

"Keady?" her eyebrows rose. "That's on our side."

"Geographic niceties aren't being observed at the moment." He grabbed her to him. "Liz, for Christ's sake be careful."

"Body contact in public, Colonel?" She smiled more broadly. "Things *must* be hot."

"To hell with the public!" He kissed her in front of it. The turbines howled. To add to her astonishment, as he boarded, he shouted over the noise of the engines, "If the world is ending I want to marry you."

"I have that on record," she yelled, indicating her grinning crew. Then his face in the fighter cockpit flashed past her, exchanging this green island and its terrors for the gray backdrop of the Atlantic. Please God, Liz thought, this was the last time either of them would have to look at any part of bloody Ireland. She turned away to answer the other man in her life.

HER BBC SUPERVISOR, calling on cellular from London Central, had only one instruction for her:

"Habeas corpus, darling. Find the damn body."

"I'm trying," she said, as the van crossed the district border from Portadown to Armagh. "I understand Gore was killed near Keady — that's another thirty miles. At this rate Maureen Nimitz may have dropped the Bomb on the beetfield by the time we get there."

"Not now that we have Pal Hal at the wheel," her supervisor said. "The Lady's State Department take their policy instructions from the morning headlines in Roper's Washington tabloid, over their Fresh-squeezed and Decaf."

London clicked off. The van lurched over a humpbacked stone bridge spanning a small frozen river. A signpost beyond had been knocked flat by a tank, and military incompetence. Armored tracks scarred the snow. The troops had obviously got lost after the accident. The tracks started off in three wrong directions before settling on the southwest. The arm of the flattened signpost pointing in that direction said, LOUGHGALL, which was northeast. She thought of the look in Hector's eyes and felt sorry for soldiers, sent to do an unpleasant job in terrible conditions.

"Got a live one, Liz!"

Her sound man pointed at a high-speed, armored personnel carrier, traveling solo, cross-country. It had just tried shortcutting across a creek and gone through the ice. As the news van pulled alongside, a tough-looking officer, with major's crowns on his winter-white parka climbed out, to be met by a bunch of jeering local farm kids with frozen-snot noses.

"Tommy Brit is in the shit!"

The major made a move towards his tormentors... then saw the camera in the van and thought better of it. He put his hands to his mouth and called up the bank: "Have you people got two-way communications?"

"Cellular phone," Liz shouted back. "And a thermos of coffee."

The major stumped through knee-deep snow while the kids danced over the iced crust alongside him, singing: "Tommy Brit's still in the shit!"

"Just the phone," the major said curtly, when he reached her. "I'll have to ask you to leave while I use it." He pointed at the camera. "And turn that damn thing off me."

She couldn't blame him for being bloody-minded. Her team climbed out of the van and asked the kids to do their Tommy Brit act again, for posterity, but faced with the lens they became as camera shy as their former target and ran away giggling over the fields. The major slammed the van door and rolled up the window, standing with his back to it. Liz noticed a boy-scout insignia of a dagger crossed with a rocket on his shoulder. The half-submerged personnel carrier had one-man launchers strapped either side of its conning tower. From the scorch marks on the paintwork the vehicle had recently seen action.

"Against the Americans?" she asked, when the major emerged.

"Not bloody enough. And you never asked that question. Got it?"

"Got it."

"Good." He kicked a tire on the van to dislodge frozen snow from the cleats of his boot then trudged through more of the same thing back to his stranded vehicle. Halfway down the bank he paused at the lightweight footprints made by the kids, and turned to her. "One other thing — any cute footage of me and those foul-mouthed little farts is D-Noticed. Got that?"

His parting piece of gratitude meant that under the latest re-incarnation of the Official Secrets Act all her footage was dead.

"Up the Army," said her camera man.

Liz glanced in the rearview mirror. Behind them, trying to re-board his carrier, the major had also broken through the ice and was wet to his waist. She thought again of her Royal Marine Commando and decided that the major, with his boy-scout badge, doing a shitty job for half her salary, was only three-quarters of a total bastard.

At least someone was concerned for his welfare. As the van made the turn for Armagh, a helicopter with medical markings flew over them in the direction of the personnel carrier. There had been a war on: a stretcher with a body bag was strapped to one side of the chopper.

She didn't find John Gore's body. Beyond Armagh the British Army had closed the country. Liz had to be content with a hilltop long shot, maximum zoom, of a black patch in a beetfield, against a backdrop of weary young Americans sitting around a campfire just beyond it... watching her own reported explanation of what they were doing on Aunty Beeb's television!

Pal Hal • Downing Street

ROPER LOOKED AT the forty faces gathered around the long table in the Cabinet Room. The common denominator staring back at him was beyond fear. It was panic. The national fabric had been ripped so badly that they could see no way of stitching it together again.

He could, he told himself, *But gently. Gentle as hell.*

"Hal, you must keep on..."

"For God's sake, no more changes..."

"How did it happen? What's the situation...?"

The almost hysterical voices came at him from all sides of the table. He raised his hand. Obediently, his colleagues fell silent, like children.

"I can tell you where we stand at this moment. According to a military report from the Craigavon District, Sir John's plane appears to have been shot down by a heat-seeking missile, fired accidentally by an American fighter escorting their paratroop battalion. His aircraft crashed in the Border zone between Monaghan and Keady. The Prime Minister's body hasn't yet been recovered, but I have been able to speak to President Nimitz, through the security of the Hot Line."

"Yankee murdering bitch. That's big of her!"

The predictable explosion came from a red-faced junior agricultural minister and landed country squire, at the far left end of the table. Roper allowed a tight smile of sympathy in that direction.

"In wartime such terrible things happen," he said, "but the President has assured me that there will be no further act of hostility between our two forces."

"But after the Compound incident...!"

"Can we trust the Army...?"

The doubts broke out again all around the table. Just as they would in every home and workplace in Britain when news of this latest disaster was released. First their Monarchy, now their trusted Prime Minister. British Law and Order would be hanging by a thread.

"Of course we can trust our Armed Forces," Roper said reassuringly. "There isn't a man or woman in them who isn't completely loyal to the democratic foundations of British Parliamentary government. The incident with the prisoners was in the heat of battle conditions — and I remind you, it was an *Irish* reaction. Our troops shot no one. The solution to the recent disasters is to bring the lads back where they belong. Home. Here, with us.

But to make a fresh start we must have first things first. I ask you now to nominate a new leader."

There was only one nomination. Roper graciously accepted.

AFTER THE MEETING broke up he proceeded to the Prime Minister's inner office. He sat in the Prime Minister's chair and placed his hands, palms down, on the Prime Minister's desk. In his mind he could see that long-ago nursery table ... with its cracked top being heaved into the bailiff's truck. He saw the look of shame on his father's face. The contempt on his mother's ...

"Excuse me, Prime Minister."

Slade's slippery voice on the intercom was the first use of his new title. Roper pushed the privacy button to Video and saw the secretary's slippery image as well. "What is it?" he asked.

"First, may I offer my congratulations on your assumption of office, sir."

"Thank you, Mr Slade, but it has to be ratified by Parliament."

"A formality, Prime Minister, I'm sure. I have never recorded the minutes of a more effectively conducted Cabinet meeting."

"Well then, you'd better stay on to record some more."

"Oh, thank *you*, Prime Minister." Slade's image gave a slippery smile which managed to pretend surprise at the offer, while expressing considerable self-satisfaction.

"Is the job all you wished to discuss?" Roper asked him. "I'm still waiting for that Australian information."

The smile changed instantly to a look of unctuous concern.

"My own reappointment has been the *last* thing on my mind, Prime Minister!" his new Personal Private Secretary assured him. "I shall have the other matter for you by late this afternoon."

Royal Miss Manners

MAKING THE FAMILIAR turn in off Pall Mall, nothing seemed any different to Slade at Buckingham Palace in spite of the Sandringham cataclysm. The same young footman (he'd always liked the look of him, but who unfortunately turned out to be one of the few straight exceptions on the Royal inside staff) wearing the everyday uniform of sexy snug black trousers, and tail coat, and wing collar, met him at the side door entrance by the Royal Mews. And the same routine work of brushing up the horses and household carriages was being performed (under the bitch-in-heat gaze of an aproned, overweight Household parlormaid) by the moronic shirtsleeved What's-his-name coachman who had come to Slade's office for the Royal Despatch Box, even though the King was dead.

"It's Stubbins. Afternoon, sir."

The fool smiled in the direction of the parlormaid as though Slade's look of withering contempt had paid him a compliment: which meant that the principal asset for a PPS — never showing anyone what you were thinking — was working! Walking through the quarter mile of eight-foot-wide passageways and up the specially designed, gentle stairs to the second floor, nothing else seemed changed either. The same slightly worn red carpets, the same gilt-framed Royal pictures... the same mule faces in half of them! The only thing changed, Slade decided, as he turned into the last corridor, was the presence of black mourning bands on some of the pictures.

"Roger, dear! After so long. What a true pleasure!"

Alerted by the guards from the Mews entrance, his host was waiting at the apartment door. Palace Security hadn't changed either, even though there was nobody to secure!

"For me too," said Slade, as they kiss-kissed cheeks. "Sorry not to have made it sooner, but you know what it's like..."

"Serving Master! Indeed I do, my precious, but no more wasting time. Come in and let me look at you."

The apartment was a living room, bedroom, bathroom and kitchen, all converted in the 1920's from what had been a lesser State Reception Room. The walls were papered with cozy Sanderson prints, and the Georgian-style windows looked out at the private acreage of the gardens; an oasis of calm concealed behind the rear walls of the Palace from the nonstop roaring traffic and hustle of London. "Getting it off" practically next door to the monarch's bedroom used to give a high-voltage boost to what was an otherwise lacklustre performance.

"As nice as ever," Slade said, sitting down on a chintz sofa. "Like its owner."

"Do you think?" The courtier's high cheekbones flushed slightly, accenting their touch of rouge. "Of course, one doesn't *own*, except the personal treasures, you know that, but one does try to make it Home. Although after our ghastly tragedy, with our last little darling in hospital at this very moment..."

The well-bred voice trailed off unhappily. With a slight wave of his manicured hand Slade's host indicated a black-ribboned, signed photograph of his late regal landlord. A generation earlier the fading aristocrat had been employed as a sort of male Miss Manners, the Palace advisor on etiquette and dodging the consequences of "socially awkward situations" for the late king's father, the last royal reprobate to be a Prince of Wales.

"I'm sure the government will let you stay on," said Slade encouragingly.

"Please God. And a kind word from you, Roger dear, to your new Master. But don't let's waste this happy time on horrid things. Two lumps as I remember. You be mother."

Slade poured the tea from an exquisitely engraved sterling silver pot. "I understand from the Duke of Dorset," he said between sips, as his old friend moved to sit down on the comfortable sofa beside him, "that we have a new candidate for king — from the wrong side of the blanket, and in Australia, of all bloody places."

"Marching told you about Sydney?" The courtier frowned. "He promised me faithfully . . . Sorry my dear, I shouldn't snap at you, but really His Grace of Dorset does try one's patience. I said to him when he asked: 'Any surviving issue from the Australian episode is diplomatically out of the question!' "

Surviving issue. Slade felt the same twinge of excitement that he used to when the thigh of this elegant, highborn man next to him first touched the leg of a one-time East End kid in the Tate Gallery. He pressed back with his own thigh now, and said casually, " 'The Australian Episode' sounds rather naughty."

"Boys will be boys." The courtier put down his china teacup and placed a tremulous hand on Slade's knee. "Of course we always allowed for sowing Regal wild oats, but the late King's father — and I wouldn't dream of saying this to another soul — was more *oatish* than the norm for what one has to admit, historically, is a somewhat undersexed Family. Playing Nanny on our Prince of Wales Tours one had to keep track. Mind you, the girls then were nearly always on birth control. And if they weren't, one would make it worth their while to 'take away' their little bundle."

"Royal abortions?"

"With utter discretion." The courtier's hand stroked tentatively up Slade's trousered thigh. "In similar circumstances nowadays, I'm told, it's simply a matter of the Morning After pill. At the time, I blamed the wretched Sydney girl's pigheadedness in keeping it on her being an American. You know how mad they are about our Royals."

"I thought she was Australian?" Slade placed his own hand over the stroking one, and squeezed.

"She is now, wasn't then ... Oh God, darling Roger. *Please.*"

They stood up together and moved arm in arm past the black-ribboned portrait towards the bedroom. "So this possible heir would be his younger half-brother," said Slade, nodding at the late King's picture as he turned the doorknob.

"Oh yes, there's nothing wrong with the lineage and bloodstock on that side of the blanket. But an *American!*— by now thoroughly 'Outback' *Australian!*— I said to His Dorset Grace, Teddy Marching, 'That combination may be just the ticket for a Bar Sinister to become a future President of all the Aborigenes, like his beerbrewing parent: *but the throne of England?*'"

The courtier gave a high-pitched laugh of derision and touched his withered lips to Slade's neck. The two men stopped beside the bed in front of them. It had a quilt of embroidered bluebells and yellow primroses. The courtier folded it back fastidiously and untucked a corner of the threadbare, almost antique, linen sheet provided by the waste-not Palace administration. As Slade slipped into the bed and pulled his excited elderly companion towards him, he asked again, to be sure he'd got it right, "The heir is the adopted son of the new Aussie president?"

"Not adopted, darling." The courtier's frail, veined hand reached to make the magic happen at least one more time. "The American woman was already married to the brewer when she got pregnant... by Us! I told the Chief Herald,'That's what makes it quite impossible. To this day, the Presidential cuckold Down Under doesn't *know.*'"

Two

Garter King • London

MACKENZIE SHOULD HAVE been at Chedburgh, offering strength and support where it was vital. Instead, he had been sidelined to a meeting which shouldn't even be called. Outside the car the streets of the capital looked almost back to normal. A few black banners were still draped as marks of respect from the funeral but they were outnumbered by the tabloids for Mardi Gras Soccer Madness being hawked at every street corner. He turned on the staff car's backseat television to get a broader view, and found himself looking at yet another roundup of momentous events being anchored by Liz.

"This was the scene last night in Parliament," her voiceover said.

The screen cut to the Commons chamber. Roper was standing at the Treasury table, already speaking:

"...to the nation's Members of Parliament, I say: You need no Guardian of Britain! Your leader, at most, is no more than the proverbial 'First among Equals' — and only then, with *your* support and approval. That leader needs no other name than the one we have always used in this House. Until I die nothing could make me prouder, or at the same time more humble, than to have been called by you all, even for only one day of my life: your Prime Minister."

"AYE!"

The roar went up from all sides of the Chamber, followed by:

"ROPER! ROPER! ROPER!"

For a fraction of a second, as the camera froze the outwardly calm expression on the new leader's face, MacKenzie caught a glimpse through the eyes of a brain burning on raw power.

"We're now looking at Defence Department footage showing the first arrival of United Nations Peacekeeping Forces," Liz's voice told him.

This clip was some children singing winter songs, from a sleigh. A bigwig was listening. When the man turned to the camera, once again it was Roper. Behind him there was a village street with trucks painted white and blue for the UN, and some smiling women giving the peacekeepers fresh baked bread. One of the women was asked by the new Prime Minister what she thought about all these foreigners helping?

"Sure, and isn't it something that should have happened a hundred years ago!" she replied in a thick Belfast accent. "Peace here in Ireland at last? I think it's just bloody wonderful."

The clip was soothing: it was also a lie. In the last twenty-four hours, MacKenzie was well aware, Britain's new "First among Equals" hadn't set a foot out of Greater London. The UN trucks and village background were superimposed. The blatant photo-opportunism was predictable for the creator of a media empire: coming right after the scene in Parliament it was disquieting.

"MacKenzie, hullo. I didn't expect you to be so prompt."

The man waiting for him when the staff car stopped was Edward Marching. MacKenzie only knew two things about the present Garter King of Arms: as Chief of the most ancient established practice of Heraldry, the Duke of Dorset still received a salary in keeping with the rigors of the job when it was created by Henry V in 1415 — twenty-five pounds! — and he refused to have a video phone, which he felt to be a gross breach of a man's privacy.

MacKenzie got out and replied, "The Prime Minister's message said, 'expedite', your Grace."

The Duke looked more surprised. "I can't imagine why he wanted a fighting man present for our dull deliberations. Come along, we shall be meeting in the Library."

Tucked just below St Paul's Churchyard, and dwarfed by the mighty cathedral, the Heralds' Office housed the thousand branches, like MacKenzie's, of the Nation's ancient family tree. On a normal working day it would be open for the booming ancestors business; now it was still closed as a mark of respect.

"Good morning, Garter King."

"Good morning, Clarenceux."

Another middle-aged man wearing a black armband had emerged from a doorway for this antique exchange of greetings. MacKenzie recognised the heraldic second in command: like the other college members, they were familar to him from State occasions, but with one exception, not friends. He wondered again what the hell he was doing in a place where the major decisions were who wore velvet — the Duke, and the other two Kings of Arms, Norry and Ulster; or satin — the six Heralds, York, Richmond, Windsor, Somerset, Lancaster, and Chester; or silk — for the four Pursuivants who attended them, pronounced *Percyvants,* as the yeomen porters constantly reminded visitors, Portcullis, Rouge

Dragon, Rouge Croix, and Blue Mantle.

"Do the Pursuivants have all the trees for the principal candidates in case the PM should want to study them himself?" the Duke asked the second herald, as they entered the main hall, past an old yeoman porter who looked up from the newspaper he was reading and saluted creakily.

"Every one, Garter King," Clarenceux replied, at the same time acknowledging the porter's feeble greeting with a vague wave. "Blue Mantle has them arranged in ascending order of precedence and starting in each case with the male line. I don't suppose you've seen that rag this morning?"

MacKenzie glanced at the headline:

MYSTERY PRINCE IN AUSTRALIA !!!
PROMINENT PLAYBOY SON ???

He thought again of the desperately injured boy he should be helping at Chedburgh. Against such an example of courage the blaring headline was revolting. Underneath it, the usual female anatomy covered the rest of the tabloid's front page. The Duke shook his head. "Knockers for breakfast isn't my cup of tea. This rag seems to have made our decision for us."

"I wasn't referring to the infantile headline," Clarenceaux replied in a querulous voice. "Blue Mantle also tells me, via his chauffeur, there's a readership survey inside. You know, dirty weekend and free beer in Rio for the winning entry. But instead of soccer pool results, this one's on the future role of the hereditary peerage, of all things!"

The disgruntled heralds turned into the Library chamber. The other members of the College were already assembled at the center horseshoe table. The four Kings of Arms sat at the top of the arch, then the six Heralds, placed three to a side; and on either side of them, two Pursuivants. Each place was marked with the armorial bearings and full title of its occupant.

As MacKenzie saw a small red dragon of Wales, he was greeted with the exclamation "Hector, my dear!"

He received a warm kiss on the cheek from the smiling Rouge Dragon Pursuivant, his longstanding friend, and the only female in this masculine environment.

"Lady Bron." He kissed her in return. The Lady Bronwen of Llangath was Gore's generation, huge bosomed, with a heart and brain to match.

"How is our darling boy?" she asked urgently. "I've tried ten times to see him at the Burn Center across the river, but your security is so tight they won't even let me in!"

If there was anyone MacKenzie would have bent a rule for it was this loyal woman, but the secret of Chedburgh had to be impregnable. He said only, "The Prince is stable, Lady Bron. At the moment that's as much as we can hope for."

"Garter King, the Prime Minister is just arriving." Their private moment was broken by Ulster, the stork-legged College third senior. The library door re-opened to show Roper behind it, exchanging a man-to-man laugh with the old porter. "Send in that entry," Roper called back over his shoulder. "You may win!"

The group rose. Marching said with unconcealed irony, "May I now introduce you to the less vital College staff, Prime Minister? We understand that if enough people like our porter and Blue Mantle's chauffeur so decide, most of us in this room are for the chop."

"Nothing that drastic, I'm sure, your Grace. But it doesn't hurt to take the popular pulse on these sensitive Constitutional matters. Our difficult business this morning, as a pertinent example."

Roper set down a locked briefcase and gave a warm political smile all round as he was formally introduced to each heraldic title. Lady Bronwen didn't smile back.

"Our gallant little Prince is battling for his life less than a mile from us at this moment, Prime Minister. And you would put the choice of his possible successor out for public referendum?"

"I'm always interested in general voter opinion, Your Ladyship."

From the nods and shakes of heads, MacKenzie concluded that in the shock of sudden national change, even this group's opinion was as divided as the rest of the country. They took their seats at the horseshoe table.

"Before we begin," Marching said, "let us each first pray for His Royal Highness."

MacKenzie had never stopped praying but he bowed his head like the rest and sent whatever mental strength he had, north, where it was needed...

"I should just like to remind everyone present," the Duke continued in an equally solemn tone, "that there has probably not been so significant a decision to be made by a body such as ours for almost two hundred years. As we weigh the merits of our possible alternate candidates, and if we find some of them to be apparently less than we might wish, let us remember that our predecessors must have felt much the same when they had to recommend a naive and politically ignorant young girl. Yet history can only praise the result of their labors which gave our nation and the world the inspiration for an age, Queen Victoria." He turned to Roper and added, "Blue Mantle has arranged the lesser candidates' genealogies first, Prime Minister."

The Chief Herald passed a lambskin parchment folder. Roper leafed swiftly through its pages and raised an eyebrow. "The young Victoria didn't have a police notation for using a banned substance, or alcoholic tendencies — these aren't alternatives."

"Not agreeable ones, certainly, Prime Minister. However, speaking in the vernacular, the country needs —"

"I know what the country needs, my Lord Duke. And it can manage for some time longer without Royal ribbon cutting at a new plastics factory." Roper dropped the folder. "If the alternate choice is required it must be made from the two leading candidates."

"Sir, the Archbishop of Canterbury has already attempted to persuade the Catholic Lady to Anglican conversion. She is absolutely adamant. As for the Male...!"

"There is only one possible male alternative for the hearts of the British people. The young man in Australia."

The Council heads surrounding MacKenzie swiveled in unison to Lady Bronwen.

"An *actor?* You must be joking!"

"I am quite serious." She addressed Roper. "Wrong side of the bed or not — and I don't need to remind anyone at this table that it's hardly the first time a British monarch has found himself on the throne because of such an episode — the point I am making is that if further catastrophe befalls, and if this young man should be proven an illegitimate half-brother to our late King, there is no further choosing: he *is* the Heir Apparent."

"That is pure feminine emotion," said the Prime Minister, "not logic. I don't dispute that this man's mother may have slept with the former Prince of Wales, but if every woman that was said of! Council members, you would be faced with an encyclopedia of candidates!" When the politician's jab didn't get the predictable laugh, Roper unlocked his briefcase and took out a red-slashed Secret file. "However, in this case, even if it were true, I have the unhappy advantage of having been given some background on this individual from our Special Intelligence Services."

MacKenzie recognized Love's signature. Roper began reading from the file: " 'Subject, Richard Arthur Byrd-Wilson, or 'Dicky'. Age, twenty-seven. Only child, second-rate school record, expelled from one; timid in organized sports; dropped out of university. Psychiatric profile: uncertain of gender role, post-adolescent; spoiled and dominated by an American-born mother who rode around the world in a miniskirt on a motorcycle before she married for money and became an Australian.' There are photographs."

Roper produced them. The son was made up as a grinning clown in some stage production. The mother was still a striking woman; she got points for the bike exploit in MacKenzie's estimation.

"I paraphrase the rest of the Security report: Unmarried, a skirtchaser; for the last six months lived in King's Cross — the former redlight district of Sydney — with another American female, Tatyana 'Anna' Randolph, a part time marine biologist, until she walked out on him, and flew home to Virginia. Because of an episode he had with a redheaded model less exotically called 'Sally', from Brisbane.

"*Professionally,* if we can use that word, a second-rate actor who has never had a significant stage role, even in Australia. A driving record as bad as anything in the files of the British-born minor candidates we have already rejected; an involvement with marijuana... the list is endless. And on purely practical terms, a man — a foreigner — totally unfamiliar with anything to do with the day to day reality and extraordinary demands of a ceremonial life as this nation's Sovereign."

"Thank you, Prime Minister, for that illuminating, if depressing, character outline. Council members," the Chief Herald said firmly, as Roper put away the file, "the position of Rouge Dragon is one with which we can all feel sympathy. But quite apart from the man's unsuitable qualifications, with the possible royal father long dead, even if the mother came forward today — which, given her position in Australian society as wife of their new President, would be unimaginably awkward for her — there would, of course, be no way whatever for this Council to corroborate her claim."

"Yes there would, Garter King. My husband is a chemist, and at breakfast when we discussed —"

"At *breakfast,* Lady Bronwen?"

Roper's sarcasm got a stinging response. "Happily married couples, Prime Minister, do talk to each other on such occasions. Proof can be obtained with DNA testing."

There was a sudden silence in the Library.

"I don't know the scientific details," she said, "but we can get that nonsense from any university. What I *do* know, in ordinary language the initials, DNA, hold the gene pattern of our Royal Family. If the blood of this young man in Sydney has the same pattern as the late king's father, his claim to the Throne is unassailable. Garter King of Arms, I now ask formally that this body record its vote."

The Library silence became a clamor of excited voices. Except for Roper's.

"The point your intuitive colleague has raised," the Prime Minister said cooly to the rest of the Council, "might be interesting for scientists in a university laboratory, but I remind you of a simple fact: the playboy in Australia has made no such claim."

"He will," the forceful old woman behind the Red Dragon emblem declared. "I shall see that he does."

"Debate is closed," said the Chief Herald. "Council members are advised to bear in mind the Prime Minister's remarks. I will now call for an alternate Successional vote by show of hands — myself abstaining, except to break deadlock — on choosing the female first Candidate, if she should agree to convert?"

Twelve hands rose.

"And on the male Second, if she should not?"

Six hands.

"And on the male Third, as proposed by Rouge Dragon, presuming that scientific testing can be confirmed?"

Six.

Deadlock. Roper stood up with a tight smile.

"Then as Garter King of Arms I also register for the Third."

Marching raised his own arm. Roper turned away from the table and said with icy sarcasm to the Chief Herald, "Keep me informed of Your Grace's scientific research. Meanwhile, I have a government to run."

MacKenzie stood aside, still none the wiser for being here. As the Prime Minister passed him Roper added, with the same brusqueness of a strong man thwarted, "His Royal Highness may die. You know the Real World side of what it takes to be Sovereign. I want you to visit and report personally to me on the first two alternate candidates, as soon as possible."

MacKenzie suddenly realized that Gore must have kept the secret of Chedburgh even from his senior colleague in the former Cabinet. He said, "About His Highness, before you leave, Prime Minister, there is something I must tell you... in complete privacy."

He opened the door of the Chief Herald's office. Roper stepped inside.

"Spit it out, Colonel."

"The Prince is not in London."

The look of surprise that he got was genuine.

"Where the hell is he?"

MacKenzie explained. "And I think his Highness should remain at

Chedburgh even if his medical condition permits moving him. The opposition's most dangerous threat has been neutralized, but we can't discount a revenge attack from possible IRA cells still operating here in England."

Roper nodded thoughtfully, then said, "Agreed. Visiting the boy won't stop you from vetting the other two candidates." As he was about to leave the Herald's office the Prime Minister took out the redlined SIS file again and thrust it at him. "You can shred this rubbish on the Third. Her Ladyship will doubtless begin her quest for the next King Arthur over lunch. But as an officer with such long and close links to the Throne, you must agree, Colonel: the rest of us have already been fed more than we can stomach about that clowning young bastard."

Three

Prince of Denmark • Brisbane, Australia

RICHARD WOKE UP with the half-invigorated, half-exhausted feeling that came from a really good screw the night before. He rolled over and stretched. It must be mid morning. The Queensland sun was shining through frilly pink curtains, and he heard parrakeets chattering outside the open window. He was alone in bed. It took the usual post-hangover moment to make two and two equal Sally's bed. Her bedroom was pink and flouncy, with ribbons on the lampshades, and a long-piled white shag carpet on the floor.

Shag was the right bloody word! He got out of bed and ambled to where he thought he remembered the bathroom was... but found it was a closet full of Sally's clothes. The door he wanted was next to it. He flushed, showered, wrapped a pink towel around his waist and went to find his clothes.

"I'm laundering them for you while you eat." Sally was back in the bedroom with a breakfast tray. "Have some juice. You need it after last night!"

She winked, and passed him a glass. They laughed, and she shared a piece of his toast, and then they screwed some more while his clothes were in the dryer. Afterwards, Sally drove him in her car to catch the Sydney shuttle. As they went past the Toowong Racecourse and the trotting horses being given their daily exercise of swimming in the Brisbane River, they agreed to do the same thing as last night again as often as possible!

They were sharing a last good grope at the shuttle gate when the press hyenas closed for the kill.

INSTEAD OF SALLY'S tits, Richard found his way through the gate barred by a mass of outstretched arms holding sound and video recorders! More reporters were waiting on the shuttle: another pack mobbed him when he got off the aircraft in Sydney. Their constant questions were insane. It was the kind of publicity any actor would have died for, but they didn't give a damn about his opening on the Sydney Opera main stage next week as Hamlet — just over and over and over about being the next King of England! — until finally, he exploded.

"Godamn it! I don't understand the reasons for your questions. I don't have any bloody answers. I'm just an ordinary Australian. Now let me alone."

"An ordinary multi-millionaire."

"My father is one. I earn my —"

"Have you spoken to your mother?"

The last question was shouted at him by a woman from the Global News satellite TV outfit. Richard stared at her.

"This has nothing whatsoever to do with my mother. Leave her out of it."

"The year you were born, there was a Royal Tour of Australia."

"Jesus Christ! There were royal tours of everywhere."

"Your mother went to a party with the Prince of Wales."

Richard felt the blood drain from his face and then rush back with a fury more intense than he had ever before experienced. He said through clenched teeth to the World News bitch, "If that remark is meant to imply what I think it is, my father and his money will sue you and your shit-raking outfit for so much libel damage, you'll never get another bit of your shit lies on the tube anywhere that there's a court of civil law."

He slammed past the woman, knocking her videocam to the ground. And then, mercifully, when he didn't know what the hell else he was going to do, or where to turn, an airport security policeman came up to him and said, "If you'll come with me, sir. There's a private helicopter flight waiting to take you to Canberra, and President's House."

THE HELICOPTER PUT him down an hour later on the pad in the Residence garden. For the first time he was grateful about his father's new position: the garden was completely surrounded by a three-meter high brick wall, with guards at the gate to shut out the press.

His mother was waiting for him in the shade of a eucalyptus tree. One hand screened her eyes from dust getting past her sunglasses; the other held down the skirt of her light summer dress. She was wearing pale yellow, the color he liked best on her. She looked fragile, standing there buffeted by the downdraft of the rotors, as though it might pick her up like a tornado and whirl her away. Richard felt a sudden affection for her. When the rotor stopped turning, he walked across, hugged, and gave her a kiss.

"Dicky! What a lovely surprise. Have you had a ghastly time with the bloody press?"

"I don't understand how they know where to find me." And he couldn't stand it when she insisted in calling him by his baby name, *Dicky!* He said, "I hadn't told anyone I was in Brisbane."

"The bastards have eyes in their arses," she said, with a glimpse of her other self that she normally only showed in her crazy car driving. "In Brisbane, darling? With anyone I know?"

Richard shook his head. Once she started on his lovelife her voice went back to its usual tone of pretending not to want to pry... while digging like hell about his breakup last week with Anna. She took his arm and began strolling towards the flagstone terrace on the shaded south side of the residence as though the press hassle was over and nothing out of routine had ever happened.

"You organized getting me down here," he said. "Do you have something to tell me?"

"Nothing special, love. Daddy's away opening the Capital Summer Arts Festival but he'll be back in time for tea. The two of us just want to see a little bit of our only son once in a while."

She was hiding something. He could always tell from the little patches of red that showed up on her cheeks, even when she was tanned. They reached the cool of the terrace. She sat casually onto a wicker chair by a table of iced drinks and reached for a glass. He said, "The press shits kept asking about you going to a party with the last Prince of Wales."

The glass dropped with a crash to the flagstones.

"Bugger," she said. "I'll have to call one of the servants to clean up the mess."

"I told them to go to hell. The reporters. They meant — "

"I know what they meant. It's a horrible story they've only dredged up because of Daddy's new job as our President. It's nothing to do with you."

"I told them he'd sue the roof off their bloody corporate headquarters."

"Sue?" She gave a little laugh and stared at him from behind her dark glasses. "What on earth for?"

"The obvious implication was that you slept with the Prince. I'm sorry. Saying something like this to your mother..."

"Isn't like the stage," she said, after a slight pause. "No. But thank you darling, for saying it. There's never any point in keeping things that worry us bottled up."

"It doesn't worry *me*. It's you."

"Then there's nothing for either of us to worry about."

"You mean it isn't true — going to the party?"

"I went to the party. I didn't go to bed with the Prince of Wales. That is God's honest truth. Cross my heart and hope to die." She made the sign of a cross between her breasts. "And you, my own special foolish Dicky darling, are not the missing bastard King of England."

"Of course not," Richard said, kissing her again, after a huge sigh of relief for the blindingly obvious. "Nobody in their right mind would ever think I was."

Havana

SEAN McDERMID STOOD on the salt-streaked starboard wing of the *Constancia's* flying bridge and watched the finest harbor in the Caribbean approaching. Apart from the ever-present stink of dumped fishguts, the ocean trip had done him good, letting his reflexes relax after the constant tension of dodging the invader's army. How many brothers and sisters had fallen in the Struggle, there was no way of knowing. The Cuban rustbucket trawler heaving beneath his feet had burned out its radio on the first morning: all contact with the world had been lost.

An albatross swooped effortlessly from the brooding bulk of Morro Castle on the eastern shore across the Atlantic swell to inspect the guts below him, so close that he could see the bird's cold yellow eye. His Belfast granny would have said it was the soul of a drowned sailor, and been down on her chapped knees in the confessional, praying forgiveness from a clapped-out whisky priest and a dead God for being born poor and Catholic under the boot of the bloody Brits.

A long blast sounded on the *Constancia's* siren. The Havana pilot boat was approaching from the Castillo de la Punta to the west. McDermid walked across to the other wing of the flying bridge and watched the Cuban port authority vessel swing neatly in below him. To his pleasant surprise, the pilot was a woman. A real one, not like the Russian Engineer on the trawler, with her lard-filled brassiere. The Cuban pilot had raven black hair that spilled out from below her peaked forage cap, halfway down to her waist...and no damn bra at all beneath her crisp cotton blouse. Just a pair of the finest jugs a man could dream of, cooped up in a heaving, leaking bucket of—

"Buenos dias, comrades."

The Cuban pilot swung herself lithely over the rail, at the same time allowing her eyes to flick with disdain across the crew ogling her official assets. When her gaze got to McDermid, it paused for a second to give him the same frankly physical assessment that he sent any good looking woman. For a man like himself, used to taking command in sexual situations, it was an uncomfortable feeling... yet exciting. He smiled at her and gave a slight salute. She smiled back and answered the salute by tapping the peak of her cap with the rolled up newspaper she had been holding under one arm.

"Por favor, señor," she said, in a husky voice that showed how far Cuba had come out of its shell since the days of old killjoy Castro. With another appraising flick of her eyes up and down McDermid's body she passed the paper to him and went forward to the wheelhouse.

"Gracias, señorita."

He bowed ironically, watching her slim buttocks in their tight fitting chinos disappear beyond the hatch. If he was half the judge of women he knew himself to be, a warm landfall in Havana was assured for the evening. He leaned back in the shade of the *Constancia's* bridge awning and unrolled the paper.

GUARDIAN BRITANICO MUERTO

Gore was dead? He read the astounding news of America's airborne intervention and the UN takeover. Revenge was denied him: the Brit Army butcher had been succeeded by a bloody peacemaker, the capitalist tycoon, Roper.

The evening traffic of Havana was streaming homeward along the Avenida del Puerte shore drive behind the seawall. The ordinary life of ordinary people. Needing time to think, McDermid was about to refold the paper, to pass it on to the *Constancia's* crew ... and make his next move towards his evening with the Cuban pilot ... when a shaft of the setting sun burst through from behind the Santa Clara Convent and illuminated the bottom of the inside page he still held in his hands.

"¿rey britanico dentro de australia?"

The heading wasn't large, but it wasn't the words that mattered. It was the two pictures below them. One of the faces was world famous — "Our Gallant Little Prince," barely hanging on in a London hospital, good riddance! — but the unknown Australian face beside it? There was definitely a likeness ...

And maybe there really was a Catholic God in Heaven, he thought, as the albatross swooped past again on its eight-foot wingspan. The sleek white head turned to look at him enquiringly. McDermid took a pistol from his jacket and shot the feathered prick through its yellow eye.

That took care of superstition. He focussed on his next human target.

Chedburgh

THERE HAD BEEN another slight improvement. MacKenzie sensed it immediately as he approached the bedside. Inside the sterile oxygen tent, the eyes behind the slit in the bandages had recognized him as soon as he came through the doorway of the special ward.

"You missed yesterday, Colonel Ken, but I told my Drummer you'd come this morning."

The voice was stronger too. Not much, but any progress was a miracle. Again, MacKenzie yearned to tear the medical barriers aside and gather the small figure up in his arms. Again, all he could do was somehow find a smile while he tapped the clockwork toy and said, "The last twenty-four hours I've been rather busy, Your Highness, but from now on you can tell the Drummer I shall be here every morning, and most afternoons, until you're well again."

"Have my mother and father stopped being busy too?"

MacKenzie had never been a good liar. Confronted by this look of perfect trust, he found it impossible. Yet telling the truth to the boy in his weakened condition...

"You said I will be the King, didn't you? Before, when I was sort of dreaming."

Putting off the hard choice, MacKenzie nodded, and sat down in a chair beside the bed. "So I did, Your Highness, when you were dreaming."

"But I can only be King if my father and sister are dead."

The small voice was matter of fact, reflecting the reality of history lessons taught since day one in the Palace nursery... but underneath was the terrified note of a little boy trying to be braver than a grown man. The image through the plastic was suddenly more blurred than usual as tears filled MacKenzie's eyes. He blinked them back.

"Are they dead?"

The charred Drummer stared. The three words left MacKenzie nowhere to hide. He said, "Aye, Lad."

The mechanisms of modern medicine kept on their rhythmic pumping. The eyes in the bandages stayed open to show that the young mind behind them was still working. It was MacKenzie's heart which felt like breaking.

"So my mother is too busy being Queen. That's why she can't see me."

The eyes were looking at the ceiling, not at his face. He could have let that last lie go by for the time being. To have done it in stages. But he sensed that he was being tested. That the boy already *knew.* That to lie to him now would be to kill any faith that there could be a future.

He said, "I told you in the dream, you must be brave, Lad. Your mother died also."

"But you will be here?"

It hadn't sunk in. Such a brutal, stark reality could not possibly be comprehended by an eight-year-old's intelligence. MacKenzie nodded once more. Once more he found the strength to say, "Aye Lad. I will. Always."

"Thank you, Colonel Ken."

But that — *gratitude* — he couldn't take. He managed to pretend long enough to turn things back to the Surgeon General. Outside the ward he found himself trembling in a state of shock. He went to the Officers' Mess and downed a double brandy in front of a log fire. It stopped the trembling. But when he opened his briefcase to check his next move he found the Australian candidate's file. All his rage and loathing for the people responsible for Sandringham focussed on the red-lined page of backstairs gossip. He hurled the obscenity into the flames with his personal feelings, and followed his orders.

First Choice • Dorset

CHILTON MANOR LAY ahead. MacKenzie banked his one-man helicopter, skimming it in a straight line across the country lane winding below him to his destination. The winter hardened fields, the bare limbed oaks and scattered elms which had survived the last century's blight, the stone blacksmith's forge beside the half-frozen stream, all looked unchanged since the first Elizabeth's time when the house coming rapidly towards him was created.

Three horses in a field broke and cantered off, manes tossing. He saw a stable complex beyond them, and a figure standing with another animal in the center of the yard. He set the chopper down a safe distance away and walked the rest.

"Good morning, Colonel MacKenzie. I'm glad you had enough sense not to put that filthy thing any closer."

The figure beside the horse was the woman he had come to see. They had first met twenty years ago, when he had his junior officer's romantic moment with her younger Royal sister. He had never known for sure how much this more puritanical older woman had been told of that brief affair, but as she had never used his Christian name in the two decades since, he guessed she didn't approve. Her principal love was horseflesh. As usual when he saw her, today she was wearing johdpurs and a rough woolen sweater, with a small gold cross on a fine chain around her neck, while she groomed a gray stallion. The animal's eyes rolled, following MacKenzie.

He halted just inside the herringbone brickwork of the stable yard and said, "A fine beast, Your Highness. Thank you for agreeing to see me at such short notice."

"Could I refuse?" She gave a short, sharp laugh. "After being importuned by an archbishop, and my next door-neighbor, the Duke of Dorset, a Commando dropping out of the sky won't change my mind, Colonel."

"I wouldn't presume to try, Maam."

"Then why are you here?" She slapped the stallion's rump, and began moving him towards the door of a stall.

"At the Prime Minister's order," said MacKenzie. "In case you might already have decided —"

"To abandon the one true Church in favor of getting my name in the headlines of his former newspapers, like this poor young fool in Australia!" She nodded at a tabloid left beside a groom's bag lunch on a shelf.

SALLY UP HIS ALLEY ???
PRINCE DICKY BYRD DENIES ALL !!!

A full page montage showed a young red-headed woman posed in a g-string being groped at an airport boarding gate. The man groping her had an inane grin on his face. It was the first time MacKenzie had seen the Australian's features without their clown makeup: they were regular, but unformed by any character — a typical matinee idol. He saw no resemblance whatever to the Family he had served. The unemotional face of the First Choice candidate in front of him was born to rule.

"Of course there is a total lack of privacy for the Monarch," he agreed with her, as she closed and bolted the stallion's door. "I couldn't take the intrusion in my own life — but then it wouldn't make any difference to the country whether or not I did." He indicated the tabloid, "With respect, Maam, you have all the qualities the British people desperately need at this moment."

"The people may need them, but they don't want them in an RC."

"A Constitutional formality," MacKenzie answered. "I don't think the country gives a damn any longer about the religious aspect. If I were the Prime Minister I would abolish the restriction against Roman Catholics tomorrow."

She gave him a shrewd look, from eyes that did remind him so keenly, and painfully, of everything he and the nation had lost. She said to his surprise, "I believe you, Hector. Tell Roper, if he abolishes it, I'll take the job."

Second Choice • Exmoor

THE BUILDING THAT he flew towards for his second interview looked like a pleasant Devon country house at a distance: whitewashed walls, black timbers, diamond-pane leaded windows, old thatched roof. It was only when MacKenzie approached the last hundred yards on foot that he saw the bars on the dormer windows peaking quaintly out of the thatch. A carved rustic sign by the front door below said Moorwell Hall.

The reception area inside looked just as normal. Comfortable furnishings, hunting prints, rugs on wooden plank floors. The jarring note here was the size of the shoulders of the man in a bulging tweed sports jacket, watching the other occupants of the Hall. They were a collection of genteel, elderly men and women, neatly dressed for a weekend retreat in the country. The person MacKenzie was here to see had been in retreat for almost fifty years.

The attendant in the sports jacket came over and said, "How do you do, Colonel. He's waiting in the study."

A low door opened off the central passage leading from the reception area. The room beyond looked out at the rolling expanse of Exmoor. The Second Choice candidate was staring at two of its wild ponies in the foreground. He wore an immaculate blazer and gray flannels, with a wide-striped shirt and dark green silk cravat.

The attendant said, "Excuse me, Your Royal Highness: you have a visitor."

The man turned and smiled. MacKenzie swallowed hard. The movement of the body, and the smile could have been the late King's own. This handsome man with the full head of silver hair was his uncle.

MacKenzie bowed and said, "Good day, Your Royal Highness."

The smile remained in place. The pale blue eyes looked squarely at him. The second alternate candidate for the British Throne said in a pleasant, well-bred voice, "Because I wet my bed last night they tried to poison me today."

Musical Chairs • Downing Street

BACK ON THE safe side of the Number 10 security cordon, MacKenzie was surprised to see the limping figure of Love emerge from the private exit of the Prime Minister's inner office and get into a waiting unmarked car. The vehicle's armament and antennas labeled it clearly as belonging to the head of GOCSS, the Government Overview Committee on Special Surveillance and Communications. He thought that Love must be waiting for the car's official owner, but as the security man saw him, he gave a terse flick with the scarred back of his hand and drove off.

MacKenzie continued into the building, still without a valid reason to another question: why he should have been sent to interview a certified lunatic for the Throne of Britain? There was no answer from Roper. The new Prime Minister had left for a weekend with his family.

"Only to be disturbed for matters of vital national interest," the PPS told him, with Slade's usual snide pleasure at blocking access.

The minor puzzle about the GOCSS car deepened with the sight of the man sitting slumped in the outer anteroom. The Chairman of GOCSS was another leftover from Gore's old-fashioned world: the practice of espionage had changed forever with satellites and computers but the man in the chair still believed that the only Intelligence of real value came from the minds of men and women, not machines. When anyone in Whitehall addressed Britain's top spy, no last name was ever used.

MacKenzie extended his hand and said warmly, "Sir James."

Instead of returning the handshake the GOCSS said in a stunned voice, "Roper's just made me surrender my Ivory!"

For centuries the 'Ivory' had been passed to each head of British Intelligence personally by the Monarch, to keep that vital Secret Service office above partisan politics: by custom it could only be taken back at the order of the giver, or his successor. The Intelligence chief appeared momentarily lightheaded. There was a crystal carafe of water on the anteroom desk. Sir James filled a glass with a trembling hand, took a pill, and drank.

"Did the PM act because of Ireland?" MacKenzie asked.

"Roper didn't give any specific reason." The former spy chief put down the glass. "I told him that this is an Interregnum, not a republic. I said I wouldn't surrender the Ivory except to my lawful Sovereign. And any further attempt to coerce me would result in Roper's own immediate fall from office — he has certain unreceipted Old Masters in his private art collection. That was when he dropped the other shoe. I've been summoned by the new Justice Commission investigating Sandringham." The spymaster gulped another pill. "On a charge of Grand Malfeasance! High Treason. For arranging the death of a Japanese assassin in a Norfolk jail!"

That was absurd, but MacKenzie suddenly thought of Liz, with her obsession about Britain's need for a written constitution. She would see Roper's purpose, unlike the checked and balanced office of the American Presidency, as allowing a prime minister of the New Britain to hold almost total power. To MacKenzie it simply proved that the whole world was upside down — if a man like Roper could hold the Ivory; and another one like Love was running British Intelligence; and a majority of the British tabloid public could even imagine having a post-adolescent, g-string sniffing Australian bastard actor as its lawful Sovereign!

Four

Full House • Sydney

RICHARD SAT IN HIS dressing room, staring at himself in another bloody tabloid. The latest rag didn't come right out and say he *was* the next King of England — how could it? — but the paper didn't have to say anything directly to sell a million supermarket copies.

"Last call for the Ghost. Five minutes to Hamlet."

The stage-porter's voice sounded on the dressing-room intercom. Forty-eight hours ago that announcement would have been the most incredible thing that could happen in his life.

It still was! In spite of this latest gossip crap under his picture: "Our President and First Lady having a ding-dong dragout marital tiff heard by the whole Canberra Capital District." His parents' row last night was about the Prince of Wales thing. He could understand his father's jealousy — a "colonial" beer-brewer competing with a Brit Royal! He remembered his own feelings when Anna used to get dry-raped by the lifeguard steroid zombies ogling her on the Sydney beaches.

Anna...

"Oh God," Richard said to the makeup mirror, "Anna why aren't you here?"

His mind must be snapping under the tension. After her walkout? Only a week before his biggest moment! He didn't want that disloyal American bitch Anna Randolph anywhere! As for his American-born mother, she swore that she hadn't — he still found it difficult to say, *slept with*, the Prince of Wales. So his parents had a fight. Real life wasn't Shakespeare, it was post-Freudian Australia, and he had spent four years of his life learning about Theatrical Psychological Motivation.

"Last call for Hamlet, Mr. Byrd-Wilson."

Richard threw the tabloid into the waste container beneath the dressing table and strode out on stage to meet his destiny.

IT BEGAN WHEN the King, his stage father, prepared his lead-in: "But now, my cousin Hamlet and my *son*..."

Which produced the first stifled giggles, before the doomed Prince of

Denmark replied to his stepfather, "A little more than kin, and less than kind..."

Which got a few belly laughs from drunks with too much champagne on their expense account tickets. The female director pulled him after his line, *"Hyperion to a satyr; so loving to my mother..."*

Which brought the house and the curtain down. Wave upon wave of gufaws rolled at him from all sides of the theatre.

"I've had one like this before," the director said in the wings, giving him a hug. "When the House get a bee at the start, it won't stop, darling, the bastards know the words: they can see it all coming. We'll try with the understudy. Don't hang around. Get pissed out of your skull with a nice girl and come back tomorrow."

He was so numbed by the devastating audience response that he forgot the press hyenas. They were waiting for their carrion at the stage door.

"Has your name been put before the Succession Council?"

"Would you accept if it was?"

"Hey Dicky Bird! Did you ask your mother —?"

Richard wheeled and threw a straight right jab at the last libeling sod. A hundred cameras caught it. The reporter dropped to the pavement like a rock.

BBC Central • London

LIZ PONTI CAUGHT the byte of the Sydney punchout just before she was lunched by her flowchart boss in the Directors' private dining room, which made a pleasant change from her usual cottage cheese in the "Beeb" peasants' cafeteria. Her superior in the Corporation was a man of fifty, with all the news biz credentials required to earn and hold the job... and the desperate desire of a person of his age and sex to get her into bed.

Before meeting Hector MacKenzie she had been tempted to oblige. Besides sharing the danger on several hot-spot assignment locations, and being bright, the man across the table kept himself trim and had a good sense of humor. In fact, if her Highland Commando hadn't appeared in her life when he did, she was sure it would have been "I surrender" with her Team supervisor. A Beeb working partnership in the time-honored sense.

"I've got a choice for you, Liz," her host said, as the private steward whisked away smoked-salmon salad remains, and presented plates of wafer-thin rare beef in its place.

"A choice of give in or lose my job classification?" She smiled, and helped herself, and then him, to another glass of Beaujolais.

"Darling, making you that kind of choice would get my knackers removed by the Human Rights people." He raised his glass mockingly. "I can offer you endless summer in Australia ... or the delights of February in Norwich."

They both sipped, tasted, and approved the Director's choice of wines. "What's in Australia?" she asked.

"A segment for 'Names in the News'. The Playboy Pretender."

"Not seriously?" she stared at her lunch partner. "This can't-be Prince Hamlet who got laughed off the stage in his own country?"

"But you have been following the man."

"It's impossible not to." She pointed at a tabloid left at an adjacent table.

DICKY PRINCE IN DOUBLE FLOP !!!

Liz said, "I'm just amazed we'd want to get involved."

"It's called ratings, dear. Auntie Beeb can't be as pure about money as she used to be." Her lunch host put down his wine glass and continued in a professional voice. "I had a tip-off call this morning from a titled Lady, who shall be nameless but who works in the Heralds' Office. Pal Hal agrees with your opinion of this Sydney Hamlet: my aristocratic informant thinks the man could be another Bonny Prince Charlie. You and I know that's bullshit, but half the country already wants to believe it. And if the real Prince doesn't survive ..."

After a moment of silence, Liz said, "I'm still card-carrying anti-monarchy. What's in Norwich?"

"The first British Commission of Justice looking into Sandringham."

She made a wry face, and pushed her knife and fork together. "No wonder you bribed me with a private lunch."

"I wanted the private part, Liz, but not for a fun reason. The Commission has an unprecedented mandate — whose principal aim, in my opinion, is to pin the blame for all the troubles of the recent past on military cockup, and not the civilian."

"There's nothing new in that," she said. "Besides, it could be right. I saw plenty of military incompetence in Ireland. But the day-to-day kind, like getting a tank stuck in a swamp."

"Not, 'Knowingly aiding and abetting the IRA enemy'."

She shook her head. "Is that more personal opinion?"

"Personal for you, I'm afraid Liz darling." He handed her a folded piece of paper. "It's the offence that Roper's kangaroo Commission wants to hang the people on this list with. In time of war, which was what Ireland officially was, it's the only charge in Britain that still carries the death penalty. Look at the last name."

Her intuition told her before she unfolded the paper.

Chedburgh

WALLOP WENT WITH him on this afternoon visit. A sergeant-major's basic pay needed the boost it could get from pilot hours and MacKenzie allowed him as much time as possible each month at the controls. Now he watched as Wallop eased the column to change the pitch for landing. The helicopter descended smoothly past the village of Rede, immediately to the south of Chedburgh, and dropped like a feather inside the restricted perimeter of the Special Forces base.

"As good as ever," MacKenzie told him. "I'll be about half an hour. Tell Eastern Region to give us direct clearance back to London."

"Wilco, sir." Wallop saluted, then, as MacKenzie walked away, he added, "Oh, Colonel sir, there's just one thing..."

"Yes, Sergeant-Major?" He smiled, sensing a request for weekend leave in the hesitation. He would be pleased to grant it. If anyone deserved time off after these last extraordinary days, this man did.

"I wondered, sir, after the Flight plan, when you're with the Prince, do you think I —?"

"His Royal Highness is in London," MacKenzie said sharply.

"I know, sir, officially he is. But I log all your flight movements, and these trips to Chedburgh, and none to the Burn Unit in London, well I couldn't help putting things together. You know, sir, I'd never breathe an outside word."

"Of course I do, Sergeant-Major." And he did, but he was still concerned: if Wallop could make that obvious deduction others might have. He should have fitted in more visits to the dummy sick bed. "Book a roof landing at the South Bank Hospital," he instructed Wallop, "then join me inside. It can only be for a minute. His Highness's condition is still very weak."

"I understand. Thank you, sir!"

MacKenzie's anxiety heightened as he moved towards the building, but it was probably needless. Each security barrier functioned flawlessly. Only another ground-to-ground missile could leapfrog this protection. He already had anti-missile batteries to cover all four quadrants of the compass. He ordered additional equipment to double the protective spread anyway. By the time that was done, Wallop joined him for the ride up to the sealed floor. After they had put on sterile clothing the Surgeon General met them at the Ward entrance.

"Another better day," he told MacKenzie. "I must say I'm relieved. I expected a possible relapse following your breaking the news to him about the rest of the family. The boy has the most amazing inner strength."

MacKenzie agreed, and introduced Wallop. "I think seeing the Sergeant Major would give His Highness more of a boost now than medical science or myself."

The surgeon smiled and nodded them to the door. MacKenzie heard a sharp intake of breath beside him ... and realized that Wallop hadn't seen the extent of the bandages beyond the guardian Drummer Boy before.

"We must be positive," he warned him. "The lad can only use his eyes, but they catch everything."

"Yes sir. Bright's the word!"

He allowed Wallop to preceed him to the bedside. The therapy worked. The bandaged slit of the mouth inside the oxygen tent widened in a smile.

"Hullo, Sergeant-Major!"

"Hullo, Your Highness."

MacKenzie saw Wallop's larynx move as he swallowed his inner emotion. His other outward sign was just a broad grin of total confidence in the patient.

"I knew one day soon Colonel Ken would bring you," the boy said, including MacKenzie in his welcome. "Have you been away fighting the IRA about my parents?"

A similar terrible question had rocked MacKenzie. Wallop took it in stride. The sergeant squatted on his massive hams so that his face was on a level with the bedside, and grinned again. "We had a bit of a dustup a couple of times, Your Highness."

"Were you driving your tank, or was it man-to-man combat?"

"A bit of both, Your Highness. But that's all over now."

"Can I go in the tank again once I get better?"

"All the hours God sends, Your Highness."

MacKenzie tapped him on the shoulder. Wallop rose and saluted.

Automatically the small figure in the burn bed tried to move its arm. A grimace of pain tightened the bandaged lips. "Sorry I can't salute back yet, Sergeant-Major."

"That's all right, Your Highness." Wallop blinked rapidly. "It isn't your place to salute me anyhow."

"No," said the Prince. "Perhaps you could wind up my Drummer instead."

Against the mechanical toy rat-a-tat MacKenzie managed something lightly adult and optimistic which he couldn't remember as soon as he'd said it. Once again the courage of the small figure in the bed overwhelmed him.

"Colonel Ken?" The eyes fixed on his own. "About tomorrow's visit? If I asked for it, would you bring me back something I would really like?"

He thought with dread of what the child's request must be:

Bring me back my mother, my father, my sister...

"I'd really like a chocolate biscuit. Can I have that?"

MacKenzie let out a laugh that ruffled the top of the vinyl tent. He longed to ruffle the boy's head. "Aye Laddie," he said. "Your Highness shall have a whole damn case of chocolate biscuits. I'll pick them up myself from Fortnum's."

"The doctors won't let me eat a whole case," said the patient as he left, "but I suppose I could share with the nurses."

WALLOP LIFTED OFF and banked south. Both of them were too emotionally drained to speak about anything but military flight procedures. They passed into Ipswich Control, and then Cambridge. At Harlow, on the border of North London, the bell rang to alert MacKenzie to receive on his private encoded circuit. He enabled the duplicate descrambler and waited for the signal from Anti-Terror HQ.

But the lead-in header was from the place he had just left:

From Surgeon-General. Your Eyes Only:
Deepest regret. Heart failed. Patient gone.

"Bad news, sir?"

He did not answer Wallop. He did not know if he would ever be able to speak again. But the world would not wait. The messages must be sent. He must attend another hideous event. The worst yet. As he tried to think how he could begin to cope with organizing, let alone attending, a boy's funeral the signal bell tolled again...

To Deputy Anti-Terror from British Justice Norwich: Report at once to answer Summons. Charge: Treason.

MacKenzie scarcely saw the words. In his bursting head a clockwork final drum beat throbbed behind his streaming tears.

Rat-a-tat. Rat-a-tat...

Five

Bedroom Games • Brisbane

HIS LIFE HAD turned into a black farce... that wasn't the least bloody bit funny! Richard sat with his head buried in both hands, perched on a barstool in the kitchen of Sally's apartment, and blamed Anna again for everything. From the moment she walked out on him, just when he most needed her, his stage career was shattered. He was a prisoner of the media, and when he tried to break out the press made him into a national laughingstock. A world one! The hyena pack blocking Sally's front door weren't only Australian. Brits, naturally, were the most unpleasant and persistant, but there were a slew of Americans and Canadians, French, Italian, German. Even Russians and Japanese were going ape about a possible King of England!

"I'm not a king," he said in total gloom to Sally, "but even if I was I couldn't be one — because my mother would never admit it, about her and the Prince of Wales — and if she did, I couldn't prove it. The whole thing's hopeless, and now you're being screwed too."

"Look again, cobber, I'm making coffee." She smiled and handed him a mug. "Maybe later, for the other. If you cheer up. You're not much use to a woman's fantasy life in that condition. And if you mean my career, save your worries. The publicity is a model's dream."

"From those bastards out there?"

"I'm making use of them."

"Like prostitution."

"You want to fight with me because you can't get at them," she replied in an even tone. "Acting and modeling, we're both in the same line of work. You should stop crying over spilt milk with your Hamlet and use the free PR to build the rest of your career."

"Hamlet," Richard reminded her acidly, "is hardly the same as showing your damn bum to peddle savings bonds."

"I just showed my damn bum for free to get you safe in my front door," she retorted with a flash of redhead temper. "I don't give a shit what you do with your life, but no man is going to hang around mine all day crying in his beer because the press wants to make his kisser Number One for product recognition in the world. You may as well get your stuff and poke off."

"Number One? You really think so?" The thought was appealing for a moment, but then his spirit sagged again. He said glumly, "You're right, we are almost in the same business — and the Ad people probably could sell brand-name watches, or hot cars, with my face on them. But I don't need the cash like you do. Sally, I'm an *actor.*"

"You don't think Hollywood sells faces?"

"In films."

He said it quietly because the idea was so perfectly right. He could act your average Los Angeles product offscreen with a flick of his eyebrow, and his face at any box office would carry the subliminal message: This Star was born to be KING!

"Sal, you're fantastic and I'm a bloody idiot." He jumped off the barstool and threw his arms around her. Which was great because he was wearing his bikini pants in the Brisbane steambath heat, and she still had only a light cotton shirt on. His hands found themselves automatically cupping her cheeks under the shirtail... when a flashcamera exploded outside the kitchen window, and the front doorbell rang!

"I'll shut out this paparazzi creep," she said, reaching for the venetian blind to block off the leering hyena with the camera, hanging from the branches of a Norfolk Pine beyond the second-floor window. "Remember to keep cool. See who's at the door."

"Like this?"

"You look super in your jocks, and for L.A. it's just a good career move."

Richard grinned, kissed her, and sauntered from the kitchen through the hall to open the door and boldly reveal his foremost assets to an admiring world and Los Angeles. He was ready for anything the press could throw at him...except an old dame doing a curtsey which brought her nose to the level of his crotch!

HE HAD NEVER been so embarrassed in his entire bloody life. The woman curtseying to her knees in front of his bikini was as old as his grandmother would have been, if he had one. She looked like a stage grandmother, with silver hair, glasses, a large bosom in a ruffled blouse, and a cameo brooch of a red dragon on a gold chain around her neck — and a thousand of the Press corps behind it hanging on her every pommie word.

She had to be British! No other nationality would show up in tropic Brisbane curtseying in a long tweed skirt.

"What the hell do you want and who are you?" Richard croaked, as he dropped both hands across his groin, because none of Sally's professional advice covered any part of this kind of situation.

"My name, Your Royal Highness, is the Lady Bronwen of Llangath, and I come from the College of Arms. My purpose, as Rouge Dragon Pursuivant, is to beg that you return with me forthwith to London, and there lay formal claim to your Throne."

"Lay what?" Richard repeated stupidly, for all the cameras.

"Sir, by tradition and emotion the British nation and your subjects cannot endure continued interregnum. The Proclamation must be read."

The dragon granny got up off her knees, took a rolled parchment from a carpet handbag the size of a trunk, turned to his press tormentors and, in a voice designed to ring from her ancestral battlements across the Welsh marches, declaimed:

"To all Subjects of his Realm, by these present be it known:
"The King is dead,
"LONG LIVE THE KING!"

London

ROPER LOOKED AGAIN at his two current favorite possessions: his naked mistress and Titian's Venus. Both objects were highlighted by the winter setting sun that also struck the blackened walls of Britain's oldest fortress beyond his Tower Bridge penthouse window.

The combination of upmarket feminine sensuality and brute force was a strong aphrodisiac, but neither lust nor money was any longer the prime focus of his life. Four decades after he watched the bailiff's van legally drive away with his seized childish possessions he could buy enough furniture to fill every nursery bedroom in Britain.

He stood up to get dressed. He was due at a reception for the new US Ambassador that evening. He walked through to the bathroom and routinely flipped on the satellite All News Channel.

"Good God."

The note in his voice made his mistress look towards the television set. For the next thirty seconds they stared together at the extraordinary image coming live from Australia.

"Will it matter?" The lovely woman on the bed stretched a perfect, aristocratic nude leg towards the screen. "Madness runs in Lady Bronwen's family, all the way back to 1066."

"You're serious?"

"I can't swear to the starting date. But two cousins are in a private nuthatch in North Wales."

"Good enough."

Roper took a micro auto-dialer calculator card from the inside pocket of his jacket, lifted the receiver of the penthouse phone, held the dialing mechanism against the voice transmitter, and pressed the single alphanumeric key, L.

He heard the notes of the dial tones then three double rings, before the flat voice he expected said, "Love, sir. Australia. I've just seen it. At your office?"

"In twenty minutes. The private entrance."

Roper put the auto-dialer back in his pocket. That combination of brevity and complete understanding was why he had appointed the voice on the other end to head British Intelligence. Unlike his upperclass predecessors, with their Ivory, a man like Love had no bastion of wealth or old family to fall back on. Everything he had and was, he owed to the Prime Minister who appointed him. As for the female herald's bizarre behavior, it could not have fitted better with Roper's plan. In the limited minds which formed mass public opinion, a Head of State's authority couldn't be seen to be shared: it must only have a single focus.

"I'll be at the Reception too," said the woman on the bed as he emerged from the bathroom. "Is this one where we say hullo, or not?"

"I think not — unless you get invited to the supper afterwards by the Americans. If you're with a Yank it'll be all right. As for your question about that Down Under performance," he nodded at the television, already rerunning the crotch-and-curtsey sequence, "look at tomorrow's headlines."

"I don't take that kind of paper."

"Make an exception." Roper bent and kissed her.

"For you, anything." She kissed him back. Deeply. Tasting power.

Backstairs • Slap and Tickle

SLADE WAS ALSO putting his side of government to bed for the day: transcribing personal highlights of that afternoon's first Roper Cabinet meeting (after the last Royal funeral) from the Whitehall secretarial taping system to the tighter security of his coded secret diary.

"More representative of the New Britain." That was Hal's opening cliché to explain why the revised governing group was twice as large as it had been under Gore. "But with many valued old Cabinet hands for continuity."

Cliché figures like Jane Lear, Slade noted sardonically: kept on as Home Secretary with most of her addled mind still on her dead Air Force son. Roper had also made the grieving token woman the group's Deputy Leader! Plus keeping Wilfred Jamieson, the Belfast Protestant diehard who walked out after the Army "problem" at the Compound: Hal welcomed "Wilf" back warmly... to the High Technology portfolio! On a first-name basis. Not for much longer, Slade thought. With this unification of Ireland, "Wilf" wouldn't have an electoral seat to return from! The last hold-over from the Gore days was Lawrence Brown, the Glasgow roughneck, shifted unbelievably into the sensitive job at Finance — which really meant nothing, because Roper had then announced he was splitting the job and keeping Exchequor himself: "To reassure the economic community."

Which led to a strange debate between the Right Honorable Members present on the subject of Visa and Passport fees! "No Tourists because No Royals!" Which meant no tourist money. Which led to Roper's closing quote for the diary: "No naked buffoon from Australia is going to perch his backside on the throne of this country just to bring the tourists back to Windsor Castle."

Slade was about to put the book away in its secret drawer in the Hepplewhite desk when he saw an earlier entry on the facing page.

Muwi. Love... the man with the scar on his hand, taking over the Intelligence underworld. It was imperative to know more about his background. Slade was convinced that he was a fellow gay: on his way in to see Roper he had pitched Slade one of those looks only a notch removed from peak sexual excitement. Nobody called Love could have cruised in the restricted waters of Whitehall gay life without making waves. Slade decided to pay another social call at Buckingham Palace.

A NEW FACE was doing security at the side door by the Mews, but otherwise everything was still exactly the same for the handful of tourists: the Royal ostlers, the Royal horses, the oafish Royal coachman, and his Royal parlor maid, the straight footman in the sexy trousers. Given the British love of useless dead history, Slade thought, the whole damn lot could still be doing the same useless nothing for no-one a century from now!

He walked over the scarlet carpets, along the wide passage ways with the black mourning bands still on half the gilt-framed pictures and up the shallow stairs designed especially for short-legged Royals in long ball gowns, and turned into the last corridor leading to the rear of the Palace overlooking the garden.

The old courtier from the Royal Tour days wasn't waiting this time, but his apartment door was ajar. It was going to be another of those boring Let's-Pretend-We're-Strangers? Come-and-find-me! games. Slade pushed the door open, and wheedled,

"Coo-ee?"

No answer. None in the hall, or the chintz old-fashioned comfort of the living room.

It was going to be the bathroom... but the old ponce no longer had the figure for bare-balls in soapy water! All that was left was the unimaginative normal: Missionary Position under the quilted bluebells and primroses in the yellow bedroom. Slade tip-toed across the faded Persian carpet, laid on top of what was once a Palace ballroom parquet floor, and scritch-scratched with his manicured nails on the bedroom door, to get the old popsy going.

"Guess who this is?" Slade called.

The door moved a little from his scratching. He did it again, rattling all eight fingers slowly upward, like playing a scale on the piano. Still nothing...

A stiffled giggle.

More like a little gasp of excitement, muffled by a bed sheet. The old bugger couldn't hold out any longer. No light showed under the door. The fairy queen was lying waiting for it in semi-darkness.

"Coming, ready or not." Slade pushed the door and pounced on the bed.

His hands skidded on the slippery satin sheet, turned down over the primrose quilt, carrying him forward until his face bumped the old one on the sleek satin pillow.

Not satin.

The part of his mind that wasn't playing sex-games remembered that the sheets loaned by grace and favor in Buckingham Palace were threadbare linen laundered, stitched and darned for as much as a hundred years.

They couldn't be slippery.

Or sleek. The fabric should be slightly rough, with its coarse open weave. And the smell should be the acrid tang of Palace washday bleach. Not this musty sweet odor that filled his nostrils...

His hands were wet.

And his cheek, where it touched the pillow. Something on the bed fell to the floor at his feet. It landed with a metallic thud. Another sound came from the pillow.

His mind was working on its own now. Analyzing the noises, putting his hand out to the lamp on the bedside table, stopping his breathing, racing his heart, dilating his pupils, turning on the light.

Making him gag. And then vomit.

The old man he had come to play blackmail games with lay on his back. When Slade bent double in his spewing, the courtier's parchment face rolled closer towards him on the pillow. The sound came again. A gurgle, not giggle, caused by breath expelled involuntarily through a liquid. The threadbare, bleached ivory linen sheets were made into slippery scarlet satin from drenching blood, still welling from the flabby skin of an old man's neck. The courtier's head had been half severed from the body by a cut from ear to ear.

The metal object at Slade's feet was a knife.

His hand picked it up. His eyes looked at it. His stomach heaved again. His conscious brain now did nothing except go round in circles. On one of the circles his mind realized that there was another human being in the death room with him.

The Intelligence man with the scar on his hand stood in the doorway.

Slade's voice croaked, "I didn't do it."

The man called Love walked three paces closer, limping slightly, and looked down at Slade. The expression on his face... there was no expression. For the first time in his life Slade didn't know what someone above him was thinking. He only knew that he would do whatever this man from the secret world wanted him to, forever and ever, if it would keep him at the heart of power, with a full pension, out of prison.

Norwich • British Justice

THE COMMISSION INVESTIGATING the Sandringham explosion wasn't assembled in the modern Norfolk Legal Region Administrative Center, as Liz had originally been informed, but in the town's ancient, black-timbered Guild Hall. The switch of venue was at Downing Street's insistance, a court official told her, part of the peace-making Prime Minister's determination to emphasize the continuity of British life in his New Britain.

The old hall did that. The vaulted roof was spanned by oak ribs; flags of ancient battle honors hung from the walls. On a raised dais at the north end, a gold and silver mace rested on a trestle table below the escutcheon of the City of Norwich. An elderly clerk, with white-tabbed collar and a robe like the local town-crier, walked creakily up the six steps of the dais and came to a shaky halt next to the mace.

Great visuals for the TV backdrop, Liz agreed, as she positioned her BBC crew. The hall was packed. Like murder trials before Britain's permanent abolition of the death penalty, trials for High Treason with the fear of the hangman still drew the ghouls.

"All rise, for their Lordships, the Commissioners."

Liz shivered as one of the battle flags above her waved in a draft from an opened door. A shuffling quartet emerged behind the elderly clerk on the dais. Only three of the Commissioners were male, the fourth was a woman in her late sixties. "Lordship" was a formality: none of the four possessed a title. Liz dismissed her momentary apprehension.

"Hear ye, hear ye. The Chief Commissioner will now read the warrant from Parliament establishing the terms and conditions of this lawful enquiry."

The Chief was the woman: no surprise considering that Roper had handpicked the tribunal. The tabloid masses still associated an extra degree of fairness and moderation from a female!

"The aim of this enquiry is simple." The Chief Commissioner had an upper-crust, university voice, but with none of the condescension to social inferiors that so often went with it. She looked out at her audience with a kindly expression, accentuated by a pair of antique, gold-rimmed bifocals perched halfway down her nose as though she was completely unaware of the tens of millions behind the cameras. "The language used by Parliament," she went on, "which I will read to you in a moment, may sound a little daunting, but all it really means is this: we four ordinary human beings are to do all that ordinary people *can* do to find those responsible for the terrible tragedy our country recently experienced, and what steps can be taken to see that they are brought to British justice."

A murmur of assent swept through the Guild Hall audience. The old clerk sitting by the mace struck the trestle table with his gavel. The Chief Commissioner gave him and the home viewers a soothing little gesture with her right hand.

"Common sense," she said. "Common sense tells us that in a very special situation such as this one, we must have some special rules. For example, when a person accused as a Terrorist has a record with the International Anti-Terrorist Police, and has been found guilty before of a Terrorist act? and is discovered once more to be in possession of weapons or munitions? — 'common sense' tells us that it is up to such a person to prove beyond a reasonable doubt that in similar circumstances, *this* time, he is innocent! And the same thing, naturally, for anyone helping him."

Prove you are innocent.

Liz could not believe her ears. But the ordinary British people all around her nodded, and leaned forward eagerly as their oldest legal right since Magna Carta went down the tube: in Roper's arse-backwards New Britain the State no longer had to prove that a defendant was guilty. Without a written constitution, when a person had to prove that he was innocent, everything changed.

"May I remind you, Admiral, that of course you have nothing whatsoever to fear from speaking entirely freely before this body." The Chief Commissioner was smiling through her bifocals at the former First Sea Lord, now standing at the witness box. "As I have told our other most co-operative witnesses, our joint task is simply to discover the truth behind recent events — in civilian language, if you don't mind, as I'm afraid we are all landlubbers on the Commission."

A ripple of easy laughter swept the Guild Hall, keeping everything comfortable. The British way. The man in the dock did not look comfortable.

"Madam Commissioner, to do what you ask would require me to release the most highly classified information, and this I am forbidden to do in an open court."

"You mean, Admiral, that you will not comply with the Commission's request?"

The woman's sharpness was that of a mother to her rebellious little boy. The First Sea Lord's neck reddened.

"Not, 'will not', Madam Commissioner. By law, I cannot. Initiation of the Irish blockade was enabled through the code name, King's Cross. While I can say that it permitted calling up units of the Reserve Fleet in a certain order you must be aware —"

"Admiral, this Commission is the law. We have Parliament's warrant. However," the Chief Commissioner resumed her reasonable mother's voice, "in view of its sensitivity, and in deference to your honestly stated patriotism I will not require any further specific reference to the words, 'King's Cross'. You may stop for today. We will continue with our next witness after a recess for tea."

Liz rose with the rest of the spectators and watched the Honorable Commissioners file out through the carved door at the back of the dais. The crowd in the Hall moved less formally towards the street entrances to grab a cuppa from mobile canteens. Only the nation's former senior naval officer still stood rigidly at attention, staring blindly ahead, totally alone. She went up to him.

"Admiral?"

He turned and looked down at her. His expression was one of unquenchable shame. There was a touch of blood on his lower lip where it had been bitten in his fury.

"If you're with the Press, I have nothing whatsoever to say."

"At the moment," she said, "I'm here as a close friend of Hector MacKenzie. I thought perhaps we could go for a drink."

"MacKenzie's friend?"

"Liz Ponti."

She put out her hand. The Admiral shook it. None of the tension eased from his neck and face. "I read this piece of so-called *news* this morning." Sarcastically, the First Sea Lord thrust a torn clipping at her. She saw that it was based on a release from the Chancellor of the Exchequor's Office:

> "Resultant upon a minor regulatory change in the administration of the Civil List; in future, all royal residences will be made completely accessible to the public, year-round, on a free-market basis: with the sole exception of any personal apartment actually occupied by the Sovereign, when that constitutional appointment has been filled."

The Admiral snorted with absolute disgust. "The kind of civil service mentality which could call a King a 'constitutional appointment' is running Roper's New Britain! All I can tell you, Miss Ponti: if you want to help everyone in this country, find out about King's Cross."

He stalked from the Guild Hall. The crowd returned.

"All rise," the old clerk droned. "This Commission now summons Colonel Hector Lysander MacKenzie, Royal Marines."

HE LOOKS SMASHINGLY impressive... that was Liz's first thought as she saw Hector enter from a side door, wearing his full dress uniform. And then she saw the tortured expression on his face and realized, *he must have come straight here from the boy's funeral.*

"Step forward to receive the Oath."

The clerk held out a bible. Three of the Commissioners studied some papers in front of them. Another member of the panel stared vaguely at a Regimental flag. As Hector placed his right hand on the bible, and recited his oath to tell the truth, so help him God, only the woman in the center of the group never took her eyes off him. The male member of the panel opened in a dry-as-dust voice:

"You were Chief Equerry to the late King?"

"I was."

"And military aide to Sir John —"

"With your indulgence, Commissioner." The woman cut off the dry career questions. "I think we all know quite enough of the witness's life as a Royal Marine, and we have many other people to hear. Now, Colonel, as I have said many times already —" her smile warmed — "but that can be no comfort to you, as we haven't met before have we? What the Commission has to find out from you is exactly how you did what — and more importantly, *why?* — during the blockade period."

Hector had seen her, Liz realized. The glance he exchanged with her was a mixture of defeat and resignation: after all the recent earthshaking events he obviously treated this lethal old woman's enquiry as no more significant than his mother asking if he had his oilskin with him before he went out riding as a child in the drenching Highland autumn rain.

"Thank you, Madam Commissioner. I'll do my best."

"I'm sure you will. Now, Colonel, when you joined your Anti-Terror unit in Belfast, did you have any particular thoughts about Ireland?"

"Particular thoughts?"

Liz could tell that he still wasn't concentrating on the questions.

"On the political situation?" the motherly woman said. "Or what your task might mean for ordinary Irish people?"

"I don't think I know any ordinary Irish people."

"We don't need sarcasm!" Her tone had the crack of a ruler hitting a desk in the nursery. "You have a sister, I believe?"

"I do."

"And she has two children: a boy and a girl?"

"She has."

"However the children's father does not live with the family?"

"No. My sister is divorced."

"Did you like her husband?"

"As a matter of fact I did."

"Matters of fact are what we are after, Colonel." There was another of the razor-sharp glances, but Hector still missed it. "And following the divorce, did you continue this friendship?"

"I continued to like him, but we didn't meet."

"Did you write?"

"I don't think so."

"I show you this exhibit." The woman picked up something from the table in front of her and passed it to him. "What is it please?"

"A Christmas card."

"A special one?"

"To civilians, possibly."

Liz saw that the card had the Marines' regimental badge of the Globe and Laurel.

"And is that your signature, inside it?"

Hector opened the card. "Yes."

"And the name at the top — the person you sent it to — was...?"

"My former brother in law."

"And where did you send it to?"

"His family's home."

"And where was that?"

"I don't remember the exact —"

"The town will be enough, Colonel."

"Dublin."

"An Irish town. With ordinary Irish people, like your former brother-in-law."

Liz felt her heart sink. At last, but in vain, she heard Hector trying to fight his way out of the legal quagmire, as he said to the woman, "I had completely forgotten. I didn't think of him as Irish. His family was as old as mine. They lived most of the year over here, in Hampshire. We went to the same school —"

"Where you were on the rowing team together?"

"We were."

"And you both took swimmers' lifesaving courses together."

"We did."

"And you had no knowledge whatsoever that on the first morning of the blockade your former brother in law, and old school chum, was a volunteer member of the Bangor Life Boat's crew."

There was no question mark on the end of the sentence. It slammed with the finality of a jail door. Liz heard Hector say that he didn't know, he hadn't known, he couldn't have known. And when the woman said that the Bangor boat had been carrying the most wanted terrorist in Ireland, he said he hadn't known that before, either.

Liz longed to shout at him: Take it from another female! If you ever want to head up your beloved Marines, look straight at that terrible old bitch and every chance you get, say, Sorry Mummy. But of course he didn't. He just stared with that frozen Highland Honor mask, hiding his grief for the Royal boy he would blame himself forever for having lost.

"In the absence of any expression of regret," the woman said, "this Commission must now consider whether we are dealing with merely gross negligence, in allowing the IRA's most notorious assassin to escape to South America, or the far graver charge: an act of deliberate High Treason. Until such time as we have determined that answer you will remain confined to your Regimental barracks, and hold yourself available for immediate recall."

Six

Buenos Aires

McDERMID'S FOCUS HAD narrowed. Except for a small bit in one corner about the last good-riddance Royal funeral, Australian photos covered the front page of an old *Buenos Aires Nuevas* scandal sheet tossed to him by a stevedore handling the lines of his fast tanker from Havana when she secured in the North Dock dredged from the Riachuelo River below Puerto Madero.

When the formalities had been observed between the tanker captain and the Argentinian authorities — allowing an unrecorded Mercedes Benz being offloaded without Customs duty, for the benefit of the Senior Port Inspector — McDermid paid his last respects to the ship's captain with a certified credit note on a Rio bank, the vessel's next stop, where the Struggle had an account. He had similar facilities to draw upon in Buenos Aires, but he was here: the captain's bankdraft, though guaranteed, would only be cashable there, in Rio... and there would be less point in the captain turning him over to the Argentinian Anti-Terror, should that nautical gentleman have a sudden sea change of political sympathy!

A bus came along the route of the untaxed Mercedes to take the morning shift home for their breakfasts. McDermid walked casually down the gangplank to join them. The bus was Brazillian, with important parts made in Bangladesh. Quality control was lacking. When the bus stopped at the Plaza de Mayo by the Casa Rosada, it would not start again.

The stevedores disembarked, swearing but used to such situations. McDermid drifted westward with the group past the memorial to the Disappeared Ones towards the Colon Theater and the Hall of Justice. By then his safe cover had dwindled to a handful who were more eager for the bars to open than returning to the bosoms of their families. Things were slack enough that he could take a taxi. He strolled across to a cab rank outside the theater. Three vehicles were waiting, their drivers all reading the same tabloid rag with the cheeks of Brisbane Sally McGuire's attractive bum spread over it.

He walked along the rank, checking each driver for any second-sense whiff of police informant. The first seemed okay, but stank of booze; the middle was rubbing his crotch under the newspaper and didn't want to be disturbed for another couple of moments. The guy on the end smoked a clay pipe, and said bilingually, "*Bueno,* Hi there! You want nice boy-girl *vergen?*"

McDermid took the boozer. They went west along the Rivadavia and turned north onto the Avenida General Paz, known proudly by the locals as The Longest Street In The World, and by everyone else as a pain in the arse. All the streets crossing the Avenida city limit changed their identity completely as they did so. Avenida General Mitre became Francisco de los Incas and tourists were lost. McDermid knew the city but it still made checking locations difficult. He was looking for the change from Chacarita to Municipal Museum, when the Anti-Terror hit him.

THE TWO CARS came from left and right: two dirty brown Toyotas made in Argentina, screaming in tight turns from the diagonal lanes of Rodriguez Peña. McDermid's pisstank driver knew they were coming. The man hit the brakes and threw himself sideways on his front seat to miss the bullets.

"Sit up, you fucker!" McDermid grabbed the driver's throat with one hand, yanking him vertical. "Now go! Or I put out both your eyes!"

The driver saw two vee'd fingers, hard as ironwood, coming at his rolling eyeballs... and goosed it. The first brown Toyota clipped their rear bumper. The second let off a burst that got rid of the passenger window. A shower of safety-glass fragments struck McDermid's head. A sudden foul stink meant the cab driver had crapped himself.

"East!" McDermid shouted. "District La Paternal."

The man stared straight ahead with his mouth and bowels open. McDermid yanked the wheel and just missed the ornamental entry sign for the Museum. A truck behind it was unloading exhibition cases. In a screeching explosion the first Toyota became Display Exhibit One.

"North! To Belgrano!"

"Can't breathe!" the man gasped.

"Fuck breathing! Just drive!"

The second Toyota fired again and got a tire. The cab dropped, swerved violently to the left, straight at a streetcar locked on its tracks. Now the taxi driver tried to turn the wheel. McDermid said a prayer he thought he'd long forgotten, and held the column rigid. The tram took off their right fender, and all of the second Toyota. The pursuing car became two halves, like a silent movie; three bodies were hurled out in the street before one was run over.

"Keep on," he told the taxi driver, "but more slowly."

The man gulped, and nodded. The cab lurched free of the tracks. Two blocks later, at a pleasantly shaded spot in the Parque Thomaso, McDermid stuck his thumb behind the vermin's ear and killed him.

THERE WAS NO TIME for post-mortems. The Anti-Terrors must have been on to him since landing: all his efforts now had to be devoted to getting back below the surface. The cab was shielded from the street by overhanging shrubbery. Under cover of the trees, McDermid took a dirty handkerchief out of the dead driver's shirt pocket, the man's wallet from the pants, tumbled the body into the back seat, opened the cap of the taxi's fuel line, dipped the handkerchief into it, pulled enough back out to act as a wick. Using the vehicle's cigarette lighter, he gave the treacherous Latin shit a viking's funeral.

Police sirens were wailing with a rising howl that meant they were coming in his direction. A running man was the first thing they would look for. A wheelbarrow with a shovel and rake was propped up by a pile of park rubbish where the shrubs ended at a flower bed. He lifted the wheelbarrow's handles and began trudging. The first police car passed him without a glance. The second slowed and rolled down a window. McDermid pointed after the first car, in the direction of the column of smoke rising from the taxi behind him. The second cop made a gesture of thanks and accelerated.

McDermid dumped the barrow and ran into a group of school kids. They were waiting for a streetcar, with an elderly Magdaline nun still wearing the old-fashioned, ankle-length blue habit of her Order.

He said in Spanish, "Bless you, Sister, for Mary's work," and crossed himself.

"Bless you, my son."

The nun smiled at him. The kids didn't. It was tough to fool children. From their chatter he learned that they were headed for the Zoo. He could hear the rattle of another tram approaching along the tracks. The kids were staring with heightened suspicion.

"Anyone got an apple, or an orange, or a tennis ball?"

The dodge worked. His request got their attention off himself. The children came up with a nectarine, a plum, and a pingpong ball. McDermid resurrected another silent Hail Mary from his own childhood and began to juggle. The kids loved it, but he was sweating like a pig in a blanket by the time the streetcar arrived.

As they all departed with the tram bell ringing, a police van cruised by in the opposite direction. When McDermid got off at the Avenida Santa Fe, they gave him a Three-Cheers farewell, but by now the workers of Buenos Aires were out in the streets for their long lunch and no one noticed. He found a pay phone near the entrance to the Zoo and made his call.

"Palm Beach Travel. May I help you?"

The voice was a woman's, in English: the mother tongue of butchery meant posh in the travel business.

"I need a ticket for some little people," McDermid told her.

"I see. One moment, please."

He would give her no more than half a minute. Anything longer, and they were tracing his call.

"This is the manager." A male voice came on, with a faint hint of brogue. "We can have tickets for little people. How many would you be wanting, and when?"

"One. Yesterday."

"We can't be quite that quick. Why not see if we can't come up with something satisfactory over lunch?"

"Satisfactory would be a café at the entrance to the Zoo. Order a kilo steak with four eggs, no chips, and a glass of milk."

"You must be hungry." The brogue chuckled.

"Not me," said McDermid, "I've just been at a barbecue in the park."

"Ah." The chuckle stopped. "Then be damn careful until we can take you home for supper."

He hung up and went with the crowd towards the lions and tigers. The travel manager showed up alone — a thin man, with a typical Derry face and a wart beside his nose — and ordered a steak that would have choked a gaucho cowboy. Plus the glass of milk. When McDermid was satisfied that no uninvited guests had gate-crashed, he eased forward from his observation place behind the sign pointing to the Reptile House, and sat down.

"It's good to see you." The travel manager shook his hand with a fierce grip. "When we first heard about the Compound Massacre, we thought for sure you hadn't got out."

"I wasn't in the compound. I still don't know who was. I checked the papers in Havana, but they didn't show a list."

"The Brits only released a final one yesterday, and it won't be accurate. The two-faced bastards lie about having their morning piss." The travel manager took a newspaper from a shoulder bag. "I haven't got your ticket, though. We didn't know where you're moving on to."

McDermid said, "I still haven't figured how the Anti-Terrors tumbled me. I was with a woman in Havana —"

"Sure, and there's your answer!"

"Often it's women," McDermid agreed, scanning the list of martyrs' names in the newspaper, "but not that one, I'd swear to it."

His Argentine contact shrugged and poked at the edge of the enormous steak. McDermid finished the list of dead Irish heroes. "So where's my bloody escape hatch?" he asked.

The travel manager put down the fork he was toying with, and rubbed the wart on his face. McDermid said more urgently, "Man! I'm telling you —"

"*Culebra!*" A girl's hysterical shriek pierced the lunch crowd chatter. Followed by a scream of *"SNAKE!"* from five hundred throats, in ten languages. The cafe crowd surged for the street, carrying McDermid bodily with it... and towards his new Target.

Brisbane

THE OLD DRAGON granny from Wales wasn't totally nuts, Richard now conceded. Her handling of the bikini situation outside Sally's door had been pretty good, considering that on one side she had him in his briefs, and on the other most of the media in the universe. When they were both safely back inside the apartment, and he pulled a pair of tennis shorts on, and Sally jumped into her jeans, he discovered that the Lady Bronwen of Llangath was married to a chemist and had at least a couple of bright ideas.

Richard could settle the absurd King thing by just getting a blood test. His DNA would be checked in London by the chemist husband...

You can't fool the blood.

The reality of the old woman's message came home to him. If the DNA said *Yes* ...

That scared the hell out of him. He shut himself away in Sally's bedroom, with the door locked and the blinds down, and tried to really think, for the first time, what would actually be involved if he took the blood test and it turned out...?

Negative, of course!

It was like reading your daily horoscope in the papers: you saw something good about yourself and ignored all the rest. The simple fact was that the DNA odds were overwhelmingly in the other direction. He could agree to a test but go on with his acting life. Try Hollywood, as Sally suggested. He got off the bed, unlocked the door, and went out to the living room to give her the news.

She wasn't there. Only the old woman, still in her tweed skirt and dragon brooch, who stood up when she saw him and then dropped another of her crazy curtseys.

"Where's Sally?" Richard demanded, knowing that he was sounding bloody rude, but not caring.

"She's gone to a local pub, I believe, Your Royal Highness."

"Without me? I wanted to tell her something important. Did she say which pub?"

"I'm afraid not, Your Royal Highness."

"Did she say how long?"

"No, Your —"

"For God's sake," he snapped, "don't go on calling me that. Didn't she say anything?"

"That she was tired of waiting for you to grow up." The old woman smiled gently at him. "I know how difficult this must be, my dear, but you see it won't get any easier, and I can hardly call the Monarch by —"

"You can call me Richard, like everybody else in Australia, except my mother. And it will get easier, because I'm going to take the test and it's going to be negative, and it can't be a minute too bloody soon."

He went into the front hall to look through the peephole at the media hyena pack. The old woman said after him, "If it will make things any easier, for the time being, and only when we are in private, I shall call you Richard."

"Good. Just try not to sound like my mother when you're saying it."

He put his eye to the peephole. Only about half the world press were still camped outside. A Japanese reporter was acting as point man for the media's next attack.

"Don't you get on with your mother?"

"Not at the moment." He turned away from the door to check the balcony outside the kitchen.

"You blame her for your predicament. That's only natural."

The old woman had the ability to see into his head. "I don't blame anyone," Richard said, "except those bloody jackal reporters."

He pulled the blind back at the edge of the kitchen window. The balcony and its adjacent Norfolk Pine were both Press free. He suddenly had an idea how to make his unwanted baby-sitter useful. "I need to get a breath of fresh air," he said to her. "Could you keep them busy in the hall while I use the tree?"

"I could. But it's not very wise. You may elude the reporters for the moment, but it will only enrage them further when they find out."

"So how would you handle the bastards?" he asked sarcastically.

"As they are used to being handled. You are an actor and you must have studied psychology. The psychology of reporters is to wait in the expectation of news. *You* go to the door, and you tell them you will have something else to tell them shortly, and they'll be waiting there like sheep all night."

Richard laughed and thought that he might actually be able to like this weird old woman from the other side of the world. Or at least trust her, which was more than he could say for his mother — or Anna, and now Sally who waited till things got rough and then just cleared out!

He went back to the front door of the apartment and jiggled the handle. On the other side of the peephole, the press pack almost smothered each other in their collective leap forward. The Japanese guy got the first foot in the door. Richard kept the anti-burglar chain in place and spoke to him through the opening.

"Good evening, Ladies and gentlemen. I'm sorry you've had such a long day, under somewhat difficult conditions. I know you must be bored stiff, but if you can just wait a little longer I shall have something significant to tell you. Thank you all very much."

The Japanese bowed! The mouths of the others fell so far open at this unexpected courtesy that he had the door closed again before their renewed questions reached a howling crescendo.

"That sounds like a successful counter-operation," said the dragon Herald.

"It worked a treat. And you are, too, Lady Bron. I'll only be an hour. And then we'll think about that test." He saw that she was looking at him again in a funny sort of way. "Did I say something wrong?"

"No Richard, my dear. Nothing wrong at all. It was just the name. When I was very young someone I rather liked called me his Lady Bron."

He imagined her as she must have been as a young woman, when her face was smooth and her arms were slim, and her dark Welsh hair would have glints that matched her Celtic eyes. And on a hunch that came from nowhere he suddenly said, "That person when you were young — would he have been a Prince of Wales?"

"He might have been," she said, with a trace of a young girl's smile. "Run along and find your companion, and enjoy your beer."

Captain Cook's Arms

WITH MALE AND female relations, Sally McGuire decided, Australia had moved at least some way into the Twenty-First Century. When her mother had been her age and went to a pub, all the men present massed in a rugby scrum as far as possible from the women and spent their time pleasantly vomiting or kicking beercans at the ceiling until it was time to go home for the Saturday Night Screw.

Tonight, in the crowded lounge of the Captain Cook's Arms, a convenient few suburban blocks from her apartment, there were soft lights and a piano, with a girl like herself actually playing the latest romantic pop hit... and only about half the males present were bellowing a totally different song about Frigging in the Rigging. Some of the locals had dragged along a visiting contingent from an international sailing regatta which had been canceled for lack of wind. Sally didn't see how, as one of them belched and another one farted, and the rest switched to Beans, Glorious Beans!

"Would it be disturbing you, Miss, if I shared your table?"

The voice came from slightly behind her left shoulder, so that she had to turn to check out the speaker. He was medium height, dressed in yachting casuals, but older than the average sailing yobbo, which explained the politeness of his greeting. Forty plus, she decided, because of the life experience lines at his eyes and the gray at his temples, but the trim physique and flat stomach could have been thirty.

"It wouldn't disturb me," she said, shifting to the right so that he could move by her. "I thought I heard a touch of brogue — would you be Irish?"

"Only enough to get drinks in a bar. It's mainly Boston." He smiled, set his glass down, and extended his hand. "Bill Lamb."

His teeth were unstained, and his nails were trimmed, although the fingers had scars which showed he certainly didn't spend all his time at a desk. She liked what she saw, and she was fed up with little rich boys singing songs about beans, or evading real life.

"Sally McGuire," she said. "Mainly from Brisbane."

"Hullo, Sally McGuire."

"Hullo, Bill Lamb."

They shook hands, with just a touch of extra pressure, and he sat down. The bean boys, feeling hungry, decided it was time to eat an alligator from the Brisbane Zoo and crashed their way through a glass door without opening it, out onto the terrace. The girl at the piano ignored the whole thing and began playing a medley of old-fashioned ballads.

"It's a stale line, I know, Sally, but would the McGuire be why you asked about the Irish?"

Bill Lamb smiled at her again, with a touch of apologetic shyness that she found refreshing as hell in a man who could obviously just grab what he wanted from women. "My Dad came from Ireland," she said, "like half of Australia. He died three years ago, but we still have some relatives there, and it looks beautiful in pictures, all that fantastic green, but I've never been back."

"Maybe one day." He raised his glass. "Here's to the green."

"The green." She sipped on the straw of her Margaritta. "I'm ashamed to admit, it isn't just Ireland. I've never been anywhere ... outside Australia, I mean."

"That's nothing to be ashamed of. If I lived in this fabulous continent I wouldn't move either. There's enough here for three lifetimes."

He didn't seem only to be humoring her. There was a look at the back of his eyes, which were gray, that seemed searching for something he hadn't found out of life.

"Australia's pretty bonz," she admitted, "but the grass is always greener — I don't mean just Ireland."

"That was quick! I like puns." He raised his glass again, in a mark of mock respect ... and he didn't swill it down, she noted, which was another refreshing change from the locals. "What part of the old country did your father come from, Sally?"

"The North, that's why he left. Even though we're Catholic, he couldn't stand all that endless violence. He used to say, nothing political was worth it. His brother, my favorite uncle — he's visited several times — didn't agree. 'Freedom's worth it!' The way he said it, for a moment you could almost agree. They used to argue something fierce. But Dad was right because we have every religion here and everyone gets on just fine. People can't go on living like something out of the Middle Ages." She suddenly realized how long she had been mouthing off. "I'm sorry, Bill. Nothing's more boring than politics. I don't know why I got started."

"My fault. I was asking you what district?"

"Down near the border. A place called Killylea. I think that's somewhere in Armagh."

"It is, just south of Milford. And you're right again about politics. I'd rather talk to you on a hundred other things."

He lifted his hand for a waiter. The new round of drinks came fast. Although the place was crowded, Bill Lamb was the kind of man who would always get attention if he wanted it. "What sort of other things?" Sally asked, with enough of a smile to let him know that she already knew the answer. His answering smile knew that she knew.

"Things like what a girl with such quite magnificent hair does to make ends meet?" he said, with a hint of a wink. "And if she likes dancing?"

"I model for savings bonds and I like to tango."

"No more questions. Let's tango."

"It's hardly that kind of music."

"It will be."

She knew that it would be. He got up and went across to the piano player. The pianist looked up, listened, smiled. The current ballad stopped. The Latin beat of tropic nights in Rio took its place. Sally's eyes closed. She swayed to the music and felt the taut muscles of her partner's thigh press her own more yielding flesh as he bent over her . . . and found herself being swept off her feet in a way that had only been —

"Hop it, Chum. That's my girl."

HER EARS HEARD the snobby, snooty, Shakespeare accent. Her eyes opened to see its owner standing with a boy's flushed face, and his poncey acting hand grabbing the shoulder of an adult man who would grind it up for dog meat if this ridiculous confrontation went any further. A wave of rage replaced Sally's marvelous tango feeling. Using all her self control she said to Richard, "You've obviously been boozing. We're finishing a dance."

"I thought you were waiting for me to grow up." Her little-boy lover gave his sarcastic laugh. "It took a few pubs to track you down, I admit, but all you have to do to apologize is say 'bye-bye' to your sailor friend."

"The name's Bill Lamb."

The real man still holding her extended his hand politely, able to ignore the incredible preceding juvenile rudeness. Sally moved closer to him and said through clenched teeth, "Bill, meet —"

"Bye-bye . . . baa Lamb."

"That's the sodding end!" With all her strength she delivered a slap across the little-boy cheek that almost broke her hand but was worth it, and shouted at him, "Get it through your royal head, *Dicky* bloody Byrd-Wilson! I'm not *your* anything. Bugger off!"

At which exact moment the Press caught up to them.

But five seconds before the first flash bulb exploded, Sean McDermid, alias Bill Lamb, saw it coming, and prudently ducked out of the picture before it made tomorrow's headlines.

Westminster • Power Play

"MR SLADE, SIR. His Grace, the Duke of Dorset, is here without appointment to see the Prime Minister."

A breathless youth dressed in the cute bum-freezer jacket of a Parliamentary Page stood in the doorway of the PM's office. Space at the House was divided in the same way as at Downing Street. Slade had the outer half, to head off the endless queue of political arse-lickers and favor-seekers. Roper had the inner portion, with one slight change. Instead of only one private door for appointments and getaways without the prying eyes of the Press, there was also a second exit, leading directly to the Commons' Chamber behind the PM's bench at the Treasury Table. Two colored lights above Slade's desk indicated which door was to be used for a given occasion.

"Please sir, he's in the State Guests' waiting-room."

The pretty boy Page was fidgetting. Slade looked at the telescreen. The Duke was pacing back and forth, hitting the headline of a tabloid he was holding in his left hand with the fist of his right. A copy of the same paper was on Slade's desk. Below an enormous,

BUGGER OFF DICKY BYRD !!!

was a smaller,

SHOULD THESE MEN BE LORDS ?

Since one picture was labeled a BISHOP!, and the other a JUDGE!, and the half-page picture of each man showed him wearing articles of women's underclothing, the answer for "normal" readers was obvious. To help those with poor eyesight the *NO!!!!* box in the readership poll was five times as large as the Affirmative.

"Sir, he said it's urgent."

"Very well," Slade told the agitated Page, "I'll handle his Grace."

Peers of the Realm were not a vital lynchpin of the New Britain's government! The Upper House couldn't do much more than delay non-money bills for a month and debate Saving the Water Rat. And the Law, of course. The Law Lords formed the country's highest, and final, court of appeal.

Slade pressed the muted intercom buzzer, and said, "Excuse me,

Prime Minister. The Garter King of Arms has arrived non-schedule. I imagine you would like me to stall until after the debate?"

"No." Unexpectedly, the green light flashed on above the door. "I'll see him now."

INWARDLY, ROPER BRACED himself for another major play: outwardly, he made the gesture of walking around his desk to have his hand out when his latest opponent in the power game entered.

" Your Grace," he said, "what a pleasure."

"Have you seen this?" Marching thrust a tabloid in front of his face. "The hereditary peerage is being used as a whipping boy again."

Roper gave a small smile of sympathy. "Even in my heyday as a Press ogre, Duke, I didn't read my own product. But judges and bishops in female lingerie doesn't necessarily mean abolishing the hereditary peerage."

"I'm glad to hear it." Marching hurled the paper into a wastebin. "However that's not my chief concern. What of the Succession?"

Roper waited for his opponent to be seated, then took his own high-backed chair behind his desk before replying. "The Attorney General's people have advised me that the Welsh Pursuivant's embarrassing Australian exercise might have had some meaning if it had been made on the balcony at St James's Palace, or even on foreign, but legally British, soil — such as the former High Commission which is now our embassy in Canberra — but none whatever when announced in the hallway of a Brisbane flat!"

"I agree," Marching said. "There is no choice in the matter. If the First Candidate will not convert, then the Upper House will support the government in changing the Succession law immediately."

"To allow Roman Catholics?" Roper drummed his fingers on the day's Order paper that lay upside down beneath them. "Your Grace — and now I speak with all respect for *your* position — I must be frank and say that I would not feel able to have the Government accommodate your suggestion."

"In God's name, why not? This country has been through a cataclysm!"

"Exactly." Roper leaned forward to speak with special intensity. "The country cannot heal without *continuity*. Changing these Succession Laws..."

"Is trivial!" Marching gestured contemptuously at the waste basket, "Damn it, Prime Minister, in the world of those tabloids what the hell is religion?"

"From our perspective," Roper replied, "as two educated, tolerant men, of course the religious beliefs of a figurehead in modern government are of no consequence whatever. But for the tabloid readership, Roman Catholicism sanctioned what happened at Sandringham. If we were to put a representative of that faith on the throne of this country today, we should have another Northern Ireland in the Home Counties."

"You can't seriously believe that," Marching protested.

"My Lord Duke, I tell you from the bottom of my heart: a Catholic monarch would start the Wars of the Roses all over again."

"Then she must convert. I shall call to see her on my drive home this afternoon. Our lands are almost adjoining; we share a Hunt property."

"I wish you luck," Roper told him. "Although I'm not a supporter of blood sports."

Cavalry Overture • Chilton Hamlet

THE DUKE'S BENTLEY purred Marching homeward with the effortless speed and smoothness he expected. Passing the new motorway cutoff to Ranham he turned on his radio for the program of light music he always hummed along with at this time in the afternoon. Wagner at full bore was not his cup of tea!

"We interrupt this program to bring you an important address presently being given by the Prime Minister to the House of Commons."

He had had too much politics already for one day. He was reaching to press the tape button for Suppé's familiar *Cavalry Overture* instead when he heard the words, "Reform of the House of Lords..."

His hand stopped.

"These changes we propose," said the Prime Minister's reasonable voice, "are not restrictions on the democratic process. Quite the opposite. As part of a modern United Europe, it is both inappropriate and unjust that in the New Britain those persons whom ordinary people turn to for spiritual and legal guidance in their lives should be given aristocratic titles. If plain 'Mr' was good enough for Winston Churchill — the son of a Duke, I remind you — then how absurd it is for a clergyman or judge to expect to be bowed down to as Your Lordship."

There was the sound of laughter and applause. Marching was not amused. He was astounded. Barely two hours earlier, Roper had given his solemn assurance that the powers of the Lords would *not* be ammended!

"There can be only one law for any citizen of Britain. The Ecclesiastical peers will be abolished, as will those of Justice. A new body will be created, to be named the British High Court —"

An army all-terrain vehicle appeared around the corner. Marching was still stunned by the news. Only the other driver's faster reaction avoided a head-on collision. The army vehicle shot right, climbing the embankment with all six wheels spinning, hurling loam and turf down onto the Bentley's roof. At the crest of the bank it almost rolled over...

Then crashed back, smashing a shock absorber.

Marching had a glimpse of the army driver, a man in mid-thirties, stocky, with an insignia of some kind of dagger, or missile, or both, then it was gone. Without the younger man's quicker reaction times...!

Badly shaken, he slowly reversed the Bentley and then moved forward. He drove cautiously around the next corner.

A riderless horse passed him, bolting from terror.

The animal's rider lay on the field side of a five-barred gate beneath an oak. Edward Marching had ridden in too many point-to-point steeple-chases to doubt his instinct, but on shaking legs he got out of the Bentley and walked the few paces necessary to confirm it: There would be no new War of the Roses. The lady he had come to beg to take the throne of Britain would never change her mind on religion, or any other subject.

Her neck was broken.

Seven

Royal Marine Barracks • Plymouth

MACKENZIE HAD NO choice — after the double hits of the First Candidate's accidental death, and McDermid's miraculous survival. But involving others by his actions was not acceptable. As he spent these last minutes rechecking his weapons and communications gear, his only personal regret was not being able to contact Liz. He could still see the expression on her face at Norwich as she watched him being treated like a common criminal.

"Excuse me, sir."

A familiar bulk was squashed in the Ready Room doorway.

"Good evening, Wallop. What can I do for you?"

"Well it's really the other way, sir. The buzz on the field is —"

"You should know better than to listen to field buzzes, Sergeant-Major," he said coldly.

"I do know, sir. But when we join A-T, we volunteer. If taking McDermid has to be an out-of-bounds type operation, I accept the risk of that and you can always use a spare pair of hands."

Wallop's right hand was holding a hundred and fifty pound kitbag with as little effort as a woman's purse. There was no one MacKenzie would rather have with him, but implicating a subordinate in the disobeying of a legal order was even less acceptable than telling Liz.

"I appreciate your offer, Wallop — but the risk in this case could mean your indefinite imprisonment by our own government."

"Yes sir. But he was our own Prince, wasn't he?"

MacKenzie conceded game point and stopped arguing. The Aircraft Ready lamp came on. He gave a brief nod and stood up. Wallop grinned broadly and fell in behind. They walked together across the rainswept runway. A pale quarter-moon was rising through ragged clouds to the southeast. As MacKenzie put his foot on the first rung of the cockpit ladder a communications messenger doubled towards them and handed a signal to Wallop.

"Latest update, sir! Forget Argentina. He's in Australia."

Press Conference • Queensland Hilton

IT WAS BEING held in the Hotel's main ball room, which still wasn't large enough to hold all the hyena reporters. As Richard stared out at what would have been a full house at the Sydney Opera main stage he truly couldn't comprehend what sort of group madness the Press operated under.

"Ready?" asked his mentor, with an encouraging smile.

"As I'll ever be, Lady Bron."

At least for this appearance he was dressed! While he tried to cure his hangover from the row with Sally, the old herald had summoned Brisbane's leading purveyor of overpriced menswear to show up at her Hilton suite with a vanload fit for a king, or the Cannes film festival. She selected his costume too: a blazer of dark navy barathea which was going to be a killer in the Queensland heat, and brass buttons with embossed sterling silver anchors that followed the curve of the lapel facings to the points of the flared waist, which had vented flaps showing a scarlet satin lining. The satin picked up the color of the fine pinline woven in the cotton shirt, with french cuffs and a pair of links that matched the buttons.

"Five seconds to broadcast!" A technician held up a hand.

"Right," Richard told himself, in his usual pre-performance ritual: "Let's break a leg."

He stood up to read the statement...

"Richard Arthur Byrd-Wilson?"

A man stepped out abruptly from the side of the platform. As Richard nodded, thrown completely off stride, a paper was thrust into the hand that wasn't already holding his statement.

INJUNCTION

> "At the discretion of the Supreme Court of Australia, you are hereby enjoined and disbarred from speaking on, or appearing at, or participating in any venue within Australia if such actions bear in any way on the suit for Libel and Malicious Slander brought before the Undersigned, for restitution due the Claimant named below."

The Claimant was his father. The Undersigned was one of his drinking cronies — a man who got his new job when the country got a new Supreme Court along with the new office of President — the Chief Justice of Australia.

"Your Royal Highness?"

The old woman was still play-acting. Richard showed her the Injunction.

"I can't speak a word about anything in my own bloody country."

"Is that all?" She smiled her secret little smile, as she had when he asked her about knowing the Prince of Wales. "Well then, my dear, we shall just have to get you out of it."

"I don't understand."

"We shall now go to the airport and fly to London to do the blood test there, so killing two birds at once with my husband."

Her sentences were cockeyed, but it was the solution to everything. Richard was sick to death of running between Sydney and Brisbane, and even sicker of his parents.

"What were you just handed?"

The press hyenas were slobbering. He said to them, and to all the idiots who bought and ate what they spewed out: "I came here to read a statement to you about what I was going to do next — although that isn't any of your business. And don't give me 'Freedom of the Press!' There isn't anything 'free' about standing here like this, or being hounded out of your house, or where you work, or in the pub where you take your girlfriend for an evening. Anyway, now I can't read it to you, because if I did I would be arrested." He held the Injunction up to a camera. "This says I can't speak or do anything anywhere in my own country — which is supposed to be a democracy, and more of one since we got rid of the King's representative and put in our own President. Well, the Claimant on this paper is a President." He smacked the paper with his hand; the press howl became a roar...and triggered something deep inside him.

"The claimant, so-called, *is* my father. Well, if I'm going to be arrested for saying that, I may as well say what else I want to before I'm jailed like the men and women who founded this country. I'm not a king. I never wanted to be a king. I *am* an actor, which is nothing to be ashamed of. No job is, if you try your very best at it. I tried — and I was pretty damn good — and Australia would have had a chance to see how good if this whole absurd Royalty thing hadn't been started, and kept stirred up by all of you to make a few more billions for the corporations that own every one of you. No-one owns me, or any actor. If we succeed, or starve, we do it on our own initiative. We go for broke, and most of us give up everything: a proper home life, and kids, and a house in one place for them to grow up in — and most of us actors don't finally make it. When I clear up the mess you've put me in, I'm going to go back to being an actor, and I shall try and be the best damn actor Australia ever saw the arse of — because if I can't speak freely in my own country I don't want to live here. I'm going to get a blood test which has a ninety-nine percent chance of being negative and proving that I am only who and what I've always said I am —"

"How about the other one percent?"

A British voice called from the front row, next to the Japanese he had noticed before. "If the one percent said I was the bastard son of a former king of England," Richard replied, "I should be proud of it — but I would never take the job. Although there are worse trainings than acting for such a miserable one."

"Miserable?" a woman shouted. "Living in a palace full of servants?"

"Would you want to stand around like a cow in a field?" he shouted back at her. "Never thinking for yourself, doing what you were told to every day of your life? Going where you were pointed? Meeting people you couldn't care less about, and being endlessly nice to them? — and on top of all that, the constant chance of being shot at or bombed. If the Brits want another king, they should start by looking in their psychiatric wards. No sane person would take that job for just the chance to drink tea off a silver dish served in any palace by a thousand servants. And that's all I have to say to you."

He was turning away, to find the old woman or the cops sent to arrest him by his father... when behind his back he heard an unmistakable sound: *Applause.*

FROM THE TOUGHEST audience he had ever had to face. Lady Bronwen was smiling with tears in her eyes, and a security guard next to her reached to shake his hand. It was like that all the way to their limousine, and at Brisbane airport, and even on the plane. The speed with which news traveled was unbelievable. On landing, the Sydney branch of the hyena pack was there to greet him, but at least they stayed at arms length, and the sneering hostility was no longer directed at him. None of which stopped them surrounding his King's Cross apartment when he and the old Herald finally arrived there to collect his passport and pack his things for London.

"Why don't I make us some tea while you're doing it?" Lady Bronwen asked him.

"If you can find a clean cup," Richard said. "I'm not the world's greatest housekeeper."

"Nor am I, my dear. There are more interesting ways to spend one's time than washing up, but it's one of those tiresome necessities which life requires. Rather like a constitutional monarch."

He located his passport and tossed it into his carry-on with his shaving gear and went out to the old woman in the apartment kitchen.

"Was that last bit a sales pitch?"

"Only an observation." She had found two used cups and was rinsing them under the hot tap. "In a country like Britain which has no written constitution, without some living and visible symbol there is always a tendency of human nature to want to do what it wants. When the human natures are political, that can quickly turn into something not very pleasant for everyone else."

"A dictatorship."

"That's being melodramatic. I suppose you don't bother with a teapot?" When he shook his head she placed a tea bag in each cup. "Let's just say that the kind of country you described so eloquently for the reporters — a place where we are not as free to speak as we should be, or where someone is quicker to try and stop us than they should be — it's all a very fine line. Britain's way of staying on the right side of the line has been to have a monarch, who wears a crown, so that everyone can see with their own eyes that the Crown is not an abstraction but a living, breathing human being like themselves." She passed him a cup. "It may be a cow sort of job, my dear, but if it helps to keep sixty million people free, it is surely not a useless one. Or an ignoble one."

"Maybe not," Richard agreed, "but it's not one for me."

"So you said." She sipped while he gulped. "Is this your Anna?"

It was a photo on top of the fridge, which he must have missed when he threw out the others. "Not mine any longer," he said tersely, "but yes, that's Anna."

"She looks rather a nice person to me."

"I don't want to talk about it. If we're going to catch that London flight we ought to go."

He took a last look around the King's Cross flat which had been part of him long enough to feel a home. He wondered how and when he might come back to it? Whatever the circumstances, he didn't want *her* there. He threw the last picture of Tatanya Randolph from Virginia in the trash compactor and pushed the button. As he closed the apartment's front door, he heard the glass and frame crunching with the picture ... and wished with a sharp pang that he hadn't done it.

And when he sat in the limo with Lady Bronwen, as she chatted him through the passing sights of Sydney, and the airport barrier, and the hounding Press ... for every foot of the way he knew, that she knew, what a bloody fool he was for doing it.

"Documents please."

The girl at the Quantas first-class ticketing desk was smiling pleasantly, but obviously awed, at both of them. While he dug through his carry-on Lady Bronwen calmly presented her passport.

"Thank you, your Ladyship. Sir?"

Richard handed it to her, and watched her place it in the optical scanner while the Press took another few thousand pictures of him walking out on his homeland.

"I'm sorry, sir. Your documents are invalid."

He stared at her incredulously. "They can't be. I just renewed last summer."

"There's nothing wrong with the renewal date, sir." She showed him her computer screen. "This number has been rescinded."

Trashed. Like Anna.

Roanoke Virginia

HER LIFE WAS finally her own again! Anna Randolph reached that decision when she woke up to find that the snow had melted enough on the south slope outside her bedroom window to reveal a patch of golden aconites turning their faces to the sun.

The color, and the light, made her think of Australia ... but *not* about the man she left there, which was how she knew she was cured. It had taken her longer to get him out of her system than she had reckoned on. The bags under her eyes had only just stopped staring back at her from the mirror in her girlhood bedroom. The smallest lines, the ones at her temples that she usually pretended didn't need makeup, were still etched into her skin like the gullies of the Mid-Atlantic Canyon.

Fortunately she had the Farm to herself, except for dear old Grace, the caretaker. Her father was down at his winter condo in Key Biscayne, which he bought after the death of her mother, last year. Holed up here — twenty miles east of Roanoke, on five hundred acres with the phone off the hook, no TV, no radio, no newspapers, just a wood fire and her favorite music selections — Anna had once more become independent of biology and weak-reed males needing constant re-assurance for their sagging egos and body parts. She laughed, took several deep breaths of the farm air, did some calisthenics, and went for another real Virginia pancakes and sugar-smoked ham.

She could feel the pounds going on with each flapjack, but she didn't care: hunting for Archie would soon take it off again. She waved the fax message she had just received at Grace, sitting across the plank table, and said, "It's been a dream since the first time I read Moby Dick."

"Hunt a Giant Squid?" Grace rolled her eyes. "Child, that's a nightmare!"

EIGHT HOURS LATER Anna found that winter hadn't lost its grip on the coast of New England. The Penobscot River was still frozen all the way down from the Longfellow Mountains. In Bar Harbor, on the edge of Acadia National Park on Mount Desert Island, enough snow still lay around to make the place a New England Christmas card of red-painted saltbox houses, green-trimmed steepled churches, and rounded wicker lobster pots.

Deep Six Explorations Inc. stood out like a sore thumb.

The building squatted with a flat tar roof and concrete block walls cracked by the frost. Bristling antennae of every shape and size were stuck wherever a spare vertical or horizontal spot could still be found. But the jarring lack of aesthetic design didn't count.

The *Melville* counted. The marine research vessel lay secured to the wharf that jutted out from the rocky shore by the headquarters building. The *Melville* wasn't pretty either, Anna conceded, but the ship's design incorporated everything deep-sea explorers like herself had ever hoped for. Stabilization in two axes; infallible communications and navigation aids in spite of engine failure; full laboratory facilities on board, backed by realtime computer links to any other oceanographic center in the world.

And "Moby".

The miniature submersible was the first to be completely automated, with no umbilical of any sort to the mother ship. Although two human beings could go with it on its voyages, there was no need to. The ocean floor topography, tides, currents, temperatures, salinity, and specific gravity for any possible location were already programed into its computer. "Moby" could pick its own routes through the underwater mountains of the Mid Atlantic range, or traverse the deeps of the Marianas Trench, and do both far better than any human operator.

"You think he'll find Archie for us?"

The speaker was Jack Nash, a Canadian dreamer of mad dreams and President of Deep Six Inc. He had been at Harvard while she finished her Doctorate. His roots in North America were as old as her own; one of those

United Empire Loyalist families who had to leave everything after the American Revolution and trek north to Canada. He was also the hairiest man Anna had ever seen with his shirt off — which he was now, because he was lying under the Moby boom in a suntrap formed by the *Melville's* white-painted superstructure and the submersible's gleaming stainless steel hull.

"I don't know, Jack" she replied to his previous question. "After all the tries so many other good people have made, it's hard to believe that Archie really is down there."

"But you've seen his fingerprints." Nash rolled free of the confined space below the boom and sprang to his feet with surprising agility. "Anna, those suckers ain't just a figment of drinking too much Newfie screech. *Architeuthis princeps* lives and breathes off Newfoundland, all hundred feet and ten arms of him."

"Or her," she said with a smile.

"No battle of the sexes on this man's expedition; we'll call Archie androgynous. But somewhere off the Grand Banks, that mother is *there.*"

"I believe it," Anna said, "or I wouldn't be here."

She handed Nash his sweatshirt which had an artist's likeness of their target printed front and back. The genus Cephalopoda, in the phylum Mollusca, belonged to one of the commonest species of creature in the sea, and every Greek restaurant! Only its stupendous size kept it from showing up, deep fried, with a bottle of Retsina. Another picture, this one full-scale, had been painted as a mural along one wall of the headquarters building. A life-size photo of "Moby", the submersible, had been superimposed in the giant squid's suckered arms.

Anna laughed aloud. Jack Nash pulled on his shirt and looked at her quizzically. "Woman: you laugh in the face of certain death?"

"A thought I was having."

"Just as long as it's happy. There's no room for sad ones in a head being squeezed by ten times atmospheric pressure when we go hunting. Let's break for coffee."

They strolled through the sunshine towards the building. Her amusing memory was of a poster which Richard brought home one day, stolen from the Ladies' Chorus dressing room, and tacked up in the john of their shared King's Cross apartment. *Penes of The World* — keeping the dirty bits medical with the latin plural. That she could laugh at it now proved the Australian Hamlet was definitely out of her system.

Canadian Jack Nash might be moving into it. He poured her a coffee the way she wanted — cream, no sugar — without having to be told. The company secretary, a local girl with New England's inquisitive distrust of strangers, who was doubling as cafeteria attendant, slid forward a cracked tray of fresh jelly doughnuts with a special courier-pack envelope on top of them, and said, "Mail call."

"For me already?" Anna asked in surprise.

"It says, 'Tatyana Randolph. Near Roanoke. Please Forward.' Not too many folks around here with that name and address."

Another job offer, she thought... but inside the envelope was a postcard of a white-crested cockatoo. Anna recognized the sender's handwriting immediately. Jack Nash didn't, but he sensed it, and took his coffee, plus the hovering wide-eyed secretary, into his office, and closed the door.

Richard's writing perfectly reflected his personality: a mixture of moneyed class and little-boy rush. The lines squashed together as they moved down the page and then ran off the sides in mid word.

> *Anna, I'm sorry. Everything my fault! Life is CRAZY. Anything you want. Just come back. Charge the ticket. I DO LOVE YOU.*
>
> *Richard.*
>
> *PLEASE? I mean it!*

She put down the postcard and picked up a doughnut. She read the postcard again. Then she saw the tabloid newsprint being used to sop up the jelly oozing through the bottom of the broken box of doughnuts.

BRISBANE LOVENEST !!!

A picture showed the cause of their breakup. The redheaded model she had discovered him with on that unpleasant occasion was hanging out of a window, backwards, wearing only a man's shirt. Anna ripped the postcard in half, and dropped it and the tabloid in the Deep Six office shredder.

Eight

Norwich

DURING ANOTHER JUSTICE Commission noon break Liz tried yet again to get through to Hector at Plymouth. Still with no success: he would have been more accessible in a maximum security jail than in this Gentleman's Agreement called an officer being Confined to Barracks! The military brick wall only made her more determined than ever to cover the Commission's witch-hunt proceedings professionally. The public had to know.

But the lunch-hour crowd around her were more interested by the Australian pretender's Oscar-winning performance on the large screen in the bar. Liz rated his sincerity and spur-of-the-moment honest conviction at his press conference about as highly as an American two-dollar bill, but he would look good in a crown. With his actor's training he carried himself much better than your everyday human's round shoulders and slouching gait. The thing that sold a majority at the bar was the split-screen clip of the former Prince of Wales, the Australian's supposed natural father. When the two images were superimposed, walking, talking, Liz conceded it was spooky: but unlike her fellow pub viewers she also knew how easy it was to make tape bytes lie. Slow one down, speed up the other, change the level of background lighting; as for speech patterns, lip synch. Pop singers did it all the time.

AT THE AFTERNOON session, the Commission's response continued to be unpredictably erratic. The Commander in Chief from Belfast got dealt with harshly, but the military garrison commander responsible for protecting Sandringham on the night of the explosion didn't even receive a tap on the wrist. The range of the missile had been shown to be clearly outside the perimeter of the royal estate and so not part of army responsibility.

Army don't know range of missiles?

As Liz jotted that query down, the Commission began cross-examining its first civilian witness: the owner of the rentals firm in the nearby coastal town of King's Lyn. His shop had provided the television set which had the missile's homing beacon inside it. The brother of the owner's Irish wife had been taken on as a repair technician only a month before the incident. An older brother had been shot by the army in Londonderry five years earlier. In the Irish memory that was like yesterday.

"Murdering Brit bitch! —" the technician was also the first to throw it back at the motherly Chief Commissioner — "Don't think you can get away with that Compound Massacre!"

"Add gross contempt to the other offences," said the woman. "Call Chief Commissioner of the National Police, Isaiah Dayman."

Liz already distrusted the idea of a single national police force: more so when the man in charge of it kissed bibles before he was asked to! The Chief Commissioners faced each other: a male and female English matched pair; pink-cheeked and blue-eyed. Each treated the other with the respect of two scorpions in a bottle.

"And would you tell us, Chief Commissioner Dayman, at what point you first became aware that a suspect for the Sandringham incident had been taken into local police custody?"

"Approximately forty-five minutes before his death, Madam Commissioner."

"And have you fully investigated the cause of that death?"

"I have. Suicide by chewing on a capsule of cyanide built into a tooth. It is a method common to members of Asian terrorist cells."

"And this person was a member of such a group?"

"He was. 'The Happy Anarchists' is an approximate English translation."

"And what was this person's role in the attack on Sandringham?"

"None, Madam Commissioner."

"Then why did he commit suicide?" One of the male Commission members had stopped staring at the Guild Hall ceiling to ask the question.

"We believe that he was part of a cell whose mission was to interrupt the meeting of the International Monetary Fund which was to open the next day in London."

"And yet he was apprehended outside King's Lyn?"

"He was, sir. If I might be allowed to explain —"

"But that's here in Norfolk!"

The male commissioner looked exasperated. His female Chief swiftly regained control. "Certainly you may explain," she told Dayman.

"Madam Commissioner, for the last several years it has not been easy for a known terrorist to enter Britain by any regular venue. Therefore the Wash, with its numerous coastal creeks and estuaries accessible to the North Sea, has become one of terrorism's preferred locations. Using high-speed boats and swimming gear, it has been both penetrable and close to central England. Since this incident we have redoubled our sensory capabilities in the area. Nothing is impossible, unfortunately, but I think I can say that, with God's help, penetration of our security from anywhere near King's Lyn will be most unlikely in the future."

"Thank you, Chief Commisioner Dayman."

The mutual admiration was over: the whole interrogation of this central police aspect of the assassination investigation had lasted a bare ten minutes. As Liz glanced down at her watch she saw that she had automatically recorded and underlined another question: *King's Lyn = King's Cross?*

She had no idea now what her subconscious had meant to convey with the co-incidental similarity in the names...

That must be it! Her own brain hadn't made up those names, but people planning clandestine operations often had an unconscious psychological trick of repeating themselves.

"All rise..."

The proceedings were over for today. On another of her hunches, Liz signaled her camera crew and went after Dayman. But when she reached the civic parking area behind the Guild Hall, the nation's God-fearing top cop was lifting off in a police helicopter with an antenna pack mounted on the side. She ran to her equipment van and switched on the illegal scanner which all news hounds kept hidden for just this purpose.

"NP aerial One Zero, departing Norwich. Destination, Marchings."

The name seemed familiar. She keyed the letters into her Placenames calculator. The mini-screen showed,

DORSET – VILLAGE AND ESTATE – DUKE OF

Marching was the family name of the Chief Herald, a man with an unimpeachable reputation. She was just about to call it quits when she remembered that the Duke was also the person who found the body of the leading candidate for the succession to the throne.

Sydney

THE NEW SOUTH WALES Forensic Facility looked like any other medical lab and had the usual half-sweet, half-sour smell that always reminded Richard of unpleasant medical procedures performed without anaesthetic.

"Now relax."

He unclenched his fist. The medical butcher this morning was a girl technician from Auckland, with great legs and the New Zealander's built-in rivalry that made it a bonus to inflict pain on an Australian male.

"Good. It's flowing nicely."

He felt the rubber tournaquet released on his bicep and kept his eyes averted from what was flowing. He concentrated instead on the legs... which reminded him of Sally, and the horse's ass he made of himself in the Brisbane pub when he found her with a Yank yachtsman old enough to be her father.

"Hold that, please."

Richard put two fingers of his right hand on the wad of gauze the technician had placed over the gaping wound in his left arm.

"Very brave," the New Zealander said with an ironic, but not totally unsympathetic smile. "You can watch the next part."

The technician squirted small amounts of his blood into eight glass dishes the size and shape of tiny egg shells, then, just as Richard was wondering whether he could watch after all, she slid the tray of shells into a stainless steel drawer and closed it.

"The machine does the rest." She touched a keyboard. There was a slight click and a whir. "A group centrifuge is breaking up your platelets. We want a reduced homogeneous base for the comparitor."

While that was happening, he decided to call Sally afterwards and apologise. The comparitor said, "First Sample Profile Ready: going to Second."

"How many does it need?" Richard asked.

"A group average of three, just to be sure, in case of random shadows. You'll see what I mean when we get the pictures."

The comparitor finished all eight samples; rejected two as "incompletely separated" and picked numbers 1, 3, and 4 for photo-processing.

The technician keyed, OK. The machine flashed a few lights and rattled out a couple of lines on a highspeed printer. "Good," she said, "it's developing. Sometimes the auto-cam doesn't agree with the assessment."

A thin strip of transparent film, like a row of negatives still all together, was emerging from one end of the device. The Auckland girl clipped it to a white panel of glass and flicked on a light.

"Super! Here comes your family tree."

The negatives became a row of vertical black bars, like the pricing labels on groceries in a supermarket, but further apart and not so sharply defined.

Richard said, "That's DNA?"

"One representation of it. The dark bars are the gene components of your nucleic acid. The genes are part of the chromosomes, as you probably remember from school."

He said, "If I had a half-brother, his bars would look exactly like mine?"

"Not exactly. The point of a DNA signature is that it's unique to a chance of one in a hundred billion." The technician touched several points on the film with a rubber-tipped pointer. "You see how some of the bars are wider or thinner than the others? And the sequence in which they're arranged? Those form the GPC — what we call the Gene Pool Chain. If your signature was compared to your half-brother's there would be a series of these similar arrangements. But what London will be looking for, of course, is the GPC with your father. I mean..."

She stopped. They stared at each other for a moment of awkward silence. Because he couldn't have two fathers. And this test wasn't going down for comparison to Canberra.

"But in London," Richard said slowly, "if it's the same, then they really will know? It can't make mistakes?"

"Anything in science can make a mistake; it's called the law of probability. But with the DNA signature, since it was perfected about twenty-five years ago, nobody anywhere in the world has ever made a mistake in matching. Yes, they really will know."

She took the other two strips of film, and checked and approved them. She pressed a key for "Duplicate" and slipped the originals into a lead-impregnated mailing envelope to avoid any damge from x-ray security scanners in transit.

"You may as well take one duplicate with you," she said. "We'll keep a full backup set here, just in case."

"Thanks." He took the fragile evidence. "You've been great. Sorry I was a bit of a coward with the needle."

"You did fine." She flashed her ironic grin. "I've never seen another Aussie he-man yet who didn't hit the deck."

Richard grinned back — and then thought: *If I am an Australian.*

Because it wasn't just his possible British father: his mother was American. Which gave him the brainwave.

HE WENT OUT to the lobby to find Lady Bronwen. She gazed with an almost religious reverence at his strip of DNA film but wasn't impressed by his other plan.

"I am not an expert in the field, but I think you will find that to get a

US passport you would have to become an American citizen. Which would take somewhat more time I imagine than waiting for your stepfather's injunction to be lifted."

"My stepfather?"

"Forgive me. That presumption was rude."

"But it's how you think of him."

"No, Richard. It's how I think of you."

"And the Prince of Wales?"

She smiled gently and gathered up her huge handbag.

"Lady Bron," he said, "I have to *know.*"

"You do, my dear, but I am not your mother."

"You think I should ask her again."

"I think you should talk to her, yes."

"She doesn't listen."

"Perhaps she will when you show her that piece of film. Once people realize that something is going to happen anyway, they often change their minds. Go and see her."

"And then what? I'm stuck. I can't act. I can't leave."

"Take a few days of doing nothing. You told me you liked climbing in the hills."

"I do. We have a condo cabin in the Snowy Mountains."

"Then go there and relax. I have people I need to see here in Sydney. If you want me for anything call my hotel. But after all the trouble we've gone to, don't break your neck."

"I won't."

Richard kissed her cheek and got another of her secret-smile, Prince of Wales looks, and then accompanied her in her hired car as far as the American Consulate in the new Pacific Rim Plaza of Nations near the Opera House... where a clerk of one hundred percent, native-born Australian bloodymindedness told him rudely that it would take two years minimum on the current waiting list to get his application noted by the State Department in Washington. Half the world press took his picture while he got the word, but they still had that new touch of respect and kept at slightly more of a distance than they used to in the bad old days of climbing trees outside Sally's bedroom window.

Remembering that location, he ducked into a phone booth to call her.

Brisbane

SALLY THOUGHT IT was Bill Lamb when the phone rang. She only half heard it, because she was blow-drying her hair at the same time as watching the Home-Shop channel for any summer sale bargains. She was getting ready to go out for lunch with Bill at the yacht club. He had sent the invitation, asking if he could come by and collect her with a lovely bunch of flowers, which was really sweet considering that he had nothing to do with the pub-brawl episode.

It was Richard's fault... but not completely, Sally now conceded. Her own behavior had been partly responsible. She should have made more allowance for the pressure he was under.

It was only when she saw his interview on the breakfast TV that it really came home to her what Richard was going through. Somehow, at that moment, it was as though the filthy rich, spoiled-rotten part dropped away. She switched off her blow-dryer, but by then the phone had rung more than five times and her answering machine cut in.

"*This is Sally McGuire speaking. I'm not at home right now but...*"

She had to let it do its spiel, then said, "Bill, ignore it. I am home."

"It isn't Bill. It's me."

"Richard?"

"I'm sorry about my bloody behavior last night."

"I'm sorry for mine," she said. "I shouldn't have slapped you."

"I had it coming. Listen, I can't talk properly. I'm surrounded by the usual hyena pack, although they're a bit nicer since the press conference."

"Are you in Brisbane?" Sympathy was fine: but if the two men met again, she didn't want another brawl.

"No," he said, which made her sigh with relief. "I'm stuck in the lobby of the US Consulate. I thought I could outflank my old man by getting an American passport. I've just had the blood test."

"Did you get the result?"

"Not yet. They can only do that in London. All I want now is to get the hell away from everything. I've got to see my damn mother first, but then I'm going down to the cabin. Sally, take a couple of days off from the Savings Bonds campaign and come with me."

Her lobby buzzer sounded. She put her hand over the phone's mouthpiece, and said to the intercom, "Yes?"

"Hi," an American male voice said, "It's Bill Lamb here."

"Great. Come on up." She pushed the Unlock button, uncovered the phone and told Richard, "There's someone at the door. I have to go."

"That Yank in the blazer? Listen Sally, do the cabin. It's five miles south of Corryong, towards Mount Kosciusko. The ski train makes summer runs for tourists and climbers. Get off where it says Marriot's Hat; there's a post office shop only a five minute walk. They'll show you the rest."

She heard Bill Lamb's knock on the door of the flat. "I can't promise, Richard."

"Just try. Either way, for God's sake don't tell anyone or I'll have the bloody hyenas back on my neck."

"All right," she said, "I'll try."

She hung up and went to let in her American caller. He was wearing the same blazer but he had a sailor's white tee shirt underneath, with a mock turtleneck and thin navy stripes that accentuated the muscles of his chest against the trimness of his waist.

"You look beaut, Bill. Sorry to keep you waiting; I was on the phone."

"Telling him you were sorry for delivering that knockout punch last night?"

"As a matter of fact I was. I guess in Boston they know all about Irish tempers."

"I guess." They smiled at each other. Bill Lamb said, "I've ordered a table by the river. There will be a sail past. I thought you'd like to watch."

"Super. Before we went Republic — when the yacht club was the Royal Brisbane — a girl like me could never have made it in the door." As she smiled again, a beeper sounded twice. Bill Lamb swung sharply.

"What was that?"

"Just my phone-answering shutting off; I bought it on discount from the Home Shop." Sally pointed over her shoulder at the TV screen, now showing a half-price genuine diamond ring. "I'm hopeless with tech gadgets; I forgot to hit wind-back. If the machines are so damn smart, you'd think by now they could do it themselves."

The Home Shop drum roll came on full blast for a Super Special. "Shoppers' alert!" the announcer shouted. "Never in the stores! You're seeing it here! Australia-first!"

She turned her head further... and there was Richard! At least an artist's impression of him, done up as a porcelaine figurine, wearing a blazer with buttons like the one he had worn on TV.

"This beautiful piece can be yours," yelled the announcer. "Delivery seven days, but don't wait, or this once in a lifetime chance will be gone. Call now and ask for *Our King in Waiting!*"

"I'll be damned."

Beside her, Bill Lamb was staring at the screen as though he'd been thunderstruck. "They try anything," Sally said, hunting on the hall table for something to write with, "and I know it's all junk, but under the circumstances I'll have to buy one."

"Sure. Use my pen." He removed it from his pocket and passed it to her. "I don't guess they've got a million seller in that number."

"You never can tell," she said. "Once they had a Malayan plastic canary with zircon eyes that you wouldn't have given to your worst enemy and it went *Whoosh!* — that's when every line from the Outback lights up." She touchtoned in her order, and while she was waiting on Hold, said, "Bill, if you'd rather be sailing, don't think you have to do the yacht club for me because of last night."

The Home Shop line came free and he waited while she placed her order, then said, "Sally, sit for a moment, and let's turn that thing down." He reached past and muted the Home Shop announcer. "There's something I have to tell you. I was going to put it off until lunch but it wouldn't be right."

They hadn't known each other long enough for the kind of personal implication of bad news in his voice. But she sat anyway, because of it.

"This morning, a guy in the crew gave me a copy of *The New York Times,* with the complete casualty list from the Compound Massacre at Belfast. I read it. I don't know why, because it was hardly the kind of thing you want to do to ruin a holiday regatta." He looked into her eyes with the same honest strength that she felt when he squeezed her hand. "It's about your father's brother, in Armagh."

She said, with an extra lurching throb of her heart, "Not Uncle Jack?"

"And his oldest boy."

"Cousin Bob? Both of them? Both dead?"

"Both shot, Sally. By the British Army. Or their surrogates, the Ulster murderers."

"But they were both here. In Brisbane, only two years ago..."

She began to cry. Bill Lamb held her, and stroked her hair as though he was used to this kind of totally unexpected tragedy coming into innocent people's lives. She felt his arm tighten protectively as the television screen before them exploded in a cartoon flame, with the one word: *WHOOSH!!!*

THE EXTRAORDINARY TELEVISION image of *Our King in Waiting* had changed McDermid's plans instantly. If a piece of crap pottery could light up every phone line in Australia...!

His first decision was that he would take Sally McGuire to lunch anyway. Talking about her murdered relatives would be easier with all the lovely yachts gliding in the river, and the chat of the other diners with their own jokes and little daily problems. And he could use the same time for his racing mind to think through his next step, while extracting more vital personal information about his main target.

"But why?" she asked him, once again turning teary eyes across the club dining room table, after they were seated. "Why Uncle Jack and Bob?"

"Sally, they're martyrs now, to a holy cause. Freedom for Ireland."

"It doesn't seem holy." She stared past him at the massed activity on the river. "Not being shot for it."

"Tens of thousands have been shot for it," he said. "Or blown up in their own Godfearing homes, or innocents drowned at sea by the Royal Navy."

"You sound as though it was part of you, not Boston."

"I was married to a girl from Belfast," McDermid said, with the simple directness that never failed to work. "She too was one of the innocents."

"Oh Bill, I'm so sorry."

"I wouldn't have mentioned it, but I wanted you to know I understand what it's like to be told, and to know who's responsible. And how easy it is to hate the Brit government and everything it stands for. Or that stands for it! Which is why I almost spewed when I saw them flogging your boyfriend's picture on TV — although I realize it's nothing whatever to do with him."

"With Richard?" Her eyes widened, then narrowed slightly with the inevitable beginning of suspicion that McDermid's carefully chosen remarks had planted. She said haltingly, searching for words, "I suppose, I mean if he got a positive on his blood test, but it still wouldn't mean he was personally ever responsible..."

"Not even if he took the job as King of England?"

"But he couldn't. It wouldn't — he's as Australian as I am. Those kind of things don't matter in this country. He likes swimming, and climbing in the Snowys at his cabin..."

She broke off. Their waiter had arrived with another bottle of the sweet kind of wine that young women like Sally McGuire associated with romantic strangers. When her glass was refilled and the waiter had left McDermid said casually, "You were saying about a cabin?"

"I can't. Because of the Press, I promised I wouldn't."

"Sure. But he's had his blood test done? He knows the results?"

She shook her head. "That happens in London. He wanted me to join him, but after what you've told me that's impossible."

"You mustn't change your plans for anything I've told you." McDermid topped her glass again. "That isn't what your Uncle Jack would have wanted, and this young Wilson can't help what he looks like. The test will probably turn out negative, just as he says."

"I'm sure that's right." She dabbed her eyes. "I feel better now. Let's talk about happier things. Tell me the places you've seen."

So he told her about the places young women like Sally McGuire dreamed of: Tahitian sunsets, and Mardi Gras dawns in Rio. "And Boston, Mass — where a girl like you could get a six-figure modeling contract in five minutes flat with hair like that, and the Aussie accent."

By the end of lunch, and the third bottle, she believed every word.

MCDERMID DROVE HER home, and although she asked him to come up, he kissed her cheek and declined, which made her more hot for it. He let her get halfway to the front door of the building before he patted his pocket and called after her, "I guess I will have to come up, Sally, just for a minute. I left you my pen for that shopping show."

He followed her up to her flat. Inside it, her answering machine was still winking for an incoming recorded call. He watched as she pressed the Play button.

"I'm sorry about my bloody behavior..."

He heard the half-Brit acting voice from last night's brief encounter. She smiled apologetically. "I told you how dumb I am with machines. I forgot to rewind all the way back."

"No hassle. Is that the call about his climbing holiday?"

She nodded... then shook her head. "It's too much wine. Typical of me leaving the thing stopped where anyone could hear it."

McDermid smiled back with warm understanding, then rabbit-punched the stupid bitch just before she hit the Erase button.

Nine

Free Press • Marchings House

LIZ WASN'T EASILY IMPRESSED, but to see that one individual still owned so large a piece of the British landscape, in such classically perfect condition, made even an anti-monarchist republican like herself stop for a moment just to look.

To her left, the ground rose in a wooded mixture of connifers and bare beech trees. To her right, for a greater distance grazing lands were dotted with spotted fallow deer and thick-faced Dorset sheep. A river wound through in a graceful double curve. Marching's House was built on the promontory between the curves. One end was red brick, sixteenth-century. The other end was older, all the way back to late Norman. The middle section had been restored as a Johnny-come-lately Victorian Gothic.

She released the brake of the BBC van and drove on across a humpbacked stone bridge spanning the river. The narrow Dorset road divided. A one-way arrow pointed to the left. As she took it, the sheep closed in, staring at the van with stolid eyes. But their bodies were agitated. Another warning sign urged reduced speed. She slowed, and the sheep followed along beside her, baaing, and looking towards the big house. The road became even narrower... a graveled drive leading through a gateway arch. Liz drove under it, leaving the sheep milling outside. Beyond the arch she found what had excited them.

The Tabloid Press.

The courtyard that fronted the house was crawling with papparazi firing still-camera shots at everything in sight. High-angles, looking down a housemaid's cleavage; low-angles, of an old Bentley being polished by a liveried chauffeur; wide-angles, of the impressive architectural wings of the house flanking the court — but the central photo action was zoomed on an elderly man standing on the broad front steps. Liz thought at first he was the Duke, but as she got closer she realized that he was an old butler whose antique wing collar and morning coat made him another irrisistable tabloid target.

"What did Dayman want?"

"Will the Duke fight the reforms?"

The questions were hurled from pointblank range at the butler's face.

The man flinched as a drop of spit landed on his cheek, but his voice was imperturbable.

"I have told you before. His Grace has instructed me to say that he was simply asked by the Commissioner if he would assist the police in their enquiry into yesterday's regrettable accident to our neighbor. Naturally his Grace was anxious to do so. Of course he has no intention of obstructing any act passed by an elected Parliament. And he will not be coming out. Thank you very much."

The butler's calm answers muted his inquisition. They fired off a final volley of film in the direction of a Marching family flag, flying over the central gothic turret, then departed in a rush of gravel and jeering finger signs at the BBC logo on Liz's van. That was the second thing that surprised her: except for the inevitable Satellite News, which peddled 24-hour sex and sensationalism worldwide, there was a complete absence of other network video crews. Normally, on a hot-breaking story everyone got the word together and joined the feeding frenzy, but her supervisor at London Central hadn't heard anything about this one when she checked in with him on her way down.

She got out of the van and walked across to the steps. The old butler, wiping his cheek with a spotless white handkerchief, was more disturbed than she had thought. His hand shook slightly as he replaced the handkerchief in his breast pocket. He turned on his heel, and said over his shoulder, "I have no further statement to make."

"I don't want a statement. I'd like to see the Duke about a private matter."

"Private?" As he glanced from her to the BBC logo, the butler's tone managed to be both polite and scathing at the same time. "His Grace is indisposed. I suggest, Madam, that you write a letter."

The man continued up the steps towards the center of triple front doors. Liz found a business card, scribbled on the back, and ran after him. "Please give the Duke this."

The habits of a lifetime halted the butler in his tracks. He held his hand out, palm upwards as though holding a tray, took the card, examined the writing, raised one eyebrow, and said, " 'Hector MacKenzie's friend'. Very well, Madam. If you would wait here."

He indicated an uncomfortable wooden chair just inside the front hall. Liz sat and looked at the Victorian Gothic surrounding her. Faces that must be Marching family ancestors looked back from heavy framed portraits. The oldest, of an Elizabethan in a starched white ruff, hanging over an enormous bricked-up fireplace, was a Holbein.

"What's this about MacKenzie?"

Liz turned to find herself looking at the same nose and mouth as the picture's. Their owner did not look at all "indisposed": just angry and worried. After his treatment by her media colleagues, she didn't blame him. She extended her hand and said, "Thank you for seeing me, your Grace. It isn't merely an excuse. Hector and I are close friends."

"Indeed." The Duke didn't take her hand.

"He appeared before the Justice Commission," she said. "He's been arrested."

The Duke gave a deep sigh. "Forgive my rudeness, Miss Ponti. Damned press! I don't know how they sniff these things out — present company excepted. Oh, I know you're BBC, but I thought you were probably fair from the way you picked the Holbein. Let's go along to my study."

He ushered her across the vast foyer and through a plank door into a paneled room lined with books. The "old-boy" way of doing things, Liz thought: look the right way at the right Old Master and you're one of Us. But she wasn't. Although she accepted the Duke's hospitality, and hoped to get help from him, she had no other use for hereditary titles. Roper's new administration was right about that.

"Drink, or tea?" the Duke asked, when she was seated. "I'm having whisky myself."

"A small one, please. No soda."

"Water?"

"A touch."

Marching poured the whisky from a crystal decanter into a matching glass, added the water from a silver jug, and handed the drink to her before getting his own. "I too am concerned for MacKenzie," he said, as he pressed the siphon. "However, one mustn't exaggerate. This Justice Commission has wide powers, but it isn't a court. He hasn't been formally tried, and Barracks' confinement isn't 'in prison'. Your good health."

The Duke raised his glass to her. She returned the gesture automatically and asked him, "Do you watch television, your Grace?"

"Very seldom. State ceremonial of course. Or when there's a particularly close horse race. Why do you ask?"

"Because most people do watch it," she said. "They're watching this Commission in Norwich every day, and what they see happening there, in their view *is* a trial. When that terrible old woman in charge brings down her gavel, she might just as well be saying 'Off with their head!' "

"With all respect, I don't believe that."

"Nor would I, if I hadn't sat there every day, and if television image-making wasn't my business." Liz leaned forward and said with absolute conviction, "Hector's former brother-in-law is Irish. Irish means terrorist — whether or not the man actually helped one to escape in a lifeboat. And sending a Christmas card to an Irish Terrorist means Traitor. To the mass of viewers it really is as simple as that."

"And what do you expect me to do about it?"

"I don't know." The force that had impelled her to seek this man out evaporated with his total lack of support. She finished the drink, put the glass on the inlaid table, and stood up. "I suppose I hoped you would feel as strongly as I do about what seems to be happening to real British justice, through guilt by association. I thought you could use your old-boy influence, which still really runs this country, to do something for Hector. It was an emotional reaction. I shouldn't have bothered you."

She moved towards the study door. To her surprise, before she could touch the handle, the Duke locked it.

"I may not have your knowledge of the power of television to distort reality," he said, as he removed the key, "but I assure you that the possibility of guilt by association is something I know personally, only too well."

It was her turn for disbelief. "With all respect, your Grace, except for perhaps catching a salmon that was under the legal limit in your private river, I don't see what the ranking peer of the realm whose family face got painted by Holbein could be found guilty of."

Marching gave a short, harsh laugh then, looking her straight in the eye, said, "Can we consider this exchange off the record?"

"I already said I came here in a private capacity."

"I have your word on that."

"Absolutely."

The Duke turned away and stared out at his vast acreage. "Yesterday," he said, "I found my neighbor with a broken neck. Today, I was visited by the Chief Commissioner of our National Police."

"That's public knowledge, not privileged information."

"This is." He swung back to face her. "Two hours ago, Dayman informed me that I may not leave the country because a dual charge is pending against me: accessory to murder and collusion in High Treason."

It was so absurd that Liz would have laughed... if his manner were not so grave and if she hadn't heard equal absurdities given the full weight of authority, day after day, by the British Commission for Justice. But even at that, "What possible motive could link you to such charges?"

"A conspiracy among the members of the College of Arms to install this pretender from Australia without Parliament's approval." The Duke threw his arms out in a gesture of helpless rage and apprehension that made a flock of sheep beneath the study window bolt away in alarm. "In my opinion," said their master, "and although I can't yet prove it, the real motive behind Dayman's visit is that the government of the day — which is led by an unmitigated liar — using fair means or foul, has decided not only to eliminate any last restraining power on its actions against the House of Lords, but also to take advantage of a national calamity and abolish the monarchy as well."

The sheep stopped at a safe distance and turned their heads back to stare at the window. Their group response reminded Liz of the spectators attending the daily hearings in Norwich. She said to the Duke, "I appreciate your confidence, and I share your concern about many of the government's actions, but it's only fair to tell you that my sentiments are Scottish Nationalist and Republican. There is no reason for monarchy any longer."

"Perhaps not, if a solid majority of the British people, after due consideration, voted against it in a national referendum — although I should fight such a thing with every breath in my body. But to achieve that end through the backstairs, using cloak and dagger means accessible only to Inner Cabinet, is utterly despicable. And believe me, if the Throne goes down in such a fashion, your Free Press wouldn't last the candle."

"No," Liz agreed, "it probably wouldn't. What did you mean by cloak and dagger?"

"You think I exaggerate." Marching looked towards the locked door of the study, then back to her. He said in a low but intense voice. "Dayman was right on one point. The lady's death next door was not pure accident. The army was involved."

Half incredulous, but already half convinced, she listened as he recounted the details of his Bentley's near-collision with the military all-terrain vehicle, and the man driving it. She said, "You say he had an insignia of a rocket?"

Marching nodded. "A missile in flight. Crossed with a dagger. The College records regimental arms, but it must be new; I didn't recognize it."

"I do," Liz said. "And I think I saw the same man wearing it. In Ireland, on the day that Gore was shot down."

There was a silence in the study so complete that they could hear their own hearts beating. She had no more half doubts. Only a deeper fear for the future of her country.

"An involvement in Gore's death," Marching said at last, "would make the situation rather worse than I imagined. And rather more important that it be corrected."

"I can't see how," Liz replied. "Roper holds all the strings."

"Not all." Marching gave her a terse smile, "A republican and a duke make a strange pair of bedfellows but perhaps with your image-making powers, and my old-boy net, together we can put a Sovereign back on the throne. I shall call Roper's bluff and confirm Rouge Dragon Pursuivant's proclamation of the Australian."

Sydney

THE INTERNATIONAL HYENA pack had bayed after Richard all the way from the US Consulate, but for once he was off the streetcorner tabloid front pages.

NEW BRITAIN'S OLD SHAME
RIO SOCCER MADNESS !

One of the usual British fan riots at the World Cup match in Brazil had a new wrinkle: the Brit yobos had chartered a jumbo hypersonic and flown it half way around the world. Unlike most Australians, he had never bothered much about soccer, but he felt a moment of sympathy for the majority of fans who only wanted to cheer and beer without being hounded by the Press or hit on the head by broken glass.

"Security check, please."

The turnstile attendant at the New South Wales Archives main entry stopped Richard's soccer thoughts. The barrier halted the hyenas as well, except for the same Japanese, who always managed to be up front, and had now got his squat bulk into the Archives as a single individual representing the group pack.

"But no cameras or recorders, sir."

The security attendant took two of each from the Japanese and put them into a steel bin marked with a black and scarlet sign:

In Event Of Bomb Alert

Soccer stadiums or libraries, explosive violence was everywhere. Beside the bomb sign, the floor directory listed Special Periodicals in the basement. Richard walked over to the elevator with the Japanese, who bowed, playing the game of You-First: No-You... until the door started to close and Richard lost his patience with Oriental manners and jumped on board. The Japanese just made it, and they rode down in silence, with the Japanese bowing smaller bows and smiling each time their eyes met through the gaps between the other occupants' heads.

It was only dropping through the last two floors, when the final other passenger had left, and the pair of them were alone in the elevator, that Richard suddenly wondered if the polite smile was genuine.

In closed spaces he always had to fight claustrophobia. The air seemed to get hotter every time he found the Japanese looking at him, or shifting very slightly towards him, rocking on the balls of his feet like a Sumo wrestler. The man was built like one: without the enormous gut, but his shoulders showed the strength of a bull, and his hands could probably snap —

"Please ...?"

The elevator had stopped. The Japanese was holding the door and bowing him out. The Special Periodicals desk was straight in front.

"How can I assist you?"

Richard explained. A helpful archivist proceeded to show him through the computer routine needed to recover the items from the past that he wanted to look at. The archivist had left, and he was looking at January in the year of his birth before he remembered that he should be nine months earlier!

He punched the keys accordingly. A menu file prompted, WHICH PAPER? and gave a list: *The Australia Times*, *The New South Wales Recorder*, half a dozen others. He hadn't realized so many real newspapers used to be printed before the tabloid explosion. He picked the *Times*. When the image came up, with its large pages and dense columns of news, and only an average two or three small photo shots of leading world figures, it was like looking at a museum exhibit.

Twenty-eight years ago, on New Year's Eve, he found his mother in a full color society section called "Sydney Life".

SHE LOOKED SO young. She was wearing a black jersey formal dress, but strapless, cut very low on the shoulder, and a skin-tight skirt above her knees, with a giant scarlet taffeta rose stuck on to one side. Plus a single string of huge pearls, and even bigger spike high heels...

Resting on pedals.

Dressed like that, she was astride a motor bike!

"On her way... to a party?" was the photo caption. There was a short story underneath about the new Mrs Byrd-Wilson, and her previous adventures on two wheels before her recent marriage to the Nation's largest brewing fortune. There was no other mention of his father.

The last Prince of Wales.

On the computer's next page, they were standing together on the edge of a group in the grounds of what used to be Government House when Australia still had a Governor General as the British Sovereign's representative. The former Prince was only medium height, Richard noted, level with his mother, so their eyes were looking at each other, laughing about something... and even a long shot, grainy black-and-white newsprint photo seen on a small television screen showed there was more going on than a discussion about Constitutional Monarchy.

The next day they were on the front page.

At least his mother was. The Prince was flying back to Britain "For further medical advice..."

There had been a car smash with his mother driving. She was uninjured. Her royal passenger had been treated for a cut arm by ambulance medics.

Eight months and seven days later, "Mr and Mrs Ronald Byrd-Wilson of Karamatta Estate are pleased to announce the birth of their first son, Richard Arthur..."

He zoom-magnified to look at the Government House picture again; and saw the two pairs of eyes meeting without giving a damn for who was watching. He had wanted to know. Now he *knew.*

Forget DNA tests: It was true. They were his own eyes.

More Bed Games • Whitehall

"SPEAKING VERY FRANKLY," said the mandarin lying beside Slade — the one who'd had the little problem in the Museum of Man lavatory and was now running Careers, and Commercial Investment Review — "bashing the Lords, on top of Roper virtually amalgamating Treasury into the PM's Office, on top of replacing the entire upper echelons of military leadership at a moment when Defence planning expenditures are in a total state of flux: well, I can understand him wanting soldiers with less old-fashioned ideas of loyalty but turning his tabloid dogs on the Duke of Dorset's jugular is simply too much. Marching represents enormous private capital, and if confidence in that falters! I can tell you, fiscally speaking, at this point in time your new Master scares the hell out of us."

"Hmm," Slade responded non-commitally as he got out of bed to plug the kettle in for tea. "I don't know what you mean about the Duke."

"Look in my briefcase."

It was on the bedside chair, next to the mandarin's knife-edged, pin-striped trousers. Slade flipped the lock.

SHOULD ONE MAN HAVE ALL THIS ?

Almost half the front page was taken up by the headline. The rest was a montage of Edward Marching, dressed in his ceremonial robes as Garter King of Arms, surrounded by shots of his housemaids and chauffeurs and butlers and fifty thousand acres. The arrangement was laid out so that His Grace appeared to be leering at his housemaid's tits while the chauffeur polished his bum. Superimposed at one side was a portrait of the Chief Commissioner of the National Police, holding a bible in one hand and seeming to stare as an avenging angel at the Duke.

"Dayman Demands Death Truth!" was the subhead. The death was the Catholic candidate's, who fell off her horse.

"You don't really believe," Slade said, dropping the tabloid rag on the bed, "that my new Master still has daily lay-out meetings with his former editors to produce this kind of wipe?"

"I believe," replied the mandarin, "although I haven't yet proved it, that the arms-length blind trust regulations have been breeched by Pal Hal. The synchronisation of tabloid and SGN cable coverage of events, especially those which adversely affect the restoration of a working monarchy, can't possibly be coincidence — even allowing for a politician's natural abilities for sniffing every fart from the electorate! The sooner we get this Australian playboy on the throne, and some stable continuity back in Whitehall, the better. Have you got that tea?"

WHEN SLADE'S BED-PARTNER informant had departed, he decided to record the conversation highlights in his coded diary before returning to his official duties. *More Downing Street tremors*, he concluded at the end of the entry, in his tiny, immaculate script: *Too early to jump ship!*

He locked the diary in its secret compartment, straightened the blotter so that its edge formed a perfect right angle with the front of the desk, then adjusted a rock-crystal paperweight so that it didn't reflect the bright afternoon sunlight from the window into his eye. A small but brilliant rainbow formed as he rotated the crystal. The rainbow's arrival never ceased to fascinate him. It was something to do with the speed of light: red was fast, and blue was slow — or the other way around. Except that today there were two reds, which there had never been before. The second one was below the purple band. He twisted the crystal further. The rainbow vanished.

But the red remained. Reduced to a dot. Next to it he saw the distorted image of the ceiling chandelier. He stared up at the high ceiling. Six feet above his head, the red dot was still there. Slade pulled the chair away from the desk and stood on it. From a distance of four and a half feet, the dot was a pinhead red light in a scarcely larger hole in the plaster. He climbed onto the Hepplewhite, dragged the chair up to him, rested it on the desk top, then climbed on to the chair.

Now his eye was only six inches from the hole. The red pinhead inside it was attached to a piece of glass the size of the top of his little finger. As he peered at it, the glass withdrew with a barely audible hum. The glass was the self-focussing lens of a micro-miniaturized surveillance camera. The point of focus was the spot on the desk where he wrote in his diary.

Slade's legs began to shake.

He grabbed the back of the chair to support himself... and felt the antique wooden stile collapse. He crashed with it off the desk to the polished parquet floor. Half stunned, he tried to rise. His head swam. He slumped back against the desk. His office door connecting to the Prime Minister's inner study opened. A hand which was scarred as though an animal had torn it reached towards him.

"Need help?" said the spine-chilling man encoded *Muwi* in the diary.

Friday Rush

THE MAN WHO had been Slade's partner for their lunchtime slap-and-tickle spent his afternoon on the telephone. Confirming that Roper was still actively involved in the tabloid and satellite cable interests of his former business empire was a tricky exercise. No one was going to go on record against a popular prime minister before the time was ripe to bring in a successor. However, for now, an off-the-record nod would be good enough.

Getting a knighthood...

All the mandarin's civil service contemporaries had already received their sword-tap on the shoulder: without that little morals problem at the

Museum of Man, he would have had his. Now he never would unless there was a monarch to do the tapping! Any cipher would serve for the figure-head: Roper had to be made to see reason over the Australian. The means came from a telephone call to an old army pal who had made an unusual and smart switch to Trade and now controlled advertising money for the largest global Wash-Day conglomerate.

"Of course no quoting, old boy, but I was lunching the Chief of SGN for world rights on the commercial for our new detergent. We met in his office, which used to be Roper's, and the former Big Boss himself came on through cellular. Naturally it was a scrambled call but the CEO's Girl Friday used the magic letters, 'PM', to get his attention. Which I can assure you it did. Lunch was delayed for a good ten minutes."

A scrambled ten minute personal call from the Prime Minister to the head of the muckraking Satellite Global News channel! The mandarin already felt that tap of tempered steel on his shoulder!

"You wouldn't happen to remember the day?" he asked casually.

"Thursday last. There were Breton oysters on the club menu, the season had just opened. You know, the day of the Lords' legislation, when that unfortunate woman got her neck broken."

WITH THAT LUCKY break the mandarin left his office in the restored Treasury building and took the escalator to the underground garage where his other self-indulgence was parked: the latest Japanese sports sedan whose every automated feature made driving effortless luxury.

"Our country home, Jeeves!" he ordered the car's trip computer, while the leather seat adjusted automatically to his body's configuration. He approved the choice of music the sound system suggested, and then relaxed. The four-wheel computerized steering made even reversing out of the confines of the narrow parking bay a piece of cake; on the crowded Southern Motorway it was blissful ease. The radar range calculator kept the exact distance-to-braking-ratio between the cars ahead and behind. A single finger was all that the steering control required. The calm beauty of Mozart's Clarinet Quintette lulled him...

The sign to his Kent village appeared. He swept past a military vehicle crawling along in the slow lane and tapped the steering control lightly to take him left beneath the overpass abutment. The blurred regimental insignia of a launched missile painted on the military vehicle's door made him think of his own coat of arms which would have to be designed when the royal voice would say in its Australian twang —

The steering control was not responding!

The computer panel said it was, but it wasn't. The bureaucrat pressed the control again, harder. Nothing happened. With his thumb. Really hard. Nothing. The exit ramp curved sharply left. He turned the override switch to manual.

All four wheels stayed straight.

He shouted in panic, *"CUT SPEED!"* and slammed both feet on the brake pedal with such force that something snapped in one ankle...but the dual electronic braking system ignored him. As the Mozart soared in a glorious crescendo, his marvel of Japanese engineering hit the abutment head-on at eighty miles an hour.

Ten

The Residence • Canberra

RICHARD MET HIS mother as she was coming out of her private sitting room. Trapped in the passage, she was forced to stop.

"Dicky!" Her face reflected a number of emotions, but not pleasure in being reunited with her only child. "I thought it was your father," she said, without offering a kiss. "You've caused him endless grief."

"Caused *him?* Christ, he didn't get a bloody Injunction served on national television!"

"You shouldn't have been on it. Calling yourself a bastard in front of the entire country."

"I didn't say I was — I said, 'if.' That's why I'm back. Mother, we need a serious talk."

"For God's sake," she hissed. "The servants!"

Footsteps clicked behind him. The Residence housekeeper was crossing the tiled floor of the main hall. His mother gave her First Lady smile until the woman was gone, then said, "Your poor father is the one to be serious with, but if you're going to make a scene by being such an unending nuisance we'd better use my room."

She opened the door and went inside. Richard followed. And because he knew the sneaky way her mind worked was just able to make it across to the French door opposite, before she could escape to the garden outside.

He said, "It's no good trying that. I'm sure I have been an unending nuisance all my life, but this time I want a proper answer." He took a printout of the Archives newspaper story from his pocket and handed it to her.

"Not the Prince of Wales again." She gave her little laugh that wasn't funny, and didn't bother to read the story. "I didn't mean you were really a nuisance. Now you're just being silly."

"I have his eyes." Richard pointed at the photo shot of her and the Prince looking at each other at Government House. "And I've had my blood tested."

"Your blood?"

He remembered Lady Bronwen's advice about people really wanting to let go of psychological burdens in this kind of situation. He passed his mother the duplicate film strip as well, so that she had everything, and said,

"Tested for DNA. The DNA signature is like a family tree. The original has already gone to London for matching. I thought you would want to be told."

"For matching." She didn't pay any attention to the film strip, but now she looked at the old newspaper picture. She bit her lower lip, and sank into a yellow velvet chair. "You really do think that I — that we…?"

She stopped.

Richard pulled up a matching stool and sat down facing her, so that she couldn't avoid his gaze. He said, "I don't think any more. I know."

Her hand touched the face in the printout from twenty-eight years ago. "I wasn't driving," she said. "That was a lie. I could have kept a car on that road, blindfolded, with one hand! But if the police had found *him* at the wheel…"

She stopped again.

"Did he know that you got pregnant?"

"For Christ's sake, Dicky!"

Finally, she was being herself. Richard said, "I don't care about the bastard part, but we have to be honest."

"You do care." She looked into his face. "And they are the same eyes. And, yes, he knew. At least I wrote a letter to his personal secretary. It's strange how things come around. I saw in the paper just the other day that the man was murdered. In his apartment in Buckingham Palace of all places. These days no-one's safe anywhere."

Richard had known it was true. But that wasn't the same as hearing it. He felt… he couldn't describe how he felt. Nothing was different. He was exactly the same person he had been when he came into this room. But he wasn't.

"I'm so sorry, my darling."

His mother was crying. Tears ran down her cheeks and dropped onto the yellow cushions. He felt his own eyes getting hot. "You don't need to be sorry," he said. "These things just happen, I guess."

"I guess." She sniffed, and found a tissue in her purse and dabbed her cheeks.

"Does my father — my stepfather — know?"

"He hasn't asked."

Which meant, yes-but. "He'll have to be told properly. Before the test result comes out."

She nodded. "I want you to promise me one thing. He is still your father. In every way that counts he always has been, even though it hasn't been easy for him. Because medically — well, for most of our married life he's known that he couldn't produce a child of his own. Promise you'll go on calling him — I know you hate using, 'Daddy', but..."

"I promise." Richard would think of her marriage partner as Father, because there wasn't any other possibility. The other man was just a shadow in a photograph. He said to his mother, "I'll tell him if you like. If it would be easier?"

"Jesus, no you won't!" She made a wry expression and handed him back the printout of the picture that showed her dressed for High Society on a hog motorbike. "Thanks for the kind offer, but if I could wear that hemline and six-inch spikes on a Harley, I can find the guts to tell my husband the result."

Richard put away the evidence of past history, and they both stood up. "Where is he — Father, now?" he asked, as they moved together towards the French door leading into the garden.

"Receiving new Ambassadors. It's on the Parliament channel. Let's watch and be proud for him."

She turned on the patio television set next to the drinks table. He poured them each a stiff one. "After that last scene, we can use it!"

"Thanks." She took the glass. "Swap you for the Guide. The Cable idiots have changed the damned channel numbering again."

The programing guide was behind the ice bucket. As he gave it to her, the channel supposed to be for Parliamentary Affairs was offering the usual rundown of global disaster and domestic violence called The Nation's News. Between another British Soccer Riot in Rio and Unsolved Queensland Crime, Richard said, "We should be on Eighteen, not Seven."

His mother put her hand on the channel switch. He caught the words, *Brisbane*, and *Model*, and *Murder*. He glanced automatically...

And in the instant that the picture took to change, he saw Sally's face looking at him from the screen.

BY THE TIME he reached past his mother and turned the switch back, the face was gone. The picture was now a body covered with a sheet, being carried from the pink bedroom that for a few hours he was happy in when the body was a live, exciting girl who wasn't too bright, but was kind to him when no-one else was.

"The Queensland State Police are pursuing several leads: among them, rumors of a link to international terrorism, and possible blackmail, due to the victim being recently linked with the President's son..."

He didn't hear the rest because the picture cut to the bare-cheeked tabloid shot of Sally's bum, and he hurled his glass through the tube.

Then he collapsed on a patio chair. Shaking.

"It will be all right. Drink this." Somehow his mother was holding another glass. "Go on. It's brandy."

"It won't be right. Nothing will. Ever."

"Yes it will. Now drink, damn you."

She forced the glass in his hand. He raised it and drank. Obediently, like her child.

"That's better," she said, in a new voice of absolute authority which astounded him. "I'm not having your father dragged through the mud again. We have to think, and we have to be bloody quick about it. The first thing is to get you out of here."

"Sally was going to meet me. " Richard stared at the exploded wreckage of the television. "Just the two of us at the cabin. I had it all planned."

"In the Snowys? That's perfect. Come on."

She tugged his arm. He sat rigid, unable to comprehend anything about this person she had become. "I don't know what you're trying to do. The police will want —"

"Bugger the police!" She punched his chest, hard, above the heart, where he had the newspaper story of his beginnings. "Dicky, *I've been there.* You didn't kill this girl. The police will believe what our lawyers tell them. Now get off your arse. I'll drive you in my car."

THEY GOT TO the cabin at dusk... after a drive on the new Mountain Highway that changed for the rest of his days the image that he would have of the woman who had been his mother. She listened to every word he poured out about Sally, and Anna leaving, and acting: she was understanding, and often funny — because much of it was pure farce, he could begin to see that — and through all of it she never stopped driving like the hammers of hell.

As they came down through the pass above Corryong and saw Mount Kosciusko turning pink and gold from the evening sun, she said, "Remember: no phone calls, no trips to the village, nothing! To the Press, and the police, I'll do the talking, from Canberra. Until I tell you it's okay to come out, you just stay put."

"And when I come out?" Richard asked her, when they had left the highway at Marriot's Hat, and the Mercedes was bumping up the private lane. "Then what?"

She stopped in front of the cabin without replying and watched as he got out of the car, then she reversed and pointed it ready for the long haul back to Canberra. She pulled his head down fiercely and kissed his cheek.

"You didn't answer my question," he said. "When you've handled everything and I come out?"

"Then you'll quit play-acting and take your crack at being a real king."

The Mercedes drove away, and the sun dropped behind the western foothills, leaving him alone with the gathering darkness...and the terrifying knowledge that she hadn't been joking.

And thinking, *Sally might not be dead if I had played it straight with Anna.*

Research Vessel *Melville* • Grand Banks

TO MOST OF HUMANITY, Anna thought, as she watched the topography of the New England Seamounts climbing up the screen in front of her, the floor of the sea was still as remote as the moon, and less familiar. The pictures were coming back to her from "Moby", the self-controlled submersible. In the last week he had led the *Melville* up the eastern edge of the five-thousand-meters-deep Hatteras Abyssal Plain between the Bahamas and Bermudas; then across the Hudson Canyon running at right angles out from New York across the dropoff of the continental slope; then north, along the slope to Sable Island; and then he had reversed course to the Kelvin Seamount which rose as high as the volcanoes on the West Coast.

Now Moby wanted to shift east, into the Sohm Abyssal Plain in the direction of the Atlantis Fracture Zone, breaking the axis of the mid Atlantic Ridge. Anna decided she would let him — everyone on board thought of Moby as a live male — because all the submersible's apparently random movement for the past week had a single motive: he went where the whale food was.

Where the whales were, so was *Architeuthis princeps.*

Despite the occasional, washed-up evidence of titanic struggles and battles between the two leviathans, so far as science could tell the giant squid did not deliberately attack the whales. As with human beings, the struggle was for food and territory.

That's if there was an "Archy". Because in seven days of searching with TV and sonar, all Moby's electronic genius and the *Melville*'s worldwide support facility hadn't found even a trace of a tentacle longer than the half-meter average on the drfting shoals of ordinary squid. To imagine an arm one hundred feet long... Anna couldn't imagine it, although she hoped with all her heart to see it. But not on tonight's watch. It was 03:30 and Jack Nash was due to relieve her in half an hour for the morning watch.

"Six Float, this is Six Base: am I losing you to the veil of sleep?"

She wasn't completely alone: the on-shore operator in the lab at Bar Harbor kept her company electronically, exchanging data on salinity, plus all the tidbits gathered from the fishing vessels sharing the same waters. The voice on the other end of the data link was a post-grad from the Massachussets Institute of Technology. The machines could handle the scientific data; Six Base helped her keep awake with human gossip bytes of yesterday's news.

"Not quite asleep, Six Base," she called back. "More like day-dreaming."

"Day hasn't started, lady. Got one here from Australia."

The company's nosy Maine secretary had ensured that Anna's former interest in a particular Australian had become Deep Six Inc group experience. The link signal next to her began flashing to show it was receiving the condensed, digitized video signal, which it handled alternately with its more important scientific material.

Out of a perverse curiosity Anna pushed the "window" key that would allow a second image to appear in one corner of the screen without encroaching on Moby's view of the underwater territory. A huge shoal of cod taking a sideswipe at the Grand Banks filled the main picture; or maybe the fish were smart enough to know that by going south they could miss the waiting factory fleets that ringed Canada's two-hundred-mile limit. The whales knew it. She could hear their far-off superfrequency squeaks.

"I came here to read a statement to you..."

In the middle of the whales and cod — was Richard.

The sight of him had more effect than she expected. She blamed it on being alone in the middle of the Atlantic at the lowest hour of the night... and masochistically enlarged his video image share. The cries of the hunting whales grew louder.

"This says I can't speak, anywhere in my own country..."

To compete with the whales she had to turn Richard louder. What astonished Anna was that she wanted to. In some intangible way, in a handful of words, the world's most selfish and juvenile ham actor had actually convinced *her* that he actually cared about things like free speech and humanity!

"I'm not a king..."

"You said it!" Annoyed with herself, she deliberately turned his sound off and reduced him back to his former corner of the screen, being gazed at by an old grandmother as though he was already King of —

The first whale!

A finback female, and it had an adolescent calf. The truly majestic creatures swept all interest in the puny Australian out of Anna's head and off the screen. And as she gave the whole picture to the whales, she saw the tentacle.

It was enormous! Draped across the cow whale's back, just in front of the distinctive fin. The tentacle was thicker than the fin in diameter: the suckers were half the size of the whale's massive lower jaw. Anna pushed the zoom key for Moby. Nothing happened. The picture stayed the same. At the most important moment in natural history since discovering the first coelecanth, the remote submersible communication link had failed.

She pounded both fists on the table. Which did nothing. With all the instructions crammed into its mini-micro circuits, the piece of metal junk out there in the water had never been progammed to give a shit about the Target Visual Image.

What it was actually looking for!

Almost sobbing with frustration, she altered the *Melville's* helm and increased speed towards the grid reference of the damaged whale's last position, but it was hopeless. When Jack Nash came in to relieve her, and said with idle curiosity, "I felt the wheel go over. Got something?" Anna could only shake her head and point mutely to where nothing but the cod and the Greek Restaurant variety of squid drifted on the screen below the unwanted image of her frog prince from Australia.

Marriot's Hat

THE NIGHT AIR around the cabin smelt of pine and eucalyptus gum heated all day by the sun and slow to cool. Except for some kind of nocturnal bird's hunting cry in the distance, it was completely silent.

Richard's thoughts were not peaceful. His mind raced endlessly on a locked-in track: from Sally's murder, to his unknown father, to what it would really be like to be a king... to his mother's remarkable behavior. Not just her driving ability, which he had experienced before, but her whole new personality.

Could *he* be a new person if he tried?

He could play any part — just hand him a script for the weekend, it didn't have to be Shakespeare — if nature hadn't given him any other gift, he had this weird ability to think himself into someone else's skin. But what his mother and, before her, Lady Bronwen expected was not just someone: the person they demanded was, *The King*.

The hunting bird screamed again outside the cabin. The moon must be rising because he could see the closest eucalyptus clearly through the window. As he couldn't sleep anyway, and knew every step of the surrounding territory, he decided to go walkabout like an aborigine. One of their song lines, a sort of boundary on an invisible spirit map, was supposed to cut through between the cabin and the shoulder of the hill that sloped down from the flank of Mount Kosciusko.

Stage work was full of ghosts, but in modern settings they always seemed foolish. Here, with the moon rising over the mountain in a land that time forgot, the idea of a spirit world wasn't so farfetched. Richard stared at the black shadow cast by the mountain, broken only by a pinpoint gleam where moonlight reflected off a trickle in the creekbed.

Sally's face was in front of him! Dead white, with terrible purple shadows under her eyes…

He turned and ran. Just for the action. To blot out any more thinking.

SEAN McDERMID WATCHED through his night-vision glasses as his Target suddenly took flight. He was not concerned. He was only here for reconnaisance: when the act of commemoration for the fallen Compound Martyrs was carried out, it would have a decent crowd of mourners handy!

With the combination of moon and infrared he could see the running figure clear as day. His eventual Target was following a trail which wound upwards through the trees to a bare patch piled with stones on the top of a low hill. The shape was vaguely like a crouching animal backed into a corner, and the moon shining off the piled rocks was like snarling teeth. That was the problem with night actions, imagination tended to get out of control.

Why not do it now, for instance?

Mourners to witness the avenging deed were fine, but the main thing was to nip any chance of a Brit royal resurrection in the bud. Suddenly, as though chomped by the imaginary animal's teeth, his Target vanished between the pale rocks. McDermid moved sideways from his observation spot to pick the man up again, but a minute went by, then another, with no sign of him.

If the Australian had broken his damn fool neck…!

It was *not* enough that his Target simply died, and definitely not of natural causes. The fifty-five percent of the British population who wanted another king badly enough to vote on it in the last plebiscite had to know that this one was deliberately taken from them as a human sacrifice.

McDermid went to the car for his gun.

THE HUGE ROCK animal on the hill was Dingo, Richard knew, from the myth time before history. The smaller rocks were the eggs of Mother Lizard. Dingo tried to steal them without permission and was condemned by the Great Spirit to be trapped for eternity just short of his goal. That was the Song Line legend, as Richard had been told it by an old aborigine the first time he had came to the cabin, five summers ago. Dingo and Mother Lizard were the totems of the two tribes that once lived on each side of the invisible line, and stealing the eggs represented unacceptable conduct in a landscape so harsh that only equal sharing allowed either party to survive.

He had received special permission from the old man to climb the hill and its egg-rocks as long as a food gift was provided for the spirits and nothing was disturbed. Now, having left a half-eaten bar of chocolate at the bottom, he scrambled up the wind-smoothed faces of the boulders, successfully blotting out his earlier nightmare thoughts with sheer physical exertion. The rock had the texture of fine sandpaper under his fingertips and there were barely enough lateral cracks for them to grab hold of. That, rather than the height, was the challenge. Tackling it solo, in the moonlight, increased the sense of separation from day-to-day life.

Behind and below him he heard a twig crack as something else out testing its night skills stepped on it. Or maybe it was just bone-dry gumwood splitting from the summer heat. His attention turned back to the rocks. The way to the top of the hill lay between two final "lizard eggs", the ones most sought after by the mythic dingo. One egg lay on its side; the other was upended. The climbing difficulty lay in making the leap from one to the other. It wasn't bad in daylight, but in these conditions making out the niche for his fingers was going to be tough.

Richard crouched on the horizontal rock, getting his eyes acclimatized to the light level. Now he could see the niche. It ran across the vertical rock at a slight diagonal. Another, below it, could support his feet if he took off his shoes. He slipped off his sneakers and felt the rock surface pleasantly cool beneath his sweating soles. He rubbed them back and forth to dry them for better traction. The nightbird gave its hunting cry again, much closer than it had been from the cabin. He wiped his hands on his shirt, straightened his legs, flexed his shoulders, and sprang forward.

As his fingers touched the opposite rock face, its surface exploded.

McDERMID SAW HIS target fall through the telescopic viewfinder. His gun used a silencer and non-flash powder. There was nothing to obscure his senses or reveal his position.

Was it over? Had he killed...?

He watched and listened keenly. No moaning, no movement. The single shot would certainly have done the trick in daylight. McDermid wasn't so sure of his aim under these conditions. In the moonlight everything had a slightly diffused edge.

Holding the gun in one hand he ran lightly down the gully and up its other side, where he paused for a moment. There was still no life sign from the Target. He moved on towards the animal shape of the rock above him... and froze. A figure flitted and was gone. It was too short to be his Target. Someone else on the hill was hunting.

CONSCIOUSNESS CAME BACK to Richard in waves: one moment he could see the pale rock above him, the next he couldn't. Gradually the pale wave lasted longer than the dark. He realized that he was lying in the gap between the two lizard-egg rocks, at the base of the upright one.

He moved his legs. It was only after the act that he thought how lucky he was that they moved at all. His skull could have been crushed, or his neck snapped, but miraculously everything worked; nothing was broken. Only his right hand, when he touched it to his face, was sticky.

Looked at by moonlight, it was black.

The sight of his own blood brought on another wave of nausea. When it passed he saw that his hand had been cut by rock fragments and one chip was still embedded. It wasn't serious. He gritted his teeth and removed the splinter, then licked the wound. He had no idea what kind of natural phenomenon had made the rock explode. Perhaps it was the stored up heat. Whatever, the sense of being alive was truly extraordinary. He patted the rock and stood up.

"Down!"

The voice behind him was gutteral, but soft. At the same instant an unseen hand pressed hard on his shoulder, forcing him back to the ground. After an instinctive shock, his mind put the soft voice and the ability for invisible movement together; they must belong to the hill's guardian, the ancient aborigine. Why the old man should behave like this was another Song Line mystery. Maybe in the dark the aborigine just didn't realize who he was, and figured he'd caught an interloper on the sacred tribal land.

"It's me," Richard whispered. "From the cabin. Look, I left some chocolate as an offering for Dingo."

He reached into the depression between the lizard-egg rocks underneath him, retrieved the half-eaten bar, and turned to show it to —

The face looking back at him, although it had features which were not Caucasian, was not old: the skin was smooth, almost ageless in the moonlight, and not ebony, but nearly as pale as his own.

"Jesus!" Richard swore at the unbelievably intruding bloody Japanese reporter: "Can't you media pricks ever let me alone?"

"Silence." The word was hissed. "With respect, your life is in danger."

"No it isn't," he said with annoyance. "I've had a minor fall, but I know every foot —"

The hand of the polite Japanese clamped over his mouth. "With humility, sir, you are target of assassin. Until is safe, you must remain silent."

The rest of the man's massive torso kept Richard pinned to the ground like a thrown wrestler. They stayed in that ridiculous position until a car engine started on the far side of the gully. When it had faded in the direction of Mount Kosciusko, the man finally released him.

"What the Christ is all this assassin bullshit?" Richard demanded. "For that matter, who and what the hell really are you?"

"Kimura Itaro." The Japanese bowed. "Last is first name, so to you sir, Kimura only, at your service for how long you need me."

"All I *need,*" Richard said, "is some godamn privacy."

He turned away to go down to the cabin. In a movement as swift as his leap in the Archives, the Japanese was over the horizontal lizard-egg rock and standing in front of him.

"Sir, I must go first. Departure of car may be IRA trick."

The Asian's brain was scrambled, but his English was proficient, with a trace of American accent.

"Go where you bloody like." Suddenly Richard felt wiped out from the accumulated shocks and surprises. He wanted only to sleep around the clock.

"You suffer post-attack syndrome, sir. Allow me to offer arm."

The Japanese put it around Richard's waist and, taking advantage of the rock shadows, began moving cautiously forward. The man's other hand, seen in a brief patch of moonlight, was holding a pistol with a barrel thick enough to bring down an ox.

"Do you seriously expect to find the IRA playing flaming arseholes here in the Snowys?" Richard asked sarcastically.

"I do not fully understand your expression, sir, but man who attacked you does not play. With deepest sympathy, from events in Brisbane, you should be aware."

"Brisbane?" As Richard repeated the name, for the first time he began to believe, even if he didn't understand. "You mean Sally..." He felt his legs tremble. Kimura's grip on his waist tightened. "The man in that car killed her?"

Kimura bowed a brief acknowledgment. The night bird gave its cry again. The cabin was visible, now only two hundred yards below them. A cloud passed across the moon.

Why? There was no point to anything. Life was random and meaningless. Kimura moved towards the eucalyptus shadows providing safe cover for the last distance to the cabin, but Richard broke free of the man's supportive arm and the ox-killing automatic. He strode across the clearing and said, "If some bugger out there wants to kill me, let him do it!"

HE WAS ALMOST at the cabin door when he heard a sound that meant they were trying. The whirring throb of a helicopter's rotor: it was coming in low towards Marriot's Hat from the direction of Corryong. He saw a dark dot against the moon, mostly hidden by the trees, but something was different...

No winking navigation lights.

The chopper was running blind. Richard calmly watched it approach.

"Sir. You must move."

"Fuck them," he said to Kimura. "This is my cabin. You go. I'm staying."

The black shape came closer. The eucalyptus leaves swished furiously in the downdraft. Still no light showed from the helicopter. Its pilot was skillful, taking the risk of a moonlight landing among these trees. Richard looked up to watch it. His mind was curiously cool and detached, as though his fate was already decided.

If I'm spared, it's for a purpose. If not...?

The dark mass of the underbelly descended. A side hatch opened. There were two men inside it. They were in black, with hoods on their heads, as he expected. He felt the Japanese tug him backwards, but resisted.

"Kimura, I said, *go!*"

One of the men jumped down. The rotors slowed to a soft chuff-chuff.

"Are you Richard Arthur Byrd-Wilson?"

"I am." He stared at the eye slits in the hood. "I don't suppose you have the guts to use a name."

"Not yet."

"I didn't think so." The voice was muffled, not Australian. It was hard to tell through the hood and the rotor noise. He said to the unknown figure in front of him, "Whatever you've come for, let's get it over with."

"We've come for you."

The second black figure jumped out of the chopper. Richard straightened his back. The first figure tugged him down roughly. He felt his hair waved by the draft from the rotor.

"Not the moment to lose one's head."

The second laconic voice was definitely unexpected from an IRA terrorist: it was Brit Upper-class.

"Stop screwing around," Richard said to both of them. "Just shoot."

The first black figure laughed... and he realized there could be something worse than being shot. Something else he was totally unprepared for: *Being taken hostage.*

THEY LIFTED HIM bodily into the helicopter. Richard saw a glimpse of Kimura's face, and a final Oriental bow. So the incident at the Lizard Eggs had been staged. The polite Japanese was part of the plot all along.

The rotors roared. The eucalyptus and pines dropped away beyond the open hatch. A scattered handful of lights showed Marriot's Hat, a greater number in the distance was Corryong, then civilization was gone. They flew with the moon behind them for an hour. The masked men on each side of him said nothing. The pitch of the rotors changed again for descent. This time, with the thud of landing the engines stopped.

"Down we get."

His captors lifted him out through the hatch. He found himself standing on a private landing strip of packed dirt that could belong to any large ranch in the outback. There were no buildings. A slight breeze blew. The silence was re-enforced by the absence of engine noise.

"This way."

He was led around the bulbous nose of the helicopter. Just beyond it a small unmarked executive jet was parked on the strip. The jet also showed no running lights. A door opened behind the cockpit, and a short ladder dropped down. There were no lights inside the fuselage either.

Richard climbed the steps. The earlier resolve he had found was much harder to maintain under these dragged-out conditions. The hour on the chopper had been bad enough. How would he cope with indefinite confinement…?

The fuselage door closed with a thud. A light finally came on, and he blinked at its brightness. He was facing the bulkhead to the flightdeck. His two captors turned him in the opposite direction.

"My dear boy," said Lady Bronwen, "what a melodrama this must all have seemed. Come and sit down. "

RICHARD LOOKED FROM her familiar face to the two masked men. It hadn't been "melodrama": Sally was dead, and he was responsible. He reacted with seething anger.

"Do you know about that?" he demanded of this crazy old woman. "About Sally being murdered?"

"Yes I do," she said gravely. "We would not all be here like this if I did not."

"So why are we — and who are these sods?"

"They are loyal friends."

"In masks," he said contemptuously.

"In waiting," she replied.

"Waiting for what?"

"Your decision." She stood, only to drop one of her ridiculous full curtseys to him, which looked even stupider in the narrow aircraft. Crouched in the aisle, squashed between the rows of seats, she lifted her head and looked into his eyes. "Your Royal Highness, if you find the courage to take and wear it, these brave men offer you the crown of Britain."

"Then they can take their bloody masks off," he said. "I made that decision on top of a rock, two hours ago!"

PART THREE

Over The Sea

One

Airborne • New South Wales

MACKENZIE'S WORST APPREHENSIONS were realized. The Intelligence file had prepared him for the Candidate's tabloid clowning and non-Royal appearance: it was the man's display of cowardice that he couldn't stomach. It was easy to strut in front of a supportive old woman like Lady Bronwen but, at the first hint of rough play, following the murder of his unfortunate Brisbane girlfriend, the playboy sitting in the aircraft cabin had cut and run to mother.

Set against the example of unbroken courage that MacKenzie had witnessed during those terrible visits to the Burn ward at Chedburgh he found the Australian's behavior nauseating... but at least his predictable reactions had simplified the task of locating him. Before entering Australian airspace with Wallop, regional Anti-Terror had already provided the locations of all the private homes of the country's new President. By the time MacKenzie landed at Brisbane the Anti-Terror HQ in Sydney had ascertained that the houses in both cities were clean. Before Queensland A-T had finished briefing him on the McGuire woman's death, the terrorism unit in Melbourne reported that the President's wife's car had been radar clocked at twice the legal limit as she left her mountain cabin.

"By dead-reckoning, crossing the Queensland line, sir."

Wallop showed him the estimated position on the chart. They were flying without any navigational aids because their exit had to be undetected and even a passive Loran receiver could be used by ground intercepting forces. MacKenzie had broken one law in Britain by disregarding the Justice Commission. He was breaking the criminal code here by transporting an Australian citizen abroad without a passport.

"Very good," he told Wallop, "keep us low and west of the Great Dividing Range all the way up to the Cape York Peninsula."

Air traffic in this part of the continent was still sparse: with luck, they might avoid a mid-air collision! There was no point in worrying, MacKenzie thought. It no longer mattered whether he liked Lady Bronwen's dark horse, or the condition of the track: all that counted now was getting past the finish line.

Buckingham Palace

IN THE ROYAL MEWS Cafeteria, over his usual bangers and mash, Samuel Stubbins was having his usual morning argument with Ben, the dour Senior Ostler, about the news. Breakfast was meant to be a cheerful time, which was why Stubbins watched the TV side of things with his sausages. The telly had to show a disaster if it happened, but it always managed to close with something good.

This morning it was kids again. They were jumping up and down outside a farmyard with baby lambs and a newborn calf on the Duke of Dorset's estate. "The Duke is going to guide them personally," said the warm voice of that nice woman announcer, Liz something, "because he feels everyone should have a chance to see the part of Britain he holds in trust, particularly the country's most precious asset, its future generation."

"Mindless pap!" the Senior snorted. "Here's what this country's 'future generation' appreciates." The ostler reached over the blue leather Despatch Box waiting for its day's run and shook his paper in Stubbins' face.

MINDLESS MAYHEM! LAGER LOUTS!

More soccer violence. The full-page color pic had blood pouring down an old man's face. "I don't know why you read it, Ben," Stubbins told him. "Not with your digestion problem."

But he filled in the Poll of the Day anyway — DO YOU APPROVE HELPING BUILD A BETTER BRITAIN? with the ordinary-sized letters explaining "by a period of national community service for young people" under a photo of some smiling teenagers clearing rubbish in flashy overalls — and picked up the Despatch Box to take it back with Dolly to Downing Street.

Market Forces • House Of Commons

"THE CHAIR RECOGNIZES the Prime Minister."

"Thank you, Madam Speaker." Roper gave her, and the television camera, his most reassuring smile. "I am happy to report that Tourism revenues are sharply up and bookings for the Royal Residence Program are already filled at the four principal houses for the remainder of the year. Extra staff have had to be recruited, helping unemployment levels in several difficult rural areas..."

He waited for the predictable Hear-Hears, then:

"I continue now to a related matter: the excessively large holdings of British land by a tiny minority of its people..."

The reaction this time was a disbelieving silence, waiting for:

"Of course," he said, "this Government totally supports the principle of private ownership of land. The large rural estates are the glory of our island, as well as its prime tourist attraction; however, it is completely against the spirit of the New Britain, or the expressed desires of its people, to have fifty thousand acres in one man's hands. As I have already said, every man and every woman should have the equal opportunity to land ownership — *through venture capital.* Honorable Members, the legislation now introduced before you allows precisely such an opportunity. Rural land must remain unaltered, but all estates of more than five thousand acres will be formed into publicly held corporations. Minority control can be retained by the present owners. All remaining shares will be offered on a free market basis to any British citizen. I should add that the Royal Estates are also included...."

Beeb Central

THE LATEST PARLIAMENTARY pandemonium reached Liz as she was having an end-of-another-week drink with her supervisor at the Wire Pullers Bar in the basement of the Corporation's headquarters. Her little countercoup of improving the Duke of Dorset's image with viewers on this morning's breakfast show had seemed successful, according to the rating meters: the chaos being transmitted from Westminster showed that she had been spitting into a hurricane.

"Roper's ability to control events is total," she said. "Since he can act without warning, but only does it when he knows the result from the polls in advance, he's unbeatable in Parliament. The bastard has the absolute authority of a Russian Tzar."

"Nothing's changed." Her supervisor gave a cynical smile and signaled the barman for more vino. "Roper isn't doing anything any prime minister holding a solid majority and the balls to go with it hasn't always been able to do."

"They haven't always been able to arrest people and hold them indefinitely without a proper trial."

"My Highland competition." The man across the table poured from the new bottle, then added, "In point of fact, Liz, Courts Martial are different. Military people like MacKenzie can be held. Power is where power lies — as someone said, or if they didn't I just have. Take Madam Speaker up there," he pointed at the screen, "she's in the job because her first cousin lies outside marriage with the People's Friend."

"Roper has a mistress? How do you know?"

"The lady in question is my first cousin, too. If you want some distaff help with your Commando, I'll arrange a meeting."

"God bless you!" Liz kissed him with a wet wine kiss which could have led to more trouble if it hadn't been interrupted by a beep on her supervisor's pocket cellular. He put the receiver to his ear. One eyebrow rose, then the other.

"That was Sydney," he told her. "Their Young Pretender has been kicked out of the fouled Australian nest by Mum. The hot buzz Down Under has him winging his way here to plop his unwanted arse on our throne."

"It's not mine," Liz said, with a nod at the storm still raging in Parliament. "As far as I'm concerned, Pal Hal can rent out the last Royal bedroom to a honeymoon couple from Iowa."

Airborne • Phillipine Sea

THEY REFUELED THE private jet at Merluna, on the far northern tip of Cape York. Their flight path was declared as due-west to Darwin... then, still blacked out, they went north again instead. The last thing Richard saw of Australia was a flashing light on Prince of Wales Island.

"When coincidences like this happen, it's hard not to believe in omens," he said to Lady Bronwen, in the seat across from him. The two masked men still hadn't shown their faces. Except for the refueling, the pair had remained hidden on the flight deck. "When am I going to meet the rest of your team," he asked the astonishing old woman who had somehow recruited them, as the Torres Strait passed below and the dark mass of Papua New Guinea emerged beneath clouds in the first hint of dawn light.

"You can meet when we enter the American Trust Territory. It would hardly be suitable for the future sovereign to acknowledge persons responsible for an illegal act committed on the territory of a state friendly to Britain while he was still within that territory. Your Australian passport had been rescinded, if you remember."

"Of course I do. But isn't it just as illegal for me to leave without a passport?"

"For whom you were. Not for whom you *are*. The Sovereign is the one British citizen who does not require a passport."

"But I'm not a Sovereign yet."

"You are," she repeated. "I have proclaimed you. It is now up to Parliament to show proof, in law, why Your Royal Highness's claim to Succeed is invalid."

The old Herald's wordgames made Richard's head throb. He shut his eyes and managed to doze. The rising sun woke him up again. They had left the northern coast of New Guinea behind at Wewak. The Phillipine Sea was shimmering gold. The cabin to the flight deck opened. His two hidden guardians appeared. The tall one pulled off his hood, and saluted.

"Your Royal Highness," said Lady Bronwen, "may I present Colonel Hector MacKenzie, Royal Marine Commandos."

A typical Colonel Blimp, Richard decided immediately. Pickle-arsed and stuffily humorless, the stage military appearance was what he could have expected from hearing a la-de-da Brit trying to pass itself off as a Scot.

"We have just crossed the Line, Your Royal Highness," this Commando automaton advised him in its clipped hybrid accent. "The Equator forms the boundary of the US Trust possessions. As we're now on auto-pilot, I should like you also to meet Regimental Sergeant-Major Wallop."

The shorter figure yanked off its hood, stamped its foot so hard that the fuselage rattled, and bellowed in Cockney as it saluted, "At Your Royal Highness' service!" The Sergeant-Major at least looked human. Wallop's nose was spread across most of his square face. He had hands the size of pewter plates, black eyes, and an amiable gap-toothed grin.

"Good morning, Sergeant."

Richard shook hands — and then didn't know what else to say. He was struck again by the impossible enormity of the whole deal. How could either of these Englishmen truly accept an Australian actor as their *King?*

"Do we have some breakfast for His Royal Highness, Colonel?"

Lady Bronwen came to his conversational rescue, but it could only be for a couple of minutes. Somehow he had to handle the situation. While the Royal Marines provided trays from the cockpit, he willed himself to feel the strength of conviction that had come to him for that strange moment when he was standing on the old aborigine's Song Line.

"Ham and eggs, Your Royal Highness."

Wallop presented the tray with another hull-shattering salute that seemed even dumber than a curtsey in the narrow and fragile aircraft cabin. It was no use anyway, Richard thought: mentally he remained still just himself. He ate the food and watched Eauripik Atoll, the first of the Caroline Islands, appear outside the window.

"It will come, my dear." As though she could read his thoughts, the old woman leaned across and clasped his hand.

"It won't, Lady Bron. I might get used to the bowing and scraping, but I won't ever believe it's genuine. On stage that doesn't matter, but in real life..."

He looked down at the other green dotted atolls in their circles of white where the rolling Pacific broke against their coral reefs. Life was simple down there. Fish and swim; make love and eat coconuts...

"What you have yet to realize," she said, "is that nothing in the Monarch's life is easy. Forms of address are the least of it. For now, simply accept what people like these brave soldiers offer you in good faith, and be yourself — as I have seen you in your better moments."

She smiled and kissed his cheek. At the same moment the jet's nose dipped as they began to descend. The door from the flight deck opened again to show the happy Highland granite visage of the pickle-arsed Colonel.

"We shall be refueling in Guam," MacKenzie declared with no greater enthusiasm than last time. "Then we shall do a long hop to Adak, in the Aleutians, and follow the Great Circle from there, over the pole to home. Your Royal Highness's presence has not been announced in advance, there may be some Press flap when they know that you're on board, but nothing that Wallop can't handle."

Richard didn't doubt that part. Sergeant-Major Brick Shithouse could probably even tackle the Japanese maniac, Kimura!

"I have a question," he said to MacKenzie. "Correction, before that I have a request. No: make it an order. Out of the public eye, 'Sir' is plenty for my title, and that in small doses."

"Yes sir. And what was the question?"

"I want to know the real score about Captain Sumo, the Japanese so-called reporter."

"Kimura Itaro, sir, is a senior personal bodyguard for the Japanese Imperial Family."

"So what was he doing with me?"

The Colonel gave him a smile of razor-thin ice and said, "The Japanese still hold rather old-fashioned ideas about honor and obligation, sir. Because a Japanese was involved in the Sandringham affair, they've taken it on themselves to guard you. I regret if Kimura got underfoot."

"He was lying on top of me like a ton of solid rock." Richard added for Lady Bronwen's benefit, ignoring the previous Highland sarcasm. "Kimura thought he was saving me from a man called Bill Lamb. The IRA assassin who murdered Sally."

"Then sadly, we must assume he was right. Ah, there is Umatac! Magellan called in here on his circumnavigation."

MacKenzie took his unfunny Blimp ha-ha about honor and Kimura back to the cockpit. The jet banked steeply. Richard heard the thud of the landing gear dropping into position. A village with a Spanish looking, twin-cupola church came into view below his window. A ridge of hills inland was wooded. Most of the rest of the coast seemed to be abandoned US military installations from the Cold War era, now being converted into condo units with golf courses and swimming pools.

As the jet leveled onto its approach, Richard wondered how the old woman across from him knew so much about remote Pacific geography, and what the hell she was doing keeping company with Imperial Japanese hitmen, and stand-up comic Marine Commandos. The jet landed with the lightest swish of rubber, reversed thrust, decelerated past a row of tourist jumbos waiting to take off, and turned in to a bay marked, Independent Arrivals. The engines died. Richard stood and stretched.

"I'll be glad of a walk before that grind over the Pole," he said to Lady Bronwen, as he helped her up.

"If you don't mind, sir." MacKenzie already stood in front of him, blocking the door. "I shall check things out. The Sergeant-Major will stay with you."

It was an order. He watched the dour senior commando climb down the steps to the tarmac, then Wallop's body filled the vacant opening, except for a fringe of daylight which let in heavily humid tropic air, perfumed with flowers and aviation fuel. A tanker truck came up to replenish them, with a sanitation pumper behind it. Richard looked through the cracks around his watchdog as the tanker driver buttoned on a filler hose.

As the pumper did a U turn and came in beside it, Wallop said, "Christ! We're off, sir! Pardon my French."

A battery of flashbulbs exploded from the sanitation unit. The sergeant bulldogged Richard back from the hatch and slammed it shut. Thirty seconds later there was a pounding outside it. Wallop grunted, "Not bloody likely."

"It's MacKenzie."

Wallop re-opened the hatch. "Sorry, sir."

The Colonel's long face looked grimmer than ever as he turned to the Welsh Herald. "I didn't get further than the Gate when I was met by that crowd outside and the Governor of the island."

"The Governor, himself?" said Lady Bronwen. "That was kind, but I don't think we should start on any protocol before our final destination."

"It wasn't protocol," said MacKenzie. "His Royal Highness has been declared *persona non grata* in Britain, by London. The American State Department is deciding how to respond."

If it took two years to get a passport out of them, Richard thought, he could be in for a long wait.

Two

Melbourne • Airport

McDERMID HAD A real ball-crunching problem. The Americans were holding his Target for him, on Guam — but the island was too small. The chance of getting in undetected was tiny. Getting out, after a successful operation, made it a suicide mission and finding himself in the Australian bush with the Anti-Terror living legend, Kimura, had been close enough! With the help of the Japanese and a loonie old Welsh woman the Brit commando bastards had managed to grab his Target, but what would they do with him when the Yanks let the man go?

That would have to be soon. The Irish vote in the States was powerful but voters had short memories. The bastard had an American mother and Yanks were permanently on heat for any Brit Royal. With her re-election coming up, President Maureen Nimitz would give in. McDermid sat at the bar in the airport lounge and examined a Quantas route map. There was no short way back to Britain. The kidnappers could go east, to Hawaii, and the States: or west, via Indonesia, and all the Middle East hot spots!

It would be to America, but...

McDermid looked again at the tiny green dot representing American sovereignty in the South Pacific. To leave a mark in history that would serve as an adequate memorial for all the Martyrs of the Struggle, he was prepared to die. But the Target had to go with him to hell. The odds of bringing that off in Guam were not acceptable.

And yet...

"Attention passengers on Quantas 151: we are now boarding at Gate 5 for Honolulu."

He might never get another chance. Hawaii was halfway to America, and one jump ahead of the opposition, but...

"Last ticketing call for passengers wishing to take Flight 176, now preparing at Gate 7, for Hong Kong, via Guam."

Guam, or Hawaii...?

A woman with quite magnificent tits walked by him.

McDermid made his decision.

Guam

THE HEAT AND humidity grew steadily worse inside the cabin of the jet. If the fuselage door was opened the air outside was almost as bad. "Not helped by the howling of a thousand bloody hyenas!" Richard remarked to MacKenzie.

"There aren't a thousand Press, sir. Possibly three hundred."

That literal correction was another example of Highland humor. Either figure, more media were arriving every minute. And there was no movement from the American government. Being cooped up for five hours was tough on him — but it was Lady Bronwen that Richard was worried about. Her face was drawn; her skin had lost its bloom of English roses and had become sallow, almost transparent. She was finally showing her age.

"They can't keep you here," he told her. "You must go to a hotel and rest."

"I appreciate your concern, Sir, however my place is with my Sovereign."

"That's bull, Lady B."

"No, my dear," she gave a wan smile in the direction of the closed hatch, "with that crowd outside, it's public relations."

Which gave him the idea.

"Open it," he told Wallop. "The hatch, man! I'm not going to escape. I want to talk to them."

The Sergeant-Major looked at his superior. The Colonel nodded, but stationed himself on the other side of the doorway, in case. As it swung outwards the familiar battery of camera flashes exploded.

"Are you a prisoner of the US government?"

"Why did you run?"

"When did you last see Sally McGuire alive?"

The last question cut through all the rest and stopped Richard dead. It was shouted by a young woman of about Sally's age. He had never seen her before, yet she glared at him with a hostility that was personal.

"The Queensland State Police have put out a wanted-for-enquiries bulletin," she shouted. "Wasn't your reason for running because you knew you'd be wanted for murder in Australia?"

He started to back away from the door, from the question... and then he thought: *If I don't face this down, I'm finished.*

His actor's instinct helped him. Against this kind of audience shouting was pointless: speaking quietly would compel them to listen. Looking directly at the hostile bitch accusing him, he said, "I saw Sally the night before she was killed. We had a disagreement, which I bitterly regret, but it's no secret. Because the Press was there, the whole world knows about it. She was with another man, called Lamb, an American who probably had IRA connections. If you really want to find the truth about her murder, I suggest you look for him."

"So you were jealous."

The female reporter's expression was as implacably hostile as it had been before.

"A waste of breath, sir." MacKenzie said tightly from the sidelines. "Sergeant-Major, close the hatch."

The door began to swing closed. Another reporter shouted,

"She's fainting!"

Richard looked sideways in time to see Lady Bronwen collapse in the opening beside him.

The hyenas surged forward, cameras and recorders grinding. Once again, his pent-up rage at their insensitivity exploded.

"Get away and give her air. If you bastards, and the American government, had a scrap of humanity or decency you'd find a doctor, not persecute a wonderful old woman."

He dropped to his knees and took her head in his hands, stroked her brow, and white hair. He thought of how much she had been through to help him and felt tears prickling.

"Wallop! Stretcher from the flight deck!" MacKenzie pointed forward to a red cross, with an arrow. The sergeant had the stretcher unstrapped and back in thirty seconds. Between them they lifted Lady Bronwen onto its canvas. And finally an airport medic team arrived.

The stretcher was eased out through the fuselage. Richard had to let her go. He stroked her hair one last time, and was about to push himself up off his knees when her lips moved. He put his ear down towards her mouth again. Her breath was faint, barely a whisper. He bent closer to catch her last words. To his total astonishment, one translucent, tremulous eyelid of this amazing person unmistakeably winked.

"I'm fine, dear boy," she said. "Ask Washington for Political Asylum. That should prod Hal Roper where it hurts."

Downing Street

FOR ROGER SLADE, his situation since the mandarin's car accident had been like sitting on the lip of a volcano primed to errupt. The coroner's enquiry this morning had blamed the sophisticated electronics of the car for the crash, but Slade knew it was the photographic sophistication in the office ceiling above him that had produced the Commercial Investment Review mandarin's sudden and violent death.

The pinpoint red light above the Hepplewhite desk had disappeared, and the hole in the plaster had been closed. Which only made the terror worse! Now Slade didn't know where to look. He had immediately burned his coded diary, abandoning his dream of adding to his pension by its contents, but he didn't doubt for a second that "Muwi", with his scarred hand and hangman's eyes, still had him under constant —

"Come in please, Roger."

Roper's voice was normal... but when Slade went through the connecting door, Love was there before him. The Security man was sitting in a perfectly tailored banker's suit as appropriate as it would be on a butcher in a slaughterhouse.

"I'd like to finalize the order of business for this afternoon's Inner Cabinet meeting," Roper told his PPS.

"Of course, Prime Minister." Slade checked his shorthand notes, and tried to ignore the fact that his hand holding them was shaking. "The new Land Corporations Act," he said, "allotted time for discussion, ten minutes. The Youth Conscription Act, to control sports attendance violence, surtitled 'A Better Britain', fifteen minutes. The revised list of new Justices, five minutes. I don't think there's anything else."

"Just this." Roper slid a paper across the desk. "I don't expect it to be controversial. Five minutes more for discussion should be enough."

Slade took the paper. The provisional title was a non-comittal, CAA.

"The initials refer to College of Arms abolition," the PM elaborated, "but only as an official adjunct to government. As a prime earner of hard currency in the Ancestor business, the College's status of a publicly held corporation will remain. That's all."

As Slade left the office, Roper gave his man-of-the-people chuckle. Love's eyes were as cold as his slaughterhouse suit.

Tower Power

LIZ NORMALLY NEVER used the Bridge — it was always up for a cruise ship — but to save five miles in the evening rush she changed her mind. Which was why she was now stuck looking at the Thames growing dark and the "De-regulated" taxi meter clicking past twenty pounds. She could see her destination, less than half a mile away on the other side of the river, with the setting sun gleaming off its western-facing windows. Her helpless immobility was like her life.

WANTED FOR MURDER !

The tabloid being peddled beside her said four people out of five thought the Prime Minister was their Most Admired Man in Britain. Only two out of five wanted a King. With a Queensland warrant for his arrest, only one-fifth still thought they wanted the runaway Australian. In the light of all that, Liz thought, her republican's conspiracy with the Duke of Dorset to bring Lady Bronwen's candidate back to sit on the Throne in Westminster Abbey could be described as an uphill struggle.

Hector's situation was truly serious.

The bridge siren sounded. The deck began dropping. A small tug appeared, pulling an antiquated pile driver which was broken. A chorus of fury sounded from all the rush-hour horns. At last Liz moved forward.

The name she was looking for wasn't on the names board at the entrance to the building's lobby, but the flat number she had been given by her BBC supervisor was listed, against Riverside Holdings Ltd. She positioned herself in front of the entry camera and pressed the tele-buzzer.

"Yes?"

The voice of the unseen tennant inspecting her was neutral. Not welcoming, but not fearful either. This was a woman sure of her position.

"It's Liz Ponti. I telephoned earlier."

"From Cousin Beeb. I'll send the lift down. Come on in."

The building was expensive, but not flashy. When the door to the penthouse opened, its resident fitted the pattern. Liz detected a family resemblance to her supervisor in the width of the woman's brow, but his cousin was her own age. The ashblonde hair of Roper's mistress was long and swayed across her back as she walked past what Liz recognized as a mega-million *Venus* by Titian. The live one was wearing a simple, floor-length dress of patterned green silk that hung loosely, yet managed to show that the body underneath wore nothing else, and was smashing.

"A drink?" the woman asked. "I'm having one?"

"Please. Gin and tonic," Liz replied, thinking, She doesn't look that way for me. It surprised her again that Roper could have kept such an arrangement under wraps — or his ownership of such an incredibly valuable painting as the Titian.

"Cousin Beeb was rather hush-hush about you," the woman said, passing the glass, and sitting into a suede chair in a single graceful motion. "He mentioned the Speaker. I suppose it's something Parliament?"

"No," Liz said, "it's personal."

"Surprise surprise." The woman raised her glass in a gesture that was relaxed, yet more guarded at the same time. "Not an unpleasant one, I hope. Since you're with my cousin's investigation team at BBC."

"I'm not here for anything to do with work. A close friend has been caught up by the Justice Commission and I want to help him."

The woman sipped, then tapped the side of her glass with a perfectly shaped nail in natural polish. "I don't know what on earth I can do, Liz, but we're all girls together. Tell me the close friend's story. "

"He's a Royal Marine colonel, in the Anti-Terror side. Or he was, before that deadly old hag and her Commission got at him. The point is that he's innocent. He happened to have a brother-in-law whom he still liked after a divorce. It could happen to anyone."

"Not to me. I'm an only child."

"But you have a close friend as well."

"Ah." The woman smiled ironically, and glanced at a clock with the lights of the Embankment and Westminster showing behind it through a window beside the Titian painting. She said to Liz, "I don't like the Justice granny either, but someone has to decide these matters."

"Your close friend, the Prime Minister."

For the first time, a hint of insecurity showed beneath the poised facade. The woman's perfect skin flushed on her cheekbones. She put down her glass with a click, stood up, and said "We don't use that name here."

"Then we won't use it again." Liz rose as well. "The only name I want to see is Hector MacKenzie's before the weekend, released from wherever they're holding him."

"This week my close friend has rather a lot on his mind." The woman suddenly swung around to face her. "Did you say MacKenzie?" Liz nodded. "Then I can't help you."

"I'm sure such a capable *friend,*" Liz emphasized the last word, "can always find a moment to squeeze an extra thing in on the side."

"Not when it's on the island of Guam, my dear. I saw your Royal Marine there, only ten minutes ago."

Three

Agaña

THE GUAM CAPITAL was relatively safe, MacKenzie concluded, as he rode in a closed US Security van with the Candidate to visit Lady Bronwen in the local hospital. He found it a constant mental effort to think of the Australian *as* a Candidate, but doing so was the only way to perform his task. Since his charge's puerile nickname of "Captain Sumo"... only a blind fool would treat Kimura Itaro with anything but the most complete respect. Especially when the Japanese had saved that fool's life! The single positive facet displayed by the Candidate since leaving Australia was his apparently genuine concern for Lady Bronwen. But even that could be mere acting.

Honor and obligation.

MacKenzie understood exactly the attitude of the Japanese people. His own duty at the moment was to protect the Candidate but, until royal blood was confirmed by scientific proof, he was not obliged to serve him.

RICHARD WATCHED his taciturn Commando bodyguard nod brusquely at the two overweight US security personnel in the front of the van. It stopped. He got out to find four sidewalk palm trees sagging under a sullen gray sky and the weight of humidity. March was a typhoon month and the hospital had plywood shutters ready outside its entrance. His allied security nursemaids formed up beside the shutters in a triangle: MacKenzie leading, the Americans behind, and himself in the center.

"Have you been granted asylum?"

"Where will you go if you don't get it?"

The hyena pack was already in place and baying. He shook his head at the first question, and didn't have any answer for the second. As he was taken up in the hospital's emergency elevator he thought that at certain moments, like the last talk with his mother, or getting his DNA blood test, or on top of the Lizard Egg rocks, his goal and the reasons for attempting it seemed clear, but afterwards...

"Three cheers for His Royal Highness!"

"Hip hip hooray!"

The ragged cheer came from a little group of nurses, unmistakably

British, even without their waving Union Jacks. Taken by surprise Richard stopped. The two US Security people behind pushed him on.

"Good luck!"

"God bless Your Royal Highness!"

The women's calls sounded ridiculous and pathetic. He was a total stranger to them, not a royal anything. And yet he couldn't help being moved by their display of loyalty to a symbol so far removed from this tiny, out-of-the-way dot of American territory.

"To your right, please sir."

A bigger surprise. The speaker was one of his US bodyguards. The women's display had made an instant change in the man's behavior. And the altered perception of his own image was contagious: somehow it was transferred in advance, so that each door Richard now went through found hospital personnel running, or standing on tip-toe to see him. They didn't cheer like the British, but some clapped and suddenly he realized, *They all believe!*

Even on television. The video crews hadn't been fooled by Security using the Emergency elevator. Ten cameras recorded his hand turning the knob and opening the door to Lady Bronwen's room.

"You look happier, my dear."

"So do you, Lady B."

The Welsh herald was sitting up in bed reading a pile of newspapers. Her eyes sparkled and the color had returned to her cheeks. The grim MacKenzie closed the door on the press, remaining outside with the US security to guard it. Lady Bronwen patted her blanket. Richard went across and sat down on the bed. He told her about the nurses' cheering, and the extraordinary general change of attitude.

"There's nothing extraordinary about it," she said firmly. "I told you before, other people aren't the problem. They *want* to believe. It's you who have had trouble accepting that you can be their symbol, but now you see that you are, and that's all there is to it. The press will be next, and then the job's done."

"King of Guam?"

"Ah yes." She smiled at his irony. "There is the small matter of persuading our American friends to behave as hosts, and not jailers."

"With the Queensland State Police wanting me for murder," he said, "and the British government refusing entry to a criminal, persuading Washington to do anything except kick me out seems like a bloody enormous matter."

"You have not been charged by the Brisbane police."

"But traveling without a passport —"

"The Whitehall fuss about that is a trumped-up piece of nonsense. Once the Americans recognize you, such bureaucratic rubbish will be given very short shrift by your loyal subjects."

"One in five of them." Richard jabbed the front page of the top newspaper. "In the last edition the bastards were accusing me of killing Sally, and now they're back on Anna! Look at this —." He held it up. " 'Grandmother a Russian Countess! Was her blood too blue for him?' " He threw the rag down in disgust.

"I understand your feelings towards the reporters," Lady Bronwen told him, "but their prurient interest is our main weapon."

"About Anna? You're not serious? For God's sake, when my life was falling apart she walked out on me."

He got off the bed and went to the window to try and cool down. The fronds of the palm trees outside the hospital were slapping the sides of the building. The wind had risen.

"I want you to write her a letter," said the woman behind him.

He swung around. "I have nothing to say to her. I don't even think of her. And she bloody well doesn't waste any breath over me."

"The hospital have kindly provided a room with a writing desk. Colonel MacKenzie will escort you."

"No he bloody won't." Richard glared at the stubborn old body in the bed... and realized that he was responsible for her being there. "Look," he said, "I know you've done so much, and I must seem very ungrateful, but this is my private life. To put it without being rude, you just don't understand about a couple in our situation."

"Possibly not, my dear, but in that case humor a foolish old lady. It may help you to write if you remember that while Anna's grandmother may or may not have been a Russian countess, her father is a most influential United States Senator. And don't be afraid, the words to Anna will be there when you see the paper."

IT WAS CREAM beige, and said Agaña New Hospital on the letterhead. The rest of the page was as blank as Antarctica. Five minutes crawled by, one digital blink after another. The muffled noises of a hospital came faintly through the door. A call bell, wheels on institutional flooring, rapid footsteps, approaching and departing. A refuse truck backing up in an alley outside the window, sounding a bleeping alarm. Then the whine as the container was lifted, and the rattling crash as the garbage was emptied, and then another whine as it was crushed...

"Dear Anna," Richard found himself writing, *"I don't know why I threw out your last picture. It was the one when we were at Bondi Beach that first time, when you had just arrived in Australia, and wanted to see the closest salt water, do you remember...?"*

HE HAD TO sleep overnight in the jet, not the local Hilton. The bloody American government had finally made a decision and refused to let him use it! The plane was tolerable. Two seats at the rear came out and their cushions made a narrow mattress which split into a crevasse every time he rolled over. His Royal Marine bodyguards took equal watches dozing in the cockpit or guarding the door.

The wind rose and fell in gusts that rocked the fuselage: morning produced a Typhoon Preliminary Caution from the airport tower. Breakfast was brought to him by the US security team, specially prepared in the local FBI kitchen. When he hadn't been poisoned, he was actually allowed by their government in Washington to go to the Hilton to take a shower.

His allied guards formed up in the same triangular formation as yesterday's at the hospital to take him through the press. The pack had grown large enough to line both sides of the route across the tarmac to the hotel lobby.

And Kimura had rejoined them.

He spotted the Japanese as soon as the door in the fuselage opened. The Imperial bodyguard was disguised again as a newshound, but his massive shoulders were constantly identifiable, weaving through the ranks of his media colleagues, parallel to the line of advance to the shower.

Richard was permitted to take it by himself! Afterwards he felt clean enough to scan the papers which Wallop bought at the hotel magazine stand to see what new muck the tabloid world was spreading about him.

KING OF GUAM ?
LOVE LETTER TO ANNA !

"Jesus Christ," he swore to the sergeant. "The bloody boom-mikes pick up everything."

"It's not all that bad, sir. This one from New York says, 'Hip hip hooray! Let him in.' "

It was true. Since the cheering nurses, even one of the British papers seemed to have changed sides. Its headline was, "WHY NOT?" But then he made the mistake of reading the print and saw that it was meant to be funny. *"If it walks like a duck, and quacks like a duck..."*

The accompanying cartoon showed a trio of duck bodies. Richard's head was stuck on the middle one, between the last King's and their supposed mutual father's. Inside, on the pages no-one read, an editorial pontificated, "Nonetheless we support the monarchy."

"A strange way of showing it," he said to MacKenzie, as they were preparing to walk back under guard through the media pack to the jet. "I want to make another visit to Lady Bronwen. Miking our private conversation doesn't bother me, but it may have upset her."

"We no longer have clearance for a hospital visit."

The colonel's manner was even more brusque than usual. As though he was hiding something —

"She hasn't died?"

The old Herald's support and guidance was the only thing that made going on seem possible.

"Certainly not," MacKenzie replied, with another iced smile. "The Lady Bronwen is completely herself again. She left us by commercial air, last night."

Bar Harbor

ANNA HAD BEEN alerted by Six-Base's overnight transmissions that she was in the news. What she had no idea of as the *Melville* entered the harbor was the scale of the press reaction. The Deep Six dock was clear, but the parking lot outside the security fence behind it was jammed. She could see the logos of four TV networks, and at least a dozen vans with satellite relay antennas. The still cameras were too many to count.

"My God," she said, aghast, to Jack Nash, "if that's all waiting for me, I can't cope."

"I can," the Canadian replied with a grin. "We need more financial backing for next month's run. With free publicity on this scale we could get enough cash to hunt Archy for a year! You stay out of sight. I'll tell them we let you off at the Swanns Island Nature Reserve on our way in."

A helicopter picked that moment to come overhead and take her picture with two zoom lenses at a height of fifty feet.

Anna went inside the wheelhouse to try and think. She could stay on the company side of the fence for now, but sooner or later she would have to come out. *Godamn Richard!* she thought, as the first heaving line touched down on the dock. *I waste a year of my life and this crud is what I get.*

Jack Nash reversed thrust on the bow prop. The *Melville* drifted the last few inches and barely touched the bumper log beside the pilings. Normally Anna would feel elated that for a while there was no wet deck heaving beneath her feet. The combination this time of no Archy, and too much Richard, took any pleasure out of the homecoming.

Nash arrived at the foot of the ladder. He grabbed his kitbag, slung it over his shoulder, looked at her, and said, "Ready?"

"I guess."

She gathered her own things and followed him through the hatch.

THE NOISE THAT followed was like feeding time at the zoo. The reporters all yelled together through the fence. Any questions that Anna might have heard from the closest ones were drowned out by the bull horns of the people standing on vans.

"I can't handle this after all," she told Nash, as she stepped off the gangplank. "Go on without me. I'll wait a while in the office."

"You don't think I'm leaving you to go it alone?" With the hand that wasn't holding his kit bag, he gave her a bear hug, which got a new howl.

He opened the door of the lab building. When it closed behind her, the noise from the parking lot was miraculously cut. For this moment she could pretend that her life was her own again.

"Oh good!" exclaimed a female voice in a pronounced British accent. "My name is Lady Bronwen of Llangath. And you, my dear, of course, are Anna."

The speaker appeared from a corner by the fax machine, smiling and holding out both hands, as though they already knew each other.

"You're wondering how this strange old body recognized you." The woman took Anna's right hand and squeezed it reassuringly. "Your picture on the refrigerator."

"In our apartment? In Sydney? You were there?"

She recognized the old woman now, from the distinctive red dragon brooch which she wore on her ruffled blouse. It had caught her eye while she was watching one of Richard's relayed appearances on the news. Despite her white hair, and dowdy tweed skirt, the grandmotherly figure in front of her was something to do with deciding who became the next British monarch. Lady Bronwen gave another smile, kind but tired.

"I've been traveling rather a lot. I wonder if we might sit down."

"Use my office." Jack Nash ushered them both into it. "I'll be here when you're through," he said to Anna, as he closed the door.

The gesture was thoughtful but his office was furnished for people in wet-weather gear. There was only a single crack-bottomed, armless plastic chair with steel legs, and a stubby vinyl-covered chesterfield. The two women took opposite ends, and then sat looking at each other sideways, awkwardly, with Lady Bronwen's oversized tapestry handbag between them.

"I should start —"

"This has to be —"

They both spoke together, then broke off and laughed.

"That's better," said the old woman. "Although I knew from your photograph that we should be friends."

Her manner was so warm and sincere that Anna found herself automatically nodding in agreement...

"Hold it!" she said. "You've come a long way to do this, and I'm prepared to listen, but you should know right now, Richard and I split, and that's that. In fact, I'm amazed he kept my picture."

"It was in a refuse compactor, I'm afraid." The old woman patted Anna's knee in sympathy. "There are certainly moments when His Royal Highness is less than loveable, but he's improving. Despite his difficult circumstances, in the last forty-eight hours he has only had one tantrum with me. Which brings us to why I'm here with you."

She reached into her huge handbag, rummaged around, and withdrew an envelope. Anna saw her own name written in large capital letters.

"If that's from him, I'm not reading it." And then she saw the printed address, *Agaña New Hospital*, in the upper left hand corner, and said, "Has he been hurt?"

"Except for a trifling wound from rock splinters when the bullet missed him — physically, no. Psychologically, however..."

"*Somebody shot him?*"

"We believe the assassin was an agent of the IRA, acting in some bizarre form of revenge for events in Ireland. He had already killed a girl called Sally McGuire, in Brisbane."

"The redhead in the papers."

With conflicting emotions she opened the letter.

"Dear Anna. I don't know why I threw out your last picture... The one when we were at Bondi... Do you remember... ?"

She had not, but now she did. In ten pages he listed all the stupid things he had done to her, and all the great times they had; and what it was like to be shot at and cheered by total strangers: to be wanted for murder and refused a passport, and publicly jeered at worldwide and banned from your country.

"And to find out that you aren't your father's son. I know it doesn't make any difference, but it does. If your own mother can keep a secret like that from you — Anna, I don't know how I can ever believe or trust anyone anymore, but for life to go on I know that I must. I can! People like Lady Bronwen — and you. Because losing you was all my fault..."

She found herself crying. The old woman beside her on the cramped chesterfield passed her a tissue, which she accepted gratefully. And then she got angry, to be manipulated in this way. And then she thought what it must be like, to be in his situation. An ordinary man, suddenly called a Royal Highness.

"I won't live with Richard again," she told the Welsh Herald, "because I don't love him. But if he wants to find some kind of new home here in America, of course I'll help him."

Guam Field

RICHARD WAITED IN his jet prison for some word from Washington, but it never came. The US security people did install temporary fencing to keep the reporters far enough away so that he could exercise on his corner of the tarmac without being hounded by their questions. It didn't stop the lenses. The money the hyenas wasted on footage of him stretching, and kicking the jet's nosewheel tire would have paid for a bungalow on the runway, with all the comforts of home.

That thought made him wonder about his mother, and how the Prince of Wales explanation between her and his father had gone. If she did explain. More likely, she would have relapsed into her ordinary self and dodged the issue by going to a tea party for the Canberra Opera Society! He couldn't blame her. And he was certainly her son: not just for wanting to avoid facing unpleasant facts, their characters were alike in so many —

"No further, if you don't mind, sir."

Wallop's voice called out behind him. Richard turned and saw the sergeant doubling across the tarmac in his direction. The jet was about five hundred yards away. A garbage truck like the one at the hospital was backing up towards the gate through the fence, flashing warning lights and sounding a claxon. A handful of black-and-white birds following the truck weren't put off by the alarm. The wind had dropped. The sky was dark. There was a curious sense of peace.

"Sorry, Sergeant-Major," he told his arriving watchdog, "I didn't realize I had gone so far." He added with a smile, "Not too many IRA killers out here."

"Not letting the bastards get you down, sir, that's the ticket. But no need to stretch our luck. The Colonel requests you to join him in the cabin."

Two strides later, with a collossal clap of thunder, the sky opened. Visibility fell to less than a hundred yards. Vague half-shapes of unidentified aircraft or support vehicles loomed all around him. Without Wallop he would have been lost. Only a couple of media vans still remained beyond the fence. On this side of it, his aircraft sat between the sanitary pumper and a pair of abandoned luggage tractors; they corraled the private jet like a settler's wagon-train circle with one wagon missing at the nose. Head down and soaked to the skin Richard ran up the ladder two steps at a time and leaped through the open fuselage door into the cabin... where he smashed into a body made of iron, and collapsed on the deck.

"My apology, sir, for such clumsiness."

He found himself sitting in a small lake, looking up at Kimura! The Japanese bowed. MacKenzie stood in the aisle behind, wearing his usual grim expression. A shrieking gust of wind filled the cabin. Wallop got blown in with it and slammed the hatch.

"Weather warning is now Typhoon Imminent, Colonel. Field closed. All ground support canceled."

MacKenzie grunted, then said, "Go on," to Kimura.

"Thank you, Colonel." The Japanese gave another abbreviated bow. "And for Your Royal Highness's kind attention, as I have just explained to my British colleagues, I have been fortunate enough to confirm identity of assailant who fired at you near your cabin. Although gun is not his usual weapon. He prefers explosives."

Richard said, "The son of a bitch murdered Sally with his bare hands."

"He is not predictable, sir. He has many aliases. His true name is McDermid. He has functioned for many years as IRA's principal assassin against defined political targets. Specifically, single individuals of prominence, such as yourself."

Kimura bowed yet again, but the Asian politeness only deepened the fear that Richard felt trickling with the rain down the small of his back. He said to MacKenzie, "What else?"

"McDermid was seen at Melbourne, beside the boarding gate for Guam."

The fear reached the base of his spine. Wallop handed him a towel. He pulled his soaked shirt off and dried his head. "Go on, Colonel."

"Two hours ago an occidental male of a similar description, dressed as a laborer, was reported by a kitchen worker, near the Guam hospital."

Richard tried to remain calm, toweling his armpits. They stayed ringing wet. Outside the closest window, one of the flashing lights on the garbage truck was backing slowly through the fence gate.

"In Anti-Terror," MacKenzie said, "one of the major problems is the phenomenon we call contagion, or the power of misplaced association. Once a description starts the rounds, there will always be a reported sighting."

"You mean we don't really know whether he's here or not?"

The refuse truck had lost its escorting birds. The storm had done what the warning lights and klaxon could never —

Misplaced association.

He pointed through the window and said to the Colonel, "Wallop told us all ground support is canceled. There was a garbage truck like that one, yesterday, at the hospital."

HIS BODYGUARDS REACTED in a single blur of motion. MacKenzie slammed forward into the cockpit. Wallop grabbed an automatic rifle, flung open the fuselage door and braced himself against it. Kimura said, "Please excuse, sir," at the same time dropping Richard to the cabin floor, then throwing his massive torso on top.

Pinioned by the weight, Richard could scarcely breathe. Under his heart he felt a shudder run through the jet. Its engines were starting! But the screaming wind from the typhoon's approach was even louder. Through a small gap between his right arm and one of Kimura's shoulders he saw the flashing light of the garbage truck drawing closer. It was past the sanitary pumper before he realized its aim: If it filled the gap in the wagon-train circle, the jet couldn't move.

But MacKenzie was already applying throttle. The fragment of fence beyond the garbage truck was sliding backwards. Only creeping, a man could walk faster, and the truck was backing up at twice the speed. The fence crept ten yards back, twenty. The truck came forward fifty.

Wallop fired.

A rapid burst. Trapped beneath Kimura, Richard felt his ears crack from the bullets, yet the noise seemed to be absorbed, half by the turbine howl and half by the wind.

"Got him, sir! Right rear wheel. Both tires."

The light on the refuse truck dropped abruptly one foot lower. But it was still moving, at a right angle to the jet, almost in position to close the gap. The turbines' howl was now louder than the wind, full throttle. The fence shifted faster. But the truck was already in line with the starboard wing.

"I can make clearance," MacKenzie bellowed from the cockpit. "Sergeant, aim for the cab!"

A second volley burst from Wallop's automatic. Kimura's weight pressed down so hard that a welding ridge in the cabin floor beneath the carpet dug into one of Richard's ribs. Getting shot was better than this slow death from suffocation. With his free hand he grasped the base of the closest seat and yanked as hard as he could. The Japanese fell off him, sideways into the aisle. Richard got to his feet. The truck had disappeared from the fuselage opening. Now he could see it ahead through the door to the cockpit.

"Sir, you must allow!"

Kimura blocked him against the seats like a one-man line of football tackles.

"Godamn it," Richard shouted. "If I'm going to die, I want to see it happen. And that's an order."

Kimura hissed himself away to a six-inch screening distance. The garbage truck was beside the starboard cockpit window. Wallop fired a third time. The safety glass of the truck's windshield turned white. But the flashing light was right against them.

"They're going to detonate!" MacKenzie turned his head, and saw Richard standing. "Wallop, Kimura, put him down!"

Four hundred pounds of muscle flattened him. As he went down again for the count, he saw the leading edge of the jet's wing scrape sparks on top of the truck.

This time he truly could not breathe. A weird pattern of black lines and deep blue dots formed on the inside of his closed eyes, to become brilliant yellow, slashed with crimson. The deck under him felt as though a huge fist outside it had punched him in the groin. He was submerged by a rolling wave of nausea...

"So deeply sorry."

"Sir?"

He opened his eyes. His allied guards were bending over him. The fuselage door was somehow closed. The jet had stopped moving. MacKenzie had arrived from the flight deck. Wallop said with concern, "We could only protect the top of the body, sir. His Highness took the hull concussion."

There was a stench of something scorched. Richard saw that the hair on the right side of the Sergeant-Major's head was frizzed like a singed chicken. Kimura's right cheek was bright red instead of pale amber. And the insulation on the door panel had melted.

He murmured to MacKenzie, "So there was a bomb."

"Thank God!" exclaimed the nerveless commando colonel, "Your Highness can speak!"

THEY LIFTED HIM into a seat, and stripped off the rest of his soaked clothes. He had a massive welt, already bruising, from his navel down to his upper right groin, but it stopped at the line of his pubic arch. MacKenzie probed his abdomen carefully, with evident medical skill, then produced the verdict with an almost human smile.

"Nothing smashed in a delicate area, but you came unpleasantly close to not being a father."

"In that case, Colonel," Richard replied with a weak grin, "you would have needed a new candidate. I'd have been off the hook."

"There is no other candidate, sir. After your subjects hear of this attempt, I'd say you're hooked for as long as you want the job."

His subjects.

The thought was almost as astonishing as MacKenzie's revelation of some human emotion. Richard pulled on a pair of dry pants that Wallop provided. The wreck of the refuse truck was still flaming on the tarmac a hundred yards away. And people would hear about it. The two media vans behind the security fence were piercing the typhoon gloom with additional illumination from high-intensity lights. He said to MacKenzie "At least the negative PR may talk the Americans into letting us stay at the Hilton."

"With respect, sir, I cannot chance our opponents re-grouping by Your Highness remaining static."

The jet rocked in the latest gust. Richard said, "But the typhoon warning? All flights are canceled."

MacKenzie was already returning to the cockpit.

THE RAIN WAS once more so solid that they could only see one blue light at a time to follow the taxi strip. Their own running lights were off again. No one from the control tower could have seen them anyway. After passing only three of the blue lights, even the flaming wreck of the truck was absorbed by the storm.

At fifty blue lights the bulbs changed to red.

"Cautionary hold, for closed runway," Richard heard MacKenzie tell Wallop. "From here it's Hobson's Choice. Using the East-West strip, we get the crosswind. North-South, it's up our arse. Cross at this velocity would wipe us for certain. The tail-wind will only do it if I can't hold the nose."

That didn't sound like any choice. Buffeted sideways despite twenty degrees of opposite rudder, they moved beyond the red lights of the East-West runway, and found another row of blues. Then the reds of the North-South hold. The sideways buffeting changed to a peculiar see-saw motion, front to back. The red lights became amber, the see-saw stopped, and the rain lessened. Richard counted ten amber lights stretching ahead on each side of the runway. Take-off might not be totally suicidal.

Wallop said, "Running final instrument check, sir."

Now there were twenty ambers. For the first time the whining hum of the jet turbines was audible instead of the wind. The typhoon must only have grazed —

"Guam Tower calling. This is a military command. Private Flight on runway Two, stay where you are."

"No reply!" MacKenzie snapped at Wallop.

"We've got a problem, Colonel."

"Let the diplomats fight it."

"Not the Tower, sir. I'm getting a hydraulic fault signal from our right brake."

All the runway lights went out.

THE FULL FURY of the storm returned. To MacKenzie the night outside his cockpit window was as black as his sabotage clothing. Only the green phosphor glow of the instrument panel broke the darkness. A single red LED lamp on the right side revealed the brake hydraulic line fractured by the explosion.

"How bad is it?" he asked Wallop.

"No sweat at this end, sir. Coming down at the other…?"

"Private Flight, hear this. The field is being blocked with vehicles. Do not attempt —"

MacKenzie switched off the circuit. Two things had changed about his task: the young man behind him possessed true courage; and when his eyes opened after the bomb blast, their expression looked Royal.

"Prepare His Highness," he said to Kimura in the cabin. "We're going."

RICHARD SAT IN the seat closest to the open cockpit door. In addition to his seat belt he was protected by a parachute pack, two life jackets, and a dozen spare flotation cushions forced on him by Kimura. Because of the mechanical fault the jet couldn't first build engine power while holding on its brakes. They had to start from zero thrust, seeing nothing. Their floodlights were off in case the Guam military decided to give a really stupid order.

Open fire?

Anything seemed possible. If it came, Richard thought, there would be no way of knowing. No radio. No runway lights. No radar echoes of deadly moving vehicles or lifesaving navigational aids either: the torrential rain made the tubeface of the ground-control radar solid green.

And even if there were no human obstacles against them, a mere three thousand yards ahead was the typhoon driven rage of the Pacific...

"Brace for impact!"

The back of the jet was lifted as though the invisible hand which had socked Richard in the belly had now grabbed the aircraft's tail and tugged straight upwards. The nose dipped, slewed violently left, then right — the hand let go. The tail section slammed down. The nose bounced up . . . then leveled.

MacKenzie's voice said in its usual calm tone to Wallop, "Please read my range-remaining counter."

"Twenty-three hundred, sir. Twenty-two hundred. Twenty-one. Two thousand..."

The sergeant's voice was equally unruffled. Fifteen hundred yards. In three-quarters of a mile, one way or another, it would all be over. Richard unclenched his hands. There was nothing he could do. And in this minute between earth and heaven, suddenly he believed in God. Or fate. He just knew absolutely that something had marked him for a special —

"So!"

Kimura's breath hissed. The Americans must have changed their minds. The airfield was ablaze: every bulb had been turned on. Searchlights and runway lights all converged to mark the last of their strip, and the sky had cleared.

"Eight hundred, sir."

Caught in the searchlights the breaker line of the ocean ahead of them was a brilliant phosphorescent white... but then, black against the surf, Richard saw that not everyone had got the new word. A line of emergency and support vehicles were still ranged across the runway.

"Airborne." MacKenzie's voice was laconic. The last of the blocking vehicles which could have killed them swept by beneath the wings.

MacKenzie turned on the Tower circuit. "Thanks for the warm send-off, Guam. Request you ask Adak to be as kind at our arrival."

With salt water trailing from the undercarriage they turned north, to the Aleutian Islands.

Four

Beautiful Waikiki

McDermid strolled along the beach in front of the Diamond Head Hotel. He appeared calm but his mind was racing. He had guessed wrong on three counts: his target wasn't in Hawaii; there was no catchup flight McDermid could take from here to the Aleutians; and the bombing in Guam.

The attack had been meant to look like his trademark and for that there was only a single explanation. Britain and Guam were as far apart as it was possible to be on a route map, but British governments were used to running wars in remote corners. Hell, the bloody Brits invented cloak and dagger. Obviously this commando team who kidnapped the Target had rigged the bomb attempt themselves, to drum up sympathy among the royalists at home!

There was a flight leaving for London in three hours. Meanwhile, Waikiki was a pleasant spot to wait. The imported silver sand had been freshly groomed overnight and the first sunworshipers were already frying their skins. The Asian ones weren't good camouflage for a freckled Irishman, but a quartet of Caucasian females next to the catamaran concession looked promising.

McDermid strolled closer and saw that their shoulderbags all had Lufthansa logos, and their average age was mid-thirties. Flight attendants on stopover from Europe, mature enough to know how they wanted to fill their day off, and not going to waste any time getting started. They were watching a portable TV and looking dead bored by it.

"Gutentag, mein damen," he said to them, with a smile. "Would anyone want to share a catamaran?"

"You like sailing catamarans." The woman in the center of the group smiled back at him, and then at her companions. She had broad hips and a spandex hot-pink bikini, small enough to show that she was a natural Nordic blonde. The other three women giggled, and whispered to each other.

"I can get the beasts started," McDermid said, slapping one hull of the catamaran, "but when it comes time to turn for home, I never know what string to pull."

"You need some help pulling it?" The broad-hipped blonde laughed, and stared even more frankly at his crotch than the Cuban harbor pilot. Her companions giggled some more, then turned their attention to the mini television. On a news re-run his Target was being bombed in Guam again. When the bastard's Royal profile was shown in the next cut, the German women all sighed in unison.

"Okay," said the blonde, "let's go out on this beast, as you call it, and see what we pull."

She stood up and brushed sand off her thighs. The Hawaiian kid managing the boat concession slid the catamaran into the emerald water of the shallows. The blonde jumped up on the canvas platform stretched between the twin hulls, revealing more of her ample Teutonic charms. McDermid followed. The other German women waved and giggled. The Hawaiian kid pushed the cat out into deeper water. It glided a few feet and then stopped.

"Too early in the morning," said the Hawaiian. "You need the onshore wind in the afternoon."

"We don't care," the blonde replied in English, but looking at McDermid. "We shall have our beast-pulling lessons where we are."

She lay on her stomach and scissor-kicked lazily to get the cat a little further from the beach. The sail flapped once and then hung motionless. The double hull bobbed gently. The blonde rolled over, and up onto her elbow. McDermid dropped beside her on the canvas. She traced a finger on his chest, and down his belly...

"Ach! Mein Gott!"

The scream came from the women left behind on the beach. In a huddle of feminine excitement they were pointing at the television.

"Vas ist das?" the blonde called to them, while keeping her eyes and her finger both moving lower on McDermid.

"Der Prinz von Australier!"

The last word came as the blonde's finger slipped inside the waistband of McDermid's trunks. "What about the Prince?" she asked, keeping her eyes locked on McDermid's, as his prayers were answered.

"Hawaii!" the women shrieked. "He comes *here!*"

Midway

TO MACKENZIE, THE final island in the Hawaiian chain was a scimitar-shaped trace on his radar; at three hundred miles distance scarcely more visible than the sea return. Immediately after leaving Guam's airspace he had turned east and set the jet's indentification transponder to indicate a

Japanese civilian aircraft. With luck the double ruse should at least allow touchdown at Honolulu before the media got word.

At a hundred miles range the radar echo was solid. At fifty, the atoll was visible to the eye. Kimura, sitting beside him in the copilot's seat, said solemnly, "Here was our turning point, in Pacific War."

From a height of thirty-eight thousand feet, MacKenzie thought, it was hard to believe —

"No more screwing around, Limey!"

An American voice squawked from nowhere on the navigational radio net. Without a trace on the radar, a black boomerang shape suddenly appeared off each of the private jet's wingtips. There was nothing MacKenzie could do to evade this interception. The other aircraft were a pair of super Stealth Five fighters.

"Follow us down," said the American. "Make it now."

"No argument," MacKenzie replied. "You lead, we follow."

The black craft to starboard whipped upwards and took station above the private jet's nose. The fighter to port dropped and began a long glide. Midway appeared at the end of it as a pair of islands sharing a lagoon. MacKenzie rolled to a stop on the runway. The two escorting Stealths lifted off again and resumed a low altitude patrol. A military staff car drove up on the tarmac through a flock of mating Laysan Albatrosses.

"Bloody Goonies," said Wallop, opening the fuselage door. "On the bright side, sir, we've got His Highness halfway home."

That was no comfort to MacKenzie. He watched in silence as a gray-suited civilian got out of the staff car. The albatrosses clacked their beaks at each other and rolled their heads like drunk Marines after a week-long binge. The civilian walked through the birds without paying any attention, stopped at the foot of the private jet's ladder, held out a document, and said: "Empowered by this warrant from the Secretary of State, I must ask your passenger to accompany me."

MacKenzie unstrapped his seat harness and stepped down the ladder.

"Without British escort, Colonel."

The man put out an arm. MacKenzie struck it angrily aside. He said, "His Royal Highness goes nowhere —"

"On the contrary. The Prince goes exactly where the United States government says he goes. And how he goes."

Armed American combat troops in camouflage materialized from the dunes.

RICHARD SAW THE GI's and heard the title. Now he was being called a Prince, but as a jail Midway was even worse than Guam! One low building, a few Norfolk Pines, and ten thousand crazy birds bowing to him like Kimura as he climbed into the staff car. Ramrod-stiff, the Colonel and Wallop saluted. He wanted to shake MacKenzie's hand but with the cordon of troops between them he couldn't even do that.

Behind the pines a small helicopter was waiting. Richard climbed out of the car and got into the chopper with his new American civilian escort. The machine lifted off and flew across a narrow channel. On the far side was a second runway. A mid-sized jet aircraft was parked on it. A badge on the side was painted with some kind of US government insignia. He wasn't going to stay on Midway. The jet's engines were already idling.

The plane started to move even before he was seated. He couldn't see where it was heading because the shades were pulled down. He lifted one. All the windows had been painted on the inside with white paint. He could tell that it was daylight outside, nothing more.

"You will find reading materials, bite-size food products, and non-alcoholic beverages in the cabinet at the rear of the compartment, adjacent to the onboard hygiene facility," said his bureaucratic escort. "There is also a fold-down cot, midships, equipped with an anti-turbulence harness for retirement mode."

The civilian went forward through a door to the flight deck. Locking it. In spite of the American government's long-winded courtesies, Richard was still its prisoner. He walked up and down his flying cell, ate some food products, drank a non-alcoholic beverage, tried to scrape some of the white paint off one of the windows with his thumbnail. It didn't work, and the bite-sized food meant there weren't any knife-blades for a prisoner to use for scraping. Or slitting his wrists. Honolulu must be about a two hour hop. He decided to try some retirement mode.

HE WOKE TO feel gravity forcing his body against the anti-turbulence harness which he had fixed loosely across the cot. The aircraft was banking steeply beneath him. A small overhead spotlight shone down into his eyes. He reached up and tilted the light at a different angle. The rest of the cabin was dark. So was the space beyond the painted windows.

He couldn't be landing in Hawaii. The American government must have taken him to the Aleutian Islands after all. Like Napoleon exiled to St Helena, he would be stuck indefinitely on a volcanic rock in the Bering Sea.

The door from the flight deck opened. His civilian jailer said, "Landing will be in ten minutes, sir. Tooth-cleaning and shaving apparatus are in the onboard hygiene facility if you wish to freshen up."

"I don't. If any Press shits want more pictures they can have me as I am."

"The Department has gone to some pains to ensure that the media will not be present."

"I'll believe that when I see it."

The civilian shrugged and withdrew. Richard knew he was being childish, but feeling helpless brought out that kind of behavior. The wheels thumped down, the thrusters roared in reverse, the plane stopped. The fuselage door opened.

The night was black. It had been raining. The air felt bitter after the tropics. And his traveling wasn't over yet. Another helicopter waited, rotors swishing, lights blinking. He followed the man in the suit past two rows of armed guards to this latest chopper, felt the inevitable downdraft, climbed onboard, lifted off. He no longer cared where it was taking him. All his senses were numb.

It seemed only minutes before the next descent. Open the door again. Inrush of air. Down the ladder. Raining again. Shapes in yellow slickers were waiting to hustle him to his next prison cell. The navigational strobe light on the starboard engine pod flashed intermittently across the waiting faces. One moved forward, then stopped, as though uncertain how to greet him, then moved again. He was tired to death of protocol or Press games. He ignored the figure in the slicker... until he saw the face was Anna.

HIS FEET STOPPED. His mouth dropped open. He had nothing to say. *He wanted to ask her everything.* But she was biting her lip, and he knew that look. Already she was sorry she had come — wherever it was they were — and was wishing she was somewhere else, doing something more important like trolling for five-foot sea-worms.

"I don't know how to tell you," she said in her tense tone of voice that meant she didn't give a damn anyway. "I wanted it to be just the surprise of getting you political asylum on the Farm."

"Your father's farm? I'm in Virginia?"

She nodded. He couldn't believe. He said, "Asylum? The American government granted it?"

She nodded again. The Yank bureaucrat behind him was actually smiling! Her hands reached out hesitantly. Richard grabbed, and pulled her to him.

"No." She pulled back, away, maintaining her distance. He had been right the first time, she might have done something through her father to get him here to America but she didn't care personally. Not really. She said in the same tight voice, "There's no easy way to say this. We just heard ten minutes ago. From Canberra. Your mother is dead."

Five

Virginia

ANNA'S WORDS WERE simple enough for any child to understand, but their meaning wasn't clear to Richard. He heard her explain about a traffic accident, at high speed, in the Mercedes, coming off the Canberra-Sydney motorway, and it all made sense.

But not that his mother was dead.

That part wasn't possible. His mother always drove fast. She always took chances. She always made it.

Why hadn't he told her last time, when she drove away from the cabin, that he loved her?

"You're in shock," Anna said at some point. "Let's go inside."

He was still standing in the rain. He felt Anna hug him, and take his arm, and lead him away from the helicopter in the rain to a warm farmhouse kitchen, with a glowing wood stove and low beams, and strong coffee in an enamel pot and a bottle of brandy.

"Drink this," she said, after pouring both into a mug, because he was only standing staring, seeing nothing.

"Was she hurt?" he asked.

"I don't think your mother suffered. Apparently the police ambulance arrived almost at once. Drink your coffee, darling."

Richard took a gulp that burned, but he didn't feel it. He knew that Anna had called him darling. He sat down hard in a chair and spilled some of his coffee, and apologized.

"It doesn't matter," she said, "everything's old and comfortable here at the farm. Grace will fix things up in the morning."

"What time is it now?"

"Around two. Or it was when you landed."

An hour had passed. It was three now. A grandfather clock struck in the corner of the kitchen. He told Anna about the last ride with his mother, through the Snowy Mountains to the cabin, and her motorbike mini-dress with the huge red rose that she wore to a party for the Prince of Wales, who truly was his natural father.

"There was a traffic accident that night too," he said. "But she wasn't driving. She told me it wouldn't have happened if she had been."

The clock struck four. Anna said to him, "Don't talk any more. Come to bed."

She walked with him through the sleeping farmhouse and helped him take his clothes off. "I can't make love," he told her when she got in bed beside him under the quilted feather comforter. "Not after..."

But some time later, with her naked body warm against him, Richard found that he could. And they did.

He drifted to sleep on a wave of relaxation induced by sex and brandy, which blanked out the reality of life and death, until the nightmares started.

Westminster

SLADE'S DREAMS HAD been horrific since the slit throat of the old courtier, with the blood welling on the threadbare Palace sheets. Now they were joined by unspeakable images of the mandarin bureaucrat's head being smashed against a motorway abutment...

Unable to sleep he went in early to the office. Even there, he could feel the ground trembling. Roper's personal popularity was still eighty per cent in the tabloid polls but since the bombing attack against the Australian, the support for his candidacy to the Throne, which had dipped sharply, had jumped back even more so. Overnight, with this death of the man's mother, three out of five moronic Britons were now sure that he was suitable to be their King. Of course, anything from discovering that the man had a wart on his genitals to a change in his hair style could swing public opinion back again!

"PPS, come in please."

The PM's call light had been blinking. As Slade entered the inner office, Roper passed across a tape cassette.

"Put this into my usual quick reference form for delivery, and then alert the television people. You can say my speech to the House this afternoon will respond positively to this latest racial incident in Devon."

Slade hadn't noticed it. There were always racial incidents.

CURRY TOO HOT FOR LITTLE HOOKER !

The press clipping was only front page news on one of the worst tabloids, and as usual the the sex tag was misleading. A Pakistani family had opened a restaurant in a tiny and remote Devon village — Little Hooker, naturally. A molotov cocktail had subsequently been thrown through the kitchen window. Damage was minor. Slade read the label on the cassette:

" 'Best of Britain Areas Act'. Very well, Prime Minister."

He took the tape back to his office...just in time to meet the Coachman oaf, Stubbins, collecting the empty daily Despatch Box to deliver to nobody at Buckingham Palace.

"Morning, Mr Slade, sir," the fool said cheerily. "Won't be long now, eh?"

Slade ignored the greeting and said with annoyance, "What won't be long?"

"Before the old Box here is in harness again." Stubbins picked up the blue Morrocco case by its brass handle and gave a cretinous grin. "Like I told my Dolly-girl, with His Royal Highness in America, you and me could find ourselves back in regular business any day."

"The man is nobody's Royal anything," Slade reminded him sharply, "and the Aleutian Islands can scarcely be described as America."

"You know best, sir." Clutching the empty Despatch case, and whistling a pop tune, the coachman waddled to the outer office door, where he paused, turned, and said, "Of course, you lot won't get the on-the-hour news in here. Not like me and Dolly with our headset!"

"What in God's name is that supposed to mean?" Slade demanded.

"Well sir, I'm sure you're right about these Islands, but now His Royal Highness — begging your pardon — only my Mabel's got a cousin in Virginia and that's in America. Right near where the Prince is staying. She'll be going over to give him a cheer, I shouldn't wonder."

Exasperated, Slade kicked the door shut. Then he loaded the cassette of Roper's afternoon speech into the player, to trim it for the file cards the PM used as memory aids in the House. He was about to press the Play button when a Computer Priority came in from the Foreign Secretary's hotline.

Asylum granted by Washington.
Applicant already in place.
Location, Roanoke Virginia.
Ball in our court.

That explained the coachman's apparent insanity. The call light immediately went On again from the inner study... then Off. It was going to be one of those days! Slade pressed the Play button for the speech. Only tape hiss came from the speaker. He hit fast forward.

"...immediate cover is being provided re Guam King's Cross action. For PPS: Best of Britain Areas. Speech starts: Honorable Members —"

Slade stopped the tape, reversed, re-ran it. There were two voices. The first was Love's. The second Roper's. By an error, the Prime Minister had used a tape containing a privileged conversation without first wiping it in the demagnetizing machine. The implication of the "King's Cross" code-words was unmistakable: Love was involved with the Guam bombing. So was the highest level of the British Government. And now Slade knew about it.

If Love knew that he knew...

Slade's only hope of escape now was to find a very public ally.

Heathrow Airport

LIZ PONTI HAD been saved a twelve-thousand mile goosechase to Guam by an aircraft engine failure. When she called her supervisor to tell him of the delay to her schedule, she heard in return that the Australian was now a guest of the American government, in Virginia.

"For someone wanted for murder by Australia that's quite a change," she said. "Does this mean official US recognition?"

"Fence-sitting," her supervisor replied. "We've just had a leak here, high-level, through one of your male spies in Whitehall. He wanted you, but got me: our Kangaroo Prince is being kept incommunicado at this private ranch outside Roanoke. Which has to mean CIA, as the spooks own most of the real estate in Virginia. When you can get airborne again, scoop the pool by an in-depth personal with His Royal Highness."

"Thanks," she said. "Just me and the ten thousand."

Her aircraft wouldn't be ready to dare death again for another two hours. As usual in such circumstances she joined her fellow media truth-seekers at the bar. Via satellite, large screen, they were watching flood-lights shining on a split-rail fence flanking an iron gate with a sign saying Randolph Farm. She checked her notes and verified that Randolph was the name of the American woman who dumped the Candidate in Sydney.

"Tatanya (Anna): half Mayflower Pilgrim, half Russian Aristo."

And only daughter of a powerful US Senator. The tabloid mix was a natural for trans-Atlantic Royal matchmakers. A solid line of American Secret Service blocked the farm gate. There was no sign of life in the night beyond it.

Nor of the man Liz really wanted to see.

Washington

MACKENZIE ENTERED the new headquarters building for the International Anti-Terror Co-ordination Group on Massachusetts Avenue, still trying not to let rage override common sense. The bureaucratic infighting between the American security agencies had now separated him from the Candidate he had to protect by a time lag of four hours!

"With a protection gap that large," he said, tight-lipped, to the Dutch current chief of I.A-T, "McDermid could be through it like a fly in Fort Knox."

"The US behavior in holding you at Midway was regrettable, Hector — but you know our American allies: they only feel secure when they do it all themselves. And I'm bound to say, on this occasion they have a point. The action by your own government on Guam seems far more threatening to His Highness than McDermid."

"What action?" MacKenzie demanded.

"CIA didn't tell you about the bombing?"

"Only that they had the body of an underwater swimmer, still unidentified."

"Then I'm afraid I have a shock for you."

The I.A-T. chief passed a dossier. It showed that two swimmers had come ashore on Guam, near the port of Apra. They had expected to go back via the same route but the weather blocked them. One had killed herself. The second was in US custody. Both agents were employees of British Special Operations. The dead swimmer had worked for Love when MacKenzie headed the torture case tribunal. He returned the dossier to the foreigner across the desk, and said,

"This doesn't mean that the elected British government knew or approved of the Guam action."

"If you were talking about France, perhaps. But England?" The Dutchman shrugged. "Be grateful, Hector, that President Nimitz is not extraditing you for disobeying this equally bizarre British Justice Commision."

Randolph Farm

IN RICHARD'S NIGHTMARE he was riding on the motorbike behind his mother, faster and faster along a wet black road with hairpin bends winding down through the mountains to the cabin, and then a brilliant beam of light sliced across the midnight sky to show a huge white cliff straight ahead of them, and he screamed at her to turn, but she drove headon into it and he flew out alone, without her, into the endless blackness...

"It's okay, I'm here."

He opened his eyes to find Anna looking down at him. She stroked his brow. The bright light was the spring sun streaming in through the farm bedroom window. He remembered where he was and what had happened. He said to Anna, "I had a dream. I have to go back for her funeral."

"You want to," she said gently, "but it isn't reality. You don't have a passport. They won't let you back in Australia. And if they did, there's a police warrant outstanding in Queensland."

"For something I had nothing to do with — and if I followed reality I'd never be here! I have to go back. That's all."

He got out of bed and realized he was naked. That Anna was. It seemed so natural that they were together again, and yet it was a miracle.

"Maybe it can happen," she agreed as he went into the bathroom, "going home to Sydney for your mother's funeral. We'll ask Washington, everybody's sympathetic. But there are other people too in your life now. A whole lot of them."

"If you mean the British," he said in disgust, "read their papers. Half of them couldn't care less, and the other half change their minds oftener than their underwear."

"And some people in Britain are totally dedicated to helping you. Listen to their point of view before you decide."

"That sounds easy." Richard stepped into the shower and turned on the tap. "Your helpful government marooned my British support in Midway."

"Not all of them," Anna said through the curtain. "You'll find a robe behind the door, and use my razor."

Richard grinned, and dried himself, and shaved with a little pink unit from a case marked, "For those Ultra Feminine Places." The robe was a man's, probably her father's, of heavy chequered flannel. He decided to believe it was her father's! He put it on and walked out of the bathroom back to the bedroom. The sun was blinding on the white wall. Nothing else was visible. He felt disembodied, alone in space: total isolation.

Like the dream.

The meaning of it struck him. With his mother dead, there was no one alive to vouch for her Prince of Wales story. There was no way to prove he was not an imposter.

A TELEPHONE RANG somewhere in the house; a smell of freshly percolated coffee wafted from the farm kitchen. The everyday events broke through to Richard's frozen senses. His moment of panic passed. His mother's word was not what counted in proving his paternity. The DNA match in London would do that.

The bedroom door at the end of the hall was open and he heard Anna speaking, and someone laughing. He knocked. When no one responded, he entered.

To his astonishment Lady Bronwen was sitting up in bed, at the far end of the room, holding a cup of coffee. Anna sat in a chair next to her. Already they had the "just between us" look that women did when they were close friends.

"Your Royal Highness!"

Richard said with an answering smile, "Better not try a curtsey from that position, Lady Bron."

He was relieved to see how well she looked after the hospital episode in Guam. He still didn't know how much of that had been part of her plotting, and how much genuine illness. Now her skin was fresh and pink again, and her eyes sparkled.

"I'll get you a coffee. Take my chair." Anna got out of it, kissed his shaved cheek, said, "That's better!" and left the room in a way which signaled another pre-arranged, Us Girls maneuver.

"We must have seemed unbelievably callous to be laughing when you entered," the Welsh Herald said to him, when they were alone. "My dear, I am so terribly sorry about your mother."

"The world doesn't stop," Richard said, "I realize that, but thank you. It still hasn't sunk in that she's gone. I hope you understand why I have to go back for her funeral."

"Have you spoken to your father? You must, you know."

The question jolted him. He had not thought once of what his mother's death would mean as a wife to her husband. The telephone rang again, and he heard Anna answering it in the kitchen, but not what she was saying. "I've never been able to really speak to him," Richard replied to Lady Bronwen. "Now, after the embarrassment in the Press, it would be impossible."

"You might find that it was just the opposite. Now that there are only the two of you."

"But I'm not even his own —"

"Sir, I must interrupt. The very fact that you can now appreciate his position changes everything. If you make the first move, I'm sure you will find that he will respond."

Anna came back with a mug of coffee and the same excited look Richard had observed at the beginning. She tried to hide it when she saw his own expression.

"You don't need to put on an act," he said. "I've told Lady Bron, I don't expect the world to quit spinning because of my problems. If you have some good news, share it."

"All right." She passed him the mug. "The last two calls were from the White House. They've confirmed your invitation tomorrow in Washington, with the President. It's a charity dinner. A big affair, the whole diplomatic corps, so you don't need to worry about your stage fright. You can hide in the crowd."

"Sir. You realize the implication. American recognition!"

The two women were so pleased for him, and all he wanted was to get away from them. "Tomorrow," he said tightly to Anna, "I intend to be at my mother's funeral. And now I need to use the phone. In private, please."

ANNA TOOK HIM to the Senator's study, her father's, whom Richard had never met. The Senator's favorite possessions were placed where they were needed: pipe and tobacco, and a handcarved whalebone paperknife at the desk; an antique brass and leather telescope by the window. The room was paneled in cherry wood, and looked out at a sunken lawn with beds of daffodils and hyacinths. He phoned direct to the Residence in Canberra and found that his own father — his stepfather — was not at home.

"The President is at the New Capitol," the Residence duty receptionist told him. "If this is an official condolence call, a log is being kept there."

"It's not official," Richard said, and rang off before he remembered to ask for the other number. Beyond the lawn the farm fields sloped gently, with plantings of chestnut and oak trees just starting to bud. He saw something moving in the distance, and looked through the telescope. A figure with camera equipment slung around its neck was being pursued by three security guards. They had guns.

The media intruder suddenly froze. A second later the muffled sound of a shot came into the study. He watched the figure with the camera being marched away, hands in the air, from this beautiful spot. He had been invited out to a dinner in Washington, but the rest of the time another name for political asylum, he realized, was prison.

He keyed long distance information and got the New Capitol switchboard in Canberra. After considerable confusion and a lot of being put on hold, he heard the male voice he was trying to reach.

"Hullo?"

"Hullo," Richard said. "It's me."

"Yes."

"How are you?"

"I'm well, thank you."

"I'm sorry about..."

"Yes."

Lady Bronwen had said things between them would be fine. This conversation was so terrible that he only wanted to hang up.

"Were you there?" he asked instead. "With her, when she..."

"No. I was informed by the hospital. The senior administrator. Afterwards."

"Look," Richard said, "this isn't right. We have to talk properly. I'm coming home for the funeral."

He waited. There was only silence. He said, "Did you hear me? I'm —"

"Yes, I heard you. It isn't a question of embarrassing me, Richard. Returning before the family lawyers have settled with the Queensland authorities would be unwise for you. You may not be aware: there is a State warrant outstanding for your arrest."

"Christ," he shouted in fury at the phone, "Father, why won't you ever listen? I don't give a damn about any of that. I'm going to be at her funeral."

"No you are not," said the man he had finally called Father. "Even setting aside the fact that I was confidentially informed last night by our Attorney General that British Intelligence now claim to have proof of your direct involvement with Irish terrorism. Your mother was buried in a private ceremony at Karramatta, this afternoon."

With the International Date Line, today was already tomorrow in Australia. The Virginia flowers waved. The sun shone. The men with the guns patroled the split-rail perimeter of his perfect prison. He could not go home. He could not move forward. He could not even mourn.

A voice behind him said, "May I come in, Sir?"

MacKenzie was back. His jail was tighter.

Six

Dulles Airport

EXCEPT MAYBE FOR London, McDermid thought cooly, as his plane touched down on arrival from Honolulu, he couldn't be taking a greater risk than sticking his head in the noose of Washington. Even disguised as an American citizen from the South, passing into the US mainland these days was no routine matter. Under the authority of the latest sweeping Anti-Drugs Act, the Yank agents were empowered to look at every arriving passenger, domestic or foreign, for any sign of pressure.

"Where from?"

He was stopped by a young black woman, hired as a "minority" to fill a quota, unaware of how she was really manipulated by the capitalist system.

"Why, I'm from Honolulu, Officer," McDermid answered, in a laid-back southern drawl.

"Citizenship?" Her dark eyes challenged him.

"Of these United States." McDermid shut his own eyes in a moment of reverence, and added softly, "Praise the Lord."

"What was the nature of your business in Honolulu, please?"

"I was at a gospel convention, Officer."

"Are you a minister?"

"Only a lay preacher, Maam."

"Okay, Reverend. Have a nice day."

The Lord's name had done something useful for a change. McDermid strolled on with his one piece of luggage towards a passengers' coffee bar that had a magazine stand and a screen showing 24-hour news overhead. He bought a coffee and a selection of local tabloids, and sat down to scan them.

HE'S HERE !

Keeping track of his Target's physical whereabouts was too easy, but getting close enough to do the job was still a nearly impossible challenge. This farm the Target was staying at was out of the question. The place crawled with armed guards. The TV showed a bunch of them collaring a newsman who had jumped the fence. The picture cut to a super-long zoom through the trees to the farmhouse...

The face!

It was blurred behind the window, slightly shadowed by a curtain, but the profile he had last seen in his gunsight was unmistakeable. The screen changed back to the press mob at the farm gate. Letting the Target come to you was always the best answer: just find the optimum intercept position, and wait. Time only improved the shock value. McDermid was glad now he hadn't taken the man in Australia: with the Americans' misplaced Royalty worship, doing it in the USA would get incomparably better coverage.

But do it where...?

"Late flash! A Royal dinner!" The TV reporter standing in front of a White House backdrop was bug-eyed with excitement. "The man most of the world is already calling Prince Richard will be coming here! Tomorrow night! For an all star gala with President Nimitz!"

With a little bit of Irish luck McDermid had just enough time to round up the necessary pieces. He gave his collection of tabloids to a smashing looking woman with a BBC logo on her flight bag and went to catch the Boston shuttle.

One on One

LIZ WAS ALSO astounded at the pro-Royal hysteria in Washington. The otherwise normal, average American businessman with the Southern accent, just leaving, had been scouring a teenage fan's supply of "Prince Richard" headlines and photo-stories at the coffee bar. Viewed from Britain, the Australian had still seemed an actor playing a part at a remote distance. In America, with his physical presence only fifty miles away and each blink of his eye instantly transmitted to every resident of the US capital, to say nothing of the three hundred million watchers elsewhere around the country, the American people had simply accepted: He *was* Prince Richard.

For the first time Liz began to think that the task she had agreed to with the Duke of Dorset — seating this young Australian on the Throne, in exchange for a written British constitution — might not be completely insane. If she got the right kind of interview; if her subject responded with the genuine personality she had glimpsed perhaps twice out of all the miles of garbage tape footage that were already built up in the BBC files...

"All set, Liz. We've rented a van."

Her team waved from the U-Drive booth across the lobby. She went over and joined them for the ride to Roanoke.

"Any ideas yet how we break the bank?" her sound-tech asked.

Liz shook her head. In Britain, just arriving with a BBC Depth Team would have been enough to get through security; the American police had never heard of her and she was competing with at least half a dozen equally skilled group efforts. She had already spotted Japanese NHK, Canadian CBC, and Moscow One. She decided to wing it. The pleasant but unspectacular Virginian countryside east of Roanoke changed into the striking terrain and magnificent views of the Blue Ridge Parkway.

"Other side," said her second camera, who was driving. "Not exactly Sleepy Hollow."

A whole small town had been assembled in a field: recreation vehicles, trailers, transmitter-dish trucks, generators, Porta-Potties, and numberless tents surrounded by about fifty flashing State Police cars. A trooper in a Smokey Bear boy scout hat directed the BBC van off the road.

"Lane three, on the right. Watch the ditch. Go slow."

The van lurched forward cautiously over a mass of snaked cables. They found a billet between a government-run team of TV Brazil, and a freelance outfit from Kuala Lumpur. The Malaysians had a telescope the size of Mount Palomar Observatory's mounted on top of a super-streamlined mobile home and invited Liz to use it in exchange for a spare kit bag with the BBC logo.

She climbed a ladder onto the RV's roof. The farm was at least a mile away, on a slight knoll, almost obscured by intervening trees. In summer, with their leaves out, the house would enjoy total privacy. Today —

"There he is!"

Liz didn't like the young man; she didn't trust his story; she didn't believe in the institution he would represent if the rest of Britain bought it... and yet she stared like a star-struck teeney-bopper at the face looking back at her through the giant lens of the telescope.

It was the Family face.

She had never thought that from the news coverage...but news never was the same as seeing with her own eyes. His were grieving, with a kind of trapped sadness, at a moment when otherwise, with this invitation to a State Dinner with the US President tantamount to American recognition, he should have been wildly happy.

If I could get that look, Liz thought, but it was gone. The Australian had turned away and walked towards a young woman standing by a log fire. His American girlfriend, the half Mayflower Pilgrim, half Russian Grand Duchess. The pair embraced briefly, blurred and out of focus, but the intrusion in their lives gave Liz a second unpleasant voyeur feeling.

This kind of titillation was the tabloids' bread and butter: she was here for something deeper. She still had no idea how to get it.

"Can we use any more Loony Lady?" her First Camera asked. "You know, that Pink Dragon herald shit."

"Rouge Dragon," she said. "The Pursuivant. Are you sure? I had no idea she was here with him."

The camera operator shrugged, and gestured back at the telescope. Liz looked through it again, and knew that she was home and dry. Hector was standing beside the Herald.

MACKENZIE SAW HER as she entered the farmhouse. He nodded at Wallop, who closed the door behind her, leaving them alone. Before she could speak, he took her in his arms. Somewhere in the middle of a kiss he managed to say, "Wallop can give us cover for about another thirty seconds before the FBI break the door down."

"Then don't let's waste it on talk," she said, but then broke her own instruction. "Hector, what will happen when you get home to Britain?"

"The country will have a Coronation."

"I mean, you personally?"

His answer was interrupted by a knock.

"Colonel sir, it's Wallop. His Highness is waiting."

MacKenzie hugged her hard. "Time's up."

LIZ CONDUCTED HER interview in the absent Senator Randolph's study, the room with the log fire; its comfortable masculine trappings were a natural setting. Her subject was anything but natural. When MacKenzie introduced her the Australian was stiff, defensive, obviously hostile. In a contemptuous glance over his shoulder at the window he referred to "Those leering bloody hyenas."

"You dislike the Media," Liz said.

"Wouldn't you, if they climbed trees outside your bedroom window?"

She thought of herself using the Malaysians' telescope, but her next hurdle was what to call her subject. The title could put off more British viewers than it attracted, so she decided to use nothing. His accent, on the other hand, was not as much of a problem as she had thought it would be. He had the Aussie twang on words like "hyenas", but it gave them a suitable robustness. His acting training had moderated the rest, and his voice had the actor's instinctive and expressive range of tone — more engaging, in fact, than his late half-brother's. If he *was* a relative of the last King, Liz reminded herself as the on-air light went red.

"I'm sure you realize that many people watching will not be prepared to accept you only on the basis of physical appearance," she said for her opening. "Have you considered what would happen if the DNA test you put so much faith in should fail?"

"It won't. The odds are astronomical."

"But that must mean there is a slight chance."

"Everything in life is a chance. You flew over on a plane that could have crashed. Someone could have left a bomb in a suitcase at the airport. Your car could have gone off the highway on a curve..."

His voice stopped, slowly, with a sigh. His head turned back, in three-quarters profile, his best angle, to look past her, towards the window, and the sunlight, and the flowers waving in the spring breeze. Liz prodded gently: "Your mother must have been an extraordinary woman. Could you tell me something about her?"

"She was scatty most of the time. I would have given up everything to be at her funeral."

His eyes blinked... and Liz had "The Look." There wasn't a viewer anywhere who could fail to sense and share its emotion. "This is terribly difficult for you," she said, "but 'scatty' sounds rather appealing to me. There must have been lots of fun times, with a person who rode a motorbike around the world and went to a dance with the Prince of Wales?"

"She rode a bike on the night she met him. She said that was what appealed to him... Her crazy dress with the red rose. But it would have been more than the bike and what she was wearing."

"Yes?" Liz relaxed: her subject had been triggered.

"My mother had a way of behaving, as though nothing in the world mattered except this particular moment, and if you were with her then you would just be swept along with her. I'm sure he was, the Prince, rather than the other way around. If you look at the picture of the two of them together, you can tell. The mystery is why all the rest of the time she could be this other person, going to those endless damn society teas when what she wanted was to take a bunch of gifted abo kids — our aborigines — and turn them loose in the Sydney Gallery with a bucket of paint and see what happened to the Art World. I suppose I'm a lot like that. Not much social consciousness. It's only when life socks it to you that you begin to see..."

His voice stopped again. He smiled diffidently at Liz, in a way that would be ringing ratings bells off the hook in London where this was being received live at Central.

"Life has been pretty tough recently," she agreed, "with your mother's death, and being the target of a bomb attack, to say nothing of all this publicity, however there are of course some people who say — to put it bluntly — that you are simply milking this for all it's worth as a good career move."

"They haven't been speaking to the Board of the Sydney Theater!" He laughed ruefully, and she joined in. His self-modesty was unexpected. Liz found herself not only liking, but respecting him. "What else do people say bluntly?" he asked her.

"Apart from political motives, that you're trying to embarrass the British government, it's very difficult for ordinary people watching you now not to think that acquiring huge estates, a vast amount of money, to say nothing of the trappings of Monarchy — crown jewels and so forth — that that isn't a reason."

"That's crap."

With which four-letter word he had either gained himself a lot more friends or blown himself out of the water in Britain.

"Then if none of those reasons motivated you," she asked, "can you tell me what else could make a person in your position — living comfortably, a career about to take-off — why turn your whole life upside down for a country with which your own had just severed its last Monarchical connection?"

"Because Lady Bronwen convinced me that a majority of the British people still want a King in *their* lives. Oh, I realize they don't want me — or they wouldn't, if they had a choice — but by a blind fluke and a single night in my mother's life, I'm here: and following the rules of the Succession game they don't have another choice. If they had a written constitution, like Australia, America, and Canada it would have been spelled out."

"Can you elaborate on that?"

"On the need for a written constitution in Britain?" He looked at her with surprise. "Surely it's self evident in your line of work. With the manipulation that's possible through the mass media today, a parliamentary prime minister and cabinet operating without written rules could get away with murder. You asked me before why I would do what I'm doing, well that's part of it. In a world that's changing so fast that their heads are spinning, the ordinary people you speak of want something to hold to: something tangible, yet mystical, that represents stablility, and honesty, and decency, and fairness. One human being can't begin to be all that, but the Crown can as a symbol. All I can say to the British people watching is, that if and when their government decides that I'm not a common criminal, and gives me the chance to prove it, I shall give the job of being their King the best that I can until the day I die."

LIZ WRAPPED IT with a shot of Our Prince with his American Girl, standing together, hand in hand outside among the daffodils and hyacinths while their old fairy godmother, Lady Bronwen, looked on fondly at one side. Hector and her crew gave a unanimous thumbs-up, but Liz didn't need anyone to tell her that it was good. She made her farewell to her subject, who might be her King, and went outside to the van to call her supervisor at Central via satellite to London. She got the switching desk first, and could sense the excitement from the BBC operator's voice.

"I saw it coming in on the monitor, Liz. Marvelous. We didn't have any idea he was like that before, from Australia. Control's busy for a moment, I'll just put you on hold."

She didn't mind the wait. It gave her a chance to unwind and bask a little in the glow.

"Hullo?" said the voice of the man she had once almost moved in with. "Are you there, Liz?"

"You bet," she said. "How are things in Glocamorra?"

"Remarkable. It really was. You were fantastic. No-one else could have drawn him out like that. We're vastly impressed."

But her supervisor didn't sound it. "I'm a big girl," she said. "You lost the feed, yes?"

"Not exactly."

"It doesn't matter. We've got a full tape here, we can just send it again."

"It isn't that we didn't get transmission. There was an interception."

"You mean it got hung up on one of the relays?"

"On government. Liz, there isn't any easy way to say this. We got a Security Notice at the opening credit. It came through on-line direct from Government Communications Counter Intelligence, at Cheltenham, highest level. Under the gag law for anything remotely connected to Irish Terrorism, the subject of your interview is banned. I'm sitting on the best thing you've ever done and we can't show one word or blink of it in Britain."

Seven

Downing Street

ROPER HAD BEEN expecting today's Cabinet revolt. The warning of it came from Love, at Security headquarters, together with a second useful dossier. The trigger was the Australian's Virginia television performance: although it had been successfully banned in Britain, two ministers had caught it elsewhere. The group mood at the Cabinet table was expectant, but not apprehensive as it had been during the earlier crucial turning points in the country's new direction.

"I have called you all together," Roper said, "because some of you may be understandably concerned about the difficult situation with regard to the Succession. I gather that our acting volunteer from Australia made a small hit in America yesterday. Although I haven't seen the interview."

"I have. The man was damned good." The Foreign Secretary stretched his neck inside his collar with a typical ostrich-like gesture. "The State Department are applying heavy pressure to lift our immigration ban. Frankly, I support such an action."

"I don't understand why we banned him in the first place," Brown said, in his pugnacious Glasgow accent. "No one's showed me hard proof of anything criminal from Australia, and if the Yanks love him, it'll do wonders for tourism."

By the murmur of assent from other places at the table, about half the group supported the free entry position, Roper concluded; the same percentage as the latest poll of the population at large.

He said evenly, "I appreciate everybody's frankness. It seems the Lady Bronwen's candidate has undeniable charm, but that's the definition of a psychopath." The last word got the predictable shocked reaction. "I would not use that term lightly, and following on the regrettable death of the mother and the highly embarrassing nature of the circumstances for Australia, I am reluctant to add publicly to what most decent people would quite justifiably feel was a heavy personal burden for the young man. However, I am also bound to protect the reputation not just of this political administration but, far more importantly, the name of our late and revered Royal Family."

That got silence. Roper picked up the dossier from Love and opened it. "What I will show you now — and what we shall be providing the American government — is unequivocal evidence of this man's ongoing connection to Irish Terrorism. As you will see from his file, in the three months before the Sandringham incident he made a series of telephone calls from Sydney to the number in Ireland of a principal IRA assassin, a man named McDermid. We have taped intercepts of conversations which reveal how Byrd-Wilson then proceeded to meet with, and subsequently recruit, the young woman who was later murdered in Brisbane by this same lethal agent. Murdered because she had been couragous enough to attempt to go to the anti-terrorist police division of that city with information. The brutal killing was carried out with the active support of Byrd-Wilson, who met McDermid again following the death at a pre-arranged rendezvous in the Snowy Mountains of the State of Victoria."

"But why?" demanded Jamieson, from Belfast. "What possible reason could the son of the Australian President have for a link with the IRA, or to hold such a grudge against us, for that matter?"

" 'Extreme Oedipal reaction together with a Messianic Complex' is the psychiatrists' explanation," Roper answered. "Both are typical, I gather, in the development of the psychopathic personality."

He passed the file first to his Deputy, Jane Lear. She read through it rapidly, shaking her head. "The man is the age of my late son," she said. "But if he gets to Britain, after the appalling loss this country has already suffered, what more can he possibly hope to achieve by going on with this impersonation?"

"If you will look again at the last page, Jane, under the subheading, 'King's Cross', there is a quoted section of a telephone call. Please read it aloud."

She turned the dossier. "*'King's Cross is agreed then, Sean. At the Coronation, like Guy Fawkes. Nobility, politicians, media. Skyhigh! The whole bloody lot of them.'* " She looked aghast around the Cabinet table, and said, "Blowing up Westminster Abbey? This is absolute lunacy!"

"I think you can all now see," Roper said gravely to her equally stunned colleagues, "why every possible resource at our disposal must be used to keep such a person from entering this country."

Randolph Farm

THE WEIRDEST RESPONSE of the American public to his BBC interview was a live baby alligator sent from South Carolina with the British Royal coat of arms painted in waterproof enamels on its belly.

"Here, you're the biologist."

As Richard passed the baby crock to a laughing Anna he realized that Lady Bronwen wasn't sharing their amusement.

"Come on, Lady B, it isn't like you to be glum."

"Forgive me, Your Royal Highness. Your performance was everything I could have hoped. I do congratulate you."

The audience reaction had been beyond anything Richard had ever imagined from the wildest theater crowd! Within an hour of his broadcast on the US channels truckloads of letters, flowers, million-dollar job offers, and freak presents began arriving at the farm gate where they were all run through baggage x-rays and ion-sniffers to detect any explosives.

"There was nothing hostile," he reminded the old Herald. "What's our problem?"

"I have just heard from Liz Ponti. The interview was banned in Britain."

The glow went out of his day. The sun dropped behind a bank of black cloud massed over the Blue Ridge Mountains. He walked out into the garden. Anna tried to follow but he shook his head and went off by himself through the leafless chestnut trees. The flowers and fanmail from Americans meant nothing. No matter what he did, the British Government was implacably against him. And tonight he had to go to the White House and be happy in front of two thousand social climbers and the woman who had put him under plane arrest in Guam, kidnapped him on Midway and, in spite of all the protocol bullshit, was keeping him a prisoner here at Anna's farm.

He watched numbly as another intruder, who might be an assassin, broke through the perimeter security barrier and leaped the split-rail fence, this time only three hundred yards in front of his position. MacKenzie materialized from the trees with his usual split-second Commando skill to stop the latest threat to Richard's life. She was a stark naked, gorgeous girl who cried out between gasps that she was in love with him.

"Let her go," he said tersely to the Colonel. "Love can't kill me."

Maryland

THE UNDERGROUND COMRADES of the Struggle in Boston had been able to provide McDermid with everything he wanted. A borrowed light aircraft returned him solo from Massachussets as far as a private landing strip on a dairy farm outside Cockeysville, north of Baltimore, where a Maryland supporter had a recreation vehicle waiting for him in the middle of a herd of Jersey cows. The RV was a monster: thirty feet long, carrying Florida plates, plastered with Shriners' scimitar decals and bible bumper stickers.

"Quite magnificent," McDermid told the Maryland comrade. "You'd best buzz off now and leave me to it."

He waited until the man had turned away towards a farm jeep parked beyond the Jerseys before killing him, and then transferred his supplies from the aircraft to the RV. There weren't many, but some of the pieces were delicate and didn't like joggling. McDermid left the two most sensitive items in their boxes, cushioned with extruded foam, and assembled the rest into something that looked businesslike. The cows watched patiently.

"So what do you think then, Bossie?" he asked the closest dumb brute, pointing the sharp end of the device at her amber eyes. "Will that do the job for us?"

The cow dropped a wet pat. McDermid grinned, debated using the beast for a dry run...but decided against it. There wasn't much correlation between a purebred Jersey and his Target.

"Even if your old man did get it off in a test-tube, Bossie," he told her, "you had a Dad to be proud of — not like my Royal bastard."

He slapped the cow on her rump and climbed into the RV. He put the device and its remaining separated components on a double bed fitted in the rear of the vehicle, covered both with a satin quilt embroidered with more Masonic symbols, then blew up the light aircraft and the body of the helpful farmer by remote control before driving slowly away from the cows, across the field, towards Highway 83.

Where a State bike cop was waiting for him...!

Only a fellow Mason. They exchanged fraternal waves and a helpful guiding to the first freeway sign:

STRAIGHT THROUGH WASHINGTON

Oval Office

MAUREEN NIMITZ RECEIVED the British Government's secret file on her evening Guest of Honor ten minutes before the helicopter she had sent to bring him safely to the White House was due to take off again from the lawn of the Randolph Farm. A picture of it was showing on every channel. She read the report and said to her Intelligence and Security Director, "Is this thing true?"

"Not in our opinion, Madam President, but what we think doesn't matter. We can't afford to take the risk to your person of being wrong."

"Guy Fawkes wanted to blow up the English Houses of Parliament," she said wryly, "not 1600 Pennsylvania Avenue. Roper has sent across the tapes of these calls to Ireland. It's the man's own voice. God knows I've heard enough of it on television. How could the Brits fudge something like that?"

"Through a process of micro-editing," her Director replied. "Given a sample of a subject's speech, for any words not in inventory you take individual syllables and re-splice them to form a complete new whole."

"*You* take?" She raised her eyebrows at her Intelligence chief. "We do this too?"

"We possess the capability, maam."

"Sure," she said, "and I'm from Missouri!" On screen her guest was climbing into the waiting helicopter. She tapped the file impatiently. "If we know the technique, why can't we be certain that this shit from Roper is a forgery?"

"Because there is no way of *proving* that the vocal pattern is a reassembly. We can show that the inflections are abnormal in comparison with the subject's regular speech, but no one's voice is absolutely constant. Under pressure, or stimulus — fright, sex — even if the man did make the calls from Australia, on such a sensitive topic his voice would have been considerably stressed. The fact that we know he did not make them —"

"Hold it," she said, as the chopper on the screen rose into the night. "Now I find out that we listen in on all of Australia's private phone calls!"

"Some," her Director conceded. "And for those dates our microwave traffic records do not verify with the British. We have calls from Australia, and to Ireland, involving the telephone numbers in Belfast, Canberra, and Sydney, but not a completed electronic link between them. Brit security obviously got in and adjusted the international telecomm data base."

" 'Adjusted' " she said, "meaning another forgery. The Prime Minister really doesn't want this guy." Maureen Nimitz stared at the image of the retreating helicopter's winking lights. "And I don't like Brit agents tossing bombs around on US soil. I accept your warning, Mr Director. Let's go to dinner."

Arlington National Cemetery

McDERMID WATCHED FOR his Target's approach on a television instaled in the RV's dinette area. The huge vehicle was parked all by itself just below

Robert E. Lee's Memorial. The deserted spot was put aside by the National Parks Board for overflow peak season visitors to the cemetery for America's fallen heroes. An appropriate base for his operation, McDermid thought, with a momentary amusement. In front of him was the main axis of official Washington: the Kennedy Flame, the needle of the Monument, the reflecting lakes, the gleaming tourist-trap home of the ballbreaking Mrs Nimitz.

"Any minute now!"

The voice-overed image on TV was showing the same view as the one outside the RV's windows. McDermid walked back to the double bed and threw aside the satin quilt covering the device. He placed it on the formica table in the dinette area and put the two last boxes beside it. With great care he removed the contents of each one from its extruded foam cushion and fitted it into the appropriate slot of the main housing. He unfastened the catch on a small bubble skylight in the vehicle's roof, immediately above the table.

"Here he comes!"

The telephoto lenses had caught the Target before McDermid could with the unaided human eye. He lifted the device and pointed the business end out through the skylight. And now he could see the winking navigation lights approaching.

"The President's Guest of Honor is just passing over..."

It would be live, to a nation-wide audience. If the first viewers could have been the Brits, things would be perfect, but it was never possible to have everything. The real enemy would get the picture soon enough. McDermid squeezed the trigger. He didn't see the problem until the device was clear of the bubble opening. For the first time he lost his cool and shouted.

"Bloody Yanks!"

There were *two* US Marine helicopters — and the device he had so meticulously assembled couldn't tell more than a fart in a hurricane which one of them held his Target.

History Repeated

FROM THE AIR the view of Washington at night was breathtaking. MacKenzie stared down at the floodlit buildings ahead of him and wanted only to be rid of them. The airspace above the capital was frozen to all traffic during Presidential Flights like this but any one of the million road vehicles moving through the streets below could house a lethal weapon. If the threat had been only from one IRA lunatic he would not have been so concerned for the Candidate's safety, but the almost certain fact that British security forces were also ranged against them.

"Over there!"

MacKenzie whipped his head around. But Anna Randolph was only pointing out the Mansion.

"A great-something grandfather Randolph fought with Lee," she added, as the building's Southern columns passed below them. "And look, there are fireworks!"

In a repeat split-second of frozen horror, for the second time MacKenzie saw an arcing trail streaking through the blackness.

"Evade missile!" he bellowed to the US Marine pilot, and hurled himself forward.

RICHARD WAS SMOTHERED again at the bottom of a human pyramid. The chopper lurched sideways. Again he heard an explosion outside an aircraft and felt the concussion. Wind and noise rushed in beside him. The helicopter twisted back the other way. He saw a ball of fire through the hole in the hull. The craft escorting them was going down in flames. Seconds later it shattered the mirrored surface of the reflecting pool by the Washington Monument.

His American pilot said, "Our tail rotor feels damaged, Colonel. I'll try and make it over the fence. Is *he* all right?"

"For Christ's sake," Richard shouted, as the pile of bodies released him. "I'm fine. It's Anna."

"I'm fine too." He heard her voice, but couldn't see her. All the lights had gone out. The pilot said,

"Lost power. Hang on. With luck we can feather."

Traffic along the parkway blurred in two long streams of red taillights. The flashing blue of police cars joined in from every direction. At last he found Anna. He touched her face and said, "Tell me you really are okay. I felt so useless."

"I really am. My God. Your jacket!"

She was holding his left arm. Richard ran his right hand up it. Half the fabric of the sleeve was missing. The pilot said,

"Last warning!"

The car lights disappeared. He gripped Anna with all his strength to hold her into her seat. His bodyguards braced their bulk against him.

The landing was anticlimax.

Feather soft. Outside, two US Marines in dress blues appeared with a set of steps as though none of the earlier horror had happened. Only fifty feet out of position. There was even a red carpet.

WHAT FOLLOWED WAS more surreal. As he and Anna were escorted by the Marine Guards across the South Lawn towards the floodlit White House, Richard had the feeling that he was part of a gigantic theater production.

Hail to the Chief sounded from a band inside the building, a plummy voice announced, "Ladies and Gentlemen, the President of the United States."

To some polite hand-claps a tough-looking woman appeared at a pair of French windows which opened outwards. Her face was set in a grim expression that relaxed slightly as she saw the two of them, and then tightened again after noticing the missing portion of Richard's sleeve.

The invisible major domo announced, "His Royal Highness, the Prince — I beg your pardon, Madam President — Mr Richard Byrd-Wilson, and Miss Tatanya Randolph."

"You've had quite a trip," said the woman whose armed forces were responsible for him surviving it. "Come and join your party."

"Thank you, Madam President," he said, "but perhaps I should do something first about the state of my dinner jacket."

She looked at him, and her face finally relaxed. "Son," she said, under her breath, as she ushered him forward, "I don't know what kind of King of England you could make, but the Aussie stage has lost one hell of an actor. Wear the tux the way it is: as a badge of honor."

Following Maureen Nimitz's example, the applause started...as it had at the Sydney Opera House...but this time it continued, and no-one was laughing.

THE WASHINGTON NIGHT became a whirl of introductions, and smiles, and congratulations, and dancing with Anna in front of the cameras. The whole world seemed to want to have them to supper, or sign them to Hollywood. When Maureen Nimitz excused herself and retired the crowd thinned; but more than half stayed on as if it couldn't get enough of just looking at the pair of them.

"This is worse than a wedding night," Anna whispered in Richard's ear. "Ask your commandos to run some interference and help us out of here."

He found MacKenzie with a thickset American who had Secret Service stamped all over him. They were talking behind a carved Oriental screen, while Kimura listened inscrutably. The two men broke off their conversation as Richard walked up to them. He saw that MacKenzie was holding a message form with his name at the top of it.

"Anything interesting, Colonel?"

"A fire in the Southern Regional Public Records Office outside London. The building was destroyed."

Richard yawned... before he realized that his bodyguards weren't huddled in the White House to worry about bureacracy catching fire three thousand miles away. "What was in the building?"

"Primarily over-classified excess that could go up in smoke with no-one missing it. Unfortunately —" MacKenzie handed him the message form — "all the confidential medical records of the Royal Family for the past one hundred years were also lost. Without physical proof of the blood classification and DNA signature of your natural father, it will no longer be scientifically possible to confirm your claim to the Throne."

Eight

Virginia

ONCE MORE, RICHARD and Anna weren't speaking. He had insisted she drive back to the farm by car from the White House, rather than airborne with him, and she said, "No. That's all. No."

He knew she thought sharing the risk would help him get over the bombshell about the medical records, but having her on board only made his depression worse. He had put all his faith for British public acceptance of his claim in the DNA matching test; now, in a puff of smoke it was gone. With nothing to go on for, the constant Marx Brothers presence of MacKenzie, Kimura, and Wallop really got under his skin. He turned his back on all of them and went walking with his head down among the leafless chestnut trees again...

"The moment has come," the voice of Lady Bronwen said, some time later, "for you to snap out of this self-indulgent nonsense. If Your Royal Highness won't talk to Anna, you will to me."

He looked up to see the Welsh Herald in front of him. She was sitting ramrod-straight on a garden bench made of teak, placed out of the wind, facing the sun.

"You think that things are hopeless," she told him, "just because of another temporary setback. This is not the 1930s, with Mrs. Simpson: news today can't stay blacked out of Britain, even under Henry Roper's ownership! But what you must grasp is that the scale of time is different for *you* now than it was as an ordinary man. The Monarchy runs in centuries; as individuals we will all die after a few years. Whether you move on from Washington this week or next month is of no consequence. When you finally land in Britain the result for history will be the same."

"I don't know how," Richard said. "Losing the medical records isn't temporary. It's a total bloody roadblock."

"For heavens sake boy, the destiny of the Royal House and the British nation isn't going to be stopped by losing a piece of paper. Or burning it deliberately, for that matter."

"You think it was deliberate?"

"Convenient accidents seldom happen in my experience — and perhaps I should tell you a little about that. My life. You must have wondered what an old woman is doing mixing with Royal Marine Commandos."

He nodded. "I thought you and MacKenzie might be related. He has the same kind of eyes."

"We're in no way connected by blood, it was my profession. As a young woman, before the end of the Cold War between the Great Powers, I was involved in work behind what was known then as the Iron Curtain. I was never a Mata Hari!" She laughed, then added, "Nor do I want to exaggerate. What I did was seldom dangerous, and probably not very important in the scheme of things, but once you work in that line you never really retire. You know people..."

" 'Seldom'," Richard said, "must mean that there were other times when it was dangerous."

"One or two." She smiled dryly.

"What sort of people?" he asked.

"From every walk of life. Certainly not only the mighty. That is why when I tell you that you will be received and helped in Britain at every level, you must believe me." She leaned forward and took his hand. "My dear, that is what I meant about the fire. Medical records and written constitutions have their place, but the emotional life of a people does not rest with a piece of paper. From the moment I first saw you, I knew our mission could not fail. If a man looks like their King, then in his people's hearts he *is* their King. They don't need a lab certificate to tell them — or even a television interview!" She released his hand and touched his cheek. "Don't worry. You performed brilliantly at the White House last night, and for the ceremonial of British life I shall be beside you every step, until I see you stand before God and your loyal subjects in Westminster Abbey. Now go and find your Anna, and thank your lucky star you have her."

RICHARD WALKED BACK towards the house with his head up. The chestnut trees were not leafless after all. Their buds had burst and a bird trilled. He grinned at his bodyguards, Wallop and Kimura, when that odd pair rejoined him. When he looked back, as he stepped into the building, the extraordinary old woman he had just left was still sitting on the teak bench, smiling gently, with her eyes closed in the warm spring sun.

Even the grim-news face of MacKenzie couldn't take the glow off the day. Richard bumped into the senior commando at the study door as he was about to patch things up with Anna.

"Okay, Colonel, let's have the latest gloom and doom."

"Two items, sir, and I assure you that I don't like having to relay either one of them. However, you have to know the full extent of the opposition. Please read this document."

MacKenzie held out a file folder, with SECRET stamped in red at the top of it. Richard opened it. FROM PRIME MINISTER: PERSONAL FOR THE PRESIDENT. The rest said merely that he had a Messiah complex, was involved for months with an IRA murderer, and intended to blow up the entire British Establishment at his coronation.

"And they think *I'm* crazy?" he said to MacKenzie. "I never made one of those phone calls. Hell, I've still got the bloody bills."

"Really?"

"Sure. They're in a kitchen drawer by the fridge. If you've got connections in Sydney, tell them to break into my flat and check out —"

He stopped and looked again at the false transcription of the message he was supposed to have sent to Belfast.

"*King's Cross*?" he said. "Why on earth would they think I'd pick my own district as a code name?"

"Possibly for misinformation." MacKenzie took back the file. "This could be a cover for a counter operation. Which brings me to the second item. The missile residue from last night's attack has been recovered. It was not one previously used by the IRA."

"Not McDermid. Then who?"

"The Americans informed me this morning that a similar weapon was used to shoot down Sir John Gore's aircraft in Northern Ireland." MacKenzie's jaw was grimmer than ever. "I bitterly regret having to say this, sir: that missile was developed for the exclusive use of the British Army."

"But it could have been stolen."

"No such theft was ever reported. And there is one final thing that you should know. Two members of our own Special Intelligence were apprehended by US Security after the bomb attack in Guam."

The sun still shone. The birds sang. There were no dark clouds this time outside the window. Richard was determined to stay cheerful. "The fact that both the IRA and the British government want to kill me only changes the odds from hopeless to impossible," he said. "Try those phone bills."

He went to find Anna in the kitchen. The black housekeeper told him, "She gone to meet that dear old soul restin' *her*-seff in the garden."

Old Grace was even more ancient than Lady Bronwen. Richard smiled at her, then shadowed by his Japanese watchdog, he walked back along the path between the banks of daffodils and hyacinths. He was surprised that he could accept MacKenzie's information with such equanimity. He saw Anna ahead, and waved, but she was talking to the Herald and didn't see him. In the distance, beyond the fence, the perimeter guards were keeping up their running battle with the media. He caught a brief glimpse of Kimura slipping with a Judo expert's amazing lightness from tree to tree as unnecessary cover, and wondered if the IRA killer, McDermid, had ever been anywhere closer to him than Brisbane?

Anna straightened up and saw him. "Hi," Richard called, waving again. "I hope Lady B told you. I'm talking again."

It was going to continue as a one-sided conversation. The old woman's face still wore the same slight smile as when he had left her, but Anna's was as stiff as it had been in the chopper.

"I'm sorry," he said, halting beside her. "It was just that I was worried for you, taking the risk, and I feel so damn helpless at not being able to do anything to stop it."

"I understand."

Richard wondered if he would ever understand the female psyche! "I'm resigned to waiting here," he assured Anna. "If I have to be jailed indefinitely —"

"She's gone."

"Who has?"

"I know how you felt about her. And coming after your mother."

"Anna, what are you talking about?"

"Don't try to block, darling. Grieving has to accept the reality."

She took his hand and moved it towards Lady Bronwen's face.

"Excuse!" Kimura's iron grip came from nowhere to clamp his wrist. "The dart is still present in Her Ladyship's flesh."

A needle-sliver of shiny metal was stuck in the papery skin of the Herald's neck, just below the right ear. And as Richard saw that macabre evidence, but could not comprehend it, the head of the woman who would have guided his steps if he ever got to Britain, lolled in the same direction, east, towards the fence, and the media watching through their high-power telescopes. In front of his stunned gaze, the body of Lady Bronwen of Llangath sagged off the teak bench, and fell as dead weight into the bright flowers.

Nine

Heathrow Airport

LIZ WAS WAITING for her luggage to be lost. Through the baggage area window to her left a trio of obviously upper class, elderly males wearing long black overcoats stood holding archaic bowler hats over their hearts. Abruptly, a cardboard shipping coffin rolled out on the conveyor. As the box was loaded into a waiting hearse, Liz saw the red dragon of Wales stencilled on its lid. Unwittingly, she and Lady Bronwen had ridden home together.

She had no knowledge of Hector's whereabouts either. Before she could try to pump him on the subject of the man he was guarding, her tight-lipped commando had once again vanished behind his impenetrable Security curtain. The Kuala Lumpur crew had caught the Herald's heart attack through their Mount Palomar telescope while they were filming another Keystone Cops chase by the State Troopers. The Malaysians had given her a tape copy but she hadn't viewed it: since the banning of her own interview, her enthusiasm for Royal voyeurism was at a low ebb. Bags started spilling out of the chute. The hearse doors closed. As the bareheaded man in the center of the group turned away, she saw it was the Duke of Dorset, Edward Marching.

Liz gave her baggage stub to her crew chief for collection. "Unless they've sent it to Bahrein by mistake! I've got to catch someone."

She headed for the Arrivals exit and saw the Duke climbing into the back of an old Bentley waiting at a No Parking section of the curb.

"Your Grace!" she called.

Marching looked around, then said vaguely, "Oh yes. BBC..."

"Liz Ponti." He had aged since their last meeting. His hair was whiter and deep lines were etched down his cheeks. He had also lost weight, and she wondered if he too might be ill.

"I've just come in on the flight from Washington," she said. "I thought you and I might be able to talk about the subject of my visit there."

"Ah." The Duke glanced along the curb with an uncertainty that didn't square with his car's aristocratic monopoly of the No Parking zone, then, making up his mind, said loudly, "Nice to see you again. May I offer you a lift?"

It's fear! Liz realized: *The leading peer of the realm thinks he's being tailed.* She climbed into the rear seat of the Bentley beside him and closed the door. Marching rapped on the glass divider. The chauffeur nodded at an Airport traffic warden, who nodded back, then merged out into the traffic leaving the Arrivals area. Liz checked the rearview mirror but couldn't see anyone following them.

"Sorry if I seemed rude," said the Duke. "Between Roper's Estate Incorporation thing, and the possibility of being charged with complicity in the death of my neighbor, my life has become a legal hell."

"The Catholic candidate?" she asked him. "Surely that business of you finding her body isn't still dragging on?"

"Only when I speak out on keeping the House of Lords in a written constitution! By remarkable coincidence," Marching added, with a note of bitter irony, "the police invariably call afterwards for 'further help with their enquiries'. Which of course gets me further headline treatment in Roper's 'arms-length' gutter press."

The chauffeur swung into the passing lane of the motorway. A giant screen showing that day's cover of the largest circulation tabloid appeared on the wall of an office tower in front of them.

WHITE HOUSE DENIES TERROR ORGY!

Female stockinged thighs covered the rest. "If they want to smear the Prince," Liz said, "telling readers that he was invited to the White House for any kind of reason seems counterproductive."

"The Prince. From a Republican?" Marching raised his eyebrows. "Perhaps you should tell me what you thought of him!"

Her account lasted until they reached South Kensington, where the chauffeur stopped the Bentley in front of an impressive Georgian residence, looking across a private lawn to the river.

"Television impact beats print ten to one," Liz concluded as she got out. "If I could air that interview in this country it would be game over for Roper. But with the Anti-Terror restrictions on broadcasting, I don't know how to do it. The commercial satellite side are controled by the same people who run that front page Orgy we just saw. At the BBC, we're under so much pressure financially — the Director General wouldn't step out of line if his life depended on it."

"He has my sympathy." Marching looked along the quiet street with the same anxiety he had shown at Heathrow. "I retain the best legal advice available, but falling foul of the Anti-Terror section of the law is like being trapped in a tarpit. Once innocence has to be proven..."

The Duke grimaced as though a pain had stabbed him. He was seriously ill, Liz decided. "The law still works both ways," she said. "With the people you know, isn't there *something* that can be done judicially to force the government to lift the ban?"

"The judges I knew," Marching replied, "are no longer in office. But if you could present me with evidence of a purely criminal act committed by this government, one that doesn't pull us into the Security tarpit, then it might still be possible to bring pressure to bear. In politics, public embarrassment is the only deadly sin."

SHE GOT TO her Camden Town flat to find flowers waiting from the Beeb man she had once almost moved in with. Liz smiled at her supervisor's gesture and tossed her shoulderbag on the bed, wondering if she would ever see her other luggage. She ran a bath, stripped off her grimey traveling clothes, threw them in the laundry hamper, and rummaged through her shoulderbag to find her razor. She chucked out hotel brochures, matches, freebie soaps, haircaps, the Malaysians' video tape.

The razor was under it. And there might be something on the tape that her supervisor could trade for. She loaded the casette into the VCR slot of the bathroom TV set, flicked it on with the remote control and immersed herself in marvelous hot water.

She closed her eyes to wash her face. The tape's background soundtrack returned her to the carnival atmosphere of the media village keeping watch at the Randolph Farm. She lathered her right leg. The screen was showing the familiar spring beauty of Blue Ridge Virginia. As she rinsed off her leg, the chatter of Asian voice-overs heightened. Liz glanced. The troopers in their Smokey Bear hats were in hot pursuit of yet another intruding Royal groupie. The police weren't getting anywhere. While the cops stumbled and reached for their guns the groupie vaulted the split-rail fences like an antelope. Liz started shaving her calf...

Her hand stopped. Then let go of the razor and reached for the remote control in the sponge rack instead. She ran the tape backwards at high speed. Halted it. Advanced it at normal, then single frame, then froze it.

THE GROUPIE WAS not another pretty girl on the make. It was a thickset man in a windbreaker and wraparound sunglasses. He carried a small tube. In the next frame the sunglasses fell off as he threw the tube away... but it wasn't the tube Liz cared about, it was the face: without his glasses, she thought she had seen it somewhere before.

She advanced another frame to get more sunlight in the shot. The picture cut abruptly to the old Herald, sitting on her bench. Liz reversed three frames. The light was better. Not perfect; half the man's face was still in shadow from the tree branches. The half she could see clearly showed the eyes. Cold and flat. She advanced one more frame. The eyes were suddenly contemptuous.

"Tommy Brit is in the shit!"

It was the Major the kids had jeered at with their jingle in Northern Ireland, on the day Sir John Gore died. Now, the man was dressed as a civilian. Then, he had worn a uniform battle jacket with the insignia of a missile crossed with a dagger.

"Crossed," she said to the chilling face on the set. And then, to herself, *"King's Cross...?"*

She went back to the tape again — and caught an agent of Roper's government in the purely criminal act of murdering a defenceless old woman.

Virginia

MACKENZIE FELT A deep sympathy for the young man in his charge. Three close deaths so quickly would be a terrible loss for anyone: the additional constant personal threat must make it almost insupportable. He also felt increasing respect. The biographical outline Love gave Roper had been deliberately biased. Not just in describing what was now the trendiest district of Sydney as a collective brothel, for the Candidate had not dropped out of university for a life of hell raising; he had taken private stage tutoring for the ambitious goal of being the youngest Hamlet ever in Australia.

Now, as MacKenzie shepherded his charge from their latest Farm walk into the Senator's study, the young man blurted, "Don't tell Anna, but I'm not going to hang around here in the States, just waiting for nothing to happen. You're part of the cloak and dagger business, Colonel: get me whatever false papers it takes to fly solo, Dulles to London."

"Alone, sir?"

"I'm an actor. I can disguise myself to get through Heathrow Immigration."

"Yes sir. How soon do you you wish to leave Washington?"

The Candidate had obviously expected an argument. He said with surprised relief, "As soon as possible. I'll go as an old man, Eastern European, a beard. If you can get me some makeup supplies, and suitable clothes, we can do a dress rehearsal for the passport photo."

"Certainly, sir," MacKenzie said, "I'll begin immediately."

RICHARD WATCHED THE starched figure of his chief jailer salute and withdraw. The grim commando's actions were a constant mystery to him but none of that mattered. Now his decision was made, and a deadline set, he felt calm. Anna was in Roanoke but there was no point in telling her anyway; she would only pull another helicopter scene and insist on coming too.

To kill the time he went back to the study and leafed through the cleared mail. Apart from the business contract offers the letters which passed the x-ray inspection were overwhelmingly from women. Some had photographs of the senders in various poses. Often they came from socially prominent addresses and were blatantly erotic. Richard grinned at the latest one, in nothing but fishnet stockings, and opened another black-bordered bereavement card.

"If you do not immediately,
and publicly, renounce any
claim to the Throne,
Tatyana Randolph will die
like the others."

No signature. It had to be a hoax. He looked at the postmark on the envelope: Boston. The antique clock on the study mantlepiece struck the hour. Anna wasn't back. He saw Wallop passing in the hall and said, "Please get the Colonel for me."

"Sorry, sir. He's gone to Washington. Anything I can do?"

Richard shook his head. The Sergeant-Major saluted and moved on as old Grace arrived. "Miss Anna bein' so late, I'll just hold supper another while."

"Fine," Richard said.

It wasn't fine. His heart pounded and his gut felt as if it was being gnawed. He tore open the rest of the mail for any follow-up message but the letters were just the usual: "Travel *immediately* to Ottawa to be proclaimed King of Canada and then marry me." Another half hour had passed. He moved to the study door to find Kimura —

A car was arriving in the stable yard.

Anna!

He was about to rush out and say Hi — when he realized he couldn't say anything to her at all. If he did, she would insist he proceed. If he proceeded...

He put the death threat in his pocket and picked up a condolence note from British Columbia. Anna came in from the garage and kissed him.

"Hi, you look worried." She glanced at the pile of letters on the study table, and the one in his hand. "You've been reading the sad ones, again. I wish you wouldn't."

"I have to. Grace said you were going to be home an hour ago. Where the hell were you?"

"I got a flat. The jack wasn't in the car. I had to wait until a guy came along and helped me change it."

"A guy?"

"You don't need to snap. I'm freezing." She moved to get closer to the fire.

"I'm not snapping," Richard said. "This guy — did you know him?"

"No. What's got into you?"

"Nothing."

She shrugged, and bent down to warm her hands over the flames. In the fire's glow, her face looked unbearably special to him.

She picked up something from the hearth, and said in an accusing tone, "So that's it!"

"I don't know what you mean."

"Why you started a fight. Well let me tell you, if you want the rest of this person, it's fine by me."

She held out the unburned lower half of the fishnet stockings photo. Richard said in amazement, "You think I want *that?*"

"I know you didn't want me to see it."

"Miss Anna," old Grace called from the kitchen, "supper's on. You children better get your-seffs together."

THEY SLEPT APART: or rather, Richard lay awake on the divan in the study, watching the glowing embers and waiting for MacKenzie to return. If the FBI were given the threatening letter, they should be able to trace it. But the colonel didn't get back. The fire died.

Gray light was beginning to show through the study curtains. Richard got up and helped himself to coffee from a pot left on the kitchen stove by the housekeeper. He went to take a shower, in the guest bathroom, not the one attached to Anna's bedroom. He stripped and stood under the hot water, trying to force away the black depression which he felt returning. He made his mind concentrate on his disguise, and the solo trip to London, and where he would go when...

It was pointless. He couldn't go anywhere if Anna's life was in danger. He got out of the shower stall.

"I've found what you were really hiding." She was sitting on the closed lid of the toilet, holding the death letter. She said, "Do you think for one moment I'm going to let you give up because of this garbage?"

"That's exactly why I didn't show it to you," he told her. "Anna, I can't allow —"

She kissed him on the lips. "Come to bed."

WHEN HE WOKE it was nearly noon; Anna was already out with her horse, and Wallop, in the stable yard. MacKenzie had returned from Washington with the theatrical supplies. The commando also knew about the threat and had passed the letter to FBI Headquarters.

"Whatever the outcome of their investigation, sir, in your absence the Bureau will givc Miss Randolph continuous protection."

"Like Lady Bronwen?" Richard said bitterly.

"Regrettably, the Lady Bronwen was never under personal direct surveillance."

"The farm was meant to be protected."

"The State police were limiting access. There is a considerable difference."

The extent of it was in place after brunch. Six special agents were assigned to guard the house. Two of them were to accompany Anna at every moment outside it.

"Plus your three," she said to him. "When we go out riding together this afternoon, we'll be dragging a small army."

"I can't this afternoon," he told her. "MacKenzie has some information he wants to discuss with me."

"Okay." She smiled. "You won't be jealous of my G-Men?"

Richard laughed, and hugged her, and watched her ride out of the stable yard with her escorts uneasily jogging on either side. MacKenzie produced a small suitcase. "If you would care to get into your disguise, sir, I'll take the passport photo for your documents."

The case contained everything Richard had requested. He went into Anna's bathroom, sat down at her dressing table, and started applying the makeup. He stared at the new old face appearing in the mirror and a deep feeling of nostalgia swept over him.

This used to be my life.

"Ready, sir?"

MacKenzie's clipped voice cut off the reverie. "Almost," Richard replied, putting on the shabby coat and cracked shoes. He painted on a last age spot and said to the mirror for a last time, "Break a leg."

He unlocked the bathroom door. MacKenzie was waiting with a Polaroid camera. "If you'd step into the kitchen, sir, I can take the picture with natural light."

"Fine." The kitchen was deserted. At this hour old Grace always took her afternoon nap. He stopped by the antique maple cookery table with its built-in slab of marble for pastry. MacKenzie shot the picture.

"When will the documents be ready for me to leave?" Richard asked.

"By the time you reach the airport."

"But —"

"Your instructions were, sir, as soon as possible."

There were no buts. Not even Anna to say goodbye to.

A WINDOWLESS DELIVERY van, bearing a sign saying "Roanoke Family Market" was parked on the herringbone-brick paving of the yard. A driver dressed in a foodhandler's white coat sat behind the wheel. Wearing his disguise Richard climbed in on the passenger side. MacKenzie got into the rear where Wallop and Kimura were already squashed among crates of Mexican endive and lettuce. And an old East European male grocer, who looked just like Richard himself!

"Go!" MacKenzie snapped.

The van turned out of the yard. The farmhouse vanished. Richard saw the gate and the media horde ahead of him. Five hundred yards away to his left, riding through the chestnut trees, he saw Anna, with her FBI escorts. She was galloping, with her hair streaming behind her... then the gate posts arrived, and she was gone.

The van slowed. A bored TV-Malaysia crew absent-mindedly pointed a huge telescopic lens at Richard's gray-bearded face. The State Troopers routinely waved the van forward.

The driver swung on to the Blue Ridge Parkway, heading northeast, and dropping down to the level of the Virginia plain. Traffic was light. Richard tried to blank out his last sight of Anna by thinking about the genuinely old man in the back. Presumably he was part of MacKenzie's plan to deceive the press. The van curved right on an off-ramp to bypass Roanoke.

"Trouble!"

The driver slammed the brakes. A trailer-truck was slewed across the ramp. The van screamed to a stop ten feet short of it. By that time three masked men with machineguns had them pointed at Richard's window.

Behind him MacKenzie said tightly, "Sit still, sir. Take things very easy."

A burst of gunfire ripped into the van's engine compartment. There was a dull *thump*. A cloud of gray smoke errupted. Richard's eyes began to sting, then stream. His stomach heaved. He couldn't think. He had to have air. Ignoring MacKenzie's order he flung open the door, bent double, and threw up.

More gunshots. Shouting. Arms grabbed him. A hood dropped over his head. He felt himself being carried towards the unmistakeable *whoosh-whoosh* of helicopter rotors. He was dumped on a vibrating floor which rose beneath him. Some time later it dropped. He was carried again. Put on a softer surface, like a camp cot. He felt a strap thrown across his body, and then tightened. More time passed. The strap was unfastened. He was lifted into an upright position. The hood was removed. He looked around. Two of the masked figues were barely visible.

"Where am I? Who are you?"

No answer. In the dim light space seemed to stretch upwards. He heard an echoing sound and realized that he must be in some kind of cave.

"Is your name McDermid?" he asked the closest figure. "Are you going to kill me?"

"No sir," said the unmistakeable, clipped voice of MacKenzie. "With the assistance of my colleagues and with a quantity of luck we have no right whatever to expect — and overcoming problems of whose difficulty you have not the remotest idea — I intend to carry out Your Royal Highness's impossible order and deliver you safely to Westminster Abbey, for your rightful crowning, so help me God."

SEEING KIMURA BOW in greeting, and Wallop stamp, Richard's lack of comprehension became humiliation, then rage.

"God damn it," he shouted at MacKenzie. "You not only scared the shit out of me, you made me a total bloody fool. If my idea for London was such bullshit why did you stand there in the kitchen going yes-sir, letting me dress-up in this outfit like a second-rate hack — and what happened to the other one in the van?" His questions echoed around the cave.

When they died away MacKenzie said, "I understand your anger, sir. What you don't understand is the extent of the power ranged against you. With modern interception equipment every brick and teaspoon in that farmhouse becomes a transmitter. From the moment of your arrival in Virginia you didn't speak a word, or make a sound inside the building which wasn't picked up and relayed instantly to British Government Communications HQ in Cheltenham, outside London."

"Every sound?" Acute embarrassment was added to Richard's other emotions.

"Privacy is not one of the possessions of royalty," replied MacKenzie. "As to your last question, the other man with a theatrical beard and accent was arrested immediately upon his landing at Heathrow, thirty minutes ago."

WITH THAT BOMBSHELL, MacKenzie left him. Kimura provided a plastic pail of hot water and a bar of soap. Richard washed his face and rinsed the sour taste of the teargas vomit from his mouth. When he was finished, his Imperial Japanese bodyguard produced a box lunch of sushi and a small jug of saki, all stamped with a stylized chrysanthemum logo and the name of a Georgetown restaurant. The slight kick of the liquor helped to steady Richard's nerves. He held out the porcelaine jug to Kimura.

"Will you join me?"

"With honor." The Japanese bowed, then raised the wine and said gravely, "In anticipation of Your Highness future."

"The future."

They drank together. In the sudden glow of comradeship, heightened by his isolation, Richard had a hundred things he wanted to discuss with this imperturbable man.

"Why do you risk your life for a complete stranger? Particularly one from Australia?"

"Our Emperor's grandfather had much respect for British Royal House. Following Pacific War, thirty years later they awarded once more Order of Garter which had been given first in 1920s, but was taken away by British government during hostilities. This gesture of restored respect made deep impression in Japan. Such action imposes obligation."

"But not to die for it," Richard said.

"Surely offering life in cause of lasting friendship between peoples is more worthy than in war, as Your Highness own example shows."

Kimura bowed again, and finished the last of the saki. Richard drank what was left in his own cup, and still didn't understand.

An aircraft engine.

Half muffled, half magnified by the cave, it was approaching in waves of rising and falling sound. His heart rate, already elevated from the saki, beat even faster. He felt his palms break out in sweat and rubbed them on his trousers. The engine noise declined, roared once, then steadied. A beam of light appeared, shining erratically off the stone walls. Then footsteps, and whistling. The tune of the Royal Marines, *Life on the Ocean Wave.*

Wallop's cheerful voice called, "Anyone home?"

"Over here, Sergeant-Major."

The light beam swung across and caught him. In the shadow Richard saw that the amazingly agile Kimura had somehow managed to position himself behind the commando... in case it wasn't! Wallop dumped a bundle he was carrying.

"Flight kit, sir. Colonel's compliments. Please put it on."

As well as the previous dual life jackets and parachute pack, for this leg of the trip there was a day-glo orange, one-piece, cold water immersion suit. Wallop was already wearing one, and Kimura took another. Dressed, they looked like a trio of rubber-tire Michelin men, ready to land on Mars.

Wallop checked him: "Right. You'll do, sir."

They began walking towards the entrance of the cave. The bulky immersion suit made him sweat even more but neither of his bodyguards seemed at all uncomfortable. The noise of the aircraft engine got louder again. The beam of Wallop's light stopped reflecting off the rock. He felt a cool breeze on his face. Fresh air! They were outside. It was night. He couldn't see the plane. The threshing of propellers suddenly seemed right on top of him.

Wallop flicked on the beam: "Whoops a daisy."

The decapitating fan of a prop was only five feet away! A short ladder appeared.

"After you, sir."

Richard climbed clumsily into the darkened aircraft. When he bumped against a seat and sat down it seemed tiny. Wallop arrived next to him. Kimura pulled in the ladder and closed the door.

"Ready back there?" called MacKenzie's voice.

The sergeant-major did another check of Richard's seat belt and paraphanalia, like a nursemaid checking out a child. "Ready, sir."

The twin engines roared. The hull shook, held by the brakes. Then they were off. Richard felt the ground under the wheels. Irregular, a grass strip. A single low intensity light went by the window. The bouncing wheel motion stopped. They were airborne.

"Piece of cake," Wallop said, "but keep strapped in, sir."

There was no moon, or stars. Nothing to see inside or outside. The noise from the old fashioned piston engines was hypnotic, or perhaps it was the last kick from the saki. Richard wondered why they couldn't have used the private jet again to shorten the journey, and where they would land when it was over, and what would happen...?

FIVE DRONING HOURS later he woke up as Kimura went forward to take over in the cockpit. Another dark gray dawn was showing beyond the window, but nothing else. He could just make out the cabin. It was only wide enough for a single seat on each side of a narrow aisle, which meant that one of his bodyguards must have been squatting uncomfortably in the cramped baggage space behind. MacKenzie appeared. The commando's face should have looked exhausted but, except for an added tenseness to his mouth, the colonel seemed as parade-square clipped as ever.

"Good morning, sir."

"Good morning, Colonel," Richard replied. "Are we on schedule for wherever we're going?"

"Pretty well. We've been bucking a bit of surface headwind because of our low altitude but the weather's very obliging otherwise. At this time of year the Atlantic can be dodgy."

He looked down through the window. The starboard engine housing and the propellor fan were visible but he still couldn't see anything below them. "My guess is Iceland for next stop, to refuel," he said.

"Not necessary. We have extra tanks. I don't mean to be deliberately mysterious," MacKenzie added, "but the hull of an aircraft is another perfect transmitter. Onboard conversation can be monitored just as easily as on the ground if one of Cheltenham's satellites is listening in our direction. Thank you, Sergeant-Major, I'll park in the baggage."

Wallop was standing to offer his superior a seat. MacKenzie acknowledged the gesture with a nod, but moved past to crouch in the rear. Wallop sat down. With the daylight, Richard thought, the sound level seemed less inside the cabin. He looked out again at the grayness.

The starboard propeller had stopped.

And as he saw that, and tried to convince himself that it was routine, Kimura's impassive voice said from the cockpit, "No ignition. Both engines dead."

MACKENZIE RETURNED IN one stride. The other two pilots huddled for an emergency systems check. Their passenger was the only person with nothing to do but think about the icy water below.

The other men exchanged rapid-fire professional suggestions. Nothing changed the stalled propeller outside the window. The plane's nose dipped. Richard heard the words, *No joy,* and knew this was the end.

"Stand up please, sir." Wallop was in front of him.

He remembered all the commercial flights he had ever taken, with the attendants telling people who never paid the slightest attention to straighten their seat backs and fold up their tables. He said, in what he tried to make a calm voice, but which sounded cracked as hell, "Shouldn't we stay seated for a crash landing, Sergeant-Major?"

"If you don't mind, sir. Colonel knows best."

He got awkwardly to his feet, cramped from sitting, encumbered by the bulk of his equipment.

"Facing aft, sir. So I can check the jacket."

He turned clumsily around. He felt Wallop doing something to one of the straps on his back. He said, "Don't waste anymore time on me. Start looking after yourself."

MacKenzie said calmly, "All set?"

"Roger, sir," Wallop replied. "Whenever you like."

If Richard had to die, he couldn't do it in finer company than these men.

He half turned back, and held out his hand as MacKenzie said, *"Now!"*

Instead of gripping him in a last gesture of friendship, the commando sergeant's sledgehammer right fist slammed down on the handle of the cabin hatch: the left punched Richard out through the howling opening.

Ten

Whitehall

FOR SLADE, A NIGHT of crisis was initiated by a two-word message from Love to Roper:

Target broken.

The Australian had escaped from his American farm prison. By the time Slade got to the War Room an expanded follow-up said:

Disguised local grocer.
Boarded commercial hypersonic Dulles.
Standing by to detain Heathrow.

But before the flight was even half over, the picture had changed completely.

Grocer a dummy run.
Original taken by terrorists.
Believe US intervention.

Two hours later, as the dummy grocer was arrested by Love at Heathrow, Intelligence headquarters at Cheltenham reported:

Vocal detection, Atlantic.
Small aircraft.
Preparing interception.

Except for requesting tea instead of coffee at his 03:00 Prime Ministerial briefing, Roper seemed unruffled. The electronic plotters showed the present position of the Australian's aircraft. It had been picked up by an RAF airborne early warning radar south of Iceland. Four fighter planes were immediately vectored to intercept from a base in Scotland.

"Using minimum force," Roper emphasized calmly, with his tea. "The purpose is to escort, not to shoot down. Mr Slade, I want that fact recorded very clearly in the Operations log."

The distance between the Australian and the fighters lessened. The tension in the War Room mounted. Suddenly, with the range between them only three hundred nautical miles, the airborne radar crew voice said, "Target reports twin engine failure."

"Genuine?" the air force duty officer enquired.

"Affirmative. Both stopped."

Slade could see the proof on the screen. The speed of closing had slowed perceptibly. The airborne radar voice said, "Target standing by for ditching."

Roper asked, "How soon can any of our people reach the area?"

"Ten minutes, sir. But that's only for flyover. To get rescue teams in the water, two hours. With the temperature at this time of year, survival isn't likely."

"Make every possible effort — and Mr Slade, record that also."

The distance between the fighters and the Australian was one hundred miles. The screen went to an expanded scale. The rate of closing appeared to increase, then, "Target lost on radar."

Only the fighter blips showed on the screen. The Australian's last position was marked with the macabre symbol of a cross. The blips passed over it. The airborne voice reported, "Nothing visible."

"Low level vector search all four quadrants," ordered the air force duty officer, adding for Roper: "When the target dropped below the radar envelope, sir, it may have continued in free glide."

The fighter blips broke apart in four curving arcs centered on the cross-shaped symbol. Ironically, the pattern reminded Slade of the shape of the ostrich plumes in what once was the Prince of Wales coat of arms. Perhaps others saw the same thing. Silence filled the War Room. The maritime search expanded...

"Wreckage sighted," said the flat voice of the airborne radar co-ordinator. "No survivors"

A saw-toothed symbol appeared on the screen, fifteen miles northwest of the cross. Only Slade seemed to detect the note of hidden triumph in Roper's voice as the Prime Minister asked quietly, "Are they absolutely sure that the wreck is the former target?"

"Provide method confirmation of identity, your last," ordered the duty officer.

"By body sighting," the flat voice stated.

Slade shuddered.

Atlantic

RICHARD'S EYES SAW the side of the aircraft flying upwards, away from him: his mind didn't grasp that he was falling. It was only when a tug on his back jerked him slightly that orientation returned. His legs began to drop...

Another tug. Harder. Something whipped up around his head. He felt a third shock: a parachute billowed above him. As he finally began to take in exactly what was happening he saw Wallop and MacKenzie leap out through the hatch. He waited for their chutes to open.

Nothing.

They plummeted towards him, then fell past like stones. His gaze followed them... and saw the sea.

It was not far below as he had thought. The gray-black surface seemed almost at his feet! At last, at an impossibly low level, the commandos' parachutes opened. Their bodies swung to and fro... had barely stabilized, when the pair hit the water.

Only two of them!

Richard looked back at the plane.

Ice-cold blackness engulfed him. Panic. His arms flailed frantically...

His head broke the surface. He gasped, choked. Something exploded with a bang.

"Relax, sir. We've got you."

He heard Wallop's voice behind him. The bang had been his lifebelt inflating. MacKenzie's face bobbed up in front and said, "Well done."

"Where's Kimura?" Richard shouted.

"On his way. Not to worry."

"But he isn't!"

"Bit late, sir, that's all."

Wallop treaded water and pointed reassuringly. Kimura's orange suit was visible in the aircraft's fuselage opening. But the plane was so low.

"For God's sake, jump!" Richard yelled.

The patch of orange stayed where it was. The aircraft continued nose-down, towards the horizon. A patch of white finally appeared as well, but he knew it was too late: the parachute silk was caught on the tail. A wave broke over him. When he came up again, the orange and white blobs and the plane had disappeared.

A lump formed in his throat. He looked mutely at MacKenzie.

"Heads down!"

Wallop's hand forced him under and kept him there. His chest was bursting. Just as the panic was starting again, the hand released him. When he came up this time he heard the howl of jet engines fading in the distance.

He couldn't see anything except water. In spite of the immersion suit he felt a deepening chill in his legs. He said to MacKenzie, "I don't think I'm going to be able to keep doing this much longer."

"You're fine, Sir. Watch his head, Sergeant-Major!"

Now Wallop was supporting, instead of drowning him. But even the commandos' stamina could not stop the inevitable from happening. The chill moved into his thighs and upper arms. His eyes stung from the salt. He didn't know whether he was looking at gray sea or gray sky, but the chill was getting less. The immersion suit was working. Gradually warmth replaced the cold. He relaxed, and closed his eyes...

"Wake up!" A hand slapped his face. MacKenzie bellowed, "And bloody well stay awake!"

"I am," Richard said. "You've done enough. Sorry. Help yourselves."

"Self pitying young bastard. *Kimura gave his life.*"

He shivered violently. The chill was back worse than ever. His arms and legs thrashed. He began to halucinate. Something black rose up in front of him. Something else snaked around his legs. A strange voice in his head said, "Get him aboard."

SOMEHOW HE WAS out of the water, lying on his back in a metal cigar. The roof above him was rounded, and so low that if he reached up he could probably touch it. Richard raised his arm —

"Good lad."

Unbelievably, MacKenzie's stern face was looking down at him with a smile! Wallop was crouched behind. A third man was in front. For a moment, because of the size of the man's back, Richard thought it was Kimura, and then he remembered why it could never be.

"Things will seem a bit hazy for a while," said MacKenzie. "You've had a couple of shots to help the warming process after your brush with hypothermia."

"Were we rescued by a ship?" he asked.

"Indirectly. Meet the chap responsible."

The third man turned his head, and grinned. "Good morning, Your Highness," he said, in a North American accent. "Jack Nash: welcome to Moby."

"You can say that again!" Richard gave a weak grin back. "Whatever Moby is."

"A research submersible, sir. Deep Six Incorporated, out of Bar Harbor."

"Deep Six?" He repeated the name in astonishment. It was Anna's giant squid hunter from Canada! He said to MacKenzie, "Talk about lucky accidents!"

"Nothing accidental about this rendezvous," Nash replied, with a laugh. "Your Colonel had it planned for a coon's age. We're just about to make contact with Big Mama."

The mother ship. Its real name, Richard remembered from Anna, was the *Melville.* A television screen beyond Nash showed a U-shaped hull with those letters split either side of it. The Moby submersible eased into the U. Locking arms extruded automatically. The walls of the U began moving downwards, which meant that in real motion, he was moving upwards. Water streamed past the screen. The motion stopped. A green light came on. Nash spun a dial overhead, threw open a hatch, and climbed out. MacKenzie followed.

"Now you, sir."

Wallop helped Richard to his feet and up the ladder. His legs were rubbery, but after the terrifying sensation of bottomless nothing from treading water in mid-Atlantic, walking like a drunk on a heaving steel deck was unlimited pleasure.

"Your Highness can use my cabin." Nash gestured him inside a doorway.

"Won't you need it?"

The Canadian shook his head. "Even with full automation, driving Mama to the UK single-handed is a full time operation."

Richard's legs were giving out again. He stripped off his damp clothes, lay down on a bunk in Nash's cabin, and pulled a blanket under his chin. Wallop thumbed a high sign and closed the door. Engines started to rumble for the next phase of his journey to another undisclosed destination. He dropped his head back on the pillow and found himself looking at Anna.

Her photograph: with his favorite smile. It was stuck with tape above Nash's bunk. In the middle of nowhere, when he should be grateful to be saved from drowning, Richard was insanely jealous. He had never thought of her sharing that smile with anyone else.

Melville

MACKENZIE STOOD IN the vessel's sophisticated control center, watching the approaching northern tip of his homeland. Scotland was shown in three color display by an automatic navigational plotter worked from the computer console which calibrated the salinity and temperature readings from sea water samples gathered by the research vessel.

"Coffee, sir." Wallop held a mug out to him.

He drank some and once more calculated the odds of getting the Candidate across this portion of the Gulf Stream undetected. Britain's underwater defences against submarine warfare were maximum here, but Kimura's sacrifice...

"Colonel, I'd like to speak with you alone."

MacKenzie turned and saw his charge standing in the doorway. His clothing had been washed and pressed by Wallop. Ten hours sleep had done their restoring work physically, but sacrifice and danger made indelible demands on the mind. For the first time the expression in the Australian's eyes truly reminded MacKenzie of the Family he had lost at Sandringham.

"It's about Kimura. In the water you said he gave his life for me."

"I said that for shock effect, Sir. You mustn't take it literally. A parachute hanging up on a fin happens in this kind of exercise. Kimura knew."

"But why didn't he jump at the same time as you and Wallop?"

"He was in the driver's seat. He had to clear the cockpit."

"He just stood there, by the opening in the fuselage, I watched him."

MacKenzie had watched it also.

When he made no answer the Candidate said, "By staying in the cockpit, Kimura made sure the plane would glide as far as possible from our position, didn't he?"

"If he wanted maximum gliding distance, sir, he would have stayed at the controls."

"But then there probably wouldn't have been a body to find with the wreckage."

MacKenzie watched the track symbol approaching the passage between the Shetland and the Orkney Islands. He said to his charge, "What you believe, may be true. We shall never know — but if we suppose that it was, you are still not guilty. Everyone who participates in this operation is prepared for such an action. If lives are sacrificed, they are given for the Crown, not you, as an individual."

"Lady Bronwen told me the same thing, but it doesn't help. I *am* the individual."

"No sir. You are the Sovereign. Or will be, very shortly."

A printer attached to the plotter was issuing an *Emergency Notice To Mariners in Scottish Waters.* Two small dots seventy miles to the south of their position, MacKenzie observed, were Sule Skerry and Stack Skerry, with a third, Rona, to the west. Oil rig symbols appeared beside each one. The *Melville's* course was between them towards the Pentland Firth, separating the Orkneys from John o' Groats on the northeast Scottish mainland.

"I may be a king. I don't want any more 'sacrifices'."

"I understand your feelings, but I'm afraid, sir, that is no longer a decision of our making."

MacKenzie tore off the Notice to Mariners and handed it across:

OPERATIONAL IMMEDIATE

ENTRY TO THE FOLLOWING MARINE AREAS PROHIBITED: OUTER HEBRIDES, INNER HEBRIDES, THE MINCH, THE LITTLE MINCH, THE SEA OF THE HEBRIDES, INNER HEBRIDES, PENTLAND FIRTH, AND FIFTY MILE EAST COAST OFFSHORE CORRIDOR NORTH SEA.

As though Roper's barring the whole of Scotland was not bleak enough, the door to the weather bridge slid open. The blinding light of a magnesium flare went off beyond it.

"Colonel," said Nash's unexcitable Canadian voice, "we've got company."

RICHARD SAW THAT a military reconnaisance aircraft was circling them. Nash switched the bridge radio to an emergency frequency which immediately ordered, "Unknown vessel, report your identity and mission."

"This is the *Melville,* ocean research. Conducting sesimographic survey for oil-bearing strata."

"Roger, *Melville.* Proceeding further on present heading is denied. Reverse your course at once and leave the area."

The aircraft banked steeply. Another of the brilliant flares went off. MacKenzie's face was taut.

The radio said, "Repeat: leave this area immediately."

"Acknowledged. *Melville* departing."

Nash punched a new course into the automated steering system. The wheel began spinning as though handled by a helmsman's ghost. The vessel's bow swung around into the swell. The coast of Scotland, and beyond it, London, and Westminster Abbey, receded. The flares died out leaving only blackness. The attempt to land in Britain was over.

"Okay, Mama!" Nash slapped the console. "Right, Colonel, she's got it. Let's go."

The ship's skipper and MacKenzie jumped down the ladder to the lab compartment. Richard stared after them.

"Double quick please, sir!"

Wallop's politeness came with a thump between Richard's shoulder blades. Nash was already disappearing through the opening to the Moby submersible's dock. Richard followed, and climbed back into the claustrophobic steel cigar. The hatch closed. The green light turned red. The dock walls moved upwards. The holding arms retracted. Black water surrounded him again.

They traveled through it in silence. Asking questions was pointless and cracking jokes wasted the carbon-filtered air supply. The Moby's smaller version of the navigational plotter showed the Pentland Firth drawing steadily closer with purple Danger warnings for spots marked Stroma and Pentland Skerries, and a red vector arrow labeled Maximum Flood Tide.

"Eight knots," Nash said, with satisfaction, when they were five miles from Stroma. "It's doubled our speed over the ground."

But on the plotter it doubled the rate at which the rocks offshore were coming towards them. And as Richard kept that thought also to himself, a sound which he couldn't describe struck the submersible, and his head, and set both ringing like a bell.

"Bbbbad nnnnews, ccccolonel!" The Canadian's shouting stammer was caused by the hull's continuous vibration from the skull-crushing sound. "Nnnnavel aaaatack ssssonar! Ttttry wwwwith iiiinflatable!"

Riptide

RICHARD GRIPPED THE lifelines of the inflatable boat with one hand, a pair of night vision binoculars with the other. All around him he could hear the terrifying roar of invisible riptide whirlpools. He was supposed to be looking for the submarine on the surface but nothing appeared in the glasses. Finding anything in these conditions was impossible: there was no horizon, no sky, no land...just blackness, or blurred green smears as the lens cups either smashed against his eye sockets, or leaped away from them while the tiny rubber and canvas craft plunged and bucked through the waves created by the tide against the current.

The binoculars jerked away again. The bottom seemed to drop out of the boat. One freezing wave splashed over him. The glasses slammed back.

An object.

Dead ahead. It was there, then it wasn't, then... *"Rock!"* Richard shouted over his shoulder. "No. More like a log. Sticking straight up."

"Periscope?" MacKenzie yelled the word back at him.

"I've never seen one. It could be."

It must be. For a moment the boat steadied and he saw the object clearly. It was three feet out of the water. Slim, and flared with a shark's fin lethal streamlining. "The top is round, like an eyeball. Covered with something rough, maybe rubber."

"Anti-radar coating," MacKenzie said grimly. "Hang on. Helm hard over."

The inflatable's bow started swinging to port. The tide swirled in the opposite direction. The object in Richard's glasses remained static. He realized: *Someone is looking back at me.*

The shark's fin was pulled down. The eyeball vanished.

"It's gone!" he shouted. "They didn't see us!"

And the tide had slackened. The surface was suddenly like glass. The inflatable surged smoothly forward. He let go of the lifeline. The fingers of his left hand had been clenched for so long that they would scarcely unbend. He blew on the knuckles and rubbed them in his armpit. A slight feeling of circulation returned. He wondered if Moby would make it safely back to the *Melville*... and once again, why so many people like Nash, and Kimura, risked their own lives to save his.

Zipp.

The noise was like that, and just as short. He felt a slight bump at the same time he heard it. He put the binoculars back to his eyes. The water ahead was still like glass.

"Did you feel that?" he asked Wallop, behind him.

"Feel what, sir?"

"A bump, on the right side, where I'm sitting. After a kind of zipping noise."

"Colonel, sir! Trouble to starboard!"

Wallop's hand grabbed him and pulled him to the left. The inflatable slowed. MacKenzie said, "How bad, Sergeant-Major?"

"Checking now, sir." Wallop reached over and ran his arm along the starboard side. "Must have been razor barnacles on a rock. Slit for two compartments — make that three, sir."

The marines didn't say that if it was a rock Richard should have seen it. They didn't need to. Already the extent of the damage was equally obvious. The right hand side of the craft had deflated to the water line.

"The port buoyancy chambers will hold us," MacKenzie said, "but we shall have to make for the closest shore, rather than the sand at Dunnet Bay as I had hoped."

The bow swung around to the right until the heading was ninety degrees off their previous course. The speed increased but was only half what it had been. Water began slopping in over the low side. Wallop said,

"Sit up here to port, sir. On the rounding."

Richard lifted himself onto the still inflated side. The sergeant did the same, beside him. The flooding stopped. A hundred yards further on it began again.

"I'll try reducing speed," MacKenzie told them.

It helped for another short distance. "Too much weight inboard, Colonel sir. I'll just fasten His Highness, then do myself."

Richard looked to his left and saw Wallop snapping one of the hook fasteners on his life jacket onto the port lifeline. Then the sergeant did the same thing with a piece of doubled nylon cord for himself. The action was a morale booster: it didn't change the rate of flooding. Richard raised the binoculars again and turned forward to search for land. There was a splash behind him.

Wallop was over the side!

In the sea, with one arm through the lifeline. The sergeant's fist gripped the doubled safety cord. The flooding stopped. The boat had gained buoyancy... but their speed was reduced by the drag of the commando's body. Richard remembered the way the chill froze his own in the open ocean. No-one could hang on for long in this temperature, not even a man as tough as the commando.

He prayed silently, *Oh God, find us the land,* but nothing appeared: after all the times he hadn't believed in God, there was no reason why it should.

"Come back inboard, now," he said to Wallop. "We'll take turns."

"Kind offer, sir. Suit keeps out cold. Doing fine."

The black rubber suit wasn't keeping the cold out. Wallop's face was white. The hand clenched on the doubled cord had turned blue.

"Make him do it," Richard implored MacKenzie in the stern. "If you give a direct order."

"Sergeant-Major Wallop already has his orders, sir."

"Then cancel the bloody thing," Richard shouted. "I'm going to relieve him anyway."

He tried to stand but the snap fastener from his life jacket wouldn't let him. He went to undo it. The spring had been twisted to ensure that it stayed jammed.

"Give me your knife," he told Wallop.

"Gone, sir."

The knife wasn't gone. He could see it in the sheath on the commando's leg. He hung onto the lifeline with one hand and reached down for the knife with the other.

It moved away from him. He reached further. The sheath moved again. He saw the reason. The doubled safety cord was slipping out of the commando's clenched fist!

And then he realized it wasn't slipping.

"For Christ's sake!" he shouted. *"Wallop, no...!"*

The sergeant had deliberately released the cord. The boat moved faster. The distance between them widened. Richard turned back in horror to the man at the helm. MacKenzie's expression was a tombstone. Then the bow of the damaged inflatable dropped into another bottomless pit and the senior commando's face was also lost to him.

FROM THE MOTION and the roaring Richard knew that he must be in the vortex of a whirlpool. The roaring seemed to come up from underneath him. The rotary motion threw his body outwards. His feet jammed under the collapsed compartments opposite. His head swirled through the blackness. He clung to the lifeline. The whirling slowed.

He saw the back of the boat.

The engine was gone — *but MacKenzie was still there!*

For one moment...until the monster hurled the boat straight upwards and the colonel vanished for a second time. The boat slammed upside down. Richard was pinned beneath it. The drowning sensation started again. Squeezing his chest harder, harder, harder...

SOFTNESS, SMOOTHNESS, SLIPPING through his fingers and around his head. He was lying on his back on a sand beach with water flowing gently past him. There was starlight. The constellation of Orion's sword was immediately above him. He tried to sit up and found that he was still attached to a large chunk of wet rubber. Part was a last buoyancy chamber of the boat and part was his lifejacket which had automatically inflated.

And now he realized, when it was too late, how simple it had been all along to eliminate the jammed spring of the snap fastener. He didn't need a knife: he just had to undo the straps holding the lifejacket around his waist.

He did so and stood up. The water lapped at his feet. The sea had changed its mind with the tide. There wasn't even a murmur to recall the terrible roaring. He turned and began to walk blindly in the opposite direction. The sand got firmer. Some kind of vegetation brushed against his ankles. A dim outline of a structure loomed in front of him. A stone wall, an open doorway, part of a roof which blocked out the starlight intermittantly. And a smell which any Australian had to know: a welcoming stench of wet wool and sheepshit.

The flock were huddled beneath a corner of the broken roof. Richard sat down among them for warmth. They baa'd but stayed put. He leaned back against a soft flank. His hand felt a hoof, and then another hard object, with fragile sections. Rusted metal. It was half buried in the rubble. He pulled it out and traced its shape. He thought he recognized it from an adolescent production of *MacBeth.* He held the object up against the faint starlight of Orion: It was a claymore. The weapon of the Scottish kings.

PART FOUR

Kingdom Or Republic?

One

BBC • London

WATCHING A VIDEO tape of State murder with her Supervisor, Liz felt an intimacy almost as close as lying together after sex. It was a closeness produced by the frightening realisation of how lucky they were to be here, alive and together, when sudden and brutal death could be ordered and carried out on the whim of their democratic government.

"You know I'll back you all the way on this, Liz," her Supervisor said after their second viewing, "but this 'King's Cross' affair is obviously deep Special Intelligence — going up against that crowd we're going to have to be bloody careful."

"We made it through Central America," she reminded him. "I don't think anything in Britain could be worse than those death squads coming at us from all sides of the political spectrum."

"So where are you going to start?"

"I suppose with backtracking related deaths; the Duke of Dorset's neighbor, and that homosexual murder in the Palace."

"We got an anonymous tip on a third while you were away. A mandarin's car ran itself into a flyover abutment."

"What part of Whitehall was he bossing?" Liz asked.

"Commercial Investment Review. Specifically Roper's blind trust. That was the informant's other angle."

"Male or female?"

"Hard to tell, the voice was disguised. High pitched, but I'd guess male. An angle on arm's-length divestment must be well up in the bureaucracy."

The Late Breaks light began blinking on her supervisor's phone. He picked it up, listened, said, "And they're allowing us to run it? Then start at once."

"What's up?" Liz asked.

"The gag law is lifted on your Australian."

"That's wonderful! I can air my US interview."

"You may not want to. The Ministry of Defence has put out an immediate release saying that he's dead. The hostage taking in Virginia was a decoy apparently. He was trying to make it across in a light plane, and didn't. Defence are releasing a complete transcript of their Operations

Log and a video of the wreckage. There's at least one body. Liz, I don't know how to say this. Your Commando was with him."

Her eyes flooded. Her head whirled...but her heart refused to believe that Hector was dead. Somehow she controlled the choking in her voice and said, "I want to run the interview anyway."

"If that's what you really wish we can slot it for next weekend's People segment. That should get you at least a sixty rating."

"Roper may have the gag on us again by next weekend." She looked at her watch. "Put it on instead of the Beautiful Bodies slot on the Breakfast show."

She walked away blindly to go and powder her nose, and restore some professional composure before she had to watch the Defence Ministry tape of the Atlantic crash site, and their sanitized version of the hours leading up to it. As she was bathing her eyes with cold water she heard her name being paged on the washroom loudspeaker. She came out to find her supervisor waiting for her at the Director's Console.

"You must have intuition. Roper didn't wait till the weekend. Not only are the bloody gag laws back on in spades; halfway through their briefing presentation Defence killed it. And our people in Edinburgh say all hell's breaking loose with the army in Scotland. Don't ask me how, but your boy must have landed!"

She knew how. Her faith in Hector had been rewarded. There was only one course of action. "Bugger the gag laws and the army," Liz said. "Scotland is my home turf. The Candidate was my subject. I'm going up there to find him."

The Highlands

THE SHEEP BEGAN to stir at first light. When Richard opened his eyes the stars had faded and he could make out the timbers of the roof above him. They had originally been burned — there were still black scorch marks on the stone walls behind the sheep — but now the beams were weathered gray with spots of yellow lichen clinging to them. The ruin must be one of the croft cottages abandoned after the forced expulsion of the Highland population two hundred years ago.

"To make room for you lot," he said to the waking sheep. In history books, swapping wool and Scotch whisky for the local human residents seemed just another inevitable bit of progress. Now, seeing the burned roof, feeling the scorched stones, looking at the rusted claymore which had been used to drive the evicted people from their ruined homes and send them across the world to places like Australia — being a fugitive himself! — Richard suddenly understood the reality of what had happened.

The black depression thoughts began crowding back on him. Lady Bronwen, Kimura, Wallop, and MacKenzie were gone. He was utterly alone in Britain, as far as it was possible to be from London. He had no food, and no money: just credit cards in a name he couldn't use. He reached for his wallet... It was gone too. The only thing left in his pocket was the soggy envelope containing his spare DNA signature from the New South Wales Lab. Which, because of that other burned-out building and its destroyed royal medical records, he could never use either. In his mood of bleak hopelessness he was about to throw the lab envelope away when he saw that it also had the remnants of the newspaper story of his mother and the man who was to blame for everything, his natural father, the Prince of Wales.

His mother was dead as well. He buried his head against the sheep beside him, and let the tears fall into its stinking, oily wool.

A dog's bark broke in on his grief. The sheep jumped to its feet in alarm. Richard wiped his nose with his sleeve and stood up more cautiously. He looked through a ruined window. The croft cottage was in a hollow. The ground in front was a spongy turf of grass and heather, rising slightly. He couldn't see the dog, or the sea. He must have walked over the rise when he came from the beach.

A whistle.

He ducked his head back. A man with a shepherd's stick was approaching across the heather. The dog barked again. The sheep began pouring out of the cottage. Richard saw that there were two doorways. The shepherd appeared in front of the one to his right. Richard dropped to his hands and knees and crawled out with the sheep moving to his left until he was clear of the cottage. The land was deserted, just more boggy heather. The daylight was brighter to his right. East. He ran up the rise in that direction. He heard another sharp whistle, and a shout. He ignored it and kept on to the top of the rise.

A narrow sheep track led over it. He knew that mountains covered this remotest part of the British Isles. If he got into that kind of territory he could hide for as long as he needed, until he could think of some other —

Wire.

Heavy steel link fencing. As he came over the top he ran straight into it. The wind was knocked out of him. He fell to the ground.

"Did we no try to warn the gentleman, Glencora?" a softly lilting voice asked behind him.

The shepherd and his dog blocked his way back along the sheep trail. The man was pointing with his stick at the fence. Beyond it Richard saw what progress had really swapped for the evicted Highland families.

Huge flared concrete chimneys had menacing steam whisping from them.

"Laddie," said the shepherd, pointing his stick at a yellow death's head radiation warning symbol, "can ye no read either?"

PATROLLED AT ALL TIMES
UNAUTHORISED ENTRY
STRICTLY FORBIDDEN

Richard couldn't go on: the dog's bared teeth stopped him going back. Slamming into the fence must have triggered an alarm. A four-wheel drive vehicle was already approaching from the concrete buildings. The only weapon he possessed which might help him avoid capture was his acting ability.

"Art Richards," he said in a Roanoke drawl, extending his hand as he got to his feet. "I'm American. A writer. I was mugged by this hitchhiker I gave a ride to last night. The guy took my wallet as well as the car, and then I got lost."

"D'ye hear that, Glencora?" The shepherd exchanged an ironic look with his dog; "It's from America this unfortunate writing gentleman has found his way to us."

The approaching four-wheel had closed half the distance. The dog was a black-and-white border collie female who might be an ally if Richard had the time to work on her. "Say," he said to her master, while letting her sniff his hand, and trying to keep the desperation out of his voice, "you and Glencora here wouldn't know a local place I could maybe get some breakfast on credit until I can phone American Express and arrange for new cards?"

"Breakfast on credit. Would that be all you're after, Mr. Richards?" The shepherd reminded him of MacKenzie; tall and spare, with the same almost white sandy hair, and pale blue eyes, and the same sardonic laid-back way of asking his never-ending bloody questions.

"If you could swing it, a ride to the nearest town where I could pick up another U-drive would be a real help."

"Ye didna lose your driving licence then?"

"Well, yes. I guess I'll have to organize that too."

The dog had decided to like him, but the four-wheel was only five hundred yards down the hill. Richard could see two armed guards in it. And then he realized that was what the shepherd was doing: hemming him in like one of the man's sheep until it was time for the slaughter. If he made a break for it now, he would only have the dog to worry about: if he waited any longer he would be shot. He plunged back down the hill.

"No so fast, Laddie." The shepherd's crook came from nowhere to grab his elbow. The man's other hand held up the DNA envelope as he said to the dog, "If his Highness is after some breakfast, Cora girl, we first have to get yon nuclear damn Sassenachs off his tail."

The shepherd gave two piercing whistles. The dog dashed to the left, herding a group of sheep along the fence, and down into a large ditch. They started up the other side. At a third whistle the collie reversed, ran beyond them, turning them back by nipping at their heels. A fourth whistle, and the dog jumped to the uphill end of the ditch. The sheep milled for a moment, then somehow began pouring through to the other side of the fence.

As Richard noticed that there was a washed-out hole underneath it, the four-wheel bounced over the heather and slammed to a stop. Its red-faced driver shouted furiously at the shepherd, in a nasal English midlands accent, "You Jocks and your bloody tick carriers! How many fucking times do we have to come up here? The perimeter alarm is ringing off the Jesus control room wall again!"

"How many times do I have to mention yon ditch, and spring flooding?" replied the highlander calmly. "Your crowd in London should get off their bums and pay a fraction of their millions they have to spare for poisoning the guid earth, and use it for a decently installed culvert. My wife's nephew, here, and mysel', are going to be all day in there getting the flock."

"Not if he hasn't got a pass — and you'll pay the bloody fine, first. Now call that bitch back."

The sheepdog was growling at the Englishman's left leg where it rested on the open runningboard. The shepherd gave a crude gesture of his stick at the driver and said, "Ye'll be hearing from my solicitor. Come, Glencora."

The dog ran back below the fence. The four-wheel roared away throwing up chunks of peat and heather. The highlander watched it depart then, patting his animal helper, said, "We'd best not push our luck. Och, in the excitement I forgot to return your Highness's property."

He handed over the DNA envelope. "I'm surprised reading that article was enough for you to know me," Richard said, putting it back in his pocket.

"I didna read it, sir. I have my breakfast early but we're no complete barbarians up here. My wife was missing her calisthenics. I saw you over telly with that Ponti lassie."

"They ran my interview?" It was a first ray of hope! The sun broke through to confirm it. The shepherd began striding briskly up a steep hill.

"The news before at six was saying your Highness was drowned in an aeroplane crash. Ye canna believe a word from that man Roper's government, or his newspapers. Too many damned smiles from himself, and not enough clothes on their women!"

They reached the top of the hill. The buildings of a small farm lay below them, enclosed with a low wall beside a still half-frozen pond, or tarn. A paved road wound south beyond it. In the middle distance were the snow-covered mountains Richard had expected. The highlander started down the slope. The nuclear facility disappeared again. Except for the road, once more the barren countryside seemed totally remote from the modern world.

The helicopters arrived as the shepherd reached the gate.

A flight of six, army camouflaged. Richard searched for somewhere to hide.

"Wave," said the shepherd sharply. "We dinna want our boys up there to feel any less welcome to Benn Ratha than yersel, sir."

The highlander shook his crook-stick at the choppers. Richard waved as ordered. A crewman tossed off a lazy answering salute. The dog barked in a frenzy, then led the way through a wooden gate with Croft Benn Ratha on it. As Richard came to the front door of the house one of the choppers suddenly peeled off and circled back. It landed about a mile away beside the road. He saw the small figures of troops get out. Now he regretted the broadcast of his interview.

"If my picture has been on national television," he said, "there's no way I can pass that patrol barrier."

"With sufficient faith, did Our Lord no manage to squeeze a camel through the eye of a needle? Come and have a hot bath while the wife prepares your meal."

His resourceful Scottish host opened the front door. They stepped inside a whitewashed hall with black beams so low that Richard had to duck his head to avoid hitting them. A grandfather clock ticked next to a wicker animal basket in a corner. The sheepdog went towards it, and then froze.

A man in a police uniform was standing opposite the basket.

"Angus," the policeman said in the regional brogue, to the shepherd, "it's my duty to warn you: Your actions this morn have put your household at great risk."

The policeman must also have seen the interview. The troops on the road prevented any escape but the shepherd was still trying to bluff it out.

"And what risk would that be, Constable?"

"Radioactive contamination. There has been a leak of the damned filth at the plant. When you pulled that old dodge of letting your sheep 'accidentally' graze inside the fence they could have come in contact. If they did, they'll have to be destroyed. The military are about to escort the first load of material by truck to the nuclear waste treatment center in South Wales. As for you and your family, the area is being cordoned off. All civilians are to be ready to be evacuated in one hour's time.

The constable left the news hanging like an unexploded bomb in the hall, and departed to drop another one on the adjoining farm. The shepherd thought for a moment, then said, "If those careless Sassanach bastards had any leak they wouldna have been joyriding around after a few of my sheep. It's your Highness they're wanting. Take your bath, and have your bite, while I make a telephone call."

"You're very kind," Richard told him, "but I can't do either. Now that you know who I am, under the anti-terrorism laws in this country, it's a criminal offence for you and your wife to help me."

"What is criminal, sir, is that spewing monstrosity over the hill. The tub is through yon door to your left. Pass your jacket and trousers out, and my woman will get the worst of the sheep-pen off them."

Until he saw himself in the bathroom mirror Richard hadn't realized what a mess he was in. Thirty hours of stubble on his face, grass and sprigs of heather in his hair, sheep dung on his clothes — there was little resemblance to the immaculate figure he had been for his interview. He ran the hot water, put his dirty things out as instructed, and climbed into the tub.

He could have stayed in its luxury all day. He scarcely had minutes. And every one might bring soldiers pounding —

A knock at the door got him leaping for a towel and the window.

"It's only me, your Highness," a woman's voice said, in the soft highland dialect. "Your clothes are as best I can make them, and your breakfast's waiting."

He dressed and followed a smell of bacon to the kitchen. The shepherd's wife was only half her husband's height, and slender as a girl, except for heavy legs, with the bumps of varicose veins showing through support stockings. The price of a lifetime of hard work, Richard thought. When she saw him, the woman blushed and did an awkward half-bow, half Lady Bronwen curtsey.

"Your Highness," she said haltingly, "we have never...I mean, when my man told me...such an honor for our house. Will you no be seated?"

She indicated what was obviously the shepherd's chair at the head of the kitchen table. Richard smiled, and said, "I'll be proud to, but I told your husband, you shouldn't be taking this risk."

"It's we who are proud, sir. We couldna hold our heads up otherwise. Here's your wee bite."

She put an enormous platter of bacon, eggs, tomatoes, sausages, potatoes and rye toast, all either fried, or smothered with butter, in front of him.

"Thank you," he said. "And for the clothes. When I looked at myself in the mirror, I couldn't imagine how your husband recognized me."

"Perhaps you were not looking at your eyes, sir. A body canna see them on pound notes all her life, and not recognize those eyes, although they're a bonnier blue for real. Och, excuse me!"

She blushed, and smiled again, and went back to her stove and sink, packing a hamper of supplies to carry through this latest Highland eviction. All because of him. As Richard ate his food, he wondered how many more upheavals he would cause in ordinary people's lives before his journey was finished.

None, unless he got past the roadblock waiting at the first corner!

He could see the troops from the kitchen window. Already a small caravan of cars and farm trucks was moving slowly southwards. The road wound around a low hill but the croft was built high enough on Benn Ratha to see down to both sides of it. Some of the soldiers were walking back along the line of vehicles, checking the occupants. "Those eyes" would be his problem. Without a disguise to hide them there was no way his extraordinary luck could hold.

"Do you have a pair of sunglasses?" he asked the woman.

"I'm afraid not, sir. We havena much call for such things. Up here, we prefer to see our sun when it shines."

She took away his empty platter and put a pot of tea in front of him. Then she washed up the plate, dried it, and put it on a shelf of the kitchen dresser. Her whole domestic world was being turned upside down and left behind because of him, and still she performed her regular, routine, comforting household actions.

"All ready, then?" The shepherd was back with his dog.

"Aye, Angus. When I've given a last dust to the mantle."

"Never mind that," her husband said gruffly, masking emotion. "If I can leave my beasts, you can leave your dust."

They went out to a small Japanese car. Richard got in the rear with the dog and the hamper. The shepherd and his wife got into the front. The man drove from the croft yard without a backward glance. The woman turned her head and watched, until her house was hidden by the hill, and gone...

All because of him.

The car approached the end of the line of waiting vehicles. Down at this lower valley elevation the hill appeared larger. Dense stands of conifers had been planted on both sides of the road. They hid the troops to the south around the corner. Suddenly a heavy diesel horn sounded. A large sealed truck arrived from the other direction. It stopped with a hissing of air brakes ahead of them. The sides were plastered with the yellow deaths-head radiation markers and red warnings:

RADIOACTIVE MATERIALS
KEEP OUT!

The caution was superfluous. The driver of a small baker's van, in the space directly ahead of the huge new arrival immediately tried to nudge further forward.

"Farther back, Angus," the shepherd's wife exclaimed. "For heavens sake, they shouldna allow it on the roads at all!"

The truck was so large that its left side brushed against the pines, while its right blocked the passing lane. One of the troops came towards them with a fluorescent marker cone.

Richard tensed to make a run... but the soldier dropped the cone in the blocked lane and turned back. The nuclear behemoth released its brakes and crept forward. Ignoring his wife's unease, the shepherd followed even more closely: when the truck stopped again they were practically touching. The trees did brush the car. Richard couldn't see the vehicle behind. The truck and the hill hid him from the blockade point ahead.

"I've made up my mind," he told the shepherd. "You've both done more than enough. I'm not going to let you risk prison. I'll stay in the wood until it gets dark. Then I'll go south on my own."

"Very well," said the man.

"Angus, no —"

"Hush, woman. It's best."

Richard shook hands with her and patted the dog's head for luck. He got out and stepped straight into the pine plantation.

"I'll see you started right, sir." The shepherd got out as well, with his walking stick, saying to his wife, "I've gone for a pee, if the army asks questions."

Richard moved along the massive truck body, then turned to the hill.

The crook of the stick grabbed his elbow again.

He heard a metallic sliding noise behind him. He was whirled around. A door in the side was open. A figure in protective white overalls, hood, gloves, and boots took his other arm: with the shepherd helping he was lifted and dumped without ceremony inside. He found himself between two terrifying cement cannisters marked Strontium and Cesium.

"My wife's sister's boy is driving," the shepherd said in an urgent whisper. "You'll be right for the few hours it takes. There will be friends all the way. God speed and bless Your Majesty."

The door slammed closed. Richard was left in the dark with the killer containers, and the first-time echo of the shepherd's last word: *Majesty.*

Two

Downing Street

SLADE SAW THE scrambler light come on again from Security.

"Fox positive," Love's voice said.

"Where?" asked Roper.

"The Dounreay Reactor. Also, a body of another of the escorts. ID is being confirmed from Royal Marine records."

"And?"

"Fox missed. The cordon was late by an hour. Two local accomplices are in quarantine."

"Keep me advised."

The scrambler connection was broken. Slade was left as the only person besides Love aware of Roper's unspoken instruction: in the New Britain there was to be no room for an obsolete Royal figurehead.

The office door opened to show Lawrence Brown's heavy jowled face. As the Glaswegian stormed past, one look was sufficient to tell that the Scottish representative in cabinet had gone over to the other side.

"These reports of Army cordons all across the Highlands," he said bluntly to Roper. "No air traffic whatever is being permitted in the whole of Scotland. It's an intolerable intrusion in Scots sovereignty."

"I understand that feelings are running high, Larry —"

"Feelings, Prime Minister, are damn near exploding!" Brown looked ready for a Glasgow dockers' brawl. "The Devolution for Scotland Act clearly states that British Armed Forces are only to be deployed on Scottish soil against an external military threat — and then with the joint approval of the Assembly in Edinburgh."

"If you read the wording of the Act carefully," Roper replied, "you will see that it also permits military deployment if, 'In the opinion of the Senior Government, such deployment is required immediately to respond to a Crisis situation'."

"You know bloody well," Brown shouted, "that clause was meant for Nuclear attack."

"The clause does not define Crisis."

"It sure as hell doesn't define it as one unarmed, half-drowned Australian. I warn you, Prime Minister, if this army thing isn't lifted,

Scotland will apply to the European Commission on Ethnic Group Rights, for total separation. And the votes are there for us to get it."

"Thank you, Minister, for that warning. You may leave your letter of resignation from Cabinet with my secretary."

Brown's mouth gaped. Roper's expression showed nothing as Glasgow's ex-member stormed from the room. "Bring me those latest demographic surveys," he said to Slade, "and keep a fifteen-minute time allocation on the House order paper each day for the rest of this week. The umbrella legislation will be revisions to National Police estimates."

Amsterdam

McDERMID WATCHED THE English Channel pass below him as the European Airways flight from Boston completed its descent to Holland. How insignificant that tiny gap of water was, he thought — as long as he was going this way! When he went back in the other direction...?

His latest identity should be foolproof. He had decided on Amsterdam because British Immigration would be watching direct arrivals from America that little bit more closely. Straight in to Prestwick was out of the question: all air traffic to Scotland had been halted.

The sods in Whitehall were lying as usual.

The Target hadn't got himself kidnapped or drowned in mid-Atlantic. And McDermid wasn't going to waste his time farting over Scotch mountains; let the Brit Army do that! The near miss in Washington had been a real blow, but it had one small good effect: this time he knew in advance exactly where to go, and what to do. As the aircraft rolled to a stop in front of the Amsterdam terminal, the only thing he was not sure of yet for his final run was, How?

He passed through the green light section of Euro Entry without the slightest hassle and immediately booked himself on a flight to Manchester leaving in an hour. He went to the First Class lounge and accepted with gratitude the seat which was predictably offered to him by an American woman old enough to be his mother.

"Thank you, daughter," he said, with a gentle smile. Common courtesy both ways was only to be expected with a man dressed as a Bishop of Rome. The one whose Dioscese and accent McDermid had adopted came from Manitoba, in Canada, and was traveling to an Inter-Faith gathering about to open to talk rubbish in Salisbury's Anglican Cathedral.

He ordered a glass of mineral water. The other drinkers in the lounge were all preoccupied with the Royal soap opera unfolding live on television. There was no hard news because the media had been locked out of northern Scotland, which made the lurid coverage all the better. Wild rumors became Gospel truth in the mouths of TV anchors being fed them from the earphones stuffed in their sawdust heads. Between rumors, the announcers padded with bullshit fillers like a Faithful Royal Coachman who had continued taking an empty bloody Despatch Box from Buckingham Palace to sodding Whitehall and back again.

"Every day, yes, that's right." The moron Brit was talking to a a horse in a Cockney accent as thick as his skull. "Me an Dolly here, like we always knew, sooner or later, our King would be 'ome, and fings would be right, dint we, girl?"

"Loyalty like that, it's just incredible." The elderly American woman next to McDermid dabbed at her eyes with a tissue. "I've been praying for him," she confided, "that young man from Australia, ever since I saw him interviewed before the dinner with our President at the White House. And now, when you see his subjects like that coachman, so faithful. Their government can't go on not letting him be King. I just feel so certain, *something* is going to happen to let it all end right. Don't you, Monseigneur?"

"With God's help, my child."

The correct title for a Bishop of Rome was Your Excellency, but McDermid let it pass: educating Americans in etiquette would keep the God of Genesis busy for an eighth day! Being shown the idiot coachman was enough of a miracle for this one.

Now McDermid knew, *How.*

Scotland

THE RADIATION-SHIELDED juggernaut truck rumbled its way south through the mountains and valleys of the far northern Highlands. At frequent intervals the noise of the double-axled wheels beneath Richard changed to a hollow thrumming to indicate a bridge crossing yet another river or loch, then returned to their regular rythm. More occasionally the vehicle slowed, or stopped briefly, to indicate it was passing through a village or small town.

Every time it halted his heart-rate doubled, expecting the heavy lead-lined doors to be flung open, exposing him to the gun barrels of the British army. The darkness inside the truck's body was total: it was only his overworked imagination which made the containers with the terrifying names Cesium and Strontium seem to glow so that he could see their radioactive skull and crossbone warnings.

The shepherd had said he would be all right for the time he had to spend here, but how could a remote farmer know what was safe with radiation...?

Your Highness will have friends all the way.

Richard forced himself to concentrate on that positive part of the farewell. The fact that the man had been able to arrange this escape ride at short notice was reassuring and, as the miles rumbled by, the distance to his final destination was getting shorter. It wasn't like crossing the vastness of Australia's Outback. Even if he only averaged thirty miles an hour all the way, Britain was so small —

The airbrakes hissed. The truck shuddered, then slewed sideways in a sickening jack-knife motion. He slammed against one of the containers. To his horror he felt something give as his shoulder struck it. Then a crash.

A lid had come off!

Frantically he scrambled as far back into the furthest corner of the darkness, away from the container. Voices shouted. The side door opened. Light streamed in. He huddled down. A muffled, broad Scottish voice shouted,

"I'm warning you Tommys! Can ye no see this vehicle's carrying radioactive products? You're mad wi'out protective clothing!"

The shouter must be his driver. An English voice replied in a slow rural accent, "Hop it, Jock. We're checking everything."

A man's shadow approached the doorway. The lethal snout of an automatic rifle prodded at the opening. A helmet. Part of a face, not wearing a mask. The gun barrel poked at the floor.

"What's in this here, then?"

"Och ye bluidy idiot! Making me brake like that! A Strontium 90 lid is off. You want to lose your balls?"

"Bloody hell!"

The face and helmet vanished as though a rocket-booster had removed them. The lumbering protected figure of the driver clambered in through the opening. A pair of scissor-tongs cautiously located the fallen lid and lifted it back into position, capping the Strontium container.

Richard felt exactly the same as he had before the lid came off...but he knew that feeling didn't matter. With radiation, you couldn't see it, you couldn't sense it. If it was bad enough, some random time later you just died from it.

He had been directly exposed to it.

The white-hooded head of his driver turned slowly towards his hidden corner. The unseen face behind the visor nodded slowly. "Nae fear," the muffled voice said in a low tone, "the cannisters are all empty. Yon fuss was just for Tommy's benefit. We hae' passed the cordon for Inverness and the Highlands. That was the last of the Army, this is now Tayside. It's a clear run for the Border, down through Perth, Sterling, and Motherwell to the crossing at Gretna Green. If Your Majesty should need to relieve yersel beforehand, use the Cesium as a facility. I'll stop us at a safe spot to empty it."

The driver gave a crude bow and backed out through the opening. The door closed. They started south again. Richard used the container and found himself laughing aloud in the darkness at his Highland helpers' brass-balled nerve and practicality. To prevent another accidental collision like the last one he tied a cargo hold-down strap from a hook on one side of the truck body, across to the other. He settled back behind it in his corner and ticked off the major Scottish cities mentioned, as the truck passed through them. They were easy to tell from the heightened noise of traffic: Perth, then Sterling. Only two more until...the border.

Scotland was part of Britain — a magnificent part he would admire and be grateful to for the rest of his life — yet undeniably, crossing that historic boundary would be something different.

It would be England.

The truck brakes hissed again, but not so sharply. The driver was stopping to empty the pot, as promised. The makeshift harness held Richard static. He heard the door of the cab up front open and slam shut, and footsteps.

Too many. There was a shout. The driver had been wrong about seeing the last of the Army. And this time the lids were intact, there was nothing to frighten any searcher.

Richard could fix that! Hastily he felt for the containers and knocked the Strontium lid off again. He barely got back in his corner before the door opened.

"Carrying Strontium you say?" A man's voice with a much less Scottish accent got closer. A head appeared but Richard couldn't see the features. The man didn't seem to be wearing a helmet but there was a gun.

"I'm warning you," said the driver. "You're a damn fool —"

The sickening thud of a gun butt against bone terminated the sentence. The barrel jabbed off the lid of the container. A smell of stale urine permeated the air. He must have peed in the wrong pot. It no longer made the slightest difference.

The unseen man said to someone else outside, "It's him." and then, "All right, sir: please come with us."

The *sir*, and *please* were coldly correct, in the way police used them. Richard was half helped, half pulled from his corner. He stumbled out, almost blinded by the sudden light. There were three armed figures. He couldn't see their faces because they wore stocking masks.

"This way."

He was pushed along the side of the truck. The driver was lying moaning on the ground.

"He's badly injured," Richard said. "You have to help him."

"Keep moving."

He was prodded around the front of the truck. An unmarked windowless van was waiting.

"Get in."

Suddenly he knew where he was. Beyond the frightening anonymous van a world-famous landmark rose in front of him. A steepsided hill dominating a city: flat-topped, covered with the turrets and walls of a massive stone structure. Shafts of sunlight struck through the clouds and illuminated Edinburgh Castle, on its Rock.

Richard didn't know why the sight moved him emotionally so strongly, but somehow, as the sunlight struck his face as well, it gave him back his courage.

"I'm not moving one step further," he said to his captors. "If you want to kill me, do it here, and do it now."

A figure behind the first one stepped up to him. The automatic rifle in its hands whirled up towards him —

Then straight down. The figure's heels clicked. The masked head inclined. Astonished, Richard realized that he had been presented with a salute.

"Sire," said a deeper male voice, "forgive me. Until this moment I did not believe that you were who you are."

"Bugger forgiving," he said. "What the hell do you want?"

The last masked figure laughed, and then knelt at his feet. "With all our hearts, Sir, what we shall *do* is escort you at once to Holyrood Palace; and there see you made the first lawful King in four hundred years to sit on the throne of an independent and autonomous Scotland."

Three

Edinburgh

LIZ HAD GOT no further than Carlisle when her civilian aircraft was forced to turn back from the Border by an air force fighter. The unprecedented action confirmed the rumors of a Royal landing in the Highlands: it made finding their source much tougher. Being denied the use of a helicopter to jump over the remote northern areas of her native country meant using wheels and wild mountain roads — which meant wasted precious hours. She managed to hire an all-terrain vehicle in Carlisle, packed her two crew people into it, and headed northwest on the improved Glasgow road. At Ecclefechan, the historian Carlysle's birthplace, her cellular telephone rang. She heard from her supervisor in London about the evacuation of the Dounreay Reactor area.

"The International Radiation Monitoring agency in Stockholm doesn't record any change in background levels, Liz. It smells like Army dead fish."

"Or a live Successional Candidate," she said. "Thanks for the time saver, I'll switch routes."

She swung east, across to Langholm, and the road to Edinburgh. She flattened the accelerator but the all-terrain had a governor which wouldn't go over the legal limit. She crawled through Hawick and Selkirk, and then the winding slog through the Moorfoot Hills. She knew the route like the back of her hand from her student days. She had chosen the University of Edinburgh partly because she won a scholarship, but more because almost a century and a half ago it had been one of the first universities in Britain to go co-ed. The A7 route she was now on used to bring her back from dirty weekends to grinding final exams. Today it would take her straight in on Minto Street, past Arthur's Seat and Holyrood Park, to the city center of Princes Street, dominated by the Castle.

On the horizon beyond Lasswade a heavy black rain cloud hung over the city called Auld Reekie in the days of coal fires and maximum polution. The buildings of Scotland's capital now were sandblasted and pristine, reflecting soaring property values caused by offshore investors holding them for two weeks occupation during the annual Arts Festival. Most of Edinburgh's new big wealth was oil and electronics money, from Arabs and Asians. On a smaller scale, but more important to the vibrant feel of the city, were the hundreds of little entrepreneur firms of all the former Commonwealth nationalities: the amusingly named "Raj Picture Framing and Himalayan Tours" across from "Montego Bay Jamaican Scottish Teas", both of which she spotted as Gilmerton Road became Minto Street and the springtime green of Holyrood Park appeared to her right.

"Liz! Watch it!"

Two running men were directly in front of her. She slammed the brakes. The vehicle screeched in an uncontrolled skid. She missed the closest man by inches.

"Bloody drunks," she said to her crew. The men had been running out of the main bar of the Minto Arms. Horns sounded behind her. Shaken from having almost killed another human being, she straightened the wheel and started up again.

"Other side!" shouted her first camera operator. Her second said, "Christ! It's a riot."

The window of the Raj Picture Framing shop disintegrated in a shower of glass. Liz yelled, "Start filming, both of you." The billowing flame of a Molotov cocktail errupted from Montego Teas.

Traffic was stalled all around her. Police and fire sirens were starting. She called London Control on her cellular and said, "Liz Ponti. Edinburgh. I'm getting live footage of a race riot. Can you give me a satellite frequency?"

"Control here. We can take it but not show it. Scotland is gagged."

Three other ethnic shops were burning: jeering thugs ran past, igniting others.

"What do you mean, gagged?" she shouted to London. "This is civil disorder, not Anti-Terror."

"It's under a new emergency law. Something called British Areas. Roper is about to speak —"

The cellular link broke. A petrol bomb went off in the street beside her. One of the riot's ring-leaders running by turned his head...

It was the King's Cross major from Ireland, who had become a civilian murderer of an old woman in Virginia.

"Take him!" Liz yelled to her first camera operator, "and stay on him, no matter what."

"You're sure?"

"I wouldn't say it otherwise," she snapped.

"Okay —" the operator pointed —"but look over there!"

A dark blue van was stalled ahead of them. Another group of four men were running from it towards the gates of Holyrood Palace. The closest ones to her were masked, with automatic weapons. Undercover Special Action, she thought... until she saw the unmasked face of the man they were surrounding.

Arthur's Seat

RICHARD SAW THE BBC interviewer woman running towards him but by now he was too used to constant massive shocks to be surprised by that slight coincidence. In the van, his latest captors, or protectors, had assured him that they were Scottish Nationalists: like the kilted Regiments garrisoned in Edinburgh Castle, they were loyal to him to a man! In the street, he found total chaos and Edinburgh in flames.

The torched buildings were like a war zone. Firefighting equipment was blocked by vehicles which must have been deliberately stalled for that purpose. The men escorting him were obviously shaken.

The masked figure on his left shouted, "We can't do it now, in all this."

"We have to. For Scotland."

The other two Nationalists grabbed Richard's arms and dashed him through the flames towards a wrought-iron fence. Two tall stone columns with rampant lions on top flanked a pair of gates. The lions held metal replicas of the flags with the crosses of St George and St Andrew for the union of their two nations. A tourist sign said, "You too can now sleep in The Royal Mile: Enjoy the splendor of The Palace of Holyroodhouse, looking out at Arthur's Seat, sharing the Home of Scotland's Kings and Queens."

Not tonight. The gates were locked.

Still grabbing Richard between them, his Nationalist captors flung themselves against the filigreed ironwork. The gates shook but stayed closed.

"Shoot the lock!"

A burst from the senior man's automatic ricocheted. The gates parted. His guards raced forward towards the Palace. It was yellowed stone with rounded turrets and peaked spires. He saw an octagonal monument covered with Gothic carvings: more lions heads, stags, Elizabethan style courtiers. Another sign said something about *Darnley and Mary Famous Murders.*

"Now where?" one junior Nationalist shouted.

"Throne Room."

It was insane. There was nothing Richard could do about it. As the three men swung him away from the monument he saw that Liz Ponti was still filming him at a distance. His captors ran around the corner of the Palace beyond the Murder monument.

"Halt!"

A line of troops blocked the building. No kilts and bearskin busbies: they wore battledress and riot gear. Only the thistle emblems on their helmets showed that they were Scots. The shouted command came from a young officer holding a pistol and wearing captain's pips on his epaulets.

"Do you not realize who it is that you are halting?" demanded Richard's senior masked escort.

"I don't see anyone." The young captain kept his eyes staring at some point on the top of the Castle across the valley, above the smoke of the burning buildings.

"Damn it, man!" the senior Nationalist shouted. "You hold a commission in the Royal Scots Guards! You know this is your, and Scotland's, lawful King."

"I know I have orders to arrest any person I see, who so poses. The Palace is closed. You may not enter."

It was an Alice in Wonderland standoff. Richard's masked Nationalists were outgunned. The troops' young Scottish commander could see his face clearly, and knew bloody well who he was, but wouldn't do anything about it as long as he just stood there like another historic monument waiting to be murdered.

"God curse you!" his senior kidnapper finally shouted at the captain. And then to his associates, "It will have to be the gutless politicians."

THEY STARTED RUNNING again, across the open grass below a stone knoll, shaped like a chair. Richard saw the name Arthur's Seat — his own middle name, although he had never used it. As the Nationalists plunged him onwards, back into the smoke and confusion of the rioting, he wondered whether that other Arthur had really been here, long ago...

His lungs were bursting. He gasped and staggered against the rock. The men on each side of him dragged him to his feet.

"We cannot stay here," said the senior, pointing west. "The Assembly is not far, in Parliament House. Keep on!"

They pulled him forward. A piece of the Arthur rock fell off in his hand. He clutched it as an omen. The Nationalists abruptly changed direction: the Lion gates they had used to enter were blocked solid with emergency equipment. Hoses snaked in every direction. Richard tripped over one and fell. He heard a burst of gunfire. Two other bodies fell beside him. Blood covered his hand with the rock in it. The two Nationalists were dead. The third sat gasping, with more blood bubbling out of his mouth.

On the other side of the gates, wreathed in smoke, barely visible, a heavyset man with an automatic was aiming it at Richard.

He stared slackly, too exhausted, to run or hide any further. He heard a whirring in the smoke. A black and white chequered helicopter with NATIONAL POLICE landed on the grass. The blades blew the smoke away. He could see the marksman's trigger finger squeezing...

An entire building front collapsed into the street. A billowing shower of sparks and brick-dust flew up. As the debris settled, the backdraft sucked in the smoke again. The man with the gun had disappeared. A pair of armed policemen from the chopper replaced him. Again Richard heard that coldly official, "With us, please sir."

He didn't know how many helicopters, how many guns, how many kidnappers, how many countries. They loaded him in. The machine rose. The riot scene dropped. Edinburgh Castle was beside him, and he thought they were going to imprison him there, but they didn't. He saw a single kilted bagpiper still pacing for tourists on its battlements. So much for Bonnie Scotland. The police didn't say where he was going next. Richard didn't bother to ask. He had fought as hard as he could. The British Government had fought harder.

Westminster

SLADE SAT WITH his notepad and portable fax unit in the private gallery behind Roper's place on the Treasury benches. The mood of the House of Commons was difficult to judge. The Members had been restive on the earlier critical occasions but the public opinion polls in the Press had left no doubt that they would finally vote as usual. Like sheep. For this occasion, however, the polls were equally divided.

"The Chair recognizes the Prime Minister."

Slade had to admit that there was no hint of any lack of confidence from Roper about the final outcome. And confidence was contagious: the bleaters on the surrounding benches always followed a firm leader.

"What about Brown?"

The first sign of trouble came from a government backbencher, not the small and divided opposition, but Roper replied calmly: "The answer to that question is simple. The Minister for Scottish Liason did not see his way clear to support action which would have prevented the tragic situation currently occuring in Edinburgh. Members of this House, it is not easy to take controversial positions, but there are occasions when the well-being of the nation demands it. We have all seen the tragic results of sectarian violence in Ireland. While there is breath in my body I will not see the same thing happen in Britain."

"Bravo!"

The mood was turning... but the sheep hadn't seen the Bill yet.

"What has always made this country great," Roper continued, "has not been the extent of its Empire, nor its gallantry in standing alone against global tyranny and oppression. My friends, the true and enduring glory of our country is the unity and tolerance of its splendid people."

The bleating of assent was almost a majority. Almost...

"When our Empire was voluntarily disbanded," Roper now addressed the voting sheep behind the TV cameras, "we welcomed hundreds of thousands, of every race and religion, and all were given equal benefits and treatment under British law. However..."

This pause was the turning point. Roper picked up the waiting Bill from the leather-topped table in front of him.

"However," he repeated, "there are practical limits to equality. Everyone is *not* equally entitled to disrupt the life and well being of their neighbor: to make unlimited noise at night, or to tear down an ancient building which represents the essence of the Nation's heritage. Honorable Members, when you vote for the Best of Britain Areas Act you will do two things: you will preserve for all time the essence of the British heartland which countless millions of visitors come here anually to treasure, and you will prevent future racial disturbances from occurring in cities, towns — and even hamlets, such as the recent episode in Little Hooker, in Devon — not so far affected by such tragedies."

"Don't you mean, 'infected'?" The questioner was the Leader of the Opposition, a woolly former Unitarian clergyman who seldom posed even a minor challenge. Now he bleated with surprising force, "This odious Bill denies the purchase or ownership of real property to anyone whose grandparents were not all British citizens by birth. Damn it, these are the Nazi Nuremberg Laws!"

As the fax unit at Slade's elbow began to print URGENT FOR PRIME MINISTER, the former clergyman absent-mindedly dabbed a handkerchief to sop up the spit at the corners of his mouth, neatly undercutting any strength he had gained on television.

"On the contrary," Roper replied calmly, as Slade tore off the message, starting, FOX MISSED EDINBURGH, "a Heritage Area Change of Purpose Permit is no different than the permission already required for alteration of any Listed historical structure."

"For the love of God!" the Unitarian cried, "we are not discussing the tearing down of a Victorian kitchen cupboard! These are the lives of flesh and blood people!"

"Do you think I am not aware of that?" Roper demanded, taking the message, and glancing swiftly at it. "While we *discuss*, sir, instead of acting as a government elected by and responsible to those very same people, whole cities are being torn down!" Roper held up the fax, "I have just been informed that Manchester and Cardiff are also burning."

As the subsequent sheep count passed overwhelmingly, and the Prime Minister of Britain dropped the fax message in the Treasury Bench shredder, out of the six hundred individuals present in the Chamber only his personal private secretary knew that the phrase *"ready for"* had actually preceded the word *"burning"*.

Slade lost the last illusion he had held for his own safety.

Four

The Lowlands

THE EMERGENCY RADIO frequency in the police helicopter squawked incessantly. The pilot replied with brief monosyllables to stations in Edinburgh and Glasgow. Richard saw a glimpse of the skyline of Scotland's other major city off to his right and thought he was being taken there.

Instead, the chopper abruptly landed in a field.

A chequer-marked car raced up. The policeman in the helicopter seat beside him got up and jumped out. Another from the car replaced him. The car roared away over the field. The helicopter lifted off. The whole exchange had taken less than two minutes. It was the same ploy as the dummy kidnapping in Virginia, Richard realized, except there it was to put off his enemies: here it was to stop any hope of rescue.

The helicopter veered south.

"Are you taking me to London?"

The two grim-faced escorts said nothing.

"Will I be allowed to call a lawyer?"

The police exchanged a terse glance which was its own answer. He wouldn't know who to call anyway and there was no Anna to help him here with...

Anna. How incredibly he missed her! At least now, with the Ponti woman's video from Edinburgh, Anna would know he was alive. If the tape was ever aired. The last interview broadcast had only been possible because of America's constitutional freedom of the Press. In Britain...

As his thoughts seesawed, Glasgow had vanished. The sun was setting to the west. The chopper turned slightly back in that direction and began descending. A sing-song radio voice said, "This is Prestwick Control: Identify?"

The flashing beacon of an airport appeared off to his left. The police must be going to transfer him to a fixed-wing aircraft, but the pilot replied, "National Police One Four Two. Transiting only."

"Roger, National Police. Maintain minimum altitude for us to hold you on our radar until clear."

The helicopter continued dropping. Suddenly the sea was below them, only two hundred feet: whitecaps, catching the last of the sun.

"National Police, we've lost you. Come higher."

When the pilot instead went even lower and didn't answer, Richard realized once more he was only a pawn in another round of British political chess.

THE CHOPPER LEVELED off at an elevation less than the cliff of a small island passing to the west. A shadowed peninsula appeared ahead, to the east, and after that it was dark.

"I know you aren't police," he said to the men on either side of him: "I demand that you tell me where we're going."

The pair still said nothing. Richard remembered the grimly gallant MacKenzie explaining the reason for a similar airborne silence: the Government Intelligence satellite could be listening and the men at the controls didn't want Cheltenham to hear their voices.

Thinking of Mackenzie brought back the nightmare images of drowning in the riptide maelstrom, after Wallop and Kimura deliberately sacrificed themselves. His depression deepened. Gusts of wind began buffeting the helicopter. The pilot tried to compensate for the rapid changes of air pressure, lifting the craft in advance to overcome the following sharp drop. Each time it happened Richard hung on to his seat and waited for the rising sea to grab the skids.

Flying had become constant nagging fear. He could scarcely remember the time in his normal life when air travel was sunlight and blue sky boredom. Another beacon flashed. A radio voice identified itself as the Isle of Man; a second said Belfast. He must be over the Irish Sea, paralleling the coast of the English Midlands.

"Liverpool Emergency, calling all vehicles: can anyone respond to a new riot outbreak of looting at Merseyside?"

The voice was a woman's, sounding at the end of her tether. Flickering pinpoint lights were flames from another British city burning.

"Why is it happening?" he asked his escorts.

They stayed silent. The helicopter rose, then dropped even more alarmingly. The pilot swung its nose to the right. The flames disappeared. The lights of a ship replaced them briefly. Rain hammered on the chopper's hull. The ship was extinguished. Richard lost all sense of direction. How the pilot managed, flying blind, was beyond his comprehension. The rain turned to hail. The wind kept rising. The abrupt descents got deeper. Luck couldn't hold much longer. He thought, *When it crashes, I'll be in England.*

He had come so far, to be so near, for nothing.

He had come so far, to be so near, for nothing.

A huge gust flung the helicopter over on one side. The rotors thrashed wildly. It lurched back just as violently the other way. His head hit the fuselage. He was going to throw up. He wanted to die.

The wind stopped.

The hail and rain stopped. The rotor pitch changed for yet another descent, but this one was smooth as silk. A blaze of lights flooded the night. He saw turrets, battlements, a gleaming white flagpole. An immense flag was flying from it: on a green background, a scarlet dragon.

The sight stabbed his heart. The last time he had seen this symbol it was on an old woman's scarf. The helicopter sank gently down below the flag. The floodlights showed a smooth lawn, and a sign with carved gold letters:

CAERNARVON

The door of the helicopter opened. A man about ten years older than himself stood in the opening. Like the dragon symbol on the flag, and for the same reason, Richard recognized the man's face before his introduction.

"Your Majesty," the man bowed. "I am Sir David Llangath, Lady Bronwen's son. In her memory, I have the highest honor of bidding you welcome to Caernarvon Castle, the place of investiture of your forefathers, as Princes of Wales."

RICHARD STEPPED DOWN on to the grass. The soaring walls of the castle cut off all evidence of the natural or civil disorder raging outside them. The floodlit walls were built of curiously striated bands of different colored stone that looked more like something from the Mediterranean than a Celtic fortress.

He said in bewilderment to Lady Bronwen's son, "I understand some of the historical links to Wales, and I'm grateful for your welcome — not to mention lifting me out of Scotland! — but I should be in London."

"You would have been, Sir, that has been our intention from the start. However, events in Edinburgh, and since, make it far more difficult for you to enter your capital."

"It hasn't exactly been a piece of cake getting here," Richard replied.

"Your perseverence is wholly admirable," said Llangath, "but what Your Majesty will not know is that using the pretext of the riots, one hour ago the Westminster government of Henry Roper invoked the Emergency Powers Act and declared martial law throughout Britain."

The floodlights suddenly went out. The stage set of the flag and the walls vanished. Richard was left in the dark with this latest brutal reality of the force against him. Getting from the farthest tip of North Wales to the opposite corner of southeast England, with the British army running it, seemed as hopeless as being still stuck with the sheep in the ruined Highland cottage.

"You must be exhausted, Sir. There is a bed made up for you in the Castle. Rest for the night. Tomorrow morning we shall have a council of war."

A door opened and a faint beam of light spilled across the lawn. He followed Llangath into the fortress. Inside it a small apartment of bedroom and bathroom had been restored. He turned to say goodnight to his latest supporter, and saw a picture on the wall. It was a lifesize oil portrait of the crumpled newspaper photo in his pocket. *HRH, The Prince...*

His father.

Richard stared at the painted eyes of the man who had abandoned him. They were the eyes of a man his own age. Their expression was the expression he had seen a thousand times in his dressing room mirror, in his other life.

Who gives a damn? Let the good times roll...

Midlands

LIZ HAD GOT her crew as far south as Whitworth, on the northern outskirts of Manchester, when she heard about the imposition of Martial Law.

"Roper's going live in five minutes to explain it," said her BBC partner, over cellular.

"Explain it!" she said. "The bastard created it. This Areas Act is a transparent tabloid hustle to get people's minds off the Monarchy." She described the extraordinary near misses with the Candidate in Edinburgh. "There's also a 'King's Cross' link," she said. "I was sending you the whole thing on satellite when someone jammed my feed frequency."

"That's been happening everywhere. Liz, don't get sidetracked with any more royal adventures. Just hang on to the King's Cross footage you have and for God's sake get yourself back to London safely."

"I'm trying. I can see the glow of Manchester from here. We'll take the route through Oldham, then cut east and come down the M1. Keep your fingers crossed."

She swung the all-terrain vehicle back on the road but only three miles ahead ran into a police block. Rochdale was closed off. She had to reverse, and then try another way south. All the major roads ran across the country, forming the transportation corridor between the cities of the industrial heartland — Manchester, Huddersfield, Bradford, Leeds. Only narrow lanes from Britain's agricultural past missed the urban masses. With her two crew people taking turns at the navigation, she found herself directed past signpost names she had never heard of — Lumb, Polemore, Carlecotes, and Mapperley, where she saw a tourist display for a butterfly park, then Dale Abbey and knew she was between Derby and Nottingham.

The motorway was only a short distance east. She went through a village called Stanton by Dale, then Sandiacre. The entrance to the M1 beyond it was blocked by the army.

"Sorry, Miss," said a hassled young sergeant. "All motorways are reserved for military traffic only. The A routes are still open. Suggest you try the A47, then A1 down to London — but stay clear of Leicester."

In trying to do that she hit Ashby de la Zouche, Barrow upon Soar, and Frisby on the Wreake before the porkpie center, Melton Mowbray. The situation was changing faster than the sergeant's instructions. The A606 shortcut she had hoped for was closed. She had to keep on the old B676... only to find at Colsterworth that the A1 was denied to her as well.

The National Police were doing that, using an armored car, which made it impossible to tell the civilian force from the army.

"Godamn it!" she exploded to a cop sticking his head out of the conning tower. "You can't close down the whole bloody country!"

They could. "At least Peterborough," the National Force man answered, eyeing her coldly. "You'll have to stay north of that. At present the A141 south is still open."

Except for bitching there was nothing else Liz could do about it. She found herself on a cart track designated the B1166 which crossed the River Welland — and meant that she was already lost in the Norfolk Fens.

"No you aren't," said her second camera, checking the map. "Wisbech's just ahead. Do a right at Parson Drove and you'll hit the A47 coming down from King's Lynn. And if the fuckers have shut that, we can dump this thing at March and take the bloody train."

The graveyard humor did little to lift her own spirits: in spite of her prayers and hopes, Hector was not in any of her Edinburgh footage. The headlights showed nothing but flat blackness stretching away to either side, with occasional white-washed cottages dead ahead at unexpected right-angle bends. At a place called Guyhirn the A47 was open, but only the part going north; the way she wanted went to Peterborough, and was closed.

Manpower was stretched. Local police had been given the job.

"Go A One Four One," a constable told her in a thick regional accent. "Then One Four Two, that'll see you to Ely, but I don't know about Cambridge. There's reports things aren't too good in Cambridge."

Things weren't good a mile ahead. At West Fen someone in the army had changed their tiny mind again. Another armored car wanted to push her back off the main roads, over a railway level crossing, onto B1099. She stopped the all-terrain. A sign next to the raised safety barrier said,

Beautiful Britain
Welcome to March

"Move on there! Convoy coming through."

A corporal waved angrily. A column of headlights was approaching from the west. As Liz started moving forward again the barrier swung down in front of her and several major decisions clicked.

"Out!" she said to her crew. "We're taking your advice."

Red warning lights on the barrier began flashing. The first camera operator jumped down stiffly, followed by the second. They reached into the back seat for their equipment.

"Only take one unit," Liz said, "and let me check those tapes first."

"You think leaving the other camera with the car will be safe?"

"I'm not leaving it." She found the tape cannister she was looking for. "Get the rest of this stuff back to Central as soon as you can. I'm going to check something out in King's Lynn."

Caernarvon

RICHARD'S EXHAUSTION WAS total. Consciousness faded when he hit the pillow...only to be replaced by terrifyingly vivid dreams of drowning and flying and running and hiding.

He opened his eyes. The luminous dial of his watch said that it was only two hours later. The castle room was still pitch dark. A vertical rectangle beside his bed showed faintly lighter. He sat up to look, and found that it was a slit window, open a crack for ventilation, which he hadn't noticed on arriving. He traced his hands down the stone and felt a series of small ripples in the blocks. The aperture had glass in it now, but it had been designed for archers to shoot arrows. The grooves must be for aiming them, he thought, or perhaps from using them.

History was real in a place like this. A lifetime was nothing. He put on the light and stared again at the oil portrait of his natural father.

"Are you all right, Sir?"

The slightly Welsh baritone of Lady Bronwen's son sounded muffled through the massive thickness of the planked bedroom door.

"I'm fine." He got out of bed and went across to open the door. Llangath immediately rose from a chair outside. A snub pistol lay on a small table. His newest protector obviously hadn't slept at all. Richard pointed at the weapon and said with a wry smile, "I hope your decoy dodge after Edinburgh worked, Sir David. A world-famous tourist attraction hardly seems the best place to hide."

The Welshman smiled back. "As I mentioned earlier, Caernarvon certainly wasn't our first choice for Your Majesty, although using the obvious is not always a bad idea; taking this place would keep a full Special Air Service regiment busy for a week. We had planned for Windsor, but with the imposition of Martial Law, the odds of getting through safely on an overland flight south were no longer acceptable."

"You say, 'we'. Who else is in on this with you?"

"I cannot give you their names, Sir, but believe me, there is no shortage of loyal subjects in your kingdom, especially here in Wales. You will meet some of them in the morning. Now, if I may suggest — I can provide a pill — you should try to get some more sleep."

"No pills," Richard said, "and I don't feel like sleep, but I'll rest."

He closed the plank door and went back to the bed. The hell-raising eyes of the portrait looked down at him. He wondered what the man in the picture would do in his place? He could never have imagined that one day his kingdom would be burning under martial law. Or that a son he never knew would be running for his life.

A SOUND WOKE him the next time. He wasn't aware that he had been asleep until he looked at his watch again. Another hour. Still dark. The sound had stopped. He tried to think what the sound had been. A soft rustling, like wind in spring leaves, but there was something else as well, which he couldn't place.

He sat up. Outside the open archery window twilight was just starting. Water gleamed faintly. The fortress was built on an inlet of the sea. Now his eyes could see a narrow strip of land where the tide was out, and a causeway.

The rustling noise again. Something pale went by the window.

Thud.

That was the second sound, like something heavy, hitting... another pale shape! His heart lurched. He threw himself off the bed, grabbed his clothes, dashed at the door, yanked it open.

"What —?" Llangath asked.

"Parachutes!" Richard shouted. "They've landed on the beach."

THE WELSHMAN RACED to the window, then back to one in the corridor. Another of the ghostly shapes dropped past it. The paratroops were landing on the interior courtyard lawn as well. There was a brilliant flash of flame, then an echoing explosion. The chequered police helicopter was destroyed. Richard was cut off and surrounded.

"This way, Sir!"

Llangath moved at a run along the passage and around a corner. It was a dead end, bricked up when the castle was renovated. Behind him, Richard could hear pounding on the outer door from the grassed area. He looked for any other door or window. Nothing. On the bricked-up section a varnished board with the ostrich plume coat of arms showed the dates of Investiture of his ancestors.

The dull crump of another explosion sounded from the courtyard. Then a splintering crash. An acrid smell arrived with a gust of hot air. He turned back to face —

"Through here!"

Llangath grabbed him roughly. The wall behind the Investiture board had opened. The Welshman dragged him inside the opening. Boots were crashing along the slate floor. The wall swung shut. Richard caught a glimpse of a camouflaged uniform through the crack as it closed. Standing in total darkness he wondered if the uniform had seen him ...

"Keep moving!"

A flashlight beam stabbed on. Llangath pulled him towards a set of broad stone steps leading downwards.

"You won't have to tell me again," Richard said. "Just keep going, I'll follow.

"Well done, Sir. My apologies for touching your person, but those SAS types behind us would have been a bloody sight rougher."

The stairs ended at another closed door. Llangath took a black iron key from a hook and opened the lock. This time a wave of cold dank air struck them. A passage stretched beyond the door. Richard heard the hollow sound of water dripping. More important, there was no sound from anyone behind them.

"Watch your step, Sir, there's slime on the floor."

Orange and dark green mold, growing in patches. "Where does it lead?" he asked.

"This branch only goes under the Castle harbor. There's another that crosses the whole Menai Strait to the Roman copper mines on Anglesey, but we won't be showing our heads in that island rat trap."

The water noise got louder. The drips were replaced by a solid trickle. The floor of the passage became a pool. At first only the soles of Richard's shoes were covered. Then his laces. His feet got soaked. Then his ankles. Llangath ahead of him was wet to the knees —

"A pothole, sir! Move to the side!"

Richard avoided that and got the next one. His breath sucked in as the icy chill reached his groin. He floundered out of the hole. When he wasn't falling to his death from the sky on this trip, he was drowning! But the worst was over. The passage floor rose. The patches of mold reappeared.

"Not far now, Sir."

The passage curved. The walls changed from mortared masonry to solid rock fractured with quartz veins, stained greenish-blue from copper. The chisel marks of the miners were still visible. As he turned the curve he saw an engraved initial, **R**, and a date, **A.D. 1329**. Seven hundred years ago. Was the miner's name the same as his...?

Whump.

The sound came from behind them, but not as though it was in the tunnel. It seemed to be above, or outside.

Whump.

This time the solid stone of the floor shook slightly, like the tremor of a small earthquake.

"High explosives." Llangath looked worried.

"They wouldn't destroy Caernarvon, Sir David," Richard said reassuringly.

"Anti-submarine mines. Laid permanently in the Strait. By detonating them they hope to blow the passage."

"Is that possible?"

WHUMP.

A chunk of quartz from the roof answered the question.

"Run!"

Llangath moved with the speed of a man ten years younger than Richard, rather than older. He followed, only just able to keep up. The passage rising, and stale air, and darkness, made it worse. He caromed off the walls and skidded on the floor. The explosions came continuously in a ripple effect which reinforced the previous shock wave and compressed his ear drums.

Another closed door was the reason for the pressure.

It was the same as the one at the Castle end. The same rusted hook for — there was no key. In the flashlight beam, the hook was empty. And now the noise of water was audible again. Not drops, or a trickle. A torrent, sounding like Niagara in the confined darkness behind him.

"Look for the key!"

Llangath stabbed the beam on the floor, the base of the door, the foot of the walls.

"I see it!" Richard said. "On that ledge. By the hinge."

He picked it up and put it in the lock. It went half way and stuck. The torrent was louder. A hollow rumble.

"Let me, Sir." Llangath removed the key and shone the flashlight at the keyhole. "Some fool stuffed it with oakum!"

The Welshman took a penknife from his pocket and inserted the blade. The air of the passage felt even colder and danker. The rumble was closer. Llangath pulled a strand of tarred fibre from the keyhole.

"Try it now."

Richard's hand was shaking. The key hit the sides, the top, the bottom —

"In!"

And it turned. Even before Richard finished, his guide slammed the door open with his boot. Steps rose beyond. They leaped them, two at a time. Llangath fell.

"Go on, Sir."

The roar from the tunnel engulfed them. Richard grabbed the Welshman's arm and pulled him bodily, with all his strength, four steps forward, and up, onto a stone landing.

Bubbling and swirling like a bathtub drain in reverse, the torrent came to the step below it.

And stopped.

LLANGATH STARED FOR a moment at the boiling cauldron, then said simply, "Thank you."

"Tit for tat." Richard managed to force a grin. "Isn't that what they say in this part of the country?"

"They say, God bless the Prince of Wales. And you'll hear that sentiment a damn sight louder, Sir, full throat from all our hearts, at your coronation."

"I've got to get there, first," he said.

"After this," Llangath replied, with a gesture at the flooded passage, "to use Your Majesty's earlier expression, the rest of your journey through the kingdom should be a piece of cake."

He doubted that. But the tunnel in front was dry and level. They started off again, walking at a reasonable pace. After five minutes they came to a third door. The key was where it should be, on the hook; the keyhole was unstuffed. Dawn was waiting beyond it.

Richard found himself standing in a grassy trench, with high turf banks rising all around him.

"The Roman Camp at Segontium," said Llangath. "Please wait here, Sir, for one moment."

The Welshman moved on around a curve in the trench. Richard stared at the turf banks and thought of the times he had played amateur Romans in *Julius Caesar*...

"All ready."

Almost at once it seemed he heard Llangath's call. He walked along the trench curve and found himself looking into the barrel of a gun.

It protruded from the turret of a rubber-tired, armored personnel carrier with British Army markings.

"A modern Trojan Horse." Llangath was wearing a set of camouflaged battle fatigues and a smile. "Perhaps the local legend of Maxen Wledig — our Welsh liberator from Rome's yoke, who the centurions called Magnus Maximus and thought of as one of their own — would be more appropriate." The modern Welsh patriot held out another of the British army uniforms, and said, "If Your Majesty will put these on and climb aboard, we should have you through the lines and safely in London before suppertime."

Five

Southampton

AS THE BISHOP of Manitoba, McDermid came through British Immigration with even less fuss than easygoing Amsterdam. He didn't even need the Bishop's purple dicky and dog collar. The green light was on for anyone with a white skin.

Brown was the color the Brits were after.

Anyone with even a heavy suntan was being ordered across to the red light stream, even some outraged Japanese. McDermid walked past them, carrying his Bishop's little black bag, and thinking how invariably it happened that when the crunch really came, luck was with him. This second in-flight diversion, to Southampton, for instance. If he had landed as scheduled at Manchester, he would have been locked in a madhouse.

MIDLANDS MAYHEM
MARTIAL LAW SAVES BEST OF BRITAIN !

Southampton was also under military control, he discovered from the tabloids, but the airport was north of the army's perimeter formed by the motorway. He searched the papers for news of his Target.

Not a bloody peep: the only word from Scotland was about overtoasted crumpets in Pakistani teashops! But if his Target had been grabbed, he realized, this race scare wouldn't be going on. The imposition of Martial Law was a typical Brit ploy: at least it was late justice that the British voters who elected their murderous governments were getting a taste of their own lethal medicine.

So where was the Target?

McDermid studied the tabloids more carefully. The photo propaganda shots were all of Tommy Brit and Bobby Cop predictably helping grannies and kids out of burning buildings... but there was a pattern. The datelines and areas of the news stories were linked in a steady progression out of Scotland, southward through the Midlands, then swinging west to Liverpool and down to Cardiff. So far there were no tearjerkers below Birmingham or east of Bristol.

It was Wales.

The senile old aristo, Lady What's-her-name, came from there. McDermid wasn't going to get involved in a wild Welsh goosechase any more than Scotland. When he saw the troops ringing the airport he decided he wasn't going to chance a drive in Britain either! A Bishop of Rome should travel in comfort. He purchased a first class seat on the new privately owned super-speed rail line serving the South East...

The latest edition of *Britain Today* was slapped down on the ticket counter beside him. The dateline on the helpless-grannie picture at the top was only two hours ago, at Cheltenham. If his theory was right, the army's focus of attention had just crossed the Severn River.

His Target was in England! Less than a hundred miles separated the two of them. McDermid sat back in his private compartment — after thanking the National Police bitch who had held the door of it open for him — and refined his previous plan. Wanting maximum grandstand shock effect was false pride. Now he would simply go for the earliest possible ending of his mission.

Cheltenham

INSIDE THE ARMORED Trojan Horse, Richard was hypnotized by the name on the automated tactical State Board in front of him. Cheltenham used to be associated only with exclusive schools for Nannies and Young Ladies. Now, under the bland title, Government Communications Headquarters, the town was the brain center of British Intelligence.

Viewed through the televized image provided by the vehicle's conning tower periscope, the approaches and environs still appeared deceptively tranquil, but the SAS paratroopers at Caernarvon were final proof that the electronic eyes and ears could find him through clouds, darkness, and solid masonry. He had, but couldn't ask, a hundred vital questions for Llangath: Where in London was he being taken? Who would help him once he got there? What about protocol? How would he be presented for the first time to his subjects?

Would the British people accept him ...?

The tension was unrelenting but the actual ride southeast from Wales had been amazingly smooth. There was no civilian traffic on the motor-ways. Less than two hours after leaving the Roman Camp at Caernarvon they were through the Black Mountains. One village sign said Llanigon, the next, Cusop.

England.

It still caused a ripple on Richard's neck: a mixed emotion of elation and apprehension. He was wearing the rank badges of a major. Llangath was dressed as a Lieutenant Colonel, and no one asked either of them any questions. When the army checkpoints caught sight of the painted insignia on the personnel carrier's steel sides, the guards even moved other military vehicles out of its path!

Richard's uniform had the same insignia on the shoulder: a launched missile, crossed with a dagger. He didn't know what regiment it belonged to, or care, just as long as it kept working...

"Unit Special Force, Mike Delta, this is GCHQ Control: senior rank on board acknowledge for voice check, over?"

The order came flatly from the tactical loudspeaker. Richard's stomach flipped. He mouthed a whisper at Llangath, "Can't we pretend a radio failure?"

"Mike Delta, this is GCHQ: Failure to comply with voice check will necessitate you cease transit immediately, pending vehicle physical visual inspection."

Either way Richard was finished. He watched Llangath reach to the microphone switch on his helmet. If there was cover from trees, or buildings, around the next corner...

"This is Mike Delta Commander: voice check. Am transiting Home Counties to Capital Zone, over?"

The words were Llangath's but the sound was someone else. Instead of a slightly rolling Welsh baritone, a nasal English tenor whine went out across the airwaves.

Llangath saw Richard's astonishment. The Welshman tapped a black box situated against his larynx, gave a brief wry smile, and crossed his right hand's fingers...

"Roger, Mike Delta. You have vocal acceptance and operational clearance for Home Counties Region. Suggest you avoid Oxford. Minimum routing delays currently south via Swindon, then M4 east to London."

THE NAME OF the capital kept ringing like a great churchbell in his head. Only ninety minutes later another name from history joined it: Windsor. The label which could have been his family name appeared on the tactical screen as they were swinging south of Reading. The riots had spread this far. The lefthand sector of the periscope showed columns of smoke rising from Reading into a sullen gray sky. Richard watched the symbol for the closed Heathrow Airport approach to the north, and pass by. Now Greater London district names came on screen: Ealing, Hounslow, Brixton,

Lambeth: the Globe Theater was near there, he remembered. History was everywhere. Shakespeare must have followed this same route from Stratford on Avon.

What's in a name...?

Romeo's line came back to him. Richmond went by, with a golf course, and middle-aged suburbanites putting on it. At Clapham Common kids were flying kites. London was its own separate country. The rest of Britain was burning, the capital was still peaceful, without a care.

Through the periscope he watched an empty red doubledecker bus marked Brixton Hill move ponderously aside as a police car flagged it out of the armored personnel carrier's charmed way. Llangath eased to the right, to pass.

The bus obviously hadn't seen them. It was swinging back.

"On our other side!" Richard shouted.

But the bus had seen them. The turn was deliberate, made with the steering wheel hard over, on the incline of the hill. For a frozen instant the top wavered...then the center of gravity pulled it down on top of them.

Richard was thrown to the floor, which saved his life. The periscope assembly telescoped into the space where he had been standing, snapped off, and jabbed forward like a lance into the back of the driver's seat.

Llangath grunted. Richard tried to stand up but the overhead deck of the personnel carrier had compressed so that he could barely crouch.

"Sir David, are you all right?"

No answer. He groped his way forward and felt his hands slipping. Blood was sprayed all over the compartment. The shattered periscope standard protruded from the center of Llangath's chest.

Another person had died instead of him.

But as guilt replaced shock he smelled smoke. His brain stopped worrying about other people and screamed, *Fire!*

THE CONNING TOWER hatch was jammed shut. The doubledecker wreckage blocked the carrier's forward window There had to be some other way out. They couldn't build these armored sardine cans without some secondary exit!

But the smoke fumes were stronger, like rubber, already half choking. And blinding. What little light came through from the front was blanked out by oily darkness. In mounting panic Richard fumbled his way along the side of the interior, feeling for anything that might be a handle. A First Aid kit fell out in his hand. He threw it away in disgust. The next handle was a locker of spare steel helmets. Equipment manuals —

Gas Masks!

He pulled one on. His eyes still streamed and the blackness was total, but at least he could breathe. He crawled further to the back of the vehicle. The metal under his palms was hot. Searing! He tried to keep his hands from touching it. The heat came through the fabric covering his knees. His head struck something. He yelled in terror and pain and cradled the injured part of his skull against his forearms. The top of one hand hit something else. An explosion went off.

When it was finished a round patch of metal was missing. Through the fogged mask, and smoke, there was daylight.

An escape hatch.

He fell out of it onto the pavement. Through a gap in the smoke he saw a river, and beyond that spires.

Westminster Abbey.

Smoke obliterated the sight. The bus was burning. The personnel carrier was burning. The police car was burning. He was standing for the first time on a street of his capital and the whole street was burning!

"There's one of the army bastards!"

The shout came from his right. A mob of punks were rushing at him. Richard turned towards them. They stopped. Something flew through the air. A circle of new flame exploded at his feet. He staggered out of it and tore off the gas mask so that he could see more clearly. The advancing mob was larger. Not kids. Mostly adults. Mostly blacks. He remembered that Brixton was one of the immigrant ghetto districts. The rioters carried clubs...

A brick landed beside him. He looked for the police. None. No military help either. He was alone. Fate had brought him close enough to see the place in which he would have been crowned. It was as far away as the moon.

He began to run towards the river. Away from the mob.

Towards the white man.

HE SAW THE man emerging from an alley between two burning buildings. Athletic movements. No sign of fear. Because of the gun. A silenced automatic. Richard thought that the man must be an undercover cop. He knew the gun was silenced because he only saw the flame from the muzzle when it fired.

At him.

His arm hurt. Smoke hid the man. Richard ran away in the opposite direction. Back to the mob. His arm was agony. The mob closed in and knocked him to the ground. A club was raised in a clenched black fist. A terrifying black face glared down at him. A West Indian Cockney voice shouted, "Kee-rist! Wait a minute! What we got here, then?"

Richard said through clenched teeth, "Please, I need help. My name is—"

Emergency sirens drowned him out. The mob began melting. He saw the white man at an opposite corner, aiming the gun again. At this closer range the man had a moustache.

The man who murdered Sally had one just like it.

McDermid?

As Richard realized that the assassin who had tracked him from Ireland to Brisbane, to Marriot's Hat was finally going to kill him, he repeated desperately to the enraged black face above him, "Please listen. My name is —"

"You think we're all fucking idiots? I *know* your bloody *name,* man!"

The club gripped in the black fist descended.

Six

King's Lynn

LIZ CROSSED THE River Ouse just after daylight. The ancient town was mercifully free of either the army or the urban chaos sweeping the nation's major industrial centers. Some of the local farmers and fishermen were already beginning to stock open-air stalls in the Tuesday Market but all the retail shop keepers were still asleep. She pulled in to the stable yard of the Duke's Head Hotel and parked her vehicle. She had no time to waste on sleeping, but the night porter let her have a room at half-rate to use the shower, and for an exorbitant tip arranged a pot of fresh coffee and Fen Country breakfast.

After it, with another five-pound note, when Liz said casually, "Wasn't there an electronics shop somewhere near here involved in the Sandringham tragedy?" the porter was also glad to exchange local gossip.

"King's Lynn Video," he said, "that's right, they did the leasing. Off Queen Street, by the Saturday Market, behind the new Town Hall — that's the one with the flints pattern."

"So they're still in business."

"In prison, waiting sentence, and so they should be! Even if it was the Irish wife put him up to it. The place is under receivership. The assistant manager as was, has an offer in with the accountants, and runs the place. From Birmingham, not a local."

Liz thought that anyone as keen to pick the bones off the carcass would get there early. She found her way to the town hall with its unique chequerboard pattern of flintwork, and the Video Shop behind it, by eight o'clock.

The ex-assistant manager arrived seven minutes later. A weasel-faced little shit who took one look at her equipment in the all-terrain and snapped, "Not open for returns until ten."

"I'm not returning anything," she said, taking some bills from her shoulder bag, with its BBC logo. "I'd like to ask you a few questions for a documentary assignment. There'd be an emolument of twenty pounds."

The man eyed the cash and the logo. "Fifty, and no faces."

"Fifty," Liz agreed. If he had the answer it was cheap. If not...? But she felt positive this morning. "We need a player," she said. "I have a tape I want to show you."

"Half up front."

She gave the little shit his twenty-five and followed him into the shop. It was hard to believe that with the size of its Royal fortune the Family would have rented a set from this hole-in-the-wall operation, but that was how fortunes got made. The future owner of the business switched on a bank of receivers all getting Euro satellite coverage of burning Britain on cable. The rioting had reached Reading: at least it was being allowed to be shown from Reading, which meant that it had probably got all the way to London.

Liz said, "You were working here at the time of the Sandringham bombing?"

"That's right. Service and Complaints. Use this one."

The manager indicated a used player with a half-price sticker still worth twice its true value. Liz loaded her tape and ran it on fast forward to the counter position she wanted. "I'm interested in the days immediately before the attack. In particular I want to know if you ever saw this man?"

She stopped the tape at the footage count for the Farm scene in Virginia. The assailant she thought of as the King's Cross killer was leaving after murdering the old Herald. The manager shook his head. Liz ran it again, and filmed the man as he watched a freeze-frame of the steel-jawed face of the dart-gun assassin.

"Yes and no," said the manager.

"What does that mean?"

"The other half, first."

Liz passed the bills across with her spare hand.

"He was here," the manager continued, without thanks. "Not alone though. He had an Asian in the car."

"When?"

"Night before the set went over to the Estate. Day before Boxing Day, to give us a chance at setup, before the Royals all arrived, like usual."

"You're sure."

"It was him. I was out in Service, behind the counter. He comes through without ringing the bell and wants a cheap rate. I said, 'Over Christmas? There's thirty standbys on my list. You've got to be out of your bloody tree!' "

Liz asked, "Was he ever alone here, in the Service department?"

"A couple of minutes maybe. Not more. The Asian came in the shop front and I went to check. You've got to watch. Especially foreigners. The shoplifting at Christmas is something criminal."

She stopped her camera. The information in its cartridge was worth ten times the fifty pounds. She removed the cassette of the King's Cross killer from the half-price player.

"Hold it!" The manager put his hand over hers. "That'll be another ten for using our machine."

SANDRINGHAM WAS ONLY seven miles distant and new signs had been posted to make it even easier to get to for tourists wanting bed and breakfast in the former Royal chambers.

RE-OPENING NEXT WEEK
ALL CARDS WELCOME

Liz thought she was used to the ugly side of human nature, but she wasn't. It was amazing enough that the house had been repaired so soon: that anyone would pay to sleep at the scene of such an appalling recent tragedy was disgusting. She drove through the open gates of the Estate and stopped in an enlarged parking lot created from what had apparently been a herbaceous border.

"No pictures this week, Miss! Not before Re-Opening."

An old man with a strong Norfolk accent put down a wheelbarrow of forced summer annuals he was trundling from a greenhouse, for planting out in a strip beside her vehicle.

"I'm not here to take the house," Liz assured him. "I'd just like to ask you a few questions about the Estate, the way it was before —"

"It were a proper home," the old man retorted. "That's what it were. Now it's just a danged hotel."

"I don't agree with what's happening either," she said. "Can you tell me if there's anyone still here who was on the gatehouse staff during the days just before the attack?"

"Not days. Night-times. I was, yas."

"Yourself?" His idiom on top of the local accent made it hard for her to follow. He nodded.

Liz said, without the certainty she had felt at the television shop, "I wonder if you ever saw this man? The picture isn't very clear. You'll have to look through my camera playback viewer."

The gardener squinted at the tiny screen.

"Perhaps you'd like to get your glasses," she offered tactfully.

"Don't need no glasses. That's un."

"You recognize him?" Her case-toughened heart did a little pit-a-pat. The old man gave a cackling laugh.

"See a bloke catch the bum of his trousers on a fence rail spike, my dear, you remember the look on his face."

"And what was he doing when you saw him, apart from being snagged on the fence?"

"Measuring. I thought he were a poacher out to set a rabbit line in Home Wood, but he dassn't. He had one of they little beeping thingummys with a red light."

"A laser," she said. "And he was using it to measure the distance to the house?"

"Like land surveyors, thass right. I told police Inspector when he come up before Family arrived, but nothing never gets done by coppers till tis too late."

She got him to show her exactly where on the fence. There was even a thread still waving in the cold morning breeze off the Wash, until a wren flew up and snatched it away for a nest. Liz didn't mind losing the thread. She had the tape.

She took out her cellular to call London but the microwave channels were all being jammed. She saw some wires coming from a cottage and said to the old man, "Is that where you live — may I use your phone?"

"And tea, both," he said.

While the gardener put the kettle on she tried the old-fashioned land-line. It was still open. She got through to her BBC partner.

"Liz! For Christ's sake, where are you?"

"No names," she said. "Did the crew get the Edinburgh footage to you yet?"

"No. How would they do that if you're still in the field?"

"By train. They were coming down from a place called March, just outside Peterborough. They should have been in London two hours ago."

"From Peterborough," her supervisor repeated, in a voice that already told her what was coming next. "There was a rail crash at Horningsea, above Cambridge. They're still counting casualties. That's the same line. Liz —"

"I'm driving back on the south road to London immediately."

She broke the connection. She couldn't expect any help from London and she had no time left to lose. She raced from the cottage to the all-terrain and got it moving as fast as its infuriating governor would let it go on the road east, to BBC Regional, in Norwich.

As she left Massingham Heath, across the flat fens behind her she saw in the rearview mirror the unmistakeable black killer shapes of a pair of military helicopter gunships already descending towards the A149 leading south from the Sandringham parking lot. Traffic and train accidents were now too subtle: the people who had already killed a King would shoot her outright if they found her.

Brixton

SOMETHING CRUNCHED THE pavement beside Richard's right ear, jarring his head. He felt himself being dragged by the shoulders. He opened his eyes.

"Shut them!"

The club had not squashed his skull. And the black man who had wielded it was doing the dragging. The white man with the gun was hidden by the burning wreck of the bus.

"Listen what I tell you!" the Cockney West-Indian hissed. *"That undercover pig needs you dead!"*

Richard thought he might as well be. Every time his injured arm bumped the road it was like being shot again. He heard more shouts from the mob, and sirens almost on top of him. They were suddenly muffled. There was a fresh blast of heat, and a crash.

"Okay. Now stand up."

The black hauled Richard to his feet. He was in an alley. A building had collapsed, blocking it from the street.

"This way!"

The black plunged into a narrow lane leading at right angles between two concrete tenements. Richard hesitated —

The huge shadow of a human figure loomed over the collapsed rubble. A terrifying stick-like object protruded from its hand.

McDermid...

"Man! Come *on!*"

His unlikely rescuer gestured urgently. Richard followed him into the lane. Glancing back over his shoulder at the first corner, he saw that the shadow figure behind was only a fireman, holding a hose nozzle. The black in front ran down the ramp of an underground garage. The vehicles parked there didn't need shelter from the weather. Half had no bodies, and the other half had no wheels. Wrecked chunks and random usable pieces were stacked in any remaining spaces. Trails the width of a single person wound like a spider web through the mechanical devastation.

Somewhere near the center of the web enough room had been left for a double bed mattress.

"Okay. Rest stop for Your Majesty."

The black gave an awkward nodding bow indicating the mattress. Richard remained standing. "You know who I am," he said, "but I don't know your name."

"Harry, sir." The man gave another bow and a broad white-toothed grin.

"I have to thank you Harry, for saving my life." He started to shake hands and realized that it was his right arm which was injured. Richard offered his left. Harry stopped grinning and reached forward tentatively. The change in the man's demeanour surprised him. Until that moment the black had been in absolute command of the tenement car-wreck world. Now, from just one touch of his hand —

The space seemed to whirl. Richard collapsed to the mattress.

"Let's see that arm."

The black face was in control again, once more bending over him.

"You've lost too much blood."

He realized that his right sleeve was drenched with it. Harry leaned inside the front half of a wrecked London cab and brought out a white box with a red cross on it. He removed a pair of surgical scissors from the box and skilfully began cutting the sleeve fabric.

Richard said, "You seem to have had practice at this, Harry."

"Every war-zone needs a medic." The grin flashed briefly.

"You think of your life in Britain as a war?" The sudden stab of cloth stuck to exposed flesh made him gasp.

"Your Majesty's life is a war." The black dabbed witch-hazel on the wound and wrapped it in a bandage. "I can patch this for now but we need professional stitches. You be safe here while I get 'em."

His lifesaver ducked away and vanished almost at once in the spider trails through the car wreckage. Richard lay back on the mattress and tried to comprehend what voodoo magic there was in the idea of a constitutional monarchy that could make all this happen...

Downing Street

SLADE WATCHED THE reports coming in on the scrambler line from Love. When FOX AWAY CAERNARVON was followed by MISSED CHELTENHAM, the possibility began to seem real that the Australian might actually reach London. For him to have got so far already implied powerful allies on a scale much greater than Roper had anticipated.

Could Roper survive?

Slade's instinct said, No. But then the scrambler light turned red. He acknowledged on the Prime Minister's behalf with the Clear To Send button. The screen replied:

FOX EARTHED BRIXTON. SOLUTION IMMINENT.

Seven

Black Prince Road

RICHARD LAY ON the mattress among the wrecked cars, waiting for Harry to return with medical help for his damaged right arm. Most of the time it was eerily quiet down in the underground garage. Occasionally sounds drifted in to remind him of the urban chaos outside. Sirens, dull thumps of explosions, brief bursts of rapid gunfire, yells...

The sounds echoed for a moment off the metal hulks around him but they all seemed far away. A tiny skittering noise was close. A rat popped up through the center of a pile of tires. They stared at each other. Richard's arm throbbed. The rat began grooming its whiskers. The animal's purposeful action was a sharp contrast to his own absurd position. The rat knew what it was doing. He didn't have the slightest idea. He realized that now: not where he should go, or who he could meet, or how he would ever become the figurehead he had pretended to be.

Because it was all a pretense. He understood that as well. He had never been royal — whatever being royal was! He was an actor, playing any part the people he met seemed to expect. In America, he was a gee-whiz Highness for Society to invite. In Scotland, he was Bonnie Prince Charlie come home to his people from over the sea. In Caernarvon, he was the Prince of Wales, descendant of someone called Maxen Wledig or Magnus Maximus, if any of those names had really existed either. And here in England, supposed to be a king at the heart of his kingdom, he was just a hunted common criminal waiting for —

The rat had stopped grooming.

It sat bolt upright, ears twitching. Richard's could hear nothing. The rat relaxed. He tried to settle in a position that wouldn't put pressure on his arm. It was bleeding again. Not a gush, but he could feel the wound seeping. *How much blood could he lose before —?*

Metal clanked. The rat was gone. He almost called, "Harry?" but another clanking noise echoed as something piled up fell onto the concrete. His black helper could move blindfolded along the spider trails between the automotive slag heaps, and not touch them. A footstep...

It must be McDermid.

Richard stood up. A spring in the mattress twanged. The footsteps halted.

His head whirled. He clutched at the taxi body containing the First Aid box. His head cleared. The footsteps had started again. Bending double to stay below the tops of the wrecks, he stepped off the mattress. Another spring twanged, even louder. The footsteps stopped as his hunter listened.

Richard started moving along the trail he thought led to the entrance. He went sideways, crabwise, trying not to brush against the protruding doorhandles, mirrors, and bumpers that stuck out like stubs of branches in a dense forest. McDermid's footsteps appeared to be paralleling his...

In the opposite direction!

He moved into a new trail. The dim light grew stronger. The noises from the outside world got louder. His unseen killer's footsteps were fainter. He crossed a third trail: all European radiators on one side, Far East on the other. Even a Rolls Royce winged goddess.

A muzzle flame flared from the end of the trail.

The shot should have killed him but at the same moment he accidentally smashed his shin on a chrome-plated bumper which brought down a pile, forming a shield. Heedless now of anything but escape Richard plunged ahead to the entrance. Doors, seats, hubcaps cascaded behind him, filling the trail. He heard an oath as his hidden pursuer fell over them. The trail forked. He went right. It was blocked by a wall. He went back, and turned left.

The figure of McDermid rose from the floor.

Richard spun left again into another spider web trail. He plunged through between two totalled Fortnum & Mason's delivery vans. Another flash of flame reflected from a side mirror, from two, ping-ponging back and forth. He didn't know if the flash was ahead or behind.

He plunged ahead and collided with a human body.

In a white coat. A black woman. Harry was behind her. The woman was lighting a cigarette with a lighter. The package in her hand had a red warning label: THIS OBJECT CAN KILL YOU.

"Behind me!" was all Richard could gasp.

Harry pulled on a chain hoist. A roof-high mountain of rusted engine blocks tumbled with a noise like thunder. The pursuing figure was gone.

"I told Your Majesty this country was a war-zone." Harry gave his laid-back grin and pointed at the woman smoking the cigarette. "And this 'ere lady is your professional stitcher. I got us some professional medical wheels."

A white-painted ambulance, with its engine running and the rear door open, was waiting on the ramp leading up from the garage. The woman helped Richard into the back, then climbed in beside him. Harry went forward and became the driver. Richard lay down on a white bunk and didn't ask how someone in Harry's circumstances came into possession of such a priceless object.

The ambulance rolled forward, up the ramp, and out into the civil war still raging in Brixton. The street was not the one he had started from after the bus crash but it looked the same. Burning buildings and vehicles. Jeering mobs. Tense police. Beleagured firefighters trying to save lives at the risk of their own. Bricks all over the pavements. Hoses snaking in every direction.

Harry sounded the ambulance siren. A harrassed policeman waved them ahead. The black woman in the white coat killing herself with the cigarette habit deftly removed the makeshift bandage on Richard's arm. She examined the wound, and nodded.

"Lucky," she said. "A dirty big bullet but it missed the bone."

She took a hypodermic out of an instrument case and filled it from a small container.

"I don't want to be unconscious," he said.

"You won't be, Your Majesty. This is only for antibiotic and pain."

The needle pin-pricked his skin. She used his title so matter-of-factly, Richard thought. Why didn't she know what he knew? That he was just an actor, and always would be? He could not possibly be even a figurehead ruler of this country. He would go back to his own. Australia. He hadn't let himself think how much he missed it. Compared with the urban hell outside the ambulance window his police troubles in Sydney and Brisbane were only fleabites.

A slight sensation of pressure came from his arm. With the cigarette still in her mouth, the woman was stitching up his wound.

"Another lifesaver," Richard said, with a smile, "but I'm surprised that a medical professional would be a smoker."

"When you test Positive for AIDS, Your Majesty, it would be a pleasant surprise to live long enough to die from tobacco."

She smiled back at him, and wrapped his arm in a fresh bandage. She announced her probable death sentence from the terrible disease as matter-of-factly as his rank. He was horrified for her, yet afraid to ask.

"I picked up the virus from a cut," she said, reading his thoughts, "in an emergency operation on a heroin addict, not from whoring."

He was deeply ashamed. People like her, and the firefighters — even the police — didn't lie around wondering, *What use am I?* or, *Who will help me?* Every day they did their their jobs and offered their lives. He saw a street sign pass outside the window: Black Prince Road. The smoke had lifted. The river was back: the Thames, almost beside him. On the far bank, downstream from the distinctive Lambeth Bridge, he saw the spires again of Westminster Abbey.

The medic's example settled his mind. He had no agonizing choices to make. His task was simple: like his natural father, and his ancestors, he had only to cross the river and enter the Abbey where his throne was waiting. The Black Prince could have wielded a broadsword to carve out his rightful place in history. The way for an actor to do that today was through television. He was not alone: he did still have someone in Britain with real power to help him.

Norwich

LIZ CAME INTO the town from the north, the opposite direction to her previous visits when she recorded the witch hunt sessions of the Justice Commission. The sight of the Guild Hall made her cry for Hector.

Fighting back tears, she drove through the Maddermarket where the famous medieval red dye was sold, and past the Cathedral and the grave of Edith Cavell, the nurse shot by the Germans in the First World War for helping Allied prisoners to escape. Seeing the memorial boosted her own courage. She swung up the cobbled lanes of Elm Hill to the ugly modern contribution to the city's architecture which was BBC Regional for East Anglia. The architects were only partly to blame: the main reason that the structure looked like Hitler's bunker was because it had originally been designed to serve as an alternative communications center to London in the event of nuclear war.

Liz parked the vehicle, collected her tapes, and entered the building. Minutely detailed instructions for what to do in case of the end of civilization were all still in place on the walls, she noticed, as she showed her BBC identity pass to the front desk computer scanner.

The machine said, "Accepted. Good morning." The anti-terrorist barrier rose. Behind it, the human staff of the Center were all watching riot damage from the major cities on monitors electronically surtitled, "Officially Approved For Relay" — except the pictures from London, which had vivid red diagonal, "Not Cleared: Hold." The capital looked like an armed camp. Every image had troops in battle gear, and military vehicles with uncovered weapons, moving into position around the familiar tourist attractions of Big Ben and Parliament.

"Liz Ponti!" The center's manager had caught sight of her. "This is an honor for Regional. With London burning, what brings a star up here?"

"I have some special assignment material from the North for Central," she said. "I couldn't get it through on Satellite from my portable transmitter. I need to use your fixed link."

One of the London screens, showing riot-torn Brixton, changed its surtitle command from "Hold" to "Relay". The Center manager snapped his fingers at the engineering booth. The bank of regional monitors all lit up with the Brixton image.

"Sorry, Liz," he indicated the screens, "you can see how things are. All channels are reserved for London incoming. A tidal wave could sweep over this part of the country, but the rest wouldn't know about it. We aren't cleared to send anything."

"But my stuff is internal," she said. "Not for the public."

"Only following orders." Which his shrug showed he didn't like. "Listen, if your material is really hot, have a nice cup of tea in the Caf, and I'll give you our Local News transmission feed to Central in half an hour."

The Brixton picture showed an ambulance weaving its way heroically through the opposing battle lines of troops and rioters. The rest of the country was being allowed to see that image, Liz thought, so why not Westminster? What could Roper be afraid of…?

Him. The subject of her tapes. He must be somewhere between those civil war lines and the north side of the Thames, she realized. He had made it so far! And now the master manipulator of public opinion in Downing Street was pulling out all the stops to close the noose in private, off the air.

Another thirty minutes could be too late. As the nuclear warfare instructions on the wall said: SECONDS COUNT. But the frightening yellow and black signs also gave Liz her solution.

"Thanks," she said with a smile to the Center manager, "I'll go up to the cafeteria and wait."

He waved, and returned to his staff. She walked casually towards the lift.

INSTEAD OF TAKING the elevator, Liz raced down the emergency exit stairs. There was no problem in finding her way, or in knowing what to do. The instructions had been designed for people operating on the edge of the end of the world.

OPEN DOOR TOWARDS YOU

It was six-inch steel, so well balanced that when the handle was turned, a feather could have moved it.

LOCK DOOR BEHIND YOU

When it swung softly shut, and was locked from the inside, not even a megaton dropped on Norwich could reopen it.

PUSH FOR DEDICATED POWER SUPPLY

A large red button started the generator. The lights in the passage beside her flickered once as they changed over from the main building current, then steadied. A gentle whoosh of air came from ventilator grills along the floor.

ENTER TRANSMISSION BOOTH

The inner door to the booth was the same machined construction as the outer one, but only half the thickness. On the other side of it Liz found a complete studio facility. Seats, desks, printers, microphones, monitors.

SELF-OPERATING CAMERA

There were enough seats for a full crew, but the planners had also assumed that there might only be one pair of hands left to cope. The camera required another Start button, and her voice check: robot control did the rest. The camera's red eye was already tracking her as she loaded her cassettes in the hopper and walked to the Announcer's Position. When she sat down, a sign above the camera flashed:

ON-AIR

The banked images from London showing on the monitors cut abruptly to multiples of her own face. The Nuclear Emergency satellite had unbreakable over-ride of every UK channel: as long as it was not destroyed in orbit she had a captive audience of the entire British population.

BROADCAST

"My fellow Britons," she said to the red light, "this is Liz Ponti. Unless what you and I do in the next few minutes can make a difference, somewhere in the streets beside our Parliament, a man whom a majority of us now feel suitable to be our King, will be killed by our Government. To support this terrible statement I shall be showing you conclusive evidence of similar calculated, and deliberate, acts of High Treason by agents of that Government. What you will see is so astounding, and the consequences for our country so momentous, that it can only have been ordered and approved at the highest political level. The code name given to this covert black operation in those Government orders is, *'King's Cross'...*"

Lambeth Bridge

THE AMBULANCE WAS safety: stepping out of it meant risk. As Harry drove like a pro through the police and army cordons at each end of the bridge, claiming alternately St Thomas', or University College Hospital as his patient's destination, Richard thought of trying to use the vehicle's emergency radio to call the BBC. But after his helicopter, and personnel carrier intercepts...

The radio brought death! He had to use a public payphone.

There weren't any. The last of Britain's unique, old-fashioned red kiosks had been removed as a cost-cutting measure years ago. The advent of personal cellular eliminated most replacements. There were private enterprise group-booths in major locations like airports and railway stations but although Waterloo Station was next door from Lambeth he obviously couldn't use that. Anyway, now Waterloo was on the other side of the river.

He had crossed the Thames!

Without even realizing it, he was within walking distance of his goal. Through the porthole window of the ambulance he saw a gothic monument, the Victoria Tower, and beyond it, across grass, *Parliament!*

The ambulance stopped abruptly. He slid forward on the bunk. His black guardian angel, the woman medic, had to grab a handrail. A male voice outside barked,

"Turn south. This area's closed."

"Police casualty, man," Harry replied. "For University College, acute care."

"Sorry, no civilian traffic allowed. If they can't take you right here at Westminster Emergency, try Queen Alexandra's Military, they've still got some vacant beds, it's just down the road."

The ambulance turned left. Another pair of heavy tanks rumbled by in the opposite direction, blocking out Richard's glimpse of the walls of Parliament. He lay back on the bunk. His goal, that was so near, receded.

"Try not to fret, Your Majesty." The calm woman in the white coat wiped his forehead soothingly with a cool towel, and lit another cigarette. "Something good will happen soon."

"It might," he said bleakly, "if I could just find a bloody phone!"

"You want to use a telephone?" She stared at him in surprise.

"It has to be a public one, and there aren't any."

"Why public?"

"A private line could be traced."

"Can't public?"

"Yes," he said, with impatience, "but it doesn't have an owner to get into trouble."

"The owners I know would say that Your Majesty got into a lot of trouble on their account." The woman spoke on the ambulance intercom to Harry, "Turn right at the next corner. The twenty-four hour tobacco and grocery on Marsham Street."

"No turns," their super-cool driver answered. "Have to go round the block and come in from Page. That section of Marsham is one way."

Dull government offices and a Christian Science church went by the porthole window. The sounds of military traffic increased then, as the ambulance swung left and stopped, they faded. The medic opened the rear door slightly, checked both ways, took a spare white coat from a hook, and said to Richard,

"Put this on. I won't be long."

She stepped down. The door closed. Her head passed the porthole. He could feel the ambulance trembling slightly: Harry was leaving its engine running. He heard staccato voices on the radio, but not what they were saying. Leaving his wounded arm free of its sleeve he put on the white coat as ordered. The medic's head re-appeared in the porthole. She opened the door and beckoned. Richard got off the bunk and moved forward.

"Better wear this too." She removed the stethoscope from her neck and put it around his. "People don't look at faces," she added with a wry smile, as he stepped past her, down onto the pavement, "just skin color, and badges."

The street was deserted. Narrow. Only one block long. The grocery store was right beside him; the only shop, tucked in among more drab office buildings, it had once been a house. The medic woman escorted him to the door, and gestured him inside.

The shop was tiny, probably a former parlor, opening off a narrow hall leading away to the interior. A handlettered, paper sign folded over a string said, *Closed.*

"I'll stay outside. The telephone Your Majesty can use is at the back."

The medic returned to the street. The front door shut behind Richard. He went along the hall. An interior door with a glass pane in the top of it was to his left. A space which had been a Victorian scullery-pantry was now the living area. He saw a television screen reflected in the glass. The picture was blocked by a small bald Pakistani watching it. The grocer. The phone was in the hall just beyond; an old wall-hung unit, with manual buttons.

He didn't know the BBC number. The obsolete phone didn't have a built-in electronic directory. He couldn't see a print one. Talking to the Telecom computer was asking for trouble. He tapped on the glass pane. The Pakistani didn't hear. He tapped louder. The grocer swung around but didn't leave the set. Richard made turning-pages gestures ... which worked! The grocer produced a dog-eared directory from somewhere out of sight and brought it to the door.

"Here is what you are wanting, Doctor."

The medic had been right: the little Pakistani passed the book without looking at Richard's face. The man's attention was glued to —

Liz Ponti.

On the screen. The grocer closed the door before Richard could hear what she was saying, and then once again blocked out her picture. She was here in London, that was the main thing. The doubts he had tried without success to ignore finally began to evaporate.

It was going to happen.

He found the BBC listings, but nothing for her personally, and he didn't know the name of her department. He would have to ask BBC Information. The line was busy, and busy, and busy, and...

Ringing.

"You and who else?" was the operator's sarcastic response when he said he wanted Ponti.

Richard kept his own voice level, but firm. "I'm a physician. It's most important."

"Her doctor?" The operator's tone softened. "I have no way of getting through to Miss Ponti. I'll give you her supervisor. It may take some trying, don't hang up."

It took an endless wait...until, "Central Control. Keep it brief."

A male voice, under pressure. Richard said, "I need Liz Ponti, but I'm not really her doctor."

"Shit. A nutter!"

"*Please*—" Richard begged, because in the next instant the male voice was going to cut him off — "I can't give you my name but tell her she interviewed me in Virginia."

A pause. But the connection was still there. He could hear a whistle of breath. It sounded like all hell was loose in the background. The man said in a voice which was now trying to keep the lid on, "Was that by any chance at a farm in Virginia?"

"Yes. But I have to speak to her. No one else. It's vitally important."

"I believe you, sir. She can't be reached. I want to help — if it's humanly possible, I will help — I'm afraid I can't prove it. You'll have to take me on trust."

Richard did. The voice wasn't acting. He said, "Can you send out a location crew?"

"The whole of BBC. Just say where."

This was the moment. He either trusted Fate, or...

"Westminster Abbey," Richard said.

NOW IT WAS done, he felt strangely calm. He hung up the phone and took the directory back. The grocer who was still completely preoccupied. He tapped on the glass again and held up the book. The Pakistani waved in a distracted manner, indicating, Just drop the damn thing anyhow!

Richard bent down and placed it neatly on the floor beside the door. His nerves were steady. He straightened and turned to go along the hall to the street. The Pakistani let out a small cry and clapped a pudgy hand in a gesture of shock, or horror, across his mouth. At the same time, his squat little body recoiled from the screen. A male face had replaced Liz Ponti's.

McDermid.

As the picture changed to a zoom shot of the Farm, and an old woman dying, Richard realized that the face of the Irishman, seen dimly, at a distance, pursuing him in the underground garage, was also Lady Bronwen's killer.

The assassin didn't have the disguise of a moustache in Virginia, but a false moustache was nothing. Otherwise, the square jaw, the ruthless expression, the athletic build — it must be the man who had already almost killed him at the cabin and Edinburgh.

Third time lucky...

But McDermid hadn't been! The garage attempt also failed. The three-times jinx was off. Feeling almost jaunty, Richard walked down the hall, past the Closed sign on the tiny shop.

The ambulance was gone.

A tank was parked in its place. As he stood there, unable to think, troops appeared from behind the tank, doubling across the pavement, straight towards him.

He turned to run back along the hall and collided with the grocer. The man stood at the glass-paned door, equally frozen, mouth open, staring at him. It was only an instant, but Richard knew he was recognized.

He plunged past. There had to be a rear entry. Beyond the phone. Locked with a sliding bolt which stuck. He kicked it open. Broken stone steps led down to an alley with refuse containers. To his right... dead end. He went left. The corner of the alley opened into John Islip Street.

No troops. He saw a Hospital sign. He was a doctor. He walked swiftly in the appropriate direction. It worked for a minute: the Queen Alexandra was only three hundred yards away! The entrance was crowded with shift workers and emergency equipment. He could blend: he couldn't wait. A white vehicle turned in.

"Harry!" he shouted.

Wrong ambulance. The black stranger at its wheel stared blankly. A harrassed commissionaire said, "We're full. Try up at Westminster."

The real Harry had been given the same advice: the alternate Emergency Ward must be near. The wrong ambulance swung north. Richard followed it to Page Street.

WESTMINSTER HOSPITAL

It was only another block distant. Going up Dean Ryle Street, beside the building, allowed him to cover one more block safely, to Horseferry Road.

The hospital's adjacent perimeter was full of soldiers.

They were not just the cordon for the Lambeth Bridge. A solid line of troops flanked the road, blocking all movement west, or north. He saw why. The spires of his destination rose beyond them.

He had no option. He strode across the road.

"Sorry, Doctor. Closed area."

"But I have a patient."

"Sorry, Doctor."

His disguise was fool proof. So was military discipline.

"Put in for a pass from Mobile HQ," the guard advised him. "At the moment you'll catch 'em just down the street at Queen Alexandra's. Mind the light."

He waited on tenterhooks for it to go green. On the far side, a dark-suited clergyman, in old-fashioned rimless glasses, with the rest of his face hidden behind a newspaper, gave Richard a sympathetic shrug. The light changed. He started across. The lane of traffic beside him moved as well, then halted. An army staff car honked its horn in annoyance. When it stopped honking he heard the sound of hooves clip-clopping on pavement.

An antique hansom cab was coming towards him. A top-hatted, overweight coachman in livery waved down at the army driver, and smiled.

"Hold it!" The same guard who had stopped Richard held a hand out in front of the horse. A mare. She shied sideways.

"Whoa, Dolly! Easy girl, easy." the coachman said in strong cockney. "Don't know no better, 'e don't, scarin' you sudden like that."

"Not scaring," said the guard. "Just stopping. No civilian traffic."

"Well let me tell you a couple of fings, mate. One, me an' Dolly come through Westminster every working day of our lives, rain or shine. Two, we aren't bloody civilian." The coachman held up a blue leather briefcase. "This 'ere is Royal."

Richard didn't know what the briefcase signified, but the coat of arms was beyond question: the Lion and the Unicorn, outlined in gold on the cab door. His natural father's coat of arms.

His own.

For a moment the unexpected sight of it right in front of him overcame the reality of his position.

"All right, go on through."

The guard's gruff approval snapped Richard out of his trance. When the coach moved forward again, it would shield him from view! If he was quick, and kept down by the wheel...

"Get on then, Dolly girl."

He ducked. The mare's hooves began their patient clip-clop. He jogged with her. A horn blasted.

Not at him. The staff car had almost hit the spectacled clergyman, who had suddenly tried to cross against the light.

"Bloody pedestrians. Anyone hurt?" The coachman turned his head...

His eyes met Richard's. The fact of recognition was as instantaneous and unmistakeable as it had been with the Pakistani grocer. But on this occasion he didn't have to wonder about loyalty. The coachman touched his top hat with his whip; a huge smile creased the plump face.

"Dolly and me 'ave been waiting for you — *Doctor!*" A broad stage wink replaced the smile. "Climb in." A liveried arm reached down and opened the Lion and Unicorn door on the side away from the troops. "One more stop for Your Majesty's Box and we'll drive both of you 'ome."

Eight

Downing Street

SLADE STARED IN utter disbelief at the office television monitor. On every channel he flicked to, the same man was killing the same old woman with the same poison dart... while Liz Ponti's instantly recognizable voice-over stated that on a previous occasion the man had used a British Army missile to shoot down Slade's last employer.

"A similar missile," she told every viewer in Britain as a car door slammed below Slade's office window, "was also used at Sandringham. At this very minute, somewhere in Westminster..."

Slade looked down. The chilling figure of Love was striding through the door to the concealed private stairs.

"...as they did just hours ago in Edinburgh: these ruthless people are now trying desperately in London to kill our future King."

Slade saw a picture of the same anonymous killer, this time near Holyrood Palace, shooting at the Australian with a silenced automatic.

NO CALLS flashed on the office intercom. At the same instant the lights on all incoming telephone lines went red. With a shaking hand Slade picked up the one assigned highest internal Whitehall priority and heard the Home Secretary.

"Put me through at once to the Prime Minister," Jane Lear ordered. "On second thought, just inform him that I shall be there in five minutes with my colleagues."

Slade knocked on the connecting door. Beyond it, the brutal Love was standing expressionless in the background. Roper was studying a message on the scrambler. He looked up with annoyance as Slade entered.

"I said, no calls."

"My apologies, Prime Minister. However you should be forewarned: the Home Secretary will be arriving momentarily with other members of Cabinet."

"Good."

The reply astonished Slade. Roper seemed genuinely to welcome the news.

"Then I may show them in to you, Prime Minister?"

"Certainly. At once."

The former Media manipulator he worked for still believed that he could poll his way out of unprecedented scandal! The implacable figure with the scarred hand obviously disagreed. As Slade turned back towards the door, Love took a pace forward and pointed threateningly at a dossier on the desk. Roper sighed and picked it up.

"With great reluctance, Mr Slade, there is something I have to ask you."

The formal Mister made him freeze.

"Let me begin by saying that no matter how grave the charges against someone, and in spite of our new Code for the Justice Commission, personally I always believe a man innocent until proven otherwise. Of course, as I shall inform my Cabinet colleagues, until the Commission shows such proof you may continue in my employ."

"Thank you," Slade said in a voice which he knew was trembling: "What charges?"

Roper opened Love's dossier and passed it to him.

His worst nightmare fears were there. The Palace throat-slitting of the old courtier, and the knife found beside it — with Slade's fingerprints! His secret conversations with the mandarin from Commercial Review, killed in the car crash — but *not* talking about Roper's arms-length trust! Instead, the dossier revealed discussions on Slade's own stock trading in Defence firms he had never made, for enormous sums of Swiss banked money he didn't have.

And his coded private diary.

It was definiitely his diary, and his code, and his handwriting.

But he had burned it!

So in a book he had destroyed, how could he possibly be reading a sentence which he had never written?

"D-Day for Tepfsophjen: Lopht Dsutt."

The date of the entry was last New Year's Eve. With the vowels and consonants replaced, "Tepfsophjen: Lopht Dsutt" became three words he instantly knew by heart...

Sundringham: King's Cross.

Roper took a letter attached to the dossier. Slade's business was reading letters. Upside down, when necessary. The last line typed by Love before the space waiting for the Prime Minister's signature was, "Permission to Interrogate?"

Roper scrawled one word and signed. Slade's bowels cramped violently.

The killing on television was not over. Below the phrase, MAY HOUNDS BLOOD FOX?...the same word was still showing in underlined red capitals on the scrambler telescreen:

APPROVED

Whitehall

DOLLY THE MARE clip-clopped Richard and the antique cab briskly up the appropriately named Horseferry Road until she turned right on to Chadwick Street, left into a warren called Perkins Rents, then along St Ann's Lane. The horse seemed to know her way without any commands from the coachman, who kept up a running conversation with her about the weather, or passing shop windows, as though she was human.

There was no traffic in the back lanes. No army. With every turn the spires of Richard's destination towered higher. Closer. He wondered what had happened to Harry and the black woman in her white coat ignoring two medical death sentences to help other people to live.

To help him.

So many others had also sacrificed everything. A king could give medals for gallantry: he couldn't bring back the dead. The somber thought was reinforced by the deserted streets. The military cordon sealing Whitehall also removed the noise of a great city. It was like traveling through a graveyard in the eye of a hurricane.

Old Pye Street became Abbey Orchard Street. The cab entered a stone-arched tunnel. Once there must have been fruit trees growing here, in meadows sweeping down to the river...

A green space. Dean's Yard. Richard saw a school, but no children. The area had been cleared of all civilians. He had made it safely to the center of the storm.

Could the BBC?

If they could not...

They must. And he must be positive. He had traveled twelve thousand miles to be here. The sun shone from behind clouds, on a sign:

The Sanctuary

He was almost at his destination. The mare turned to her right, away from the sign, parallel to a long south wall of deserted cloisters.

West Walk

He saw a small wicket gothic entry at the far end of it. No guards. He opened the cab door and jumped out.

"Oi! Your Majesty!"

He heard the coachman's startled shout behind him. A few strides into the muted cloisters, all noise from the horse and cab had faded. Five more paces and he was at the wicket.

Locked? It wasn't. He had tried to turn the iron handle the wrong way. The latch lifted. The wicket closed.

He was inside.

Westminster Abbey

THE SMELL OF AGE...a thousand years. It came from woodwork polished by uncounted hands, from dusty battle flags for unnumbered heroes, from velvet cassocks for limitless worshippers.

Today, only one: Richard was alone in the enormous structure. There were no priests or security attendants; no artificial lights were switched on. The roof with its magnificent fan vaulting was a dim lace tracing in the darkness a hundred feet above him. He moved forward slowly, as though the atmosphere of history all about him was not air, but dense, like water.

A black slab of marble was in front of him. A faded Union Jack hung over it, supported from a pillar. Under the flag was the U.S. Congressional Medal of Honor. *The Unknown Soldier.* Killed in the First World War, so the anonymous man could have been American, like Anna, not British. Or Canadian, like Jack Nash.

Or Australian, like himself.

Near the black marble slab was a smaller stone, for someone famous. *Sir Winston Churchill.* The great leader's body was buried in a country churchyard, but his spirit was remembered in the nation's capital. The same thing had been done for a single named American, George Peabody, whose bones were now home again in Massachussets.

The spirits and memorials were everywhere. Livingston the explorer of Africa. Robert Stephenson, the first steam engine. Franklin D. Roosevelt. A portrait of Richard II: "Earliest painting of any English King."

The eyes of his namesake stared in the strangely one-dimensional way of seven centuries ago. Richard took another pace and found George

Washington, carved in wood. And then he came to the poets, and writers, and musicians. Tennyson, Dickens, Handel... and Garrick, an actor, like himself... and a fellow Australian, another poet, Adam Lindsay Gordon. Then more Kings: Edmunds, Edwards, Richards, Henrys. And Queens: Catherines, Eleanors, Annes...

More relatives. But everyone was related, he thought, if they went back far enough. Monarchy was only a game.

Old Palace Yard

The sign pointed to an exit and explained that the Yard was the place where Guy Fawkes had plotted to blow up the Houses of Parliament, next door. It was five hundred years ago but time meant nothing in —

Twenty minutes!

Behaving like a bloody tourist, that long had flashed by. And no BBC crew had arrived. It was the silence that had made him lose track of time. Of what he was doing here.

What am I doing?

The question seared his mind. The single over-riding goal of getting to this place had completely ignored, *Why?*

Even with TV, what had he ever expected to happen? He still knew no one. He had no proof that a royal father had produced him from a one-night stand. The whole force of the British government was still against him.

A noise disturbed the silence. More a sensation than an audible note: a trembling of the ancient stone slabs beneath his feet. An octagonal, amber glass window across the nave was translucent. He went to look through it. The trembling grew stronger. He heard shouting.

Tanks.

The street area outside the Abbey was blocked with them. Troops were pouring from personnel carriers. He ran back to the door he had entered from the cloisters. A tank rolled across the end of the walkway. He ran to the Guy Fawkes exit to Old Palace Yard. Soldiers stood in a chain, shoulder to shoulder, weapons fixed, pointing inwards.

His mind was numb. His arm was hurting. Throbbing. He had banged it against a carving when he ran. He could feel it bleeding again. He looked down at it and realized he was still wearing the white coat. He could play doctor; he couldn't heal himself! The blood stain was seeping into the white fabric.

He was frightened. He went back to the octagonal window. The chain of troops was formed out there as well. He was surrounded.

Someone had betrayed him. The unknown man from the BBC?

Or the coachman? The coincidence of a horse-drawn cab arriving from Buckingham Palace to save him should have rung every alarm bell in his head. Blood was dripping from his fingers.

A tank rolled towards the window. He moved away from it. Back to the center of the church, to darkness, to safety.

To sanctuary.

The high altar. It was enclosed by rails, in a square, guarded by tombs and effigies. His ancestors. Instinct had brought him to this spot. Sun blazed through a great rose window.

The Abbey of Westminster serves
as the seat of no bishop. Nor can it
be known as any priest's Parish.
This House of God is by right a
'Royal Peculiar': its Dean and Chapter
subject solely to their Sovereign.

The sign proved that the army could not take him here. This place was sacred. When the troops arrived he would demand medical treatment. Richard stood at the rail on the North side, facing the great entrance doors, and waited.

THEY CAME FROM the south, using the small wicket he had used from the cloisters. And only a single shadow was thrown over the sill as the door swung inwards. It was going to be civilized, Richard thought, with relief, just himself and one senior officer.

The face was hidden in shadow, but the sun from the rose window flashed on nothing higher than a major's brass-crown rank badges. And there wasn't going to be any military heel-clicking bullshit. The man didn't march along the South Aisle. His gait was smooth, almost catlike, as his thickset body moved from pillar to pillar; as though the man was taking cover between trees in a jungle. In the next shaft of sunlight Richard could see the insignia on the uniform below the shoulder. It was the same as Llangath's, for the journey from Caernarvon: a launched missile, crossed with a dagger.

Richard stepped out from the northwest corner of the altar rails.

"I'm over here," he said. "You don't need to come any farther. I claim sanctuary."

A tiny sound like a bee's wings wirring flew past his ear. He saw something else flashing. A metal tube against the man's mouth.

A blow gun. It had killed Lady Bronwen. Its latest dart was embedded in the wooden frame of a hymn announcement on a pillar beside him.

He ducked behind the pillar. He had to hide. He saw the man's face in the sun. Square-jawed, a military moustache.

McDermid.

Disguised as this Major, the assassin had found him. There was nowhere to hide. His head reeled. Blood was dripping in a steady stream from his fingers. McDermid came one pillar closer. Richard moved one pillar backwards and fell over an object.

The Coronation Chair

It was old. It was wood. A chunk of rock was underneath it.

The Stone of Scone

Stolen from Scotland to crown the Kings of England. His father, and half-brother. It was Richard's final destination.

The place he would die. His blood dripped on the wood. He had no weapon. He touched the stone of history. It was soft, pudgy.

It was Guy Fawkes up to date. Packets of plastic explosive were placed around the chair with detonators inserted.

The scene was beyond his comprehension. Something jabbed against his hip. His killer approached him with the blow gun.

A latch clicked.

The sound reverberated in the vaulted chamber. The assassin's head turned towards it for an instant...

I do have a weapon.

The jabbing object at his hip was the scrap of granite from Arthur's Seat, still in his pants pocket. Richard took it out and threw it at his assassin. A piss in the ocean. His strength was gone and his uninjured left hand had no sense of direction. The granite scrap missed McDermid, barely touched the closest pillar, and fell to the floor in the opposite direction.

A PRIEST'S FOOT accidentally kicked it. He was wearing a floor-length black robe, with a gold cross on his chest. The cleric had opened the latch and was now walking from the South Ambulatory to the sanctuary.

"Father!" Richard called out, "For God's sake, save me!"

The priest paused. McDermid turned back with the blow gun. The sun shone full face on the major.

It wasn't the Irish face with Sally at Brisbane!

But it still meant to kill him. Using the Coronation Chair as a screen Richard crawled on his hands and knees towards the wider shield of the high altar. His right palm left blood prints on the mosaic floor. His vision was fading. He saw black shoes in front of him. A black robe. He looked up.

Rimless glasses and a moustache looked down at him. He had called on a God he didn't believe in. *The priest behind the newspaper at the cross-walk had rimless glasses.*

"You," Richard whispered, "you're McDermid!"

The lips drew apart in a snarling smile.

And fell. The priest's body crashed to the Abbey floor beside him. A poison-bee dart was stuck in the cheek. The army man with the tube placed another sliver of steel in it.

Richard had already been spared by fate twice too often: his death was now sealed. He saw the cloth of the altar, and for some reason he could not fathom, reached forward with his injured arm, to touch —

"You're a dead man anyway. Don't do it!"

THE VOICE RANG out like a clarion. Clean and crisp. English. Faintly Scottish. It was the voice of another dead man, drowned in a whirlpool —

A gunshot.

A second body fell beside him. More footsteps approached. Military boots, running, crashing on the flagstones. The bandaged head and pale blue eyes of Hector MacKenzie appeared above the altar.

As Richard's own eyes flickered, and closed, he heard the Commando cry, *"Medics!"* then fainter, in his ear, *"God save Your Majesty!"* and even fainter, far way, *"Hold on, Lad. Stay strong. You will be King!"*

PART FIVE

By God Annointed

One

The West Entrance

MACKENZIE'S GREATEST FEAR was averted. The young man he was now prepared to serve as his Sovereign had not been struck by a poisoned dart. The King's wound was from a gunshot. Loss of blood had caused deep shock. There was a pulse, but barely. He ordered the medics forward at the rush and then could only wait in the Abbey.

His own trip to the edge of death was still vivid: the black boiling water of the Pentland maelstrom; the sensation of bottomless falling, then basalt rock slamming his head before —

"First adrenaline, sir."

He watched the medic depress the hypodermic in the King's arm. No further moment could be wasted on himself. The country was burning and the men responsible were still in control. MacKenzie's jaw clenched for revenge, making his head wound ache.

"Administering second shot."

RICHARD FELT A pinprick. Through half closed eyes he saw that the Colonel was kneeling at his side on the Abbey's hard stone floor, in full battle kit, still gripping his hand. A blood transfusion bottle fed into his right arm. He was lying on a khaki canvas stretcher. His doctor's disguise had been stripped off. Military medical staff behind MacKenzie were monitoring a bank of portable instruments. An erratic, wavy green line oscilated on a screen.

My heart beat.

"It's true," he heard himself saying in a strangely muted voice, to the wounded MacKenzie, "you aren't dead."

"No, Sir." The pressure of the commando's hand on his own squeezed harder. "Nor you, thank heaven."

The wavy curves on the screen grew larger, their speed more regular. Richard's eyes opened fully. He said, "And Wallop?" From the pause, he already knew the answer.

"A Fisheries patrol recovered Sergeant-Major Wallop's body last night. But no more talking, Sir, you must save your strength." MacKenzie released his hand and turned to the medics. "Carry on."

The stretcher was lifted. A BBC television crew were filming the scene. Better late than never! Richard gave them a weak thumbs up, and a grin, as he was carried past the black marble tomb of the Unknown Warrior towards the west door. "I hope you tell people everything in this broadcast is live."

The camera operator laughed, so that the picture on the feed relay monitor jiggled. A group of armed Royal Marines guarding the Abbey doors snapped to attention.

"Situation report?" MacKenzie asked an officer with them.

"Stable in our sector, sir. The others, we don't know yet. Typical bloody army — waiting for Jesus and Headquarters to make up its mind."

"I'd better take a look. Stretcher party, halt!"

They lowered him to the floor again. The center door was opened. MacKenzie went through it. Richard heard a hollow murmuring noise, like the sea in the Caernarvon tunnel, and shivered. A medic pulled a blanket over him. MacKenzie returned.

"We're fine to the ambulance. Stretcher party, forward!"

As he was lifted Richard said, "I have to know, Colonel: how bad is it out there?"

"Uncertain. The Defence Ministry deliberately assigned units with the greatest sense of loyalty to patrol the Westminster perimeter. To the Brigades of Guards, 'An order is an order until otherwise countermanded by due authority'. Obeying it to the last man goes with their regimental tradition."

The pointed arch of the doorway passed over Richard's head. The sea-in-the-tunnel noise grew louder, more restless. The medics carrying the front of his stretcher carefully descended the first step.

He saw blue sky overhead. The medics halted. The murmuring sound stopped. Once more there was only the graveyard silence of the empty center of the great city. Because of the step down, his body was on an incline. He lifted his head slightly to look forward.

The city was not empty.

Directly in front of him a phalanx of MacKenzie's Royal Marines, loaded automatic rifles resting on their hips, faced outwards in a semi-circle. This side of them, against the Abbey steps, was a green-painted mobile field hospital. Fifty feet beyond the Marines, a second circle of troops, equally armed, but many times more numerous, faced inwards. Behind them, the huge gun barrels of massed tanks were trained above their heads. At the Marines.

At him.

"Put me down," Richard said to the medics.

"Sir —" MacKenzie started to protest.

"Colonel, that was meant to be an order from a due authority."

"I understand, Sir, however —"

"There were a couple of traditions in my former life." Richard pointed at MacKenzie's bandaged head and his own injured arm. "Between us we've had enough 'Break a leg': the show must go on."

"Stretcher party: one step to the rear! Lower, and assist His Majesty!"

The medics stepped back to the portico. The gothic arch reappeared above Richard's head. He felt the metal skids touch the stone under him and swung his legs off the canvas.

Blackness.

Hands grabbed him. The black became red, then the gray of the Abbey. The murmuring sound was back, much louder.

"Let me go," he said. "I'm all right."

The medics reluctantly released him. He scarcely noticed.

He was looking at the people.

THE STREET BEYOND the tanks was full of them. They were the source of the sea noise. Waves of people. Richard took a step towards them. His head swam. His body felt light. As though he was in the water. Another step.

The people took one towards him.

He moved, and they moved. They came to him through the tanks, beneath the gunbarrels, up to the regiments of soldiers. And with each step the noise grew louder, until it was the sound of London, cheering.

He felt a limitless strength flooding his body. He strode past the mobile hospital that was waiting for him; past the phalanx of Marines protecting him. He strode to the center of the open space between the two opposing lines, and stopped in front of an officer armed with a machine pistol, and wearing an emblem of a double **LG**, above a scroll, with the Royal crest of his father's Family.

And there he waited.

The cheering ceased. The officer stared past him with eyes that were brilliant blue and slightly bulbous. Hyperthyroid. Devoid of emotion. They did not see him. The lips were compressed, bloodless. When they opened, the chin thrust forward. The teeth were recessed, and ratlike. The hand holding the pistol made a sharp sideways gesture.

"Life Guards —!"

At the strident bellow, the muzzles of the automatic rifles of the center troops elevated at a slight angle, directed at Richard's heart.

"Life Guards —!"

With a second gesture of the pistol, the guns snapped upwards: at his head.

"Life Guards —!"

The pistol thrust forward, between his eyes.

"For your Sovereign: Pre-sent, ARMS!"

FOR A MOMENT his mind still thought they were firing...as he heard the crash of the feet, and the slap of the hands against the gunbutts . . . but the people of London knew from the start that the troops were saluting. The sounds of it were lost in the cheering which broke out again, rising to fresh crescendos as the battalions of the regiments on either side joined the parade in order of seniority around the Abbey.

"Blues and Royals, present arms!"

"Grenadiers — !"

"Coldstreams — !"

"Scots Guards — !"

"Welsh Guards — !

Richard stood until the roll call was over...and then he collapsed against MacKenzie, whom he hadn't realized was behind him. Plus the stretcher party. He was glad to be an invalid. His body was drained of all strength, but his mind was calm. The show had gone on. He no longer cared what happened legally.

"Without any scientific proof for my claim," he said to MacKenzie, as the stretcher approached the field hospital vehicle, "I suppose the government will deport me back home to Australia."

"I very much doubt that, Sir. There are one or two things from Sydney which this government has yet to be made aware of."

"You found the phone bills, from my kitchen?"

The commando shook his head, with a tight smile. "Somebody's house cleaners got there before us, however...Your Majesty might care to see this."

While the medics carried the stretcher up the steps of the field hospital, MacKenzie produced an envelope with New South Wales Forensic as its return address.

"Thanks for the effort," Richard said, "but if that's my DNA signature I still have the duplicate."

"Not of this signature, Sir."

The staff of the hospital swung open the door. Richard took the envelope and removed the contents.

NSWFL: DNA SIGNATURE.
DONOR ID: HRH P OF W.
BLOOD SAMPLE OBTAINED FROM: OUTER HEADS DISTRICT PUBLIC HEALTH, CRYOGENIC ARCHIVE, TRAFFIC ACCIDENTS.
DATE OF SAMPLE FOR ANALYSIS . . ."

Twenty-eight years ago, on the night of a party where his mother met a stranger. Followed by two brief moments in a car: one produced him; the other, the crash which produced the blood sample for this piece of paper. He had never needed the battle-scarred scrap in his pocket, the forensic lab had kept its own duplicate all along. The thick-and-thin bars of the two DNA signatures matched, his own and the former Prince of Wales, all the way back to those tombs in the Abbey.

He had never needed to leave Sydney! His mother might be alive, he thought bitterly, as he was carried inside the mobile hospital, if he had just thought of checking the local police and health records for himself.

"Of course I'm pleased," he said, making an effort for MacKenzie. "A bit amazed that with everything that's happened, you had the bright idea."

"I don't see what was so amazing about it," said a voice which had to be final proof of his mind wandering. "I am a biologist."

ANNA BENT DOWN and kissed him. He wasn't insane, her lips were real. So were the tears in her eyes. Richard felt one on his cheek.

"Just now," he said, as his own eyes stung, and her face shimmered, "with all the people. You ought to have seen. You should have come out."

"I did see." She pointed at a television on a medical lab bench. "And I've never been so proud, but it was your moment."

There was a throat-clearing from MacKenzie. "I'll leave you, Sir, for the time being. I have to confer with certain people."

"Yes," Richard said, "I guess you do. But tell me one thing: you talked about tradition and following orders. Your own branch of the service has all that in spades. Why were they the first to back me?"

"The Regimental badge, Sir." MacKenzie touched the silver globe within its laurel wreath, and the initials, **RM**. "The letter 'R'," the commando added grimly, "in the unanimous opinion of Your Majesty's Marines, stands for Royal — not Roper."

Downing Street

SLADE REMAINED IN the Prime Minister's employ. He recorded the calls and arrivals in the inner office of the following men and women: Jane Lear, the Home Secretary, representing the common people and the Cabinet; Edward Marching, Duke of Dorset, representing the College of Heralds, and the aristocracy; Colonel Hector MacKenzie, Royal Marines, representing the Australian — already referred to by all the Royal arse-lickers coming out of the Whitehall woodwork as The Sovereign. And the knight with no last name, Sir James...

Love's gentlemanly predecessor as Chief of British Intelligence represented the backstage coalition which had re-surfaced once all the risk had been taken by others!

Slade's mood was bitter bleak terror. Nothing he could say or do would have the slightest effect against the overwhelming manufactured proof of his guilt in the forged dossier. He heard a knock on the office door and numbly opened it.

"Oh Christ," he said. "Not you."

The oafish coachman. Slade's world was finished, yet this fool was still making his rounds as though nothing had happened.

"That's right, sir. Me an' Dolly, for the Box."

Slade looked on dully as Stubbins exchanged one empty despatch case for another.

"That's that, then. Next run, I told Dolly, now His Majesty's back, it'll be for real." The fat shape, bursting its tail coat, leaned disgustingly close. "You'll never believe what happened to us two this morning —"

"You fool," Slade screamed. *"Get out!"*

He stared at the blank intercom telescreen on his desk.

NO ACCESS: MEETING IN PROGRESS

Slade's terror was replaced by a rage which doubled for each year he thought back on his struggle from the rathole of the slums. He no longer had his diary but there must be something he could still do to the unseen faces behind the screen.

He flicked his illegal Privacy bypass switch.

Hostile Takeover

EVER SINCE THE bailiff's van, Roper had accepted risk. For this most critical meeting of his life he kept the expression on his face one of polite interest as the small-time opportunists gathered in the Cabinet room to present their inevitable compromise offer. The men shuffled uneasily and left it to the token little woman.

"Our group decision is two-fold," Jane Lear announced. "First: when we leave this office, his Grace will proceed to St James's Palace and read the Proclamation confirming our approved Successional candidate as the new King. Second: you, Henry, in your capacity as Prime Minister, will then receive His Majesty here at Downing Street, if he is well enough, to offer him our joint congratulations."

Roper nodded calmly, waiting for the other shoes to drop.

"Of course all events will be televised," she said. "After the meeting, you, together with the rest of us, will accompany the King to Buckingham Palace for his first formal presentation to his people from the balcony. Request for Dissolution of Parliament will be presented upon leaving it. The next General Election will be called for one month's time."

Roper nodded again. Financial chaos in the markets would be soothed by business as usual.

"A week from today," Jane Lear concluded, "you will resign on the grounds of ill health, and leave the country. You will agree in writing not to return. Should you break that agreement at any time in the future, a warrant will remain in force for your immediate arrest, and subsequent detention, at the Sovereign's pleasure. Speaking plainly, a life sentence."

It was less than Roper had expected. In the era of satellite communication a business place of residence was of no consequence. And the public memory grew shorter as media transmission got faster. Within six months he would be referred to only as "the former Prime Minister". In two years, his public relations comeback image would be "Good old Hal."

He hid his smile and closed the deal.

Gentlemen's Agreement

MACKENZIE HAD A very brief and totally private meeting with the reinstated head of British Intelligence. It was held at the halfway point of the hidden bookcase exit from the Prime Minister's office.

"Housecleaning this 'King's Cross' thing of Love's. I want you to head it up. But Hector... Strictly rulebook. No personal vendettas."

Knightsbridge Barracks

RICHARD WAS DRIVEN to the barracks in the mobile field hospital. Anna stayed at his side for the trip and afterwards while the military doctors patched his arm up again. Permanently, this time! He told her about Harry and the medic woman who had saved his life last time. Then he dozed from the effects of medication.

When he woke Anna was still there.

"From now on," he said, "you always will be with me, won't you?"

She smiled, and kissed his brow, and then MacKenzie returned with the real world. Richard heard how the King's Cross plan had intended him to play a modern Guy Fawkes with the planted explosives beneath the throne in the Abbey. And he heard about Liz Ponti's heroic effort in exposing the real conspiracy. The bedside television was switched on. A man in a velvet costume, flanked by thirteen others in silk and satin, took a rolled up parchment from a pillow. There should have been fourteen: only an empty space on the St James's balcony represented the red dragon of Wales.

Empty spaces. Lady Bronwen and her son. His own mother. Sally, Kimura, Wallop...

And all the other anonymous helpers: the Highland shepherd and his wife, the nuclear truck driver, in Scotland; the Pakistani grocer, in London. And the fat coachman at the end, with his absurdly British, yet somehow touching loyalty in carrying the useless despatch box through the period of waiting for this moment.

"The King is dead. Long live the King!"

When Lady Bronwen said it in Brisbane, the world laughed. The cheer today would have pleased her. It could not bring her back. Or any of the others.

"At a time and place to be by God annointed, Richard Arthur..."

"If it's possible to find them," he told MacKenzie, "I want all the people who helped me to be there on the balcony." His eyes closed again, but the darkness was no longer terrifying. "At least we don't have to worry any more about McDermid."

"Yes sir. Immigration are tight. The sod won't get back here. Now we must let you sleep."

"Won't get back?" Richard jerked awake. "He was killed in the Abbey. Disguised as the priest."

"It's over, darling." Anna stroked his hair. "Try to rest."

“The dead priest was a priest,” MacKenzie assured him. “A new dean of the Abbey. Whatever gave Your Majesty the idea that the unfortunate man was that IRA swine?”

Two

The Royal Mews

McDERMID'S RUN OF luck didn't surprise him: the dead God from his youth was making up for the thousand years of Brit butchery in Ireland. He had suffered a moment's lapse of faith when he almost bumped right into his Target at the Horseferry Road crosswalk... only to see the man get away in the bloody hansom cab! But as he watched the bullshit building on television since, he realized that the silencer shooting of a pedestrian wearing a doctor's coat and stethoscope would have been nothing. To see the Target, decked out as their bloody King, get blown away in front of his sixty million bug-eyed subjects — a billion other royalty-loving morons, worldwide — *that* would truly be an indelible monument to the fallen comrades of the Struggle.

The Horseferry Road encounter had happened by accident as he was working out the details for his main plan. It required meticulous timing, personally checking the route taken by the coachman, using a stopwatch. The route never varied because the horse chose it: Dolly-girl had the brains in that partnership!

Getting a job cleaning out her shit in the Mews had seemed at first to be the greatest stroke of luck, but in fact it wasn't. With the new Bed-and-Breakfast arrangement for tourists at the Palace, while anti-theft precautions had been heightened, in the absence of a reigning landlord, Anti-Terror security was zero. They weren't hiring Micks, of course — McDermid dumped his brogue with his Bishop's costume — but a Canadian from the RCMP stables in his former Excellency's diocese of Manitoba was a shoe-in.

He got his own room over the horse-muck. And this morning, the final icing on McDermid's cake. In honor of The Great Occasion the Palace personnel department had even installed a TV set in his stable room!

Right now it was showing where the main event would start.

Downing Street

SLADE HAD TRIED to buy a gun, but that wasn't easy in a country which banned their possession by the general public, and ensured it with the full arsenal of British bureaucracy. Owning a pistol required attending a one month course at an approved firing range and a Special Holder's permit.

Even to get a shotgun from a fine old firm on Bond Street meant a seven-day waiting period, and two sponsors to swear to the applicant's good character. Smuggling a double-bore into Downing Street was impossible, and in a week Roper would be gone...

He would never serve a day in any prison! The Old Boy sellout Slade had watched with incredulity on his intercom screen would show as just a tap on the wrist for Roper in the history books. Slade faced imminent arrest and then a plunge into living hell. The false dossier in the office safe was like a bomb, set to explode and destroy —

Get the dossier!

It was so simple. The inner office was empty. In the event of illness, or emergency, the combination to the Prime Minister's private safe was kept in a locked drawer of Roper's desk.

Slade leaped up and burst his way through the connecting door.

The keys to the desk were gone. He grabbed a steel paperknife and attacked the antique treasure. The inlaid wood around the brass keyhole lock was brittle with age. It splintered easily. He forced the knife further into the opening and wrenched.

The notebook with the combination wasn't there.

And at the same time he suddenly heard footsteps on the landing at the top of the private entry stairs. It was too late to fix the damage. He would be caught redhanded by MacKenzie or Sir James. Slade raised the bent paperknife, ready to stab down, as the private door swung open.

He was flattened to the wall. His wrist was being broken by a scarred hand.

"Is this what you want?"

The terrifying figure who arranged Roper's dirty work was supposed to be ousted from power. Instead, he was still at its center. Love's other hand held the dossier. Slade nodded mutely. He could never win his freedom.

"It's yours."

His torturer released his wrist and dropped the dossier on the desk. Slade stared. Then reached.

"Not quite so fast." The scarred hand slammed down again. "You'll have to earn it."

Knightsbridge Barracks

OUTSIDE THE WINDOW of his Field Marshall's Suite, Richard heard the sounds of orders for the guards who would escort him to Downing Street, then back along Pall Mall to Buckingham Palace. On television, ceremonial uniforms replaced khaki battledress. The rioting had stopped in the immigrant areas. Once again the British army was only a tourist attraction.

He wasn't wearing a uniform. MacKenzie had suggested it, but Richard disagreed.

"People have to get used to an Australian first. Seeing me as an Admiral of the Fleet would be too much like Gilbert and Sullivan. I'll use a plain suit off the rack."

Not quite. A Mr Symons, of *Symons and Smythe*, arrived with a van load of coatsleeves and pantlegs in assorted patterns and fabrics. Richard chose a light gray worsted — medium lapels, no cuffs on the pants — which pleased Mr Symons, except for the cuffs.

"It is not a question of style. Your Majesty has a good eye for that if one may say. The extra weight of the trouser cuff drapes the fabric..."

He let them have the extra weight, but he kept his own choice of shirt from Mr Wilkins of *Makepiece & Asham*, shirtmakers to the crown since William the Conqueror.

"Not *quite* so long, Sir. From 1905, I believe."

MacKenzie also produced a valet to help him dress. The man burst into tears on arrival.

"I'm sorry, Sir. It was seeing the resemblance..."

No one used to, Richard thought; the power of suggestion was amazing. But the idea of someone else laying out your clothes wasn't difficult for an actor to accept, and he needed the extra help because of his arm. He couldn't bend it below the elbow. Otherwise, he felt a little shaky in the legs, and the dizziness came back if he moved quickly. The wheelchair the doctors wanted him to use was out of the question.

"I'll always have you to hang onto," he said, smiling at Anna.

"Today anyway." She touched his uninjured left hand. "Don't forget to use this one for shaking.

"I won't. What's with the 'anyway'?"

"Just that it can't be 'always'. With your new life."

"But you must." His heart lurched. The dizziness returned. He grabbed her. "Anna, I couldn't do it without you."

"Sure you can. Playing Prince Hamlet, having a father who's a ceremonial Head of State, being Australian: it all fits. Darling, I'm not a Princess, this isn't Midsummer Night's Dream, and I couldn't ever be Tatyana, Queen of the Fairies. I'm a working woman, and American. You said yourself: your own background is difficult enough for the British to get used to."

"It's nothing to do with my bloody background," he shouted in desperation. "Anna, I love you."

"Richard, sweetheart, if it could be the two of us, as lovers, we could probably swing it — I could fly over — but this job doesn't allow that kind of relationship."

"Just because it never has, doesn't mean it never can. Lady Bronwen told me: this isn't Edward the Eighth and Mrs. Simpson. People today understand."

"No they don't," she said gently. "When you have your Coronation, your people will want a proper Queen."

"Excuse me, Sir," the valet intruded. "Your Majesty's car is here."

The Mews

McDERMID WATCHED THE black Rolls Royce start its journey on his stable room TV. The impregnable security forces were already formed up and waiting in a semi-circle outside the Barracks gate. As the Rolls moved smoothly forward, the other escorting vehicles swung in behind to close the circle. With wall-to-wall security like that it wouldn't be possible to flick a spitball at his Target!

McDermid's nerves were approaching their super-cooled state for the final stage of his ultimate mission...but there was still a residual trace of impatience as he forced himself to go downstairs and wait with the other Mews underdogs of the British class system. He couldn't leave them too early. The convoy had only reached Hyde Park Corner. As it swung south, onto Grosvenor Place, the sour-faced old fart of a senior ostler shouted, "The side entrance, everybody!"

McDermid followed the herd to the entrance on Buckingham Gate. A swelling mixture of shrieks and whistles from the pavement outside the Royal Mews reached a crescendo.

"Three cheers for His Majesty! Hip-hip...!"

"Hoorah!" McDermid joined in, as a fleeting glimpse of a glossy black roof went by. The rest of the ragged cheer was drowned out by the Brit army choppers patrolling overhead. As their rotors faded the Mews employees rushed back inside to the cafeteria.

At which point McDermid left.

HE WALKED CALMLY up the rough wooden stairs leading from the stable. The Royal horseflesh still had better living conditions than the staff who looked after it! He entered his "grace and favor" apartment: eight-foot square of stone whitewash, truckle bed luxury.

And television. The set was now showing an overhead of the convoy which had reached the end of Birdcage Walk and was turning into Great George Street.

Then Parliament Street.

McDermid chucked a couple of worn pillows against the cheap rails of the headboard, sat on the sagging mattress, and leaned back to watch the last stage of the trip in as much comfort as possible. The Rolls passed the Cenotaph, where the road became Whitehall. Half a block to Downing Street. The picture cut to the view from inside Number 10. With their absurd love of ceremony, the Brits were handing it to him on a plate!

He picked up the triggering device from the rickety bedside table.

The black Rolls turned into Downing Street, and there she was: Dolly-girl, clip-clopping along from the other direction, right on schedule. The camera couldn't resist this piece of tourist-trap shit. The picture and matching soundover went split-screen: Old Hansom Cab to the left, Rolls Royce to the right.

"Just wait, Dolly luv!"

"Guard, Atten —*shun!*"

Now, Stubbins climbing down on the left-side. To the right, a buck-toothed female Bobby Cop touching her helmet.

And then, for a tearjerker, a quick flash-cut to the inevitable: the Despatch Box of blue Morocco leather the loyal moron had toted empty until last night…to leave it only yards from McDermid's room.

It wasn't empty today!

The sides of the briefcase were now lined with enough wafers of Ultra-Plastic explosive to blow Downing Street across Whitehall into Richmond Terrace. McDermid's attention stayed fixed on his Target, not the means of disposal. His right index finger moved with the unconscious assurance of a concert pianist across the device.

A cheer. His Target was out of the Rolls. A smile. A wave. Another cheer from the waiting idiots. A pause.

McDermid's finger stopped.

A warmer smile from his Target, for the Faithful Coachman.

McDermid's finger hovered above the firing key. His Target still waited.

And now the coachman entered Downing —

The stable room door burst open.

A man.

Thickset.

Scarred hand.

Anti-Terror.

Won't take me!

McDermid's ice-cold assessment took half a second. He bit down hard on his left bicuspid, felt the tooth shatter, the poison squirt out on his tongue. He saw the typical toffee-nose tight-arse smile on the unknown face representing his life-long enemy... and shouted his last words:

"FOR IRELAND AND THE STRUGGLE!"

His index finger jabbed the trigger. His dying eyes watched in final triumph as, on-screen —

Nothing happened.

Downing Street

SLADE STOOD AT the top of the stairs, waiting for the moment which would give him back his freedom. Below the bannisters, he watched Britain's Prime Minister bowing to the man he had hoped to kill.

"Sir, on behalf of all of us at Number 10, it gives me enormous pleasure to welcome Your Majesty." Roper straightened, with a gesture that encompassed Slade above him on the landing. "And now, may I formally introduce someone whom I believe you met before, under less comfortable circumstances? Mr. Samuel Stubbins, the courier of Your Majesty's daily despatch box."

"We certainly have met." And the cameras beneath Slade gobbled it up: the Royalty charade. The Australian turned his perfect teeth in the coach moron's direction. "As a matter of fact Prime Minister, I have another favor to ask of Mr Stubbins."

The oaf just stood their, blushing beet red, holding the despatch box which he should have brought straight up to Slade's office! Was this going to be the one day in the cretin's life that Stubbins failed to carry out his routine?

"Well, of course, Your Majesty. Anyfink I can."

"I'd like you to fill your promise."

"Oh my Gawd. Made a promise, did I?"

Total perplexity from the coachman. The Australian gave another of his beachbum toothpaste smiles. "Yes, Mr Stubbins, you did. You told me that after you were finished your run, you and Dolly would drive me home."

"To the Palace? Now? Down the Mall. Me and Dolly..."

Words failed. But at last the fool was moving. Clomping up the stairs in his heavy boots, sweating like a pig under his thick felt cape.

"Good afternoon, Mr. Slade, sir. It's Stubbins, with the Box."

"Good afternoon, Mr. Stubbins. Yes, I have the exchange ready."

"You 'ave?" The man's coarse eyebrows lifted at the unexpected politeness.

"Of course I have it ready," Slade snapped, to keep their routine. "For the first day in months there will actually be something more for you to transport than empty air. Just give me the case."

He snatched it from the calloused hand, carried it inside his office, and closed the door. The replacement despatch box from Love was waiting on his desk. He lifted it off and set it on the velvet cushion of a chair. He put the coachman's empty case on the desk, snapped the brass locks open, then did the same for the replacement. He took out the first State document, waiting for the new sovereign's perusal, and transferred it to the empty case from Stubbins. There was a slight smell, a little sickly. Fumes from the glue of the lining, Slade thought, accumulating after such a long period without being opened.

He snapped the lid shut, grasped the polished brass handle to lift the first case which, because each was handmade, had a little more weight than the second, and carried it back to the waiting coachman.

"Thank you, Mr. Slade, sir. Time for me and Dolly's big moment. The Mall! Can you imagine...!"

The Cockney voice trailed away down the stairs. Slade let out his breath. It was over. He had done what Love told him. He was free.

A cheer from the street rattled the windows of the office. The hansom cab was about to leave. Habit died hard. As PPS, Slade should be in the lobby for any final instruction from Roper before the PM followed in the Rolls Royce. He ran down the stairs and was almost too late.

Roper had already climbed into the car. As an automated bomb sniffer crept its way along the curb, the hansom cab moved off. Another cheer. The Australian did his beachboy wave.

"Like he'd done it all his life, isn't it, God Bless him?" a middleaged woman next to Slade said. "Here! What's this then?"

The robot sniffer was flicking a metal arm between her legs. She kicked out at it in panic. A red light started flashing. A siren sounded. The woman shrieked. A plain clothes security agent raced over.

"Horrible thing!" she screamed. "Get it away from me!"

"Relax, Madam," the agent said tersely, glancing at a swinging needle on a dial. "The trace is coming from this man."

The needle had stopped at Slade. The dial said, *Ultra-Plastic.*

The agent shouted, "Colonel MacKenzie!"

Pall Mall

RIDING ALONE IN the antique cab, all Richard could see on either side was a solid line of faces: troops in front, and civilians behind, craning to look through, or around; or with children piggyback on adults' shoulders. The ranks massed twenty deep behind looked through a forest of periscopes.

Which made him think again of Jack Nash, the Canadian who took the *Melville* single-handed across the Atlantic to be at the parachute drop point, before the underwater journey in Moby, the submersible. The non-stop roar of the crowd was like the sea, rising in a wave as Richard approached, fading in a trough —

Nash had Anna's picture taped to his bunk.

Was that why she refused to stay here in Britain with him? He tried to banish the petty jealousy. The hansom cab was turning sharply left. The crowd was suddenly even higher, rising in a kind of human pyramid. He saw a marble head with heavy-lidded eyes and a stubborn double chin. The people were clinging to Queen Victoria, on her monument. His five times great Grandmother.

He had to convince Anna that being a Queen in Britain today wasn't as it had been for a woman who ruled half the world as Empress of India. She could lead an almost normal life: certainly keep up her interest in marine biology, and as far as being American, her ancestors who founded Virginia came from England. And her Russian side could only be a diplomatic bonus. The waving flags in the crowd proved it: not just Union Jacks and Old Glorys, but Italian, Japanese, Dutch, Brazilian, German, these days the whole world was interconnected.

The mare, Dolly, swung left again. The crowd disappeared.

"Guard! Pre-sent, ARMS!"

A sentry box. A scarlet tunic, a black bearskin busby. Empty space.

The courtyard of Buckingham Palace. His eyes traveled up the stone walls. He heard a new roar from the crowd behind him. Another flag was breaking from a white masthead on the roof.

The Royal Standard: the Sovereign was in residence.

My flag.

"Whoa, Dolly! Your Majesty, we're 'ome."

My home.

Stubbins opened the door. Richard stepped down. A group wearing footmen's livery and maids' dresses cheered raggedly, but sincerely. He went across to thank them and shake hands with a Senior Ostler called Ben, and a Sergeant Footman, and a Wardrobe Mistress.

"Like backstage in the theater," Richard said with a smile, as an equerry led him onto the start of a mile of red carpet. And then he remembered the coachman, still standing beside the cab with a grin on his fat face and the blue brief case in his hand. "We're going to be on television again, Mr. Stubbins. In ten minutes. Don't forget to bring the Box."

The Mews

LOVE WAITED IMPASSIVELY in the small white room above the stables. The face and hands of the corpse on the bed opposite were cyanotic; blackly purple from the effect of the poison whose action was simultaneously to burst capilliaries in the lungs and neutralize oxgen in the blood.

The exaggerated self confidence of a psychopath had always been the Irishman's weakness. In the closing stages of an operation McDermid had the habitual pattern of moving as though protected by an invisible shield which was common to megalomaniacs. Occurrences that a normal psyche would regard with suspicion — too much good luck and coincidence — became evidence of Divine intervention.

This room; and the job in the Mews; the unchallenged entry to Britain at Southampton, over-disguised as a Catholic Bishop; the ready access to the despatch box — a conventional ego would have smelled a rat and bolted for the nearest hole.

Having outwitted and disposed of McDermid, Love calmly reached for the triggering device, whose correct firing pulse had been preset on the briefcase's receiver — *before* Southampton — to initiate a detonation on a frequency one band higher than the IRA assassin's selection. Very shortly now. On the television set so fortuitously provided with the room, another excessively lucky man was about to make his next entrance.

Before the Australian's final exit.

Downing Street

SLADE HUNCHED IN a corner of his office and watched numbly as MacKenzie's Anti-Terror forces tore it apart. He had known from the start that the dossier offer was too good to be true. Love would never let him go.

"And then what?" MacKenzie shouted the question.

"I'm sorry," Slade said, "I didn't hear your last —"

"You left the despatch box courier outside on the landing. What did you do next?"

"I put in the paper for the Sovereign's consideration tonight."

"It isn't here." MacKenzie pointed at the empty briefcase on the velvet chair.

"I know it isn't. It's in the other one."

"Other what?"

"Other despatch box. The one the fool — the courier — brought with him."

"You exchanged the document. Why not just the boxes?"

"I don't know."

"You bloody do!" MacKenzie grabbed his throat and slammed him against the corner wall. "The sniffer shows Ultra-Plastic traces on your desk. Don't play your Privileged Status shit with me." The grip on his throat tightened. "Why did you break your normal routine with the boxes?"

"Can't breathe," Slade gasped. The room darkened.

"WHY?"

Slade saw crimson flashes. He croaked, "Love told me."

"Sweet Jesus." MacKenzie released his throat. "For what reason?"

"I don't know. Truly! I —"

The commando dragged him bodily over the desk and up to the roof. A helicopter was waiting on the landing pad.

"Where am I going?" Slade asked.

"You closed that fucking box," MacKenzie replied. "You can open it."

Three

The Balcony

RICHARD WAS ALLOWED a few minutes to freshen up with Roger & Gallet soap in the Sovereign's Suite on the first floor of the Palace overlooking the garden and the swimming pool. Anna was waiting for him in the Consort's Suite, separated by a convenient connecting door.

"For the sake of appearance in a more modest age," a tourist brochure pointed out for the recent royal Bed and Breakfast trade. He showed it to Anna.

"There was one in my room too," she said with a laugh, kissing him, "but I've only been offered breakfast. No bed."

Richard said, "About that, all the way in the cab I've been thinking —"

"I know. Queen Tatanya, but it can't work. I watched you at Downing Street, and you were terrific — but that's what your life is going to be. Day after day of shaking hands and being pleasant to people you couldn't really care less about."

"But *you* wouldn't have to," he said. "That's what I was thinking. You could keep on with your career, doing a real job. The people I'm shaking hands with have real jobs, they would appreciate it. At least try —?"

"Two minutes for the Balcony, Your Majesty."

A footman stood discretely outside a pair of opened doors. Anna didn't answer the last question. Already Palace routine *was* just like the bloody theater, Richard thought: *Two minutes to Curtain.*

WITH THE FOOTMAN as a guide they walked along the King's Corridor, past the Chinese Luncheon Room, and turned a corner into the Principal Corridor, past the Buhl Room Suites.

"The Balcony Room, Your Majesty."

A waiting room, like a backstage Green Room for performers. Large, rectangular, pale lime-colored wall paper, with a high white plastered ceiling, and opaque curtains hiding large windows. It was furnished with comfortable chairs and sofas in a flowered chintz on a dark green background. The people sitting in them got hurriedly to their feet as the footman announced him.

"Your Majesty, His Grace the Duke of Dorset."

Richard said the right things to the titles, but the faces which gave him special pleasure were those of the people who would never in their lives have expected to be there. Stubbins, the coachman, still proudly clutching his despatch box; Harry and the medic woman, the Pakistani grocer; and the shepherd and his wife, from the Highlands. Richard went forward to shake the couple's hands. Out of their element they responded shyly, as though he couldn't possibly be the same man as the shabby hunted figure they had entertained in their croft kitchen. Their nephew, the nuclear waste truck driver who got him to the Lowlands, was still recovering in hospital from multiple fractures to his jaw.

Richard looked across at Roper, chatting and behaving as though none of the recent catastrophic events had happened! He didn't know if he would ever truly understand behavior in Britain. The various accents of his guests intermingled, a sea sound like the crowd lining his trip from Downing Street, but more muted.

A Palace major domo of some kind came up, bowed, and said in his ear, "Two o'clock, Your Majesty. First appearance."

A footman drew back the curtains to reveal a pair of French doors and three television cameras. Richard saw sunshine and green trees from the park, and the tops of buildings beyond. A police security helicopter was flying a patrol — no, it was a Royal Marine. MacKenzie had arrived in time to join him.

Richard turned back to Anna. "Six months together," he said in an urgent whisper. "Please. Give it a chance."

"We've got to get through today, first."

She touched him lightly on the cheek. At least this time she hadn't said, No. He grinned, and straightened his shoulders. The roar began as the French doors opened.

IT WAS A wave of sound but it struck him with the force of the mines detonating on the seabed above the escape tunnel from Caernarvon. It was partly howling, partly cheering, rising and falling as the light spring wind lifted it or dropped it. When he stepped forward he saw who was making it.

The sea was more people.

For as far as his vision could reach they stretched ahead . . . the earlier crowds had been only a fraction of this one . . . along the Mall . . . and into the sides, of the parks . . . and around the circle of Victoria's memorial . . . and when they saw him the sea rolled forward. Every age and nationality and race of the people who made up the British community, or the rest of the world who were visiting it. The human tidal wave washed over the police cordon, surged to the gold-tipped iron railings in front of the Palace, and stopped.

And then Richard waved. The howling cheering sound got louder. Which seemed so impossible that he burst out laughing. And it got louder. So loud that he couldn't hear MacKenzie's helicopter now only thirty feet from him.

He turned back and shouted at the open window, "Anna, you won't believe this. You have to come out here."

She refused, smiling, but he went in and pulled her hand and brought her onto the balcony ... and kissed her. The roar went beyond impossible.

He shouted in her ear, "Now will you stay?"

She blushed, which he had never seen her do since he first met her. He turned again and signaled to the Palace major domo to bring the rest out. The crowd didn't have a clue but they cheered each face anyway.

Except Roper.

More startling because of the previous roar, a vast hush greeted the country's Prime Minister. But then, when the crowd saw that their King was ignoring his top politician, and turning instead to go over to his grinning plump coachman on the far side of the balcony....

Split Seconds • MacKenzie

HE COULD SEE the substituted Despatch Box. Now it was only fifty feet below him but the distance might as well still have been the twelve thousand miles from Australia for all he could do about it. Even before the chopper touched down on the Palace roof landing pad, he jumped out, hauling Slade's dead weight after him.

When every second could be the King's last, he had to cross the roof, leap down the stairs, race along the passage to the door of the Balcony Room. It was already open. He hurled himself through.

"You're hurting my arm!"

Slade's body had collided with the door frame. MacKenzie yanked the slimy secretary sideways.

"Colonel! One moment!"

Now a member of the Palace Security staff blocked him.

"Out of my way, man!" Mackenzie shouted.

"I thought you'd want to know, sir."

"I know there's a bomb in that case. Move!"

"There's also a new Irish groom just been taken on staff."

"Irish?"

"He's up in his room."

MacKenzie hesitated...

Slade

HE TOOK ADVANTAGE of the moment to catch a desperately needed breath. He heard the cheers begin again through the open doors in front of him and looked —

Roper.

The tabloid-reading fools were still cheering *Roper!* And the Australian was going to Roper. With his hand out! Smiling at *Roper!* And the cretin coachman, Stubbins, was smiling back.

The sight of Stubbins being adored by the crowd parted something with a physical twang inside Slade's skull. Fueled by a strength he had never possessed, he tore his arm loose, punched the commando's bandaged head, and rushed past the camera.

"You want to see what's in the Box?" he yelled at MacKenzie's back. "I'll bloody show all of you!"

Love

IN THE STABLE bedroom, only one hundred yards away, he waited for the optimum alignment. Roper was close enough, but not the Australian.

Love's focal point was gesturing the coachman to bring the blue despatch box closer. The American woman turned her head and stepped aside. The television showed a trio: *Prime Minister, Sovereign, Coachman.*

Dead center.

Love's scarred finger moved to the firing key which had failed for McDermid. This time, the conclusion to the Operation would go off letter perfect.

Anna

ALL SHE SAW was a lunatic charging from the French Doors. She had only one thought as she threw her body forward: *Protect him.*

Richard

HE FELT HIS injured arm turn to agony again. Then he was falling. Someone ran past him. His back hit the stone balcony. Anna was on top of him. In a slow-motion blur behind her he saw,

MacKenzie sinking to his knees...

The secretary from Downing Street...

Grab the blue despatch box from Stubbins...

Swing it wildly at Roper...

Both men slam against the balustrade...

Fall over it...

King's Cross

THE CROWD OUTSIDE the Palace railings saw a ball of flame, two feet below the balustrade. The home viewers saw red, from blood on the camera lenses.

No Vendetta

LOVE PREPARED TO leave the Mews. The Palace staff watching the picture in the cafeteria had rushed out to the forecourt to see the real thing. An ambulance was already arriving to collect the remains. It was not the grand slam Love had gambled for when he accepted Roper's offer to head up British Intelligence — and through it, and the mass media, to gain absolute power. But this conclusion was sanitary. With all the principals eliminated there was no longer anyone in Britain able to attach Love's name to the Operation.

He had just placed the triggering device back in McDermid's cyanotic blackened fingers when the stable room door crashed open for a second time. He had to make an instantaneous recalculation.

MacKenzie had reached the physical and mental limit of his endurance. He had been running on enough adrenaline to find the strength to kill McDermid. Now that the task had been done for him he could only stare at the body on the bed behind his other opponent, then feel his last reserve of energy drain away.

"Suicide," Love told him, straightening up.

He walked across and looked down. The evidence of cyanide was immediately apparent in the skin color. A fragment of shattered tooth was present on the lower lip. The typical bitter almonds smell was fainter than usual.

"I was able to put him off his stride with the detonator, but five seconds too late to stop him biting the bullet." Love shrugged. "It's saved the tax-payers the cost of a long trial."

"Any saving can go towards your own," MacKenzie said coldly. "I'm heading the board of enquiry into King's Cross."

"We've been that Tribunal route before, if you remember? I wouldn't expect any better luck this time."

MacKenzie had never forgotten. Love had been guilty in that torture case: today, while his action averting an IRA bomb might go some small way to mitigate —

The fingers were stiff.

McDermid's corpse had been dead for much longer than five seconds. There was only one conclusion, MacKenzie realized: a fist in rigor mortis could not have pressed the trigger; the scarred hand of the man in front of him must have done that.

"Don't expect any loose ends for your Star Chamber, Colonel. But when it's ready to go through the motions to send me to the Tower...?"

Love gave another sarcastic shrug and turned towards the door. And MacKenzie knew his opponent was right about that, too. Under the formal rules required once again by the re-instituted Magna Carta form of British justice, there would be nothing to prove beyond a reasonable doubt that this bastard who must be presumed innocent was guilty of so many deaths.

"You know where to find me, MacKenzie."

In his mind he saw a tousle-haired little boy in yellow rubber boots, before a bed of agony at Chedburgh.

MacKenzie bent his right-hand fingers at their second knuckles. "I do know," he said. "And you may remember that the Tower of London has a special gate for traitors."

Love's sarcastic smile changed to an open sneer —

A single upward thrust! His clenched knuckles struck the traitor's neck. The spinal column snapped. The traitor's body fell across McDermid's. Shuddered once. Lay still.

"*With Impunity,*" Hector MacKenzie said as an elegy to the walls of the Palace at the heart of Britain. "For Sandringham, and Sergeant-Major Wallop."

Midsummer Night's Dream

Windsor Castle

LIZ HAD EMERGED from the bunker at Norwich expecting to be arrested. Instead:

**"I USED NUCLEAR NIGHTMARE
TO SAVE THRONE FOR BRITAIN !"**

As a Free Press Heroine she was top of the news for an hour, then the avalanche of events at Downing Street and the Palace swept her off the front pages.

***Murder in front of Millions! Anna saves HIM! New Woman Prime Minister!
Written Constitution!Coalition Government! Balcony Bomber was Gay!
Last IRA Butcher!
One Year to Crowning! Will HE wed Anna?***

The man who built an empire on sensational reporting was dead. Long live Sensation! But the big questions were conspicuous by their absence: Who else had been involved in the conspiracy with Roper? What was its real aim? How had the last IRA assassin, McDermid, been allowed to get so close? Was Slade really his accomplice?

Dead men tell no tales...and if they could, the Fifty Year gag rule on Government Records would stop them. A written constitution should make that gag a little looser, but Hector was going to have to give her some big answers, she thought, as she drove to meet him through the springtime blaze of flowering Japanese azaleas in Windsor Great Park.

She swung through the huge outer walls of the world's largest lived-in castle, and was directed to a visitor's parking slot allocated to the Library, where Hector had said he would be waiting. She got out and started walking towards the entrance.

"This way please, Miss."

A young footman gestured to a different entry. Liz followed him inside, and then through about a mile of passages and Family portraits to the extreme south corner of the Castle battlements. The footman knocked on a panelled door, opened it, and said, "Your guest, Sir."

INSTEAD OF HECTOR, the pair of royal lovers were standing together by a twelve-foot high window overlooking the Great Park gardens. Anna Randolph appeared the same as she had at the Farm in Virginia, Liz decided — clued-up, vivacious, typically-American attractive. A small bandage on the back of her left hand was the only sign that she had been in any kind of physical mishap: a kitchen scrape, possibly, certainly nothing to show that she had taken the brunt of a bomb explosion.

The man Liz had interviewed was different.

His face was pale beneath his Australian tan and he had lost weight. The slight narrowing and acccentuation of his cheekbones made his features even more like the portraits in the passageways outside. His right arm was in a sling. He smiled and extended his other hand to her.

"Thank you for finding the time to come down and join us," he said, with the familiar touch of Aussie in "time" and "join". He obviously hadn't got used to the idea that in Britain a Royal command wasn't just a casual invitation.

"Thank you, Sir," Liz replied, shaking his left hand. "It was a pleasure in several ways. I took the scenic route, through the azaleas."

"Yes. They were a gift from the Japanese government, apparently. They remind me..."

He broke off, and stared out at the flowers below the window. She realized that he must be thinking of the Japanese bodyguard, sent from Tokyo by the Imperial Family and killed in the Atlantic.

"You promised you wouldn't brood." Anna stepped forward to change the line of conversation. "Kimura volunteered, so did the others."

"I know. I'm going to put a memorial for Kimura down there. One of those Japanese wooden gate shrines." Liz's former interview subject turned away from the window, towards her. "You've probably guessed why I asked you to visit?"

"My business is making guesses based on hunches," she said. "Faced with the choice of Political or Personal, I have to confess on driving down I backed the last item."

"Too right!" His face regained some of its former expression of lightheartedness, like a schoolboy who couldn't keep a secret any more. "I felt terrible for not inviting you to the balcony" — he smiled again — "although under the circumstances I don't suppose you mind! Anyway, I've been speaking to Prime Minister Lear and she thinks it's a good idea."

"My heartiest congratulations, Sir." Liz smiled warmly at Anna. "To both of you."

"What?" He stared, then burst out laughing, until his arm seemed to hurt him. He reached with his good hand to rub it. "Not us. You and Colonel MacKenzie, on my first Honors List. I understand there's a Scottish award, like the Knights of the Garter, but more exclusive."

"The Order of the Thistle?" Liz was flabbergasted.

"That's the one. It has a great motto for someone in the news biz. Or the Royal Marine Commandos: '*No-one attacks me with Impunity.*' " He laughed again, glancing sideways at Anna. "And with the Thistle, I don't have the problem of putting a garter on a lady who isn't my wife."

"Sir, I don't know what to say. The honor is extraordinary, but I'm not a monarchist. I could never take a title."

"You could borrow it," he said. "That's all any of us do, really. I don't believe in the hereditary part either. What we accomplish here and now is what counts. You may still be a republican — although I'm not sure whether someone can be who restored the monarchy single-handed! — but you are definitely Scottish. Don't use the title if it offends your principles, but be proud to wear your country's emblem."

She felt a sudden rush of affection for him, in his sincerity, seeing him touch the pain of his smashed arm...and something more, something deeper. Something that could not be escaped in a place like this Castle, with those pictures on its walls. A sense of inexorability: now the man from her interview *was* part of history. Liz bowed her head and said,

"I shall be proud to wear the Thistle. Thank you, Your Majesty."

"Super! And now I suppose you want something really newsworthy to take back to London." He shot a lovers' smile at Anna. "Why don't we confirm the rumor that this summer there will be an American Lady putting on a British Garter for her wedding present."

"Midsummer Night's Dream?" The young woman from Virginia who had truly saved the British Monarchy, in front of all its subjects, laughed at what must be some in-joke between them, then said, "Okay...but don't say I didn't warn you."

Wedding March

RIGHT ON CUE, Liz heard the chords of Mendohlson coming from behind a Chinese screen. The tune was being played on an antique spinnet, but the free jazz beat would have got the composer spinning in his grave.

"Champagne!" said the spinnet player, in Hector's voice.

One leaf of the screen folded back dramatically to show her Royal Marine sitting at the keyboard. The smiling King, who used to be an actor, took a magnum conveniently waiting in a silver bucket beside the instrument. Anna popped the cork for him and filled four crystal glasses. They each took one. The King raised his in Liz and Anna's direction.

"To two magnificent women," he said, "and in memory of Lady Bronwen."

"To Lady Bronwen. And my congratulations, again," Liz said, smiling at them both. "That's truly headline news."

"It is, isn't it? Almost as important as the agreement that's been reached with all the political parties for a Written Constitution."

"I'm amazed they agreed so soon, Sir."

"They didn't have much choice." He flashed the schoolboy grin again. "I told Mrs Lear that if they didn't go along I wouldn't take the job."

"It will make a profound change to the way we do things in this country."

"I hope so." The grin faded. The fourth King Richard stared out at the English valley beyond his window. "With the world changing so fast, people feel better knowing that the rules of the game are written down."

"They do, Your Majesty," Hector agreed. "And if I might, Sir..."

He produced a gift-wrapped package. The King took it and removed the paper to show a Victorian toy soldier, a clockwork Drummer Boy. It had obviously been through many nursery wars, but was now freshly repainted.

"It isn't much against Your Majesty's favor of the Thistle," Hector said in his Highland understatement, telling Liz that for some inside Royal reason the battered toy meant everything. "But at difficult moments it may help a little with that sense-of-continuity problem." Her Marine shot Liz a look that she interpreted as Exit Protocol. "Will you excuse us now, Sir?"

"Of course, General." The King set the Drummer on top of the spinnet and gave MacKenzie a long look, before adding, "Thanks for this. I'm sorry to have kept you."

IT WOULD TAKE her apologetic new King some time to get the web of British ranks and titles and precedence straight, Liz thought, as she followed her Palace Commando's tactful lead out into the evening beauty of Windsor's gardens. Through the long windows behind, over the last call of a cuckoo, came the faint rat-a-tat sound of a clockwork drum.

"If they can't have the Wedding March," she said, squeezing Hector's right hand, "this place and the Order of the Thistle is as close to a Midsummer Night's Dream as human beings get."

He stopped and turned towards her. "I didn't think a modern woman like you would want the Wedding March," he said, with that glint of dry Highland humor in his eye.

"Was that another confirmed proposal?"

"If you don't mind sharing marriage with the rest of my Regiment."

"Yours!" she exclaimed. "So the higher rank wasn't just a slip of the King's tongue."

"I'm afraid not. Does it make too much of a difference?"

Liz looked up at the remarkable mixture of ancestral talents which formed the character of General Hector MacKenzie.

"Sweetheart...if you don't mind sharing the bed with Auntie Beeb, this modern broad will take on a regiment of Royal Marines any day."